CONSEQUENCES

by

Ian D Anderson

First published in Great Britain
by For The Right Reasons

Copyright (c) 2005 by Ian D Anderson

ISBN 978-1-910205-86-0

Printed & published by For The Right Reasons
60 Grant Street,
Inverness, IV3 8BS
fortherightreasons@rocketmail.com

To the many friends and professionals who kindly read my manuscript and helped me improve it.

I have in this book tried to write a poignant story that decries abuse of power and highlights the impact of world events not just on the innocent but those more deeply involved.

I make no apology for its adult content as in the real world horror is visited on the many on a daily basis.

It was one such incident, described sadly by a reporter in Bosnia, which prompted me to write the book in the first place; this in the small hope that it will make such incidents slightly less likely in future.

I hope you feel what I have produced comes near to achieving that objective.

This new edition incorporates minor clarifications to certain parts of the story in response to reader's questions. However, there is no material change to the principal thrust of the text.

Ian D Anderson
New Edition 2016

Table of Contents

CHAPTERS:

5

"The Ides of March are come."

1. A Consequence

In its final turn, the tyre crushed the delicately patterned ice glaze on the frozen puddle; an unconscious act of destruction lost in the indifference of the surrounding darkness.

The approach had been without lights, no others were visible, an awakening promise in the eastern sky the sole threat to the sweep of the night.

The shape of a solitary occupant just visible inside the now stationary car leant a pregnancy to the moment: an air of expectation.

A field mouse distracted from its foraging debated the wisdom of movement, then cowered lower as the shape moved. A door opened without the automatic flash of light. The man it revealed, despite the darkness, slowly swivelled outward, and leaning down, deliberately pulled on a pair of green wellington boots. He placed them firmly on the ground, but instead of rising, he paused: looked around; listened to the silence; seemed pensive. Then in a display of decision he pulled on light leather gloves and with a stick in his left hand, he stood to loom over the dim outline of the vehicle.

Scanning right and left confirmed his intention; on either side, both he and the car were concealed by a thick hedgerow and occasional oak, ash and birch trees. Reassured, he clearly reached another decision, took a deep breath, walked up the track to the terminal gate and passed through into the adjacent field.

Here he stopped again, admiring the dimly seen green sheen of the early crop possibly, or the view, or simply taking his time, as time, for these short minutes, was not an issue that concerned him. Certainly, the view both of him, and from him was limited: the land was barely awake; the pre-dawn light still sufficient only for immediate navigation.

The man moved around the edge of the field, stooping slightly to conceal his height. He walked with an irregular gait, something he had deliberately practiced. The frost abetted this as the roughly ploughed soil was hard and unforgiving with minimal mud. Every hundred yards or so he would stop, it seemed as if to rest his elderly limbs, or to appreciate the strengthening dawn chorus, or to drink in the surroundings. From a distance, he looked like a gentleman farmer, or a local resident of advanced years: someone maybe that had decided, before the daily routine began, to walk the marches in the peace of the dawn. The tweed cap, Barbour, stick, dark brown cords, and green boots all fed this fiction.

He approached the house slowly and obliquely so, despite the relatively short distance, it was twenty-five minutes before he stood beside the dry-stone wall separating the outbuildings from the field. Concealed from the house; the danger of observation from the opposite quarter was restricted to a narrow corridor across the field, in the direction of the car.

This, the first critical decision point, required care. He leant against the wall as if for a prolonged rest, but actually studied the hedgerows for movement. He didn't think a professional was out there, his principal concern was with an innocent passer-by or an early farm worker. At the same time, almost subconsciously, gentle pressure tested the solidity of the wall.

After a lengthy evaluation, he had assured himself both that he was alone, and that the dry stones were well built. He made his decision, followed with its immediate implementation, by vaulting the wall to crouch in the gap between it and the outbuildings. Bracing his feet between the two walls, he held himself until he was sure he could step down in silence.

Any witness to this burst of cat-like movement and its clear intent could not possibly still think his behaviour innocent. The ruse of his laboured movement, the disguise, the rustic clothing, all would have been transparent; the entire enterprise threatened. But, experience had taught fatalism: the decision was made, the Rubicon crossed, dwelling on it was wasted effort.

He carefully worked his way down the narrow gap that, like all such gaps seemed to be, was a tangled rubbish heap of rusting metal, wire, rotting wood, long grass and nettles. Reaching the building's end, he found his hide, already earmarked, behind a tall, ranging tangle of several disparate shrubs. From here he could, safely and invisibly, observe the front access to the property. It also afforded an approach to the main and side doors of the house, should he so decide, on spotless concrete paving. He pulled his light, clean sneakers out of the Barbour's inside pockets, took his boots off, and put these on his feet instead.

He drew the Browning from the waistband in the centre of his back and took a silencer from another pocket. Fitting the two together, he felt the weight and balance of the result. It was not his preferred weapon; among other problems, the Browning was heavy and poorly balanced; characteristics now compounded by the addition of the silencer. However, it was the right tool for this particular task, and he was well practiced with it: on balance, factoring this into his risk assessment left it unchanged. Having earlier checked the rounds, the magazine and the action he now carefully placed the weapon on a flat stone within easy reach.

Probably with about an hour to wait, he settled back and as his body relaxed slightly he was horrified to find his objectivity slipping. He gasped at the enormity of what he planned and he struggled to regain mastery. He closed his eyes and wrenched his mind back to the task in hand, as several quiet but intense 'fucks' escaped his lips. There was no alternative; none. He had rationalised every option and all were useless but for this. He felt his rage almost escape again but immediately slammed it down, squared his jaw and forced his mind back into its operational detachment. He consolidated his mental grip with a further rehearsing of the tactical problem and the plan for its resolution.

On the face of things, there should be three people in the house: the parents and the daughter. His reconnaissance late yesterday and in the early hours, whilst too brief, had yielded further information. He had been too late to see the parents retire, but he had seen, from a distance, the daughter closing her upstairs bedroom curtains at around one am. Placing her in the topography of the house had significantly improved the operational odds. Additionally, as she had retired late, he could reasonably expect her to rise late. This further improved the odds: he was keen to address the old man first. He also guessed that if there was anyone else in the house, for example a Minder, the likelihood was that they would have sought sleep only after the daughter was safely in bed: he took some small comfort from the absence of any such sign.

Still, there were a worrying number of assumptions in this analysis. If he had had the time he would have preferred to enter the house at night: time though was scarce. It was required to disable the security system that, he guessed, provided an invisible external perimeter. It was required for a more thorough accumulation of data: in particular the vexed question of the numbers in the house. The plan, such as it was, was driven by this key imperative: the need for speed. It relied on the hope that someone, say a postman, would approach the house in the early morning and by so doing give him the opening he wished. If this did not materialise he was left with the only, and dangerous, option of going in hard, with no element of surprise.

Half an hour brought a reward: a van drove the track slowly and turning stopped outside the boundary gateposts. From it a woman emerged opened the rear van door and extracted a small cardboard box containing newspapers, milk, and a bag of probably bread or croissants. Through the shrubbery, he watched the house intently and caught the faintest movement of an upstairs curtain. The van's approach, which had been virtually silent, had obviously triggered some form of security system: confirmation of the assumption on security warmed him slightly; his mind registered a plus point - a defence which was relied upon, but which he hoped he could fool, gave him an edge. However, evidently, someone upstairs was alert, which had the opposite effect. The two revelations, broadly equal but contrasting, yielded only a score-draw he thought grimly. Forcing himself to think positively, he speculated that the lookout was one of the parents and that they would now descend and meet the visitor. If this assumption was wrong, and the person was a fourth party, his problem would become that much more complicated; but there was no other option than to address this on the hoof.

He looked at his watch; saw that it was still early; guessed the next likely visitor the postman would probably not appear for some time: this looked like as good as it would get.

The delivery woman opened the latch gate and approached the house. He checked the landscape again but they were alone; he readied himself. Simultaneously he slipped his cap off and gently slid it down a wellington leg. Once she was ten yards past, he picked up the gun gently, armed it and carefully moved out behind her. He padded toward the nearest corner of the house with the gun levelled at a spot between her shoulder blades. She was heading for the other corner where the path led around to the kitchen door. He was exposed for five or six seconds. If he had been seen, or detected, the delivery woman's consequent demise meant the immediate threat was that someone in front or in the house would confront him. However, seemingly undetected he reached the corner and reengaged the weapon's safety. While he waited for signs of alarm he swivelled left and right checking his position for danger. Where he was, no one could approach closer than fifteen yards without him knowing; a window opening above him could be countered by changing his position. Finally, he had a quick escape route to run; safe from anything save a rifle, or an improbably good pistol shot.

There was no obvious sign of alarm, something partially confirmed by the reappearance of the woman, smiling; the time taken suggested that a short conversation had probably occurred; in her distraction, she was oblivious of her concealed shadow. In less than a minute, she had reversed the van back into the track, and disappeared the way she had come. Peace, silence, and solitude returned to the immediate countryside.

He now moved very quickly. Rising from his crouch he traversed the front of the house ducking below each of the windows: six seconds. At the opposite corner four more seconds were spent in ensuring this new panorama was deserted too; then down the side of the house to the kitchen took another five.

He paused, crouching below the window, took a deep breath, flipped the safety, cocked the hammer and quickly stood straight up with outstretched arms: the Browning, in both hands, levelled through the panes of glass into the kitchen. Panning fast right then left he saw a bag of croissants lying open, with the milk, on the central kitchen table. There was no one in the room. The papers were not to be seen on the table, or anywhere else.

Thankfully he released the pressure on the trigger, breathed again, and quickly moved to the kitchen door, confirming there the simple Yale lock that he'd identified from his long-range reconnaissance. There were probably bolts inside too, but he guessed, he hoped, that these would now be open. Plan B was to blast any offending blockage with the powerful weapon, but this, if necessary, would return him to square one: a hard entry; no surprise.

De-cocking and re-engaging the safety, he pushed the pistol into his front waistband and took out his lock-picking tools. No expert, it still took him only seconds to release the Yale. As the latch clicked open he dodged, half turning sideways, back against the stone of the house wall. He withdrew the gun and re-armed it. He had been prepared for the shock of defensive fire splintering out through the wooden panels. When none came, he gently pushed the door, and it opened soundlessly. Another critical point had passed; any noise and caution would have departed on the wind.

He stepped out in front of the open space with the Browning extended once again. No one had returned. Entering the large, stone flagged, kitchen and dining area he closed the door behind him, engaging the inside lock on the Yale. Swiftly he moved to the inner door; certain that someone would be returning to prepare the breakfast very shortly.

Now that he was inside he was much less concerned about an unheralded hail of bullets; so, he gently opened this next door, looked out, and appraised the dark corridor that lay beyond; several doors opened off it.

Hearing someone humming a tune from a room to his right, he glided over and looked through the gap below the hinge. It was a utility room; an elderly woman, the wife he realised as she rose, was transferring clothing from a washing machine to an adjacent tumbler-drier. Occasionally, she picked an item to hang on the wood and black wrought iron rack that was suspended on a pulley system next to her; it was of the type that when loaded could be raised to the ceiling. The task was only half done; she would be engaged in it for at least two more minutes. With the position of one parent established he slid off to find the other, comforted by the lack of excitement: the occupants thus far unknowing, his invasion unsuspected.

So, where to look for the old man: the clue to his location lay in the newspapers. They were no longer in the kitchen; therefore, probably providing relaxation in a sitting room, or a study?

The man went to one of the two doors opposite. Heart fast, yet controlled, adrenalin sharpened, pistol readied, he opened the door: an anticlimactic empty toilet. Moving nearer to the other, he saw it was slightly ajar; he now realised he'd been sensing a faint smell of pipe-smoke; it was strengthening as he closed.

He stepped strongly, deliberately, into the room. The old man was sitting in a leather armchair eight yards away. Near, but at a slant to, the central, coal-effect, gas-fire; reading a paper, smoking a pipe. At a half angle to the man, he was able to look around and up at him without having to twist his neck.

An expression flitted across his face as he assimilated this alien presence; the threatening weapon: not fear, maybe disappointment, maybe regret. But despite this apparent recognition of failure, his body was already moving right; hand reaching leftward toward the inside of his jacket.

The bullet hit the old man's right eye beside his nose. His cold nemesis registered the abrupt cessation of the tuneful humming; it had been percolating from the utility room, down the corridor behind. He quietly cursed the Browning. She had, almost certainly, not heard the silenced report, but the louder, though more anonymous, metallic sound of the pistol's action. Even that sound, at that distance, must have been at the extremity of hearing. He was impressed: her sharp senses belied her age.

She called, "Gordon... Gordon, are you alright... oh God!" He could hear a fearful tremor in her voice, but he knew, from her history, that this wasn't fear for herself. He sensed the movement in the corridor, she was approaching rapidly. Professional respect her due: he quickly stepped behind the door.

When she came in, he reached forward and grabbed her back collar with his left hand, his right brought the muzzle of the silencer into the centre of her back, he gave her no time to react or to turn. The round's passage through her chest caused her to collapse instantly, as he had expected, and he lowered her body quickly and quietly to the floor, avoiding closure with the already spreading pool of blood.

He calculated that as only the wife had reacted downstairs, any further threat was likely to be found upstairs. Stepping back into the corridor he headed for the base of the stairs that were halfway along it. These stairs ran upward and back, past his right shoulder: forcing him to twist as he looked up along the barrel of the Browning.

The appearance of the daughter on the landing checked him for a fraction only. She was patently unaware of the events downstairs; looked to be coming from the bathroom; was dressed in a thick white dressing gown; had a white towel wrapped around her head. They were aware of each other simultaneously. Though the shot was some twelve yards, he took it immediately: she was strong and fit, potentially more dangerous than her parents. The range forced him to aim for the bulk of her body, but at sight of him, she had started back. The result was the round instead hit her in the upper neck and travelled on upwards through the base of her skull. Also, this backward momentum took her toward a three-legged occasional table with a large glass vase of flowers on it: as her body impacted, the whole paraphernalia crashed to ground in an explosion of sound and water.

With the silence so roundly disrupted speed now replaced quiet caution: the man was already halfway up the stairs and proceeded to do a classic, crude clearance of all the upstairs rooms. There were no worrisome dark corners here: the upstairs corridor, unlike the one downstairs, was light and airy with

14

sizeable exterior windows at either end. This clearance was fast as, conveniently, all the rooms opened off this one corridor. Finished upstairs he went back down; quickly checking all the ground floor rooms too. The house proved deserted but for him... and three bodies. This had all been done at high speed, but when he was finished, he slowed a little; returning to the site of each shooting, he picked up the three empty cartridge cases.

As an afterthought, he checked inside the old man's jacket and found a holstered 9mm Ruger Corporation P85; it looked possibly as much as twenty years old, so an early example of the US manufactured model: well cared for, the professional in him was impressed. Leaving it undisturbed, he walked back to the kitchen passing, as he did so, the telephone: he paused, briefly studied the features on it, and then quickly checked the call log. Satisfied he continued to the kitchen door. With the gun concealed under the Barbour, he carefully looked out at the surrounding countryside. Seeing no one, he left, closing the door behind him. At the front of the house, he sheltered at the corner, and assured himself that there was no one there either. Eased, he headed over to retrieve the boots, cap, and stick. As he went, he removed and stowed the silencer; allowing him to hide the Browning in his right pocket: still with his hand around it; still immediately available if required.

With boots and stick in his left hand, cap replaced on his head, he walked down the drive, through the gate, and out onto the track. He was moving as he had initially in the field, but now caution wasn't paramount and escape was, he was going much faster. Only eleven minutes had passed since he had left his hiding place beside the outbuildings. He was sure he could get down the track, back to the car, and away before the postman, or anyone else, arrived to see him.

His mind, for the past hour focussed solely on the job, and the target, rose like a bird. It emerged from the thrall of the Dark and flew outward; throwing off the singular, concentrated state adopted for maximum, detached, efficiency. It had been a difficult and dangerous play, one though that he had negotiated and completed successfully. He could now plan his return to the larger game: a smile pulled at his mouth at the thought.

Whilst remaining alert, he was relaxed enough to appreciate the dawn chorus; the rural landscape; the clear cold dawn air. He enjoyed the gilding of the east faces of the trees and hills by the early sun: it was going to be a lovely day. He even stopped for a few seconds to admire a solitary long eared owl perched on a branch: it studied him back, blinking occasionally, from what it believed was a safe distance.

+   +   +

Augsburg, Bavaria

Another, unwitting, player was just sitting down in a consulting room in a suburb of the city of Augsburg. The young doctor was in light mood; he was on a short day and due to meet, with his brother, an old friend for lunch. He was hoping the three of them would all go for a walk in the woods and villages west of the city in the afternoon.

His first patient, rotund, red and rustic, shuffled through the door and glowered. The doctor smiled pleasantly, as he had done on their previous two encounters, "so Herr Martin, wie geht's ihnen?" His patient's glower deepened and muttering could be heard. The young man caught the word "auslander" at which he smiled benignly but this time to himself.

+   +   +

Battersea Heliport

At Battersea Heliport, a small, colourful, mixed group decanted noisily from a French helicopter. One man, clearly the leader, marched away followed by an obsequious official, who had already decided that Monday morning should not be marred by unnecessarily upsetting this powerful man.

+   +   +

Belgrade, Serbia

In a large, still, dark Serbian government office in Belgrade a senior intelligence officer sat at a massive, solitary desk in the middle of the room. Slowly the pages of a file turned; occasionally he paused to read a section, or study, by the light of a desk lamp, a photo. Once or twice he glanced up grimly at an immaculate, bright looking, thoroughly confident though apparently disapproving, junior officer who stood to attention in front of him.

+   +   +

Belfast, Ireland

Somewhere in Belfast sat a neat man with round spectacles biting down on a piece of toast. A small wretched man held between two big men a few feet in front of him, had soiled himself as he listened with increasing despair to the dispassionate description of the horror that awaited him should he not return, find or steal, inside 12 hours, the £3,647 that had gone missing whilst in his charge.

+   +   +

Sotheby's, Bond St, London

An art specialist called Manvers had just arrived for work at Sotheby's, on London's Bond St. His habit for the last few weeks had been to leave his travelling clothes and bag and immediately visit the restoration staff where he could gloat is not too strong a word over his latest project. In its new frame and mount it was all but complete; it would be ready for sale in a few more days. Every morning it took his breath away. Every morning he discovered some new feature or nuance previously not recognised: its sheer brilliance astounding. Each time his mind added around £100,000 to the likely auction price as he redrafted the prospectus discourse in his head. On each visit he

17

again thanked God he had been the one chosen to sell it; and as the days counted down to the moment he would revealed its existence to the world's art community his excitement mounted.

+   +   +

A dirty 5th floor flat in Liverpool

In Liverpool a still attractive girl with a fresh purple and black eye cautiously pushed the man lying on top of her off. Whether he was comatose from the drink that he was probably still drunk from or just post coital was not clear. She stood and her slim body showed various other bruising to match the eye. She angrily smeared at the semen leaking down the inside of her leg; swore viciously, though quietly, at him and went to shower in an attempt to remove the rest of his seed.

2. A Mistake

Andrew Maxwell returned late on Sunday evening from a lengthy business trip to Boston and Hartford. Too late to pick up the dogs as planned; he had cracked a good bottle of Rioja, then called Cath to say he was home, would love to see her and by the way he was horny as hell. He sighed in disappointment when she described her current major crisis and ended by telling him. "Horny has to wait."

He was relegated to vegging out in front of some infantile drama on the Box.

Jean, the lady who always looked after the dogs, had said not to worry; they had agreed he would pick them up at ten am the following morning: he was assuming he would sleep like the dead until quite late.

Unfortunately, he had not reckoned on his internal body clock: it was determined to remind him that he was human. The sheer sense of fatigued wakefulness occasioned by the jet lag was an entirely new experience for him. He was used to, even blasé about, flying around Europe; however, this had been his first excursion, in any capacity, over the Atlantic.

So he found that, despite being tired, he could barely sleep: he was up making himself a mug of tea at three in the morning. Moping around, trying to ignore the mound of post, built a sense of guilt that eventually drove him to action. Fresh air was the answer; the dispatch of the cobwebs accomplished by a bracing walk in the early dawn. A strange choice, it might seem, to the somnolent majority but Andrew was a keen outdoor type, a climber and strong walker, very comfortable with his own mind. Seeking relief in the cold dawn air, once the thought was planted, the obvious solution.

He showered and dressed quickly. Downstairs he laced his boots, and slid into his snug, Michelin Man, black down jacket. Pocketing a few items that might prove useful, he was heading out when Serendipity tapped his shoulder and said, "do something different". She had proved a good friend in the past, finding him amongst others: his best three girlfriends; his current job – up there in the top two; and on at least four occasions, maybe many more, she had saved his life. This latest suggestion would not be remembered with the same affection.

He swivelled, and returned to the big bookcase, where he ran a finger along the row of maps. Finding what he sought he pulled out and spread a map of lower Wharfedale. A quick scan of the route to Jean's old farmhouse revealed several attractive possibilities. He selected a starting point a few miles short of his destination.

Taking the Landrover, he crossed the Wharfe, and headed toward Askwith, where he turned up the hill and eventually hit the Otley - Blubberhouses road. Turning toward Blubberhouses he soon pulled into a lay-by, close to the spot he had identified; the map showed there was a right of way, and several paths over the moor. It was still dark, but the eastern sky was lightening: with the headlights off, his eyes slowly adjusted to the surroundings; soon he was able to set off without the need for a torch.

It was a delight on the moor; the cold air of the pre-dawn and the scent of the heather were a joy to the senses. This was a new sensation for him here in deepest Yorkshire; his pre-dawn walking had, up until this point, only been done during the approach to some high Alpine route where early starts, and early descents, were an essential safety measure; occasionally too, on a long day in the mountains in Scotland in winter. This though was quite different: there was no looming snow-cast; vegetation abounded. The rural peace had an urban background; there was a unique texture to the distant light. He was high up, above the valley, and the illuminated streets of Addingham, Ilkley, Burley, and Menston shone in an almost continuous band like a Milky Way of red and yellow stellar dwarfs that had, in perfect formation, crashed, from the heavens, down to Earth. Further, the glow of the Leeds – Bradford conurbation could be seen through the gap between the heights of the Chevin and Ilkley moor.

He had a lot of time to kill so he wandered on the various tracks and paths that crisscrossed the heather. Immersed in nature, the scents on the gentle wind were sharpened by the cold and, as planned, as the time passed, his body regained more and more of its vigour.

The light steadily increased until eventually he could stop and study some distant scene with his tiny monocular. He watched a raptor, lazy, high above him. He studied an early take-off from Leeds-Bradford airport. He watched the sleepy, initial activity on several farms below him. Using the little device reminded him of the joie de vivre last summer of spying through it, from the newly conquered top of the Dent Blanche, two others top-out on the classic North Face of the Obergabelhorn.

Enjoying the moor, he stayed high for some time. Then after an hour or so he descended towards the walled fields on the Wharfedale side of the high ground. Consulting the map regularly he sketched out a circular route back to the car that took him generally along farm tracks and, occasionally, on narrow metalled roads. Here were whole arrays of new sensations: farm smells mingled with woodland scents as he passed small copses; the occasional pool steaming into the cold dawn air; couchant cattle with long eyelashes and distended udders slowly chewing the cud. He made a mental note to repeat this dawn walk with the dogs in the next few days.

The light had passed from pre-dawn to dawn some time before, and now he was descending a part metalled road where the grass in the middle survived, presumably, as it was left undisturbed by vehicles.

21

Suddenly he heard a crash: it tore the fabric of the rural silence that had surrounded him: nothing louder than some cheerful early birds had disturbed the calm up to this point. He frowned at the source that was clearly the isolated house on his right: definitely someone, or something significant, had fallen in what must have been a minor catastrophe.

He stopped behind the four-foot high dry-stone wall that separated the track from the grounds of the extensive property; they surrounded a sizeable stone built villa, which at its nearest point was over thirty yards away.

Many such houses are rural retreats for wealthy urbanites working in the substantial and successful centres of Leeds, Bradford, or their satellite towns. But these properties were usually immaculately maintained: a statement as well as a home.

This property though, with its half dug borders; outbuildings with slightly skew doors; faintly weathered paintwork, looked loved and lived in. It suggested more a retreat for a comfortable, relaxed retirement: so, was the crash some old-age pensioner in a spot of bother?

In no great rush, he considered this little puzzle for a short time and then slowly walked on. He arrived at a narrow gate in the wall that was connected by a paved path to what was, he guessed, probably a kitchen door. With his hand on the wood, he stopped and debated going up to enquire if all was well.

Realising that it was still early, a thought confirmed by his watch, he decided that it might seem strange calling at such an hour. Melodramatic, he thought, and with that, still ruminating, he set off slowly, once again, down the track.

Fifteen yards further, he passed an ivy-entwined gazebo built just inside the grounds and immediately against the wall. Studying its comfortable build brought him to another halt. He found himself looking at the property with a different, almost nostalgic, eye. It was idyllic. A vision of early retirement came to him: sitting in the gazebo on a warm, still summer's afternoon; with a partner of long years; sharing the view up the Wharfe valley; maybe a jug of Pimms and a good book; feeling worthy and a little tired after a busy, but creative few hours in the garden.

A couple of minutes passed until, smiling at his indulgence, he slowly carried on; picturing yet the scene until eventually his mind changed. He would go, knock, and simply say he was passing, had heard a loud crash, and was everything fine. It might be early, but it was light now; most people would be up and about: after all the crash alone indicated they had started the day. It would simply be good neighbourliness; besides, if he was honest, his reverie had made him a little curious to meet the people who lived here.

Almost halfway down the gentle hill between the side gate and the main gate to the property, he turned around and walked purposefully back towards the smaller of the two; now fifty yards behind.

Just as he was passing behind the gazebo for a second time, he saw the kitchen door open. Suddenly self-conscious, he stopped and through the construction's low walls and ivy foliage, he saw a man emerge.

The gazebo was a relatively insubstantial wooden affair, with wickerwork around that rose about three feet from the raised floor. The ivy and other climbers grew through the wicker and then around the uprights. Fortunately as it turned out, the structure and foliage was sufficient to hide his head and shoulders, which was all that was visible of him over the boundary wall.

Something about the way this man was behaving kept Andrew from immediately making his presence known. The man had his right hand inside his Barbour; was checking the area outside very thoroughly. His gaze passed over the gazebo without pause, suggesting Andrew's presence behind went unnoticed. Apparently satisfied with this survey, he closed the door, and walked down the paved path running along the side of the house. He moved in a strange way: carrying an injury possibly, or stiff with arthritis. At the corner, he gave the area at the front of the house the once over too. Then, seeming to relax, he moved out towards the outbuildings on the far side of the drive. As he did so his right hand came clear of the Barbour and he had a long black thing in his hand. His other hand moved on the front and came away with part of it. Andrew frowned at this object. He recognised the shape but it seemed to take seconds to reach his

23

brain as he unconsciously sank lower...... he has a gun; his left hand is unscrewing a silencer. Eventually the thought found shocking form in his head.

Andrew felt his bowels tighten; he had by now sunk a few inches and watched the man with only the top of his head exposed. The peace and tranquillity from the walk was swept away by a cascade of thoughts. Was it a real gun? Of course it's a real gun! Is he a burglar? Yes! Would he have used it? Everything about the man screamed yes! What had happened in the house? What was the crash? Speculation yielded images of blood and horror, which he tried unsuccessfully to shake away. His bowels contracted further, with the realisation that, probably, his life was in the balance.

Time must have stopped briefly; when his gaze returned to the man, he was fifty to sixty yards away, carrying boots and a stick in his left hand; a cap had magically appeared on his head. The man suddenly stopped, maybe ten yards short of the gates, and again looked all around: Andrew pressed forward and hugged the wall; tried to disappear into it: frozen still; cramp threatening; time, once more, defied reason. Then as before, the gunman resumed his progress; soon turning the corner down the track.

Thought returned as chaos. What should he do? Mobile, call the police, no signal.... Shit. Think....what would he say anyway: report he had seen a gun; heard a loud noise; very slim set of facts. What if someone inside needed help? Should he go and give aid....? He looked at the house again; remembered that the man had closed the door. I can't get in, probably – is that fear? Maybe but... As his mind returned to the man; remembered his manner; the easy way he had handled the gun; his heart sank.

Should he follow the man - see where he was heading? God, what if he comes back, bypasses the gates, walks up the track - I'm dead.... blam, bullet in the head. He looked around and bounded across the wall into the field on the opposite side of the narrow road. Crouching behind it he pulled out his mobile again: shit, shit! Still no signal. Andrew looked up at the wall and realised the cover it gave him meant he could follow, at least for a bit, safely hidden behind it.....the man was about to get away scot-free.....he might get some more information on him to give the police. His heart pumped rapidly at the thought: why did he

24

always feel the need to challenge his fear. O, come on!! you need to move if only to get a signal on the phone. Giving himself no time to reconsider, Andrew ran in a crouch behind the concealing wall to the corner of the track, where the man had last been seen. He warily worked his way around until he had a view down the straight beyond. The man was standing maybe one hundred yards away, gazing up into a tree to his right. Almost immediately, he resumed his rather painful looking progress down the track, which bore slightly right as it approached the narrow public road.

Still no signal…shit, shit, shit. Following at some distance, behind the wall, Andrew watched the man reach the lane. This presented a problem: There was only intermittent cover for him if he followed the man onto the narrow road. In a quandary, he checked the mobile once more and relief flooded; the display showing a weak signal. Dialling Emergency, he watched his quarry's head over the hedge, and was surprised when the man turned right into what must have been a short farm track. At the same time any hope of immediately sharing his burden evaporated; the signal was obviously intermittent. Swearing at it again, he thrust it back into his pocket.

As he debated his next move, he saw the gunman's head drop; after a lengthy pause, an engine started. Andrew swore under his breath, he had to see the car. If it came back towards the end of the track, he had a chance. If it went west, he had a dangerous dilemma. As he ran, he reached for his monocular. Did he have the courage, or the foolhardiness, to run into the lane, if the car went the wrong way?

The sound of the engine was getting louder. The vehicle had turned east and was coming back towards the end of the track. Past this junction, after about one hundred and fifty yards, the lane bent at right angles to go roughly south. Andrew was approximately fifty yards from the track's terminus and so, for a few seconds, given the sporadic hedgerow, he should be able to see the number plate, but at a distance of maybe three hundred yards.

He stopped, dropped to the ground, and, as the car sped away, tried to zero the monocular on the car number-plate. This wasn't easy: more haste made less speed, his heart pounded, his chest heaved, and even at this distance the car was both a relatively near objective, and rapidly speeding away. Frantically trying to bring the little device to bear, he first hit the car roof, lost it, hit it again, and was then able to work down the vehicle until he encountered the number plate. Too late to get the whole thing he did get 'X389 F'; with that the car was gone.

Andrew got up, pulled out his mobile and almost cried out when he saw it had a signal. It immediately started fluctuating again, so he moved still further from the house. The signal got better with each step. Tugging the map from his pocket, he thumbed redial. This time there was a ringing tone, then a voice. Which service?"

"Police."

The operator connected him and gave his mobile number to the police handler. Immediately there was a pause he spoke, "please take this down 'X389F'. My name is Andrew Maxwell. I live at five, Drumlithie Avenue, Ilkley. I believe I may have witnessed someone leaving the scene of a gun attack, at... bear with me, grid reference 376714 in Wharfedale, near Otley and Askwith. This person was carrying a hand gun and silencer; he left in a blue Ford Mondeo, I think, and the registration begins 'X389F'."

The policeman who had received the call immediately recorded the partial car registration and other details but calmly said, "how do you know a gun crime has been committed?"

He was punching the grid reference into the system, dispassionately he continued, "yes Sir, how sure are you that you saw a pistol, it is early in the morning after all? Yes Sir, a patrol car will come out, of course. And no one injured, as far as you are aware. Yes, I understand you think there might be, but you didn't actually see or hear the gun fired."

He stiffened when he saw the screen flash back with the location details. Signalling to the Duty Sergeant, he switched the mic off. Looking across the room at his superior he said, "this guy alleges a firearms incident involving a silenced pistol. The grid reference he's given: it matches the location of a house tagged as a low risk terrorist target."

The Sergeant got up, approached, and, frowning, looked over the Constable's shoulder, "where is it?"

"Almscliff View near Otley."

Sergeant Bruce took a deep breath, considered, looked at the clock. "How does he sound?" The Constable screwed his face but nodded, "legit, competent." The Sergeant nodded back and said decisively, "right, get someone out there ASAP, preferably someone with a brain and a bit of common-sense, either way NO gung ho, I don't want any heroic dead cops; There's no other guns about at the moment, so no harm in getting Armed Response moving, tell them they can burn a bit of rubber."

He straightened, went to a second screen, and studied the detailed Ordnance Survey map he pulled up on to it. Grimacing he turned to the duty-roster, the grimace became a growl: it was early morning and light on useful bodies in the Otley area. He turned back to the Duty Constable. "See if you can get Sergeant Wells out there. If there is anything in this, remind him, at his earliest convenience, to find an acceptable RV site a safe distance from the house."

He signalled to another Constable to become involved as the first was occupied with talking to the caller and in switching channels to alert both a local vehicle and two ARV's. The second, already with his notebook out, was poised to take notes as the Sergeant issued instructions. "Get onto Special Ops; if this is real, it will probably be handled as a Major Incident.

You'd better alert Special Branch.

Put the partial registration and car details, stressing 'firearms suspected' out to all patrols. This is a covert, **underline**, observe and do *not* apprehend until further notice. Then check on the PNC that all the details match, it should give you a complete registration as well, put all that out too when you have it. Warn the murder boys they may have work to do."

Pausing and turning to the first Constable he said, "tell the informant... what's his name? Tell Mr Maxwell, no heroics, to stay put and to, absolutely not, under any circumstances take any risks."

Turning back to the second Constable he went on, "also, you better warn the Paramedics they might be needed. If they want to mobilise just in case, make it clear that they must stay well away, at least two miles, until we have the RV assembly area established. We'll let them know when they can come on in." When he was satisfied that all the immediate priorities were dealt with, he picked up a phone and called his boss.

3. A Perfidious Policeman

Andrew had sat down on the corner of a boulder opportunistically built into the dry-stone wall. He saw the blue flashing lights of the squad car some distance away just over five minutes later. As it approached, the lights were stilled and it pulled up thirty yards away from him. It had stopped with its engine still running half off the road in an interruption to the verge-side ditch: the access point for the gate to the field he was in.

A burly police Sergeant got out of the front passenger seat, looked around cautiously, then walked toward him along the road. Andrew stood and walked towards him too, but inside the field's perimeter fence. When they were about fifteen yards apart, the Sergeant stopped and called. "Can you give me your name, Sir?"

"Andrew Maxwell."

The Sergeant nodded, studied him intently for a couple of seconds, looked relieved, and then beckoned to him; Andrew walked to the gate and clambered into the back of the car. Sergeant Wells got in the front passenger side and introduced conversation, "I'm Detective Chief Inspector Grieve. Thank you for raising the alarm on this one. It's a bit of a mess in there. You really shouldn't have chased after the killer you know, but it has given us a useful piece of information, so thanks for that too.

Sorry as well for keeping you cooped up here for so long, we are a bit low on personnel this early on a Monday; otherwise you would have been in a nice warm interview room with a cup of tea by now. But what's done is done, if the mountain can't come to Mohammed, the mobile canteen can come to Wharfedale.

As it is, for me, the next stage is to learn everything you can tell me Mr Maxwell. Just why you were here; what you saw; what you heard; what you felt, and at what times? When you've done all that, I want you to start again, and we will scour your mind for things you saw, heard, and felt without realising you had at the time."

So Andrew recounted everything he had seen, heard, and felt, right down to the state of his bowels. While this was going on a young man joined them; he listened to the latter half of the story. When Andrew was finished, he made to pull Grieve away. Grieve wasn't going anywhere though, "this Young Turk is Inspector Doyle, he has been doing a more detailed study of the crime scene for me and if you can stand it, it might help us if you listen to his analysis of what happened inside."

Andrew said he would do anything he could to help and so Inspector Doyle, with a quizzical look at him, then a darker look at Grieve, started on a graphic description of the executions in the house.

Seemingly, there were three bodies, all shot. The first to die was an old man, called Gordon Armstrong. Apparently, most of the content of his head was now liberally sprayed over the chair his body was in, and much of the wall behind. Like any head wound there was significant blood loss. It would appear the assassin had surprised him, when he simply walked in. His initial attempt at defence cut short by the peremptory impact of the bullet.

At this point Doyle paused, he tried to drop his voice, but Grieve simple shook his head; told him to keep going as before. Doyle frowned, looked like he might argue, but then continued.

His hesitation was explained when it emerged that the old man had been armed with a robust, newish, US made Ruger P85. Nor was it there for show, Andrew thought, as apparently he had been reaching for it as the incoming round had struck.

After this description of blood and potential, if not actual, gun-battle, Andrew sat down on the tailgate of the police Range Rover they were standing beside. His world had darkened at a frightening pace, at the same time his life; his career; his friends; his travels; his hobbies; in fact everything he knew seemed to have shrunk. From being his whole experience he now saw the reality; the dark underside that the Police and the Forces kept at bay. This was not a stylised TV drama presentation, it was immediate, in his face, and he was part of it. The three punctured, cold, white, sad bodies were lying only a short walk away; had already started their descent to dust. His mind filled suddenly with a tableau where all his experiences were a gentle sail on a calm sea, sometimes a little rough and windy, but never truly dangerous; now he had strayed too near the edge and had found, not a gentle shelving shore, but a boundary of limitless hurricane force winds; huge ravening seas. He realised he had been innocently occupying the eye of the storm; he was being sucked inexorably into the wider, true reality, where he could be dashed to smithereens in a moment.

Grieve put a solicitous hand on his shoulder and asked if he was feeling alright, at which Andrew dragged his mind away from the image and nodded. Grieve signalled for the report to continue: Armstrong's wife, Barbara, had, almost certainly, been the second victim. She must have died instantly as she had dropped so that her right leg was bent double backwards from her hip, her left was forward and the lower leg was bent backward virtually parallel to her thigh, her upper body had fallen backwards to lie almost completely covering the right leg. This was a position no living person could have adopted. Looking up from his notes, Doyle continued, "a grotesque position, not a movie death at all, it's got to some of the lads. If our friend showed up now, we would have to drag some of them off."

Doyle's voice cut off as he glanced at Andrew, who had started to shake. Delayed shock, horror at the situation he was in, or simply a realisation of recent proximity to a monster. The first part of the infamous area, it will be vandalised or stolen in minutes.

He was hoping the Mondeo would go quickly, as he had parked it near a likely group of twelve to fourteen year olds that were showing no signs of going to school. His hope was that these kids would joy ride in it until they lost interest, or the petrol was low, and then they would torch it.

Even if they failed to destroy it, their traces would mask any small traces of his. Additionally, the reason for the theft would seem apparent in any subsequent investigation.

He walked around to the garage and opened it to find his beloved car just as he had left it. Driving it out, he spent some time ensuring the garage was restored to its original condition. When satisfied, he drove off, whistling a Sting tune that was current on his CD stacker.

His cheerful mood evaporated quickly though. Lady Luck had smiled on him when he was taking horrendous risks at dawn, but had now deserted him at the most unlikely of times: there was a police car next to the Mondeo. This was not of too great a concern: his first thought was to congratulate West Yorkshire police on their response to car crime, but the next instant his mood did go into free-fall. He caught sight of a second police car and the unmistakeable profile of levelled H&K MP5's.

Passing the end of the road, some two hundred yards away and in seconds hidden again, he was sure that his presence would have gone unnoticed. Yet, now his mind was racing. Firstly, why had he had such a very close shave, less than two hours after leaving the scene of his early morning operation? He appreciated the area he was in had very regular police patrols but why was there an ARV at the scene? Was it coincidence? No, he was no believer in coincidence. Somehow, the police had linked the Mondeo and/or its registration to his operation this morning: how could that have happened?

He thumbed his mobile in its hands-free cradle. It rang several times and then was answered, he said, "John it's Matthew, how the devil are you?"

"Okay, did you succeed in completing the deal?"

40

"Yes, it was signed this morning a couple of hours ago. Unfortunately, the deal's confidentiality is in doubt. Could you ask a few discreet questions?"

"Okay, I'll check and get back to you."

The man clicked off the phone and turned the car in a direction that kept all the options open. Five minutes later, the loudspeaker switched from the Sting CD back to the phone. A voice said, "Mark it's Luke, how the blazes are you?"

"Okay, any news?"

"Yes, the deal appears to be known to your competitors. Apparently someone unconnected to the negotiation, heard something, saw you, put two and two together, and gave them a call."

"Wonderful. How much is known?"

"He hasn't confided too many details about you to them yet; though there is hope that he has more to tell. They aim to tease it out of him over the next little while.

That's all I could get without seeming too interested."

"Okay."

He clicked off the phone and Sting filled the car once more. The day had turned to ash; his normal ice cool being threatened by the cascading fury that occasionally afflicted him. What jumped up little shit had the right to threaten him: certainly not one with any further right to life.

He forced himself back into a state of calm, and considered this new problem. Quickly it was clear that instead of heading home and returning to his normally untrammelled life, he was going to have to deal with this issue too. He felt himself approaching the edge again and it took considerable effort to close his Pandora's Box: the prison where he had learnt to confine his anger.

Stopping and looking at the large-scale Ordnance Survey road atlas that he had in the car, confirmed what he had already guessed. It should be possible to see the murder house from the promontory of the Chevin escarpment. Conclusion became decision and in turn became action, as he swung the car out into the traffic and immediately accelerated off in that direction.

Parking in one of the tourist car parks, he walked from there until the desired view unfolded. Using his binoculars, he

41

looked across the valley and the activity around the house leapt into focus. There was one person who looked out of place in the hive of armed police, forensic and detective activity; standing looking lost, he was wearing a black down jacket.

Watching for some time, he became certain that the individual in the jacket was the bastard who had spied on him and who had raised the alarm. Lowering the binoculars, he thought, what would this cunt know? He had obviously seen the car; if that point was conceded then there must also be a strong possibility that he had seen him in it too. Did he see everything he might?

The man thought of the measures he had taken to disguise his appearance. The few simple tricks to changes his face and hair had been discarded as both unnecessary and risky as soon as he returned safely to the car. Now he wondered whether that had been a mistake. Should he take this pain in the arse out anyway? The issue was the risk to him, which was a lot greater now that the police were aware of his threat. He regretted not putting the sniper rifle in the car boot, he might just have been able to take him from this position and solve the problem instantly and cleanly. Sadly, that option was out and that meant he would have to kill him later. Continuing the thought process, he went on, if he was to do that, he needed to be able to find him: in turn raising the question of how? Once that was done, he could plan a rapid departure for the little cunt, whether he knew more or not.

He could phone his inside contact again, but too much unwarranted curiosity from a remote quarter risked compromising both their positions, as did transmitting sensitive information by open telephone, whether it be fixed line or wireless.

5. A Calm

Grieve took Andrew gently aside, he was quite charming and Andrew almost regretted his distrust of him: almost. Grieve put some flesh on the bones. "Now you have signed the dreaded document I can explain more of what is going on here.

The man dead in there, Major Gordon Armstrong, was a leathery old retired security officer. He was Army; then attached to the Special Operations Executive, then MI6 and then MI5: not a man to have an argument with. I met him once and he told me, if push came to shove, he could kill me with one finger." Grieve smiled, "I'm sure he was joking though."

Andrew looked at him aghast, not only had he informed on a true monster, but an undeniably capable one too if he could kill such a man. This with the shock he had been feeling and the realisation that civilised life was surrounded by dark, undermining forces began to make him afraid for his own personal safety.

His visible chagrin was totally ignored as the Chief Inspector went on, "his wife, Barbara, came from the same mould. My information is they met in MI6. She was charm itself

43

Constable Nichol introduced himself and then proceeded to check the security in the house for himself. He was very affable but that failed to fool; Constable Nichol knew what he was doing and Andrew was impressed. The policeman told him to stay in the house until at least the following afternoon when he understood DCI Grieve was going to call to see him.

As he was leaving, Andrew summoned up his courage and asked the question engendered by their arrival. He was fairly sure he had guessed the answer already. "One last question Constable Nichol, are you armed?"

"No shouldn't need it. Our presence will keep any bad buggers away. I am trained in firearms but I prefer not to handle them. If we do need guns, the armed lads are not far away. ARV's don't grow on trees and they are most often needed in Leeds or Bradford since the proliferation of heavily armed drugs gangs. Besides, we're not alone, there's a squad car on the street backing your garden too."

"So it's not because of some break-through in the investigation?" Andrew asked hopefully. PC Nichol smiled sympathetically at him. "No, I am not aware of any significant change, but we know what we are doing and the wheels will grind on. One last reassuring thought, the animal who spilt all that blood this morning is probably several hundred, if not thousands of miles away by now, and I am sure is blissfully unaware of your existence."

Andrew realised it was a valiant attempt to reassure him, and he really appreciated it; nevertheless, this last comment, failed to help at all. What was it Grieve had said? 'We think the killer comes from the old man's world, where such skills are fairly commonplace.' It must be possible, or even probable, that he would follow the police investigation to ensure they got nowhere near him. If he did this, Andrew reasoned, he was probably on to him already. It was the obvious explanation for the police protection.

He went back to his Scotch and his thoughts. After another hour of considering alternatives, he had decided on two that did not involve sitting in the house waiting for a bullet. Still, rather than act on either immediately he decided to trust Constable Nichol's assessment and test if the fatigue from the jet lag and the events of the day would yield the oblivion of sleep. So, disregarding the very early hour, he went to bed where he tossed and turned: lying on his back; on his front; on his side or in a foetal curl. No position conferred sleep. Counting several thousand sheep, normally a reliable technique, failed him on this occasion. He imagined himself in a hammock between palm trees on a warm sandy beach with the gentle ebb and flow of small waves. Sadly, it was all quite futile. Dog-tired, with no hope of sleep, no hope even of it creeping up unannounced, he conceived every creak in the house to be the prelude to execution. After thirty minutes he realised this attempt was doomed, he simply was not going to sleep, and he was now desperate to give his mind and body the rest it needed.

He rang Doyle on the number he had been given: this was the first alternative he had thought of. He begged him to take him to a 'safe house' or whatever they called it. Doyle kindly, but firmly, told him not to worry and that he should go to bed and get some sleep. No amount of pleading would sway him and Andrew dejectedly put the phone down; he simply could not sleep in this house: he knew that what he knew would keep him awake. He also was certain that if someone wanted to find him, this was the first place they would look. Reluctantly, as it was a big step, he decided to put the last alternative into action.

He dressed as best he could in dark clothing; dark blue Helly Hansen long johns, dark blue Lowe long sleeved top, the Lowe didn't have the distinctive white chevron arms that the Helly tops had, dark blue climbing socks and lastly his black woollen balaclava. He debated his footwear; his Alpine boots were very dark coloured but heavier and bulkier than his mid brown walking boots; in the end he chose the lighter ones.

He took his winter sleeping bag, which was inappropriately bright yellow and orange and arranged it in his Gore-Tex bivvy sack. Fortunately the bivvy sack, like all bivvy sacks seemed to be, was camouflage or army green. Andrew had never seen any variation from this, and if there was one shop he enjoyed browsing in it was a climbing shop. He could only assume that people lying helplessly cocooned in one probably would prefer that other people could not see them: keeping the demand for bright pink fluorescent bags relatively muted.

49

He also took his vicious looking Predator ice axe, as it was the most lethal thing he had in the house and its shaft was covered in black plastic; downstairs he put black boot polish on those bright steel parts that were not covered.

Then he quietly made his way out to the apple tree about twenty yards away in the garden, near the left boundary wall. It was surrounded by a large rhododendron, rooted between the tree and the wall, which had the great merit of being thick with maze-like branches and considerable foliage: both old and new.

He pushed the sack in under its arching frame and quietly and quickly got in boots and all. He left the bag zip fully open and closed the sack zip, in case the colour of the bag crept out, and laid the axe ready to hand in front of him.

He imagined what he looked like from the garden and decided, as he had hoped, that to see him someone would have to come to within a couple of yards or less. With that reassurance, that here he was in one of the last places anyone would look for him, and that he was well hidden, he almost instantly went to sleep.

6. A Storm

Awaking suddenly, very disorientated, Andrew was unclear what had pulled him from a very deep sleep. He could feel the shock of heavy items hitting the ground near-by, a few shivering the apple tree. Above him, there was a cloud of smoke and fire ascending and it took him some seconds to realise that the silhouette of his modest home, dark against the sky, was nothing like it had been when he had settled down.

It took several more shocked seconds before he accepted that it had been torn apart by an explosion and the heavy rain had been stone blocks flung from the walls. Shivering with shock he was about to stumble out of his hiding place, when he thought better of it. The fear of this anonymous killer was so great now that he imagined a Harpy of old perched on the wall just waiting for movement to pounce. Resolving to stay hidden Andrew settled down again: he would wait until such time as large numbers of armed police arrived.

The next hour was full of different noises: wailing sirens, the sounds of emergency personnel doing their job, the voices of shocked neighbours, and the sad sound of settling rubble in his house. Then Inspector Doyle appeared in the garden, stepping

upper lip he drove into Ilkley centre. Parking in the main and central car park, he went hunting for a car to steal.

Finding a quiet corner of the parking area he waited inconspicuously for new cars to arrive. Several came and frustratingly the drivers all bought half-hour tickets. His impatience grew, but finally, after twenty minutes an elderly lady pulled up in an old Vauxhall Corsa. She bought a ticket and then hobbled off. Following her and passing the car in the process brought a smile to crease his face: the ticket was for two hours. She made a beeline straight for a stylish looking hair salon on an adjacent street. Watching for another minute or two, he saw her being taken in to have her hair washed and smiled again.

Returning to the vicinity of the car, he checked for CCTV, whether it was overlooked, or in case the car park attendant came by. After a couple of minutes, the man decided it was safe so he quickly opened, started, and then drove the car back to the area of Drumlithie Avenue.

There he went 'For Sale' hunting in the adjacent streets, careful not to pass any of the squad cars more than once. He found three houses with 'For Sale' signs in a circle around the target house and spent some time looking at them and the locality. After a while, he thought he had found a route that would allow him to approach the target house, over two neighbouring gardens, without being in sight of any of the watching police.

As he reconnoitred, he considered the question of how best to snuff the target out. Unlike the first attack, the police were actively guarding the house. They were also heavily armed; the last thing he needed was to fight an unequal gun battle, armed only with a pistol, when they carried semi-automatic weapons. For all he knew there was also an armed police babysitter in the house. If there was, and he was halfway competent, he would be awake, with an unholstered pistol, guarding the top of the house stair. Additionally any gunfire, silenced or not, would create a flash of light that the police outside could hardly fail to notice. No, the attack had to be conducted at arms length to give him a reasonable chance of escape. On the plus side, the target's home was not particularly large, it was detached, and it was stone-built. The best solution was clear but he needed to do a little more research.

An hour had passed so he drove back to the centre of Ilkley. As the car park hove into sight he scanned anxiously for danger, but there was no obvious alarm or excitement. The Corsa was quickly parked in a space some fifty yards from where it had been stolen. With luck, the old woman would simply think she had got confused and forgotten where she had parked.

Taking some time now to shop, he bought a large-scale OS map of Ilkley: this could be done quickly, without speaking and should not figure in anyone's memory. There was also a need to check that gas was supplied to the Drumlithie Avenue neighbourhood. The reconnoitring had not provided a definitive answer, as the houses were older and had the gas meters inside. Further away the telltale sight of two small white external doors had indicated both electric and gas meters, so clearly gas was generally available in the area.

He went to a phone booth opposite one of the estate agents and called them. He asked the question in an Irish accent and quickly rang off when he had the confirmation.

Nothing more needed to, or should, be done in the town so it was back to the BMW next and there, sure enough, was the old woman. She was talking in animated fashion to the car park attendant and gesturing in the direction of where she thought her car should be. The attendant listened and then looked sceptically around at the cars nearby. The man almost laughed out loud when the attendant pointed her car out to her and stopped her in mid-gesture.

Driving some distance away he found a DIY superstore on the outskirts of Bradford and bought a mixed pack of fuse wires and a cheap electric plug-in time switch used to turn lights on and off at set times. Everything else that might be needed was already in the car.

With all the necessary equipment in place, he returned to Ilkley where the map was put to use. He needed somewhere to park his car as short a walk as possible from the route in and out of the target, with a quick getaway and not likely to excite comment. Eventually plumbing for a spot high up the hill in Ben Rhydding he went there for a short recce: it was exactly what was wanted.

The plan now fully prepared he went to a quiet spot on the road running along the north side of Ilkley Moor and took two hours sleep. When he woke at eight in the evening he drove to the Cow&Calf hotel, which served up an excellent roast dinner and a plate of cheese and biscuits. He drank the mildest of bitter shandies. The meal was made all the more pleasant by his ravenous hunger. Coming out at nine-thirty there was still time to kill and a further opportunity for a short nap.

At 2330, he drove to the selected spot. The fine, but cold weather of the day had now become a chill, cloudless, clear night. There was only a sliver of moon but with the clear sky, the ambient light was good. Therefore discarding the small torch, he pocketed the piece of card with the five-amp fuse wire, the timer, the silencer, the lock picking wires, a glass cutter, a screw driver with a selection of magnetic bits in the handle, a two foot piece of fence wire and his Swiss army knife. The pistol was pushed into his belt in the small of his back. Wearing the now relatively weighty anorak and the ski hat he walked towards the start of his route in. The aim this time was to look like a returning drinker. As the kick-off point approached, he looked from under his eyebrows for any lights or twitching curtains: all was dark. Happy that there were no suspicions he started the risky part of the operation by walking into the first garden as though he owned it.

Coming around to the back of the house there were two windows lit so he moved cautiously along the fence outside the pool of light. When a dog began to bark furiously, he dived into the roots of the row of conifers along the back boundary and sat there as the owner put their hand to the window and looked out. Satisfied with his inspection, after a couple of minutes, the owner disappeared again.

The man continued over the low boundary fence into the next garden. This house was lifeless and there was no problem crossing quickly to the fence of the target house. This was higher but sturdy so he raised himself about a foot to see and when this went unremarked continued upward and jumped easily down onto the grass on the other side.

There were no lights, so slowly he checked each of the back windows. Alas, none of these were open and they all appeared to have window locks. Leaning against the boundary wall on the left of the property he considered. Looking up at the second floor briefly he discarded the idea quickly. If he scaled the house, there was the danger of breaking into the cunt's bedroom with all the alarm and noise that that entailed, the risk of being shot in the process by the babysitter if there was one, and thirdly, with police on both sides, and only twenty or forty yards away, they might see him.

The man looked leftwards, past an apple tree, wondering if there was anything in the garden he could use for help: a ladder, or a sawhorse. But there was nothing obvious. Before resorting to the glasscutter, he went back to the side where he had come in and realised the structure abutting the fence was a short flat roofed breakfast room, or conservatory, adjacent to the kitchen. It seemed only four or five yards deep and he could dimly see an area on the other side of this that looked screened from the front road by a high stonewall. At first he considered going over the flat roof but then realised that he could go back into the adjacent garden and approach the other side from there.

Crossing the fence back into the neighbouring property, he discovered this option was not as easy as at first thought. There were more of the ubiquitous conifers along the boundary where the two houses came closest together and he had to force his way through them to get to the fence. Once there he heaved himself up and over it.

Here he was enclosed in a very private space; at front and back bounded by the front wall and by the breakfast room; behind him the boundary was the fence and the conifers and in front of him was the sidewall of the house. What was even better was there was a small utility style window in the sidewall at head height. Unfortunately, when he got near, he realised he might be too big for it. Still, the good news was it was slightly loose. He could see the window arm inside move slightly as he moved the frame. It looked like the glasscutter might not be needed after all.

The Swiss army knife was the type with a locking three-inch blade and he was able to slide this in, through the narrow gap at the bottom of the window, and lever it sufficiently apart to slip the fence wire in. With some patient jiggling, he eventually managed to flip the window arm off the pin holding it. Gently opening the window, he was dismayed to find the gap even smaller than his first pessimistic assessment. Worse still, there was a shelf on the inside loaded with glass and plastic bottles and sprays. He moved as many of these bottles as he could to the side and heaved his head and shoulders into the space where his shoulders promptly caught in the frame. Falling back, he looked around for help. The area he was in was partially open but there was a Perspex roof covering a three-yard deep area behind the front wall. This seemed to be used as a dry storage area. There was a stack of logs, a couple of old fence posts, and a folded rotating clothes dryer in the corner. Most important to him, though, were the two spare concrete paving slabs leant against the wall. He got these and leant them instead against the wall below the window. Concerned to ensure there was no danger of them slipping away, he wedged the bottom edge with some of the thinner baulks of wood from the stack of logs. Standing on the four-inch edge these gave him, raised him about two feet. Now he was able to put his head and one arm through the window. As his arms were not needed for support, he could slant his shoulder girdle through the gap. The first problem solved, the second was to get the rest of his body through and down without noise, and especially without knocking all the bottles off the shelf.

He stepped down, took his anorak and jersey off, leaving only the thin black Odlo underwear on his torso. He screwed the silencer onto the pistol and placed this, the knife and the timer on the shelf next to the window. The fuse wire was still in one of his back jean pockets. Stepping up again it took him two minutes of careful manoeuvring before he was standing in a small, closed utility area below the stair. Cautiously he opened the door. Virtually in the centre of the house, he hardly had to move to establish that whoever was in the building: the cunt of an informant; and/or possibly a police babysitter; or a wife, or children, or whoever, they must all be upstairs. That would be where he would have been in the same situation. Reassured that he was relatively safe he slipped quietly into the kitchen, and studied the gas oven and hobs there. Quickly satisfied that there was a plentiful supply of explosive, he set about creating the detonator. Using one of the short driver tools on the Swiss army knife, he trapped a piece of 5amp fuse wire in a two-inch arc between the timer's live and neutral sockets. The kettle was plugged in adjacent to the cooker, so he unplugged it and placed the timer unit in the socket. He carefully plugged the kettle back into the timer, so that the loop of fuse wire hung below the plug. A test of the device would have removed all doubts as to its function, but certainly risked alerting the occupants: there would be a loud bang when it shorted; he opted for doubt.

The next question was how much gas to release. The most explosive mix was about 9 parts air to 1 part gas. He surveyed the floor; concerned that gas could dissipate downward, then estimated the size of the downstairs area, did a quick mental calculation, and set the timer to switch on at 0110. This gave him forty-five minutes to escape. He turned all the dials of the gas cooker full on, slightly opened the oven door, and then quietly left as he had come, closing the window behind him. He returned through the gardens, this time with no dog disturbing the silence. Then working around in an arc, he made his way to a spot fifteen yards away from the front police squad car, in a patch of dense shrubs and trees. It seemed to be a no-man's-land between properties.

The plan was that the explosion should be an end in itself, but it was possible it might not result in the target's demise. If that were the case, and this time with surprise on his side, he was prepared to shoot him, any policemen, and anyone else, if he or they staggered out injured.

When the blast came, it surpassed his expectations. The relatively small house seemed to bulge outwards and then the exterior walls disintegrated in flying blocks of stone and brick. A significant piece of the roof sailed skyward, almost it seemed in slow motion. Turning it plunged down onto both the relatively small front garden and the police squad car.

No one emerged from the wreckage, not surprisingly, as he was sure no one inside the house could have survived, it now looked like something out of the London Blitz.

Happy again he quietly slipped away, the episode consigned to history as another unfortunate diversion to the main game.

8. A Frank Exchange

Andrew sat in the interview room with a cup of tea and a police officer for company. He was getting very hungry, the last food he had had was police fare at the scene of the first crime yesterday: over fourteen hours before. The pizza that had been ordered was taking its time to be delivered.

When it arrived at four am, it was attached to Grieve and Doyle. "Several pieces of good news," Grieve announced, as the pizza was unwrapped. "We're going to take you to a secure location: so you can sleep safely."

Andrew nodded appreciatively, the pizza was good, and his mouth was full. Grieve continued, "also, we have already sent for some clothes at our local twenty-four hour Tesco, so that you are presentable when you come back."

Andrew raised his eyebrows in a mute question. "We have a couple of people coming up from London to see you, and we rather hoped you could manage to be back here at eleven am."

Swallowing Andrew said, "more important for me is the question of my home. Have you established that the explosion was caused by Him?"

"Yes, we know how he, or she, blew the house up."

"How?" Andrew asked.

Grieve turned to Doyle who, Andrew suddenly realised, looked awful. Doyle said, "the Fire Service found that the gas cooker had had every valve opened. The gas was ignited by a piece of shorted fuse wire fixed in an electric timer; it was plugged into one of the kitchen sockets: very simple. They estimated that the gas probably had been going for about forty to fifty minutes before ignition. So no attempt to make it look accidental, the killer is obviously not cercerned about that."

"And how did he get in?" Doyle looked at Grieve and went on, "we think we know, but a definitive answer really should wait until morning."

The door opened and a Constable placed a cheap weekend holdall on the table. Grieve looked inside and drew out a five pack of underwear that loudly proclaimed it had only cost £5.00. "Hope it all fits. Ah good, there's a toothbrush and toothpaste in there too." He looked up, smiling at Andrew and then coloured slightly. "Not that I'm suggesting anything."

"Don't worry, Chief Inspector, I'm sure I smell delightful. I will try and smell of blossom when I return." Andrew noticed Doyle, despite his gloom, couldn't resist a slight smirk at his boss's discomfort. "Right," said Grieve, "off you go then, get some sleep, and we will see you back at eleven am."

"Gentlemen, about this 'secure' location, I shall sleep soundly, if you can assure me that it is known to only a few of your most trusted officers."

Doyle said, "you don't have much faith do you!" Then he added glumly, "but I supposed that's understandable... You can be absolutely assured. I'm coming with you, I intend baby-sitting you at least until eleven am; I was responsible for your safety at one o'clock when the explosion happened. It will be my neck too if our friend returns. Besides, I am more likely to get sleep there than at home."

Andrew looked sufficiently puzzled for Doyle to expand. "We have a teething baby," he explained. Andrew stood and took the holdall, "oh, I forgot to ask, how is Constable Nichol?"

The policemen exchanged a meaningful look and Doyle said tersely, "he died an hour ago, in theatre." The three men stood in an awkward silence for a moment and then Doyle continued, "thankfully, the other officer should recover in a few weeks."

Doyle and Andrew made their way out to a nondescript silver Vauxhall in a closed yard. Two grim faced plain-clothed policemen were in the front. Their passengers hid under a blanket in the back. They left followed by another car, also with two grim men in it. They drove a convoluted route to ensure there was no one following and at a word from the front that all seemed clear, both the men in the back sat up.

There was little conversation even when they arrived at the Parkway Hotel. All six of them went in, two took an adjacent twin room to the one Doyle, and Andrew had taken. The other two were going to stay for a while and then go and get some sleep.

Doyle and Andrew hardly talked, mainly because they were both completely exhausted. They had a very cursory ablution and quickly got their heads down. Doyle was nearest the door and put his pistol on the table beside the bed in very easy reach.

At ten am, they breakfasted in the room and left to return to the station, escorted once more by the two other plain-clothed officers.

9. A Can of Worms

Grieve had got some sleep before being called in following the explosion. He got some more before being back at Weetwood Divisional HQ at nine am.

He found the Secret Squirrels already there: Harcourt was MI6, Thompson MI5. Both were men of considerable gravitas, aged in their fifties. Grieve was at ease with them, they felt like peers. He would have been very uncomfortable with some jumped up Oxbridge kid. They went into a small briefing room that already had a big vacuum flask of coffee in it. Grieve started to pour coffee and said, "We have an hour here together. At ten, the team comes together for a review of the domestic investigation, which will give you some insight on our progress. At eleven you meet the witness who, as you know, is off-site and under protection. At twelve, you will be taken to the scene and I will brief the Chief Superintendent on progress.

We have yet to make contact with the son, Steven Armstrong, who is on leave from his regiment. We have postponed formal identification until he gets here, but I am told you have already seen the bodies?"

Thompson nodded pensively. "I knew Armstrong, I mean the Major: it is him, not that there was any real doubt." He frowned, "I never met Barbara though."

"It is she." Harcourt, deadpan, said. He and Grieve then sat with their coffees. Thompson remained standing and wrote on the board, "As we discussed yesterday morning, the options worthy of consideration at this time are:

IRA and Republican splinter groups.

UDA and loyalist splinter groups.

A Cold War issue or grudge re-emerging.

An old domestic grievance.

Crime related to these topics above.

Other crime.

One other we added for completeness, is Second War Legacy."

As he wrote it down, Grieve looked a question at Harcourt, who had anticipated the need for some explanation and expansion, "he was young then, just a Lieutenant, but did operate in the Balkans briefly. Something else, which you must understand, Chief Inspector, the Major was a hard man. He was definitely in the "omelettes require eggs to be broken" mould. He achieved a lot and as a result made a number of enemies, on both sides of the fence." Harcourt emphasised, "when we consider these topics, we must not overlook the fact that people 'on our side' might be happy to see him dead too."

Grieve was clearly a little taken aback, "surely not?"

"Absolutely, yes. From our point of view, the world is just as complex and dangerous now as it was in the 1940's. We still make decisions today that lead people into grave danger and death. Those who die often do so quite horribly. Some of these decisions are very open to criticism. Generally, those who die have friends and family, some of whom are close enough to the business to view the sacrifice as unnecessary."

"But has that ever resulted in revenge, in a murder?"

Harcourt nodded, "I carry a scar in my back from just such an attempt."

"It's a given; lets move on." Thompson said phlegmatically. "We both had teams construct likely scenarios and likely players during yesterday. We compared notes in the evening and Harcourt and I have the end result. Let's get to it.

From the lovely Emerald Isle we have four possibles, two republican splinter candidates, one Loyalist, and one internal candidate.

Firstly, Dermot Green was the sole survivor of an IRA team he led which was destroyed by an Armstrong initiated operation. He is a hard-liner and got out of jail in the Republic three months ago, having been in there for twelve years for killing a Garda officer. The Irish surveillance boys have lost him and we are speculating he is in the UK.

We think he is a very definite possibility. Recently released, brutal, capable and with a huge grudge against Armstrong.

The second is Frank Daly, another IRA hardliner, who hates Armstrong too. He is convinced Armstrong had his only son shot. Our security forces did kill the son but we know of no connection with Armstrong. This logic, which is generally accepted by both sides, hasn't deterred Daly from threatening retribution. Then again, we are fairly sure he is still in Sligo: the Garda are checking. If he is still there, then he could have had it done by a third party. However, everything we have at the moment undermines this possibility, as we think he has little access to resource. The caveat, or alternate view, to this is that the only reason we could think of for him waiting to do the hit until now was the need to acquire resources. Maybe, unbeknown to us, he has come into some money, or some friends. We are, obviously, checking that out with the help of Dublin too.

Next is Brian McVean, he has a substantial grudge with Armstrong too but we are not sure why. He is one of the nastier Loyalists, who likes to torture as well as execute. He sees no paradox in killing British troops whilst enthusiastically proclaiming his loyalty to Queen and country.

On the other hand, we know he is at home in Belfast keeping his head low as, apparently, one of the other Loyalist factions want him dead. Could be that he organised the hit on Armstrong though as, unlike Daly, he was, and is, not constrained by lack of resources. Yet, there remains the question of why he would wait until now.

73

The last one, William Hastings, is, or was, on our side. He is also one of the Old Guard. He served in a subordinate role to Armstrong in the Balkans at the end of the Second War and then stayed on in MI5. For most of their adult lives, he and Armstrong were very close friends.

Hastings had a daughter, Carol, who was brilliant academically, especially in maths. Hastings doted on her. She graduated with a first in Pure Mathematics from Oxford. Unfortunately, she met a rabid Irish Nationalist there called Cahill Hennessy. It was instant 70's love and they married very quickly.

As the young often do, she went over, lock, stock and barrel, to the 'Irish Cause'. Once Hennessy had completed his PhD, they went to live in the Republic. She became a Catholic and both were heavily involved in Sinn Fein, much to the dismay of Hastings. Despite this outturn, father and daughter remained close at a personal level and interestingly I know that Hastings and Hennessy called a truce on the politics, and got on very well as a result.

Then two events rocked the boat. First Hastings's wife Beth was diagnosed with late stage breast cancer and died very quickly. Husband, wife and daughter had all been very close, so this threw Hastings more on to Carol, and Carol more on to Hennessy.

Independently, during their preoccupation with Beth's illness and death, Hennessy started making considerable waves in the Republican movement. He had strong views on both the appropriate strategy to achieve political status, and the exploitation of the favourable publicity from the deaths of the IRA hunger strikers. As is often the way in Ireland there was a violent end to this dangerous path: he got himself blown up.

Carol immediately assumed we, British Intelligence, were responsible, which we weren't, and she and Hastings had a massive and violent bust-up. These two events - the loss of his wife and the estrangement with his daughter caused us some concern; they came close to destabilising him.

In the meantime Armstrong, who had known Carol from birth, started to compile a dossier that fairly conclusively pointed the finger for Hennessy's death at the internecine Republican feud and, specifically, on the afore mentioned Dermot Green. With this

74

dossier, some nifty footwork, and a lot of patience, Armstrong eventually turned Carol back to the 'straight and narrow'. To be fair to Armstrong, I think his principal motivation in turning Carol was to effect reconciliation with her father. Nevertheless, she flipped from one extreme position to the other and became, at her insistence, a willing insider for MI5. Neither Armstrong, nor Carol, thought it wise to reveal this to her father.

She was determined to get Green; so much so, that it was she, again at her insistence, who was the decoy in the operation that hit his team. As already mentioned Green survived. Sadly the IRA, in fact possibly Green himself, shot her in the head at close quarters three months later.

Hastings was appalled that Armstrong had involved her in the war and never forgave him for her death. He was heard to say on several occasions that he would do to Armstrong what they had done to Carol. Despite the threats, he was unable to enact a revenge: this was the last straw for his mental health; he had a lengthy breakdown from which he only slowly recovered. He retired to North Wales a few years ago, a shell of his former self. We have sent a pair to see him."

Harcourt took over reading the report. "The next category is a combination of Second War and Cold War. Our first candidate is Victor Kossuth a Hungarian national who worked in Hungary for Armstrong when he was in MI6. He ran a small network, which was sacrificed by Armstrong to protect a more valuable asset. Armstrong attempted to save as many as possible without compromising his objective and one of these was Kossuth. His thanks was to be attacked by him when they met. Kossuth's hate of the communists exceeded his hate of Armstrong though; he left Armstrong alone after that.

When the Cold War ended, Kossuth immediately went back and killed the officer that had rounded up and executed most of his colleagues. He got banged up in a Hungarian jail until September last year when he too was released. So, he has motive and has recently been freed.

The fly in the ointment is that we are reasonably sure he is stuck in Budapest, with a heart condition, and no funds. Armstrong excepted, he is a Britophile, and kept close to British current affairs whilst in jail. He had very good English before he went in, but still managed to improve it while in there. Not good enough though to eradicate the slight accent.

Next is Gustav Forman who had cause to hate Barbara. When she specialised in Czechoslovakia, Forman became a real thorn in her side after the soviet invasion in 1969, doing a lot of damage to her networks. Working deep and intelligently she succeeded in turning the tables and scored a coup by ultimately discrediting him as a potential double agent in 1971, when, incidentally, she was pregnant with Fiona.

Forman wasn't a double agent, but she did such an excellent job on the frame that he was deported to a Soviet labour camp, where he managed to survive until 1990.

Then with the collapse of the Warsaw Pact and the Soviet Union, Czechoslovakia sought his return to face murder charges dating back to 1970. So, he got banged up again. He was released in 2000 on compassionate grounds as he was and is suffering from acute prostate cancer. I almost feel sorry for the poor bastard." Harcourt smiled insincerely and went on, "however, we are virtually certain he is still at home in Brno in the South of what is now the Czech Republic and his condition simply deteriorates. The Czechs' opinion is that he is a broken man. We also cannot think of a reason why he would wait until now to spring a hit on Barbara. He has a good command of English, but has a very pronounced accent.

Our last candidate is a Serbian called Gavrilo Bulatovic. This guy has, until very recently, been a Serbian Army Colonel with a very nasty streak, and is suspected of unpleasantries in Bosnia, Kosovo, and possibly Croatia.

The link is that Armstrong executed his father Edvard in late 1944 when he was with the British mission to Tito's Yugoslavian resistance. Bulatovic was only two but carried a stigma ever since, as the field execution was based on evidence that Edvard was a spy for the Germans. To add to his grievance his mother, unable to deal with the hate that was her husband's legacy, killed herself when he was eight years old.

Bulatovic did manage, in 1978, to get a Yugoslavian court to condemn the evidence against his father as being flawed. Two years later Tito, just before he died, pardoned the man, saying his death was an injustice. Maybe it was, but then, as we

76

all know, the fog of war doesn't blind hindsight. A short time later Bulatovic appeared on television to discuss his father, the execution, his search for justice, and the pardon. The story was covered here too. He held the Major responsible for both his parent's deaths and the difficulties he had faced in his life: it was absolutely clear that a bitter revenge would follow.

The current position is Bulatovic retired from the now Serbian army six months ago due to ill health: some debilitating old wounds that we understand have brought on chronic arthritis among other things.

His body may be decrepit but there is nothing wrong with his mind: this guy has a dangerously superior intellectual capability. Before joining the army, he studied Fine Art at university and was, reportedly, very bright and very talented. That fed through to the forces where initially he prospered, but the legacy of his father's apparent crime held him back from more senior appointments.

We know that he has amassed considerable wealth in the last ten years, from his various dubious activities. With that and time on his hands he has to be considered a real possibility.

One other thing - he has excellent English; he can pass for a native, and is very familiar with London having been attached to the Yugoslav embassy from 1972 to 1975.

Unfortunately, neither the Serbs nor we have any idea where he is. They were monitoring him, as they are, finally, moving towards trying some of their bad apples for War Crimes. He is a potential candidate for arrest, which probably explains why he gave them the slip."

Thompson stood up. "And that is it from our perspective at this time. Patently, with only a day of research, the list may get longer, but we think we have the bulk of the candidates here. If I summarise."

He turned to the board and started to write,

Dermot Green - definite possibility.

Frank Daly - unlikely but Garda checking.

Brian McVean - unlikely, if so: through a third party.

William Hastings - possibility until eliminated.

Victor Kossuth - possibility. If so: through a third party.

Gustav Forman - possibility, but ill and why wait?

Gavrilo Bulatovic - definite possibility.

"All their details are in the report."

Grieve got up and poured more coffee. "You found nothing that is simple crime; drugs or fraud or laundering or something else?"

Both men shook their heads and Grieve continued, "right, for the moment, if you gentlemen agree, I will stick with investigating potential criminal candidates. As to these seven, all their trails are off the Mainland except Hastings, but you are already onto his case. So you and your foreign friends will chase down the missing ones, Green and Bulatovic?" Grieve looked at Harcourt and he agreed. Grieve looked pleased with the easy cooperation. "You will also confirm that Daly, Kossuth, and Forman are at home?" Harcourt nodded again; Grieve handed out the fresh coffee and sat down again. "We will all have to tackle whether Daly, McVean, Kossuth, and possibly Forman organised a third party hit. Communication is vital, so please liase with Inspector Doyle or me.

Another point that bears on this is the hit on our witness, and the death of one of our Constables. It has made us angry and embarrassed here in West Yorkshire and is ultra top priority too. Our killer, or a colleague, got to Mr Maxwell very fast. I want to find out how, very fast too. Not just to preserve Mr M but also because I have officers at risk protecting him.

I would be surprised if a foreign national would be clued up enough to be so quick. I think it points to Green, Daly, McVean, Hastings, or ANO. It also, almost certainly, means that our security is breached somewhere. You have tools available that I don't have. Can I ask you to use them please?" Both men nodded, Thompson said, "already been done, we want to get this bastard as much as you do Detective Chief Inspector." Grieve tilted his head in acknowledgment, "Okay, we have some time still before you meet the team so let's delve further into the detail on these seven."

10. A Dispassionate Analysis

Grieve convened the team at ten am and introduced Harcourt and Thompson.

For some of the men and women this was their first exposure to the case, so he explained how the crime was first reported and who the victims were. He knew that there were several people who had more detailed briefs to give, so he stuck to an overview. He finished his introduction with, "let's be clear regarding this case, this person, or persons, has killed, or had killed, four people on our patch inside twenty-four hours. If the first three are not bad enough, the fourth, PC Nichol, was one of us.

Be mindful, be careful, but above all work yourselves to the bone. This is one bastard we are going to nail, and quick."

He looked into the faces and saw what he wanted: people nodding, determined faces, squared jaws, everyone deadly earnest. Then he turned to the description, "as you know the description we have is, in my view, at the detailed level, probably not very useful. But some things can't be hidden; we must try to keep our minds on those.

For what it's worth we have on the face of it: a Caucasian man, about five foot ten inches, dark brown hair with some greying, medium length and well cut; Dark rimmed spectacles; Quite a good colour to his facial skin; thin dark brown moustache. He's not slim but not overweight either and possibly quite broad shouldered. He was wearing a tweed cap, a Barbour, dark gloves, dark brown cords, and light shoes. He was also carrying green wellies and a walking stick.

The eyewitness also attests that the man was lame or infirm in his movement and seemed a little bent by age. He speculated that the man might be in his fifties, or early sixties.

I do not need to tell you that someone who knows the simple tricks easily alters the moustache, spectacles, hair, and even skin colour. We can all do a passable limp and it is also a fair bet that the clothing is in a skip somewhere."

Some of his team smiled and Grieve went on, "still, as you each give your reports, I think we'll get a closer view of this person, and I mean person, I don't want anyone assuming a male gender until we have clear evidence for it.

Okay, Sergeant Banks can you take us through what we have so far on the Almscliff View house forensics please?"

Banks came forward to the front and opened his notes. "Right, sometime between six-thirty and six-forty, the subject picked the Yale lock using a standard set of wires. No forensics here other than the telltale scratches.

He crossed the kitchen and entered the central downstairs corridor. We did get some soil particles here but they seem to be from the property itself. Either by luck, or more likely, by intention, he ignored Barbara Armstrong who was, almost certainly in the rear utility area, and entered the sitting room where Major Armstrong was sat smoking a pipe, and reading the Financial Times.

The subject fired from his position by the door at a range of seven metres. The bullet entered the victim's head through his right eye and exited out of the lower skull. The trajectory had been altered slightly by its passage and it impacted the wall low down three metres beyond the body. The bullet was a standard 9mm Parabellum. Only one round was fired and it suffered only minor distortion.

Not surprisingly, the autopsy has confirmed the cause of death as massive trauma to the head. Otherwise, Major Armstrong was a very sprightly eighty-one years with a constitution and physique that would grace a sixty-one-year-old. The only chronic or acute condition being arthritis which he controlled using a drug called Celebrex.

The next victim was Barbara Armstrong, sixty-eight years. It is possible that she heard the gun, as she seems to have left the rear utility in some haste. We know from the witness that a silencer was used, so if she did hear it, it will have been the sound of the ejection and reload action, as this is louder than the silenced report, normally.

Interestingly, she didn't seek to arm herself and came straight into the sitting room. The subject took hold of her collar and placed the muzzle against her spine. Another 9mm Para was fired through her body, and through her heart; it exited and impacted in the side of the fireplace. This round suffered considerable distortion and a lot of her bodily tissues were spread outward from the large exit wound. Again, not surprisingly, cause of death was massive shock, which in turn was caused by trauma to the spine and heart. She had some signs of early heart disease, but it was not life threatening. Otherwise, she also was in good health comparable to, say, a normal woman ten years younger.

There had been some speculation that the size of the gun and silencer could be deduced from this killing, but unfortunately, any of approximately twenty-five combinations would fit the bill. Some specialist weapons can be eliminated though.

The subject then proceeded down the corridor and surprised the daughter, Fiona Armstrong, on the landing. She was the next and final victim in the house. She was aged thirty-two years. He fired from the lower corridor at a range of eleven metres, quite far, but the subject is undoubtedly a very good shot. The round hit her upper throat and exited upwards through her lower rear skull. She must have started backwards at sight of her killer as she had backward momentum; this caused her to impact with a three-legged table set against the wall, which had a large vase of flowers on it. The round continued upwards and impacted with the upper corridor wall. Again, a single 9mm Para and this round too suffered some considerable distortion. Autopsy has

81

confirmed that the bullet and the trauma it occasioned was the cause of death. Fiona Armstrong was in all other respects a very fit and healthy young woman.

Ballistic analysis has confirmed that all three bullets were fired from the same pistol.

Regarding the killer's skill with the gun, he, or she, is obviously highly accurate, but also, interestingly, only used one round per victim. I think that was a conscious decision. It might have been to minimise the sound signature that a double tap would make. It might also be because he/she wished to conserve ammunition; unaware how many people were in the house. But I think that it might also indicate a very high level of confidence, or over-confidence, in their ability. If so, that might be a flaw we can make use of as we get closer."

Grieve and several other officers seemed impressed by this point, and the Sergeant paused to stress the conjecture. Then he continued, "there is evidence that the subject went on to check each of the seven rooms upstairs, leaving all the doors open. There doesn't appear to have been any theft or any attempt at searching for valuables. However, there were two strands of hair that match the witness's description of the subject's head hair. These are human, but look to have come from a wig judging by the cuts at both ends; they are being checked for DNA anyway.

He returned downstairs and checked all the rooms there too. He didn't leave the cartridge cases: maybe he's a tidy type. We think he took a look at the Major's pistol; then he left the same way - that is through the kitchen, closing the door behind him.

So in summary: not a lot to go on, probably none of the subject's DNA, no strange fingerprints unsurprisingly, and no particulate from other locations.

That's all for now, folks."

"Thank you, Sergeant," said Grieve, consulting his notes. "Now Constable Williams: the forensics of the exterior, the subject's approach, the delivery woman, and the subject's escape."

Constable Williams was young and looked very shy standing in front of so many people, though it did not deter him from a thorough report. "The Ford Mondeo, which you have pictured, was parked in a short track off the lane; on the north side of the Wharfe, between Otley and Ilkley. The subject walked from there in wellingtons and, despite the early morning frost, the tread is clearly visible in several places in the adjacent field. He followed the border of the ploughed ground where the adjacent, narrow stand of trees hid his approach to the house.

He stopped frequently; there doesn't seem to be a reason for this other than possibly trying to look like an innocent walker, I can only speculate. Anyway, mainly for this reason the time of arrival of the car cannot be established at this time. It's certain, all the same, that there was sufficient light to see; so, the subject probably didn't arrive at the track before five am. Sorry, I mean he didn't leave the car; I suppose he could have arrived before five am, sorry.

Anyway, he went on from the first field via the gate into the next field that is adjacent to the house. He followed a line that kept him hidden from the house, most of the time, by the outbuilding roof. So," Williams looked up excitedly, "he obviously didn't choose his start point by accident: he must have done a recce. Someone may have seen him when he was doing it."

Grieve smiled, "good, but it's also clear that he was short of time, so the period to check is probably, today is Tuesday; the Sunday evening. Sergeant Banks can you put someone…" Banks acknowledged and Grieve tailed off with, "good."

Williams resumed. "While he walked he used the stick, sometimes he put a lot of weight on it; also there were varying weights put on each leg, the left leg was taking most weight most of the time so, possibly, the limp is genuine; maybe; keeping an open mind anyway.

When he got to the property's boundary wall, he leant on it for some time, possibly to look back down the field: this was the only direction with any likelihood of his being seen from, we know this as there is some damage to the lichen and moss in places on the stone. Then he went over the wall, and this is interesting; the pressure marks of his gloved hands are clear, but there is no sign of mud or scraping on the outer wall from his feet; the wall at this place is one point one metres high; this suggests a very athletic movement and some considerable

83

strength. The leap was probably done like this so that it was quick. Anyway, this makes an argument that the subject is younger and suppler than the impression given by the witness. A further point is that there are traces of mud on the two opposing walls, which suggests that he braced himself before stepping down onto the rubbish that is in the gap. All in all, this was a nice piece of gymnastic movement: vaulting from one side of the wall to standing in the gap.

He then worked his way down the wall to a spot where he could sit at the end behind a dense set of sizeable shrubs. The fact that he knew that spot existed again points towards the likelihood of a prior recce, or that he was already familiar with the layout.

Here he must have left the wellingtons and the stick; there are some forensics to support this. Judging by the degree of crushing of the grasses, he probably sat there for between fifteen minutes and an hour.

The delivery woman, Mrs Janet Lipman, who I interviewed yesterday in Otley, estimates that she arrived at the house around six-thirty; she was listening to Radio Two and thinks she remembers a time check. Besides, the Major had specifically requested that the delivery always be before six forty-five and so she always erred on the early side. She had the routine down to a tee and usually delivered at about six thirty-five; give or take five minutes.

The Major met her at the kitchen door, which is not uncommon, sometimes he didn't, but she was aware he always checked it was her from upstairs. She never drove beyond the gate as he had kindly, her word, requested that she didn't.

They had a chat about the weather and the progress of her son's piano playing but it was brief as she felt under some pressure. She had had two new customers added to the latter part of her round, by her boss, the previous day. She estimated she was back in the lane by between six-thirty-five and six-forty." Williams looked up and smiled, "I would bet my house, my wife, my dog, my bike and all my leathers that she is a lucky innocent and not linked to the murder at all!" His audience duly smiled back at him and he returned to his report,

"There is no forensic evidence between the subject's hide and the kitchen door so the rest of this is speculation. We tested

84

the proximity alarm system and it worked well for pretty much the whole property, a person moving from the hide would definitely have triggered it, but it is not sophisticated enough to distinguish two close targets. Our conclusion is that: after Mrs Lipman tripped it, as she walked to the house, the subject moved out behind her. He could have been up to fifteen metres behind her without the system being triggered a second time so we think it is in this way he could have got to the house wall without alarm. We found that at the house wall the coverage is poor: the arc is aimed outward; so as long as he got to there, he was safe from triggering it again.

So, it seems the subject took the big risk of following Mrs Lipman; he got to the wall and hid behind the opposite corner until she departed. Then he proceeded, undetected, along the front wall; around the other corner and from there to the kitchen door. Remember, as I said earlier, this is simply educated guesswork at this stage but, given that the call from Mr Maxwell came in at six-forty-nine, there aren't many other alternatives, and all the others stretch credibility.

When he, or she, left the house, the eyewitness watched him leave by the main gate; there is no forensic to support this, but also no reason to doubt the testimony. He proceeded down the access track and got back to the car around six-forty-five." Williams looked at Grieve who nodded and smiled. The Constable flushed, self-consciously, and returned to his seat. Grieve looked over at the team. "Now Jim... Jim Prentice the car etc."

Jim Prentice, a Constable, was a long-standing member of CID and there was some barracking as he walked forward. The light-hearted abuse pleased Grieve though his face remained impassive; the team had started to move from serious and introverted to workmanlike and focussed. He earnestly wanted them to solve this case, of all cases, but not because of any sermon from him. He needed them to believe they had a chance to get the bastard and needed them to want to do it for themselves. He wanted them to go beyond 'don't let the side down', beyond 'this is good for my career', and beyond 'society needs this man caught'. He wanted them to exhilarate in working in a well-oiled machine; wanted them to exhilarate in the chase; and he wanted them to bask in the brief adulation of catching and incarcerating the killer.

Jim Prentice played to the crowd, bowing to the mock applause, "the car," he started theatrically, "that you have pictured was dumped in Chapeltown at around eight yesterday morning. It had been stolen in Chapel Allerton north of Chapeltown from the drive way of Family Sym between twenty-two hundred and twenty-three-thirty on Sunday evening.

He had the keys which he took from where they were conveniently hanging on a hook inside the front door, so he had entered the house. The front door has a Yale lock like the one at the murder scene. Either he was lucky and the first house with an appropriate car on the drive of a house that looked unoccupied was the Sym's. But this is unlikely as the house is halfway down the street. There were other possibilities that he must have tried first, Some support for this with forensics. though in these cases the keys were not so easy to locate, so he moved on. The car is used by both Mr and Mrs Sym and their daughter, so it was convenient for them to leave the keys on the hook. They won't be doing that in future." He said with some weight.

"Incidentally, anyone thinking it was one of the Sym family can forget it. Mr Sym is tiny, Mrs Sym is huge in girth and the daughter is several planks short of a load."

After the laughter subsided he continued, "the theft was after dark and only six streets away from where it was dumped. That suggests to me that the subject was conducting a car switch; a dangerous business in Chapeltown as cars come and go there regularly, as you all know. Still, the fact he chose Chapeltown suggests he knew where he was and knew what he was doing.

The other possibility is that he is a local, so I have feelers out for that, but my guess is he isn't. Any local with the ability to do this hit wouldn't point us straight back at where he lives. So I thinks," he looked at Grieve here, "that he drove to the area, left his car and stole another. If he is familiar with the locality, and my guess is he is, then the first car had to be made safe from the Chapeltown animals. How would he do that? Well I have wracked my brains for options and all I can think of is one safe one: that is, he used a lock-up.

We know he can pick locks, so most lock-ups would be easy meat; a lot of lock-ups are empty and, to boot, are visited rarely by the owner. The difficulty would be finding one secure enough. So, I thinks there would be mileage in checking all the garage lock-ups between the two sites, that is the original theft site and the spot where he dumped it." He looked at Grieve for support.

Grieve was dubious, "I don't dispute your punt, it's good, unfortunately, checking all the lock-ups will take time and resource. The reason we would be doing it is to find forensics he, or she, had overlooked. The way we would know we had the right one would be by finding relevant forensics. But all the evidence so far points to our subject being very careful not to leave forensic traces. Let me think on it, okay?" Jim Prentice nodded, but was visibly disappointed and continued in more subdued style, "The car was very clean, I mean forensically, some mud and stones on the driver's well floor and pedals - this is being analysed to try to eliminate the lawful owner's traces; but I can tell you it doesn't look hopeful. Nothing in the ashtray, nothing in the boot, well nothing left by the subject, quite a lot the Sym's were able to identify. Nothing found on the tyres that suggested anything other than a Leeds-Otley-Leeds trip.

As I have already said, I think the likely escape is via a stashed car. Other alternatives are unlikely in my view; the dumpsite is a long way from the railway station; it is quite near several bus routes, but the problem there is: it risks leaving a trail in the minds of the passengers and crew; if I were the villain, I wouldn't want to do that. Anyway, just in case, we are checking these possibilities with Leeds Metro. Nothing more to add at this time."

There was a great deal of sympathy being displayed on various faces as Jim Prentice resumed his seat, and none of the barracking that had heralded his report.

Thompson, who had been listening, with some interest, to these reports, suddenly straightened and went out fishing in his breast pocket.

Grieve glanced at his departing back and then called for Sergeant Sandy Blackhall, another popular stalwart in CID.

Blackhall had been going through Almscliff View for anything that might bear on the case. He was talking before he had reached the front. "There was an old safe in the Major's study downstairs as well as a filing cabinet. These yielded a lot, but we only got into them yesterday evening; we had to get a locksmith out to open them. There is nothing to suggest that the subject either accessed them or even had time to access them. There were two copy wills in there, documents relating to assets held, documents relating to purchases made, and so on, a lot of material to sift. The wills were identical and favour both children, but two-thirds was to be granted to Fiona, double what Steven was to get. Maybe this was because she was eight years younger. I have yet to get a handle on the value of the estate and I have yet to see the original wills from the solicitor.

Nothing else of significance found downstairs.

Upstairs, unusually, the gun cabinet was in the dressing room off the master bedroom; the locksmith opened this for us too. The reason it was there and not in the usual secure downstairs site was because this room in the rear left corner of the house was set up as a redoubt. The floor, the walls, the roof, and the door were all armoured. Though it wasn't obvious until you did some digging, and I only sussed it when I went into the loft.

In the gun-cabinet, there was a second pistol, a Smith & Wesson 9mm Polymer frame. Light, nice, I guess for Mrs Armstrong. The really big surprise was the rest of the contents. There was a Colt Commando assault-rifle, I think called the M4, like a short M16. A sawn off single barrel five shot automatic shotgun, two beautiful McKay-Brown over and under shotguns, and an old but serviceable Lee Enfield mk3 .303 rifle. There were about one hundred rounds of 9mm Parabellum for the pistols and five hundred rounds of 5.56mm for the M4; several spare loaded magazines were clipped ready for use for both the pistols and the assault rifle. There were seventy shotgun cartridges and approximately one hundred rounds of .303."

There was a considerable buzz going around the team at this armoury and Grieve had to call for attention to return to the brief.

Thompson had quietly returned and Grieve looked round at him; when he blandly looked straight back, Grieve knew Thompson had known something of the illegal stash of weapons.

Blackhall continued, "there was also a fully charged satellite phone. It doesn't take a genius to deduce that they were set up to resist, if they had warning, and for a maximum of maybe an hour, an assault by several heavily armed bad buggers. I suppose that is not so surprising given that he had worked in Northern Ireland. Mind you, the extent of the defence, particularly the high-powered weaponry, goes beyond anything I have heard of in Ireland." He looked at the trio of Grieve, Thompson, and Harcourt by the door for some support; Harcourt and Thompson studied the floor. Grieve sighed and said, "well it didn't do them any good, but it evidently shows they felt that there was a tangible threat; and, team take note, not necessarily just an Irish threat either."

Blackhall resumed his brief. "The room occupied by Fiona Armstrong did not look lived in at all. A small case was open on the floor on the offside of the bed. Unfortunately, it's not possible to deduce how long she had been there as there was quite a lot of her clothing in the tumbler-drier in the utility: whether it was used here, or brought with her, has yet to be established.

Her wallet, mobile and, interestingly, her passport were all in her room. Her mobile was out of signal at the house, but when we were bringing it here it bleeped a message alert; I listened in to her messages and discovered two recent ones from what I guess is a boyfriend." He quoted from his notebook, "'Fiona, where are you, I have just got a call from Millie, she says she arrived at the flat at five-thirty pm as scheduled, with the curtain designs, and you weren't there. She tried your mobile and just like me got the message service. This whole makeover thing was your bloody idea so what's going on. The last thing I need right now is organising internal decor. Call her and me soonest please.' That call was at six minutes to six on Sunday evening, this one at nine twenty-three followed it: 'Fiona, where the fuck are you. This really is the last straw, Millie has just rung and told me where to get off, and she is, was, a mate of mine. Why can't you phone her and me? I am up to my eyes in Bristol for the launch next Monday, and it looks like I am going to have to fight a fire at Astons too. Call me ASAP. Jamie.' It was a mobile, not a hotel phone unfortunately. I checked the number and got the details a short while ago, it belongs to James Belvedere, of Flat Three, Fifteen Chelsea Place, SW3 London. Interestingly, this is the same address as Fiona Armstrong. Four things of note here:

First: they apparently live together.

Second: she was supposed to be at home in London on Sunday, at the very least.

Third: he is, apparently, away from home so we can't waltz into their flat without first getting permission; which is a shame as Fred Collins is currently on the train to London to do just that with the Met." Grieve interrupted, "tell him to stay there anyway; hopefully we will get permission from Mr Belvedere sometime today." Sandy Blackhall nodded and continued, "fourthly: Mr Belvedere needs to be given the very bad news."

Grieve said, "so he's probably in Bristol but he didn't say where. Any mileage in 'Astons'; I guess that is a company?" Blackhall shook his head. "There are two companies of that name in Bristol; neither knew of a Mr James Belvedere. So I gave it some thought: maybe we could ring him to tell him to go to the nearest police station." Grieve looked askance, "and the reason? Because we have to tell you the woman you love more than life itself is dead?"

"No sir, I thought we could make something up, say, that we could tell him his car has been reported as being a victim of a hit and run and we wanted to check or eliminate it." This gave Grieve pause, "possibility, why what does he drive?" Blackhall was pleased with himself, "the PNC says it is a silver Jaguar XK8; he has what was probably an expensive personalised number plate on it." Grieve was beginning to see flaws in the plan, "and how do you explain how you got his mobile number?"

Blackhall frowned. "Ah."

Grieve turned to Thompson. "Could you help?" Thompson nodded agreeably and pulled out his phone. Blackhall handed over his notebook so that Thompson could read the mobile number and the car registration. As he dialled he leaned into Grieve's ear. "We got a break, Dermot Green has been picked up in Toxteth, Liverpool; a tip-off from a local snout. I've asked them to bring him here, should arrive in the early

90

afternoon; maybe you should follow it up with an official request." Then he turned away to request the search for James Belvedere, his car, or his phone. When his notebook was returned Blackhall continued. "We checked her dialled, missed, and received calls log and got the info on the unidentified numbers this morning. She called her parents at home at sixteen forty-six on Sunday; very briefly, it was not more than three minutes. Possibly to say she was coming home, but that is speculation. She called a mobile listed on her phone as Steven Armstrong immediately afterwards at sixteen forty-nine and then again at sixteen fifty-one, speculative suggestion, to say something similar. I'm guessing she got an answer-phone the first time, rang off, then thought better of it, and left a message the second time around. Or possibly, she just got cut off.

She didn't call James Belvedere at any time on Friday, Saturday, or Sunday interestingly. Nor did she call the previously mentioned Millie; though there is a Millie listed on her phone's address book. She missed a call back from Steven at seventeen twenty-five on Sunday, possibly as she was driving home, but there was no message. Also listed were the ones already mentioned from James and this Millie woman. She doesn't appear to have received any other relevant calls in the period at all but we are still checking.

We found nothing in her case, wallet, or anywhere else to suggest why she was with her parents when she was supposed to be in London. When I checked her parents' home phone I found it had no dial outs in the past two days at all!

Moving on to the rubbish bin there were signs of an evening meal for three with up to two bottles of red Australian Shiraz Cabernet consumed. The dishwasher had plates consistent with this. No obvious paper disposals and no obvious signs of destruction of documents in the rubbish, the fire, or the garden rubbish fire.

Lastly, the garage or outbuildings: these are a large enclosed area with room for three cars. Two were inside: a bronze coloured old style BMW Five series, which is registered to Gordon Armstrong and a White VW Golf, which is registered to Fiona. Both looked to have been undisturbed overnight; the garage is padlocked anyway. Off to the side is an extensive

91

workshop area, with paint, tools etc; the layer of dust suggests it has gone undisturbed for some time." He looked up and closed his notebook, so Grieve thanked him, and he returned to his chair. "We will continue to mine the rich seam of motive for killing the older Armstrong's, but Sandy can you take responsibility for investigating whether Fiona was the real target. Her unexpected appearance at the house followed by the murder at some time soon after is a bit too coincidental." Sandy Blackhall nodded and looked meaningfully around at the two Constables flanking him.

Grieve then looked over at Sergeant Reilly, who came to the front. He looked very tired. "We've been working all night on 5, Drumlithie Avenue, and its surroundings, and I've come straight from there, so my notes are a bit jumbled. Please forgive me if this is a bit disjointed." Grieve nodded sympathetically and Reilly turned to the assembly. "The would be killer approached, and left the house via the gardens of two neighbouring properties, the one nearest Number 6 is occupied but empty. The neighbours say they are on holiday. Mr Bradshaw at the other, 11 Drumchapel Close remembers his dog barking between twenty-three-thirty and twelve mid-night, i.e. one to one and a half hours before the explosion.

This subject, note we must assume a different person at this time, entered the back garden of Mr Maxwell's house and was at one point about fifteen metres from where he was sleeping under, and hidden by, the rhododendron. It's not surprising he didn't see him though: I got Ron to tuck himself into the camouflaged bag and once he was squirreled away, I couldn't see him either and I knew he was there!

It's difficult to tell from the limited spoor but we think that this subject was not limping at anytime on his approach or escape.

He must have reconnoitred the approach during the day, so Ron is checking the houses now to see if anyone saw him or his car. It's a Neighbourhood Watch area, so we are keeping our fingers crossed.

In the end, he didn't enter from the back garden. He went back into the garden of Number 6 and approached the side of the house through the conifers next to the fence. He forced his way through these and we had hoped for some DNA on the branches

92

but all we got were some blue fibres, from some kind of outer garment. We should get more on those fibres today. Once he was over the fence, he entered through a tiny utility window, which, remarkably, is still largely intact. I think it was protected to some extent by the stair structure. Once the forensic boys were finished, I tried to copy the killer by entering the window myself, but I couldn't get through." Reilly, who was a relatively rotund man, had to stop until the laughter died. Somewhat defensively he continued, "Ron tried too. There were some paving slabs placed to give extra height; by standing on these and stretching one arm forward he was just able to squeeze his shoulders through, but it was very tight. Ron has a forty-four inch chest so our villain can't be much bigger than that."

Reilly described the method of detonation and the effects of the blast. He finished off with, "we decided that the subject wouldn't leave until sure that no one had survived the blast, so we looked for some sign that he, or she, had hung around. Sure enough we found some crushed leaves below some bushes, ten to fifteen metres above and to the left of the squad car PC's Nichol and Aitkin were in: no significant forensics again though.

That's me done for now, Ron got a few hours sleep so he stayed to knock the doors. I'm bushed; I'll get back in harness later this afternoon." Grieve nodded and thanked him.

Next, he indicated for Constable Abercrombie who got up, stretched, and came forward, "I spoke to Steven Armstrong's CO at the Royal Logistics Corp yesterday. Steven is currently on leave, last week, and this week, but he is expected to call in occasionally, and sure enough at nine-thirty this morning he did. He was at home in Chiswick, London so they asked him to come down to Regimental HQ at Deepcut for a briefing on an operation. Apparently, that is commonplace, especially nowadays. Deepcut is near Farnborough and is approximately an hour's drive for him, so he said he would be there for twelve Noon. They will inform him of the tragedy and will then have him driven here. Barring accidents he should be here at around five or six this evening.

Working on the assumption that there are no problems with the identification, and we can get to Mr Belvedere today, I have arranged a news conference, provisionally, for eight-thirty

93

pm, which I am assuming you will chair?" He looked at Grieve who nodded. "A twenty-thirty schedule ensures it will hit the main evening news." Grieve interjected, "are there no other relatives?"

"None alive, or sufficiently close, that I have found." Abercrombie shook his head and then carried on, "the news of the explosion in Ilkley was too public to keep under wraps and was broadcast this morning. We have said it was a gas explosion and that two people are dead, including PC Nichol, who was unfortunate to be passing at the time.

The editors know it's not the whole truth but they have agreed to layoff for the time being. Naming Mr Maxwell will have to wait. But we can't wait too long or the subject, assuming he is still in the country, will smell a rat. It might be possible to tell his family the truth without risking a breach, a further breach, of security.

Okay, that's me done for now too."

Grieve thanked him and his last man to report, Constable Hopper, stood up unhappily. "Sorry Guv, I have hardly anything to report. The options I have thought of are:

One: the subject listened to our radio traffic, but no one mentioned Mr Maxwell's name and his address was only mentioned twice and not in context. Besides, I understood the new encrypted telecoms were secure from eavesdropping.

Two: the subject was watching us at close quarters and overheard where the ARV was taking the witness, but it is almost unbelievable that he would take such a risk. Not only that, he would have to be a miraculously good stalker to get back to within earshot without being spotted.

Three: that the subject tailed the witness and ARV when they went back to Ilkley. But again, he would have had to be in a car right next to the scene of the crime to pick them up. And anyway, the ARV guys said they were on open rural roads: there was no way a tail could have stayed hidden.

Four: the most likely explanation is that he is one of us, distasteful as it sounds, or he has one of us in his pocket." There were angry words from some of the assembled officers and everyone frowned their disapproval at the unfortunate Hopper, "what about other forces?" Someone said. Hopper responded

94

dolefully, "up to this morning no one, but no one, outside West Yorkshire police knew Mr Maxwell's name or address, now those two gentlemen do," he indicated the Secret Squirrels, "but that is it."

"Okay, thanks Constable, I will give it more thought." Grieve frowned, Hopper had covered all the alternatives he had considered and discarded. Was there something else, or were they missing something simple.

Harcourt and Thompson were introduced to Andrew when he arrived escorted by Doyle. The three of them went off to a small meeting room where once again, Andrew went through every last detail of what he had seen.

Meanwhile Grieve gave the still very weary Doyle a summary of the briefing as well as the information on the seven suspects that Military Intelligence had supplied. They then started to plan the next couple of days of investigation. Grieve said he would interview Green, when he arrived at around fourteen hundred, probably with Thompson. He considered it a good idea for Doyle to go to Belfast to see McVean, when the police there had found him, which seemingly would not be that simple. Grieve would also brief Steven Armstrong and escort him to the mortuary for identification.

Harcourt and Thompson, escorted by Sandy Blackhall, rejoined them then with some news, "James Belvedere is a lot closer than Bristol: he is currently driving eastbound on the M62 just outside Rochdale." Thompson offered. Grieve looked surprised, he turned to Sandy, "see if Traffic can pick him up and bring him here." Sandy nodded and left. "Funny that he's so close now, when he said he was in Bristol on Sunday," Grieve said. Thompson looked noncommittal.

"Where is Maxwell?" Grieve asked.

"Having tea in the canteen in the care of poor Constable Hopper, who seems to have been rather ostracised by the rest of your team." Harcourt said with another smile. Grieve looked thunderous, "bloody hell, I am not happy with that, the man is supposed to be dead, the sooner we get him hidden away again the better. I think we should send him back to his secure

95

location." He punched a number on his mobile and was brief and very curt to whoever was at the other end.

When he had finished Thompson continued, "there's more news, Hastings is not at home; the neighbours said he left with a bag on Sunday. Now, it is just possible he has gone on holiday, because it seems he finished a course on ancient Greek sculpture at the local college on Friday. However, the timing is interesting don't you think?"

"Indeed," said Grieve. "Anything on Daly?"

"No, there is no further news and we didn't get anything from Maxwell, though I think he thinks he knows something else: he hesitated a few times in his narrative, it seemed as if something was trying to surface in his mind."

"Yes, I know, hopefully it'll surface soon," Grieve agreed. "Maybe a quiet time out of the way will throw it up. I'll have him back here, incognito, tomorrow morning to see if the enforced rest has prompted any fresh thinking." He turned to his young colleague, "as for you, Doyle, you get off home and get some more rest, come back in for an hour or so at eighteen-hundred to get up to date."

11. A Couple of Suspects

James Belvedere was driving fast on the M62. He was a careful and alert driver, so as he rounded the sweeping bend he immediately saw the police car, five hundred yards ahead, on the ramp at the side of the carriageway.

He slowed, and by the time he approached it, he was doing seventy mph. Hoping he could quickly return to his preferred cruising speed, he was dismayed when he saw it leave its raised perch. It joined the traffic, all of which was now solemnly doing seventy, two hundred yards behind him. The police car stayed in the streaming traffic keeping much the same distance behind him. James frowned in annoyance and concentrated on driving carefully and staying at around seventy; he did not want to be picked up. All the surrounding drivers were similarly minded and so a sizable block of cars all sedately driving at, or just below, seventy progressed gradually towards Bradford and Leeds. Eventually, when the M606 junction hove on the horizon James decided to escape this disconcerting shadow by turning on to it. Infuriatingly, the police car followed him off and the bulk of the other drivers, who had stayed on the M62, gleefully accelerated away.

Belvedere started to get a bad feeling. He turned anticlockwise onto the, euphemistically named, Bradford ring road and still the car followed him. He was sure he would lose it when he turned onto the main Harrogate road; but it was a vain hope, it was still there and getting closer. Accepting the inevitable, he pulled over into a lay-by at the side of the road and sure enough, the police car pulled in behind him. Closing his eyes briefly in frustration he wondered, why me? He had not been the fastest or the most cavalier on the road.

The officer on the near side got out and approached his Jaguar's passenger window. He knocked on it politely and James pressed the button that made it purr downward, "Mr James Belvedere?"

"Yes, officer."

"We would like you to come with us to Weetwood Divisional HQ in Leeds, Sir. We are told it's important." James looked stunned; he gapped at the policeman for a few seconds, "why?"

"They didn't tell us that, Sir. Do you have any objection?" James thought about it, then shook his head.

"Under the circumstances, I think it would be best if I drive you, Sir." James looked stunned again, "but... are you insured?"

The policeman smiled, "I'm a very careful driver, Sir. But to answer your question, yes, I am fully insured by the Force.

Now, if you could take the passenger seat, we'll be off."

With the policeman at the wheel and the other car following, they rejoined the traffic. Belvedere's mind was in a turmoil. How did they know where he was? It couldn't just have been luck. This was not good.

Unwittingly, James had been going broadly in the right direction, so it took them only a further twenty minutes to reach the large police station on the Leeds outer ring road. There he was met by a Constable and shown into a small interview room. The Constable stood at ease by the door. James was nervous, what had they got on him?

The door opened and in walked a tall, late middle-aged man; James stood. DCI Grieve saw a man in his mid thirties, short blond hair; slim, but muscular; sharp-featured face, almost chiselled, and he was slightly taller than himself so about six foot two. He looked worried.

"I'm Detective Chief Inspector Grieve, Mr Belvedere."

"Pleased to meet you." They shook hands.

"Please sit down." James frowned but sat as directed.

"I'm afraid I have bad news, and there is no easy way to say it. Fiona Armstrong, and both her parents have been murdered at the parents' home in Wharfedale. It happened early yesterday morning."

Belvedere just looked across at Grieve, a small frown slowly started to crease his forehead. Grieve went on, "please ask any questions you want, I will try and answer them as best I can." But James Belvedere's mouth only worked in silence; he seemed paralysed. Eventually he stammered, "but... Fiona's in London, not up here, it must be a mistake?"

Grieve smiled sadly, and compassionately, at the young man's disbelief; looked down at the folded paper in his hand; opened it and put it on the table. "Does she drive a white VW Golf with this registration?" Grieve pushed the piece of typescript across the table; it was a description of the car.

Belvedere studied it for several dumbstruck seconds then looked up, "yes... yes..." he frowned and shook his head, still disbelieving.

"That car is in the garage at the house." Grieve explained, he went on, "there has been nothing on the News of it yet as we have to inform relatives and, of course, yourself. Also, there has yet to be a formal identification. We intercepted you as we learnt you shared an address with Miss Armstrong."

James still looked nonplussed, but slowly he dropped his head into his hands. His shoulders began to shake. Grieve was used to the behaviour of the bereaved, "I am so sorry for your loss." He signalled to the Constable by the door. The young officer had anticipated him and immediately went out for some tea. When he came back, he placed the tea on the table, sat beside James, and took his hand. Tears were streaming down

Belvedere's face. Grieve said, "this officer will stay with you for as long as you need. You can also go with him and see Fiona in the Mortuary, if you want to, and feel able." Grieve stayed for a further ten, solicitous, minutes answering the obvious questions as they randomly emerged, and until the immediate shock had worn off the grieving man. He then said, "I need to do something else now, but I would like to have a longer talk with you later today. I suggest that you book into an hotel tonight, again this Constable can help you with that." Belvedere nodded and thanked him.

Grieve left the room and learnt that Dermot Green had arrived as expected. Now for something completely different, thought the DCI. Thompson was going to come into the room but sit mute at the back whilst Grieve and Sergeant Banks were to conduct the interview, if they could get the Irishman to talk. He met Banks in the corridor and the Sergeant said, "we may have a break: Ron called in to say they have just found an old lady, a Mrs Moore, that he thinks saw the killer and a car in Ilkley. She lives about one hundred and fifty yards as the crow flies from Mr Maxwell's house at Eight Drumchapel Close. This is almost opposite the property our subject started from last night. Apparently, she spends hours at the window and notes everyone and everything that comes into the street, suspicious or not. She sees nothing at night, though, as she goes to bed early, at around nine every evening.

There is a property for sale on the Close, Number Four, and someone wearing a blue anorak, remember the blue fibres, and looking similar to the Almscliff View killer, i.e. Glasses and dark thin moustache, had a good look at Number Four and the Close yesterday afternoon.

Mrs Moore isn't up on her cars but she got the registration. Ron had it checked and it is listed as a 1994 Green Vauxhall Corsa."

Grieve frowned. "That doesn't sound right."

Banks smiled, "I think it does, its owner is listed as a Mrs Mary Blythe of Wharfe View Gardens, Ilkley. Our subject must have stolen it in the town. Ron's checking it now."

"Ah." Said Grieve in understanding; "I will await developments, Ron and company, done good!"

"Yes, but he's tuckered out, so I sent Jim Prentice to take over with strict instructions to send him home."

"Okay, good, lets see what Jim throws up.

Now, lets turn to the delightful Dermot Green. This news, from Ilkley, may well mean he is innocent, at least of these murders. It would be good to get some confirmation from the interview though. Thompson warned me that, like most Republican prisoners, Green will probably say nothing to us, no matter how we prod him. Having been through the mill often enough, he is now an experienced interviewee. So, I will adopt the guise of the pedantic plodding policeman and see if I can surprise him. I think it sensible if you say nothing and simply watch his reactions."

They headed off to the interview room where they met Thompson and all three trooped in. Dermot Green was slouched back on a chair, which was creaking, at an angle, on its two back legs. He still had handcuffs on and the Constable in the room stayed put, keeping a wary eye on the prisoner.

His longish black hair was tousled; he had a black leather jacket open, and a blue check shirt also open at the neck. His jeans looked surprisingly clean, though the desert boots were dog-eared and very dirty. He would have been quite handsome, but for his most telling feature: the misshapen jaw, a disconcerting disfigurement that was further accentuated by the dark stubble. Grieve knew from Thompson that the damage had been the result of an SAS bullet. Two inches higher and the annihilation of Green's IRA team would have been complete. He also had information that Green had a limp stemming from another of the bullets that had hit him.

The DCI introduced himself, Banks, Thompson, and the prisoner to the recording device. The Irishman managed to make himself look even more disgusted. The two policemen sat down opposite him and Grieve started immediately. "How did you get onto the Mainland?"

Green sucked his teeth and rocked the chair back to a perilous angle. Grieve waited for some time before going on, "what was your reason for coming here?"

Green looked at his boots. Grieve let a further suitable period pass. "What were you doing yesterday?"

Green began to study his cuticles. The silence lengthened and Grieve asked, "where were you last night?"

Having established that the cuticles on his right hand were in a reasonable state of repair, Green turned his attention to his left hand. Grieve persisted, "have you seen Gordon Armstrong in the last few weeks?"

Green's eyes narrowed and he stopped rocking the chair; there was no suggestion that he would break silence though. Grieve pleased at the reaction, sought to develop it. "How do you feel towards Gordon Armstrong?"

Green's eyes narrowed further and a thin smile appeared on his lips. Grieve saw that the prisoner was learning a lot from the interview, but he had got what he wanted. Green resumed the rocking of his chair and Grieve called a halt. The three men left and outside Grieve shrugged his shoulders philosophically. "We have nothing on him: nothing to squeeze him with, at the moment. Anyhow it may be pointless." Turning to Banks he said, "tell Mr Thompson what has cropped up in Ilkley."

Banks told of Mrs Moore and her daily activities. Grieve said, "it's a good bet we now can be fairly sure, all four killing were committed by the same person and we are pretty certain that that person was still in Ilkley at five past one this morning. Remind me, someone, when Green was picked up?"

"At seven-thirty-five this morning in Toxteth. More importantly, the snout said he went to the flat around eleven pm with a prostitute, after having downed several pints of Guinness in the local pub."

"So if we firm up on those facts, especially the veracity of the snout, then Dermot Green is probably not the killer."

"He could be behind it yet," Thompson said. "Though, it does seem unlikely given our profile of him. We included him on our list because we thought he was a direct threat to Armstrong. We didn't think he would want, or be able, to get someone else to do it."

Grieve was thinking, studying the closed interview room door, behind which, he guessed, the IRA man was still nonchalantly see-sawing on the chair. "We didn't get much from

102

that interview, but one small thing I did glean, which I was fishing for, was he seemed surprised when I mentioned Armstrong. My guess is until that moment he didn't know why he had been brought to Leeds."

12. A Breakthrough and a Faux Pas

Sergeant Banks chased Jim Prentice an hour or so later. Jim was excited, "Mrs Blythe was actually quite relieved to learn her car had been stolen, she thought she was going potty. Our subject had the gall to return it to within fifty yards of where he had taken it. He must have seen she had bought a two-hour ticket and was confident enough to trust that. I had hoped for some CCTV but there isn't any overlooking where he took it from, or anywhere else in the car park either.

We've firmed up on Mrs Moore's description and we're checking the shops in the vicinity to see if he bought any supplies here. I've already checked the hardware store and they don't recall anyone in a blue anorak and purple ski hat. But I do feel I am close to this guy."

Banks said, "have you any reason to plumb for a man?"

"I'm getting a feel, I'm sure he is."

"You need something more substantive than that for Grieve," Banks warned.

James Belvedere had returned, in the company of the Constable, from the Mortuary. He was nursing a mug of tea. Grieve asked him if he was up to talking to him. Reluctantly, James agreed. Grieve got hold of Sandy Blackhall and they sat with the still visibly affected man. Grieve and Blackhall engaged him in small talk initially but after a few minutes Grieve decided he could be more direct. "Tell me about Fiona, but do it in your own time?" He coaxed.

"She was wonderful, I can't believe she's dead... God." The tears returned and streamed down Belvedere's face to drip from his chin onto the table. It was all too easy and all too hard, when it was too late, to say all the things you should have said, before it was too late, "I was going to ask her to marry me, I bought the ring in November, I had told Barbara, her mother, and she was delighted. I was looking for the perfect moment to ask her. It never seemed to come, Christmas came and went, then Hogmanay, then never."

Grieve frowned. "Surely in the two or three months since you could have found the right time..."

Blackhall glanced at him, what an evil bastard he could be sometimes. Belvedere frowned, shook his head, "something seemed to change, she seemed to lose the plot; often didn't get home until late. She would fly off the handle for no reason; miss dates with friends; always seemed tired: I don't know. I guessed it was Winter Blues, you know SAD, and suggested a skiing holiday. Though that would have been a big problem for me, things have got difficult again in the business; the economy is a nightmare at the moment. Anyway, she dismissed the suggestion, said she couldn't leave London. Work was piling up. I began not just to question marriage, I began to question staying together!"

"What would that have meant?"

Belvedere frowned, "what do you mean?"

"If you had split up, presumably one of you would have kept the flat in Chelsea?" Blackhall looked at the floor and closed his eyes. Belvedere didn't bridle, he just looked puzzled, "well, I hadn't thought that far, I mean, when I said I began to question staying together, I wasn't altogether serious, I loved her... God, I loved her." The tears flowed once more. Grieve offered a not very clean handkerchief. "Well let's leave that for the moment, why don't you tell us about yourself; give us a bit of background?"

Belvedere sniffed and then nodded. "Where should I start?"

"Your parents, home etc."

"Is that relevant?"

"It just paints the picture, if you know what I mean." Belvedere looked perplexed but began to talk. "Well, I was brought up in West London, my father was an accountant, with a City firm, and my mother was a teacher."

A few seconds of silence forced Grieve to say, "where did you go to school?"

"They sent me to Harrow; it must have cost them a fortune: they had high hopes for me." Belvedere shook his head, as if he failed to understand their faith in him, "I did well there, getting 4 good A's. I went on to do Psychology, at University College, London. I actually enjoyed it, unlike some of my friends."

His shoulders dipped and he supported his head in his right hand, "it seems like only yesterday and yet it all seems so unreal; distant; a whole different innocent, optimistic joke." His head sank, but he raised himself once more after a few seconds of introverted thought, "I got a 2:1 and then pleased Dad no end: I said I wanted to join the Army."

"Really." Grieve said, inadvertently letting his tone flag his interest.

Belvedere noticed and frowned, "yes, so I went to Sandhurst."

He stopped again and in diverted mood went on, "God, I've led a charmed life, I would, if I could, trade it all in to get her back."

"I take it you did well at the Military College too then?"

"Yes, I did well there: near the top. I was invited to join the Royal Dragoon Guards. Within a year, I found myself in command of a troop of tanks in the 4th Armoured Brigade in Saudi Arabia. Eventually we took part in Operation Desert Storm, that is, the liberation of Kuwait early in 1991."

"Was that unpleasant; frightening?"

Belvedere laughed bitterly, "God no, it was more of the same charmed existence. It was a huge buzz: I was a twenty-three-year-old Lieutenant riding a tank in the desert. It was Boy's Own stuff."

He was remembering and then grimaced, "I'm being unfair. It's easy to forget the fear and the worry when you look

107

back. We saw some action, which was really nerve wracking at the time, but I was lucky; I lost no men." He thought for a few moments. "With hindsight it spoiled me, much of Army life after that was dull: except for Ireland, of course."

"So you left?"

"I started to think on it, but no, I stayed on for a while. We merged with the Inniskillen's; despite that, I got my Captaincy quite quickly. After that, well, after that I began to plan the start of my own company, in 1998 I resigned and set it in motion."

"What do you do?"

"We provide management and leadership training. It's designed as programmes that are run in-house. We aim at medium to large companies."

"And the name of the company?"

"Bel Leadership Ltd or BelL Ltd."

"Successful?"

"It's very up and down, very down at the moment. It's hard work, harder than the Army, but yes, after a rocky first two years, we started to motor. It was helped, sadly, by my parents' death in 2000." Belvedere sighed, "life's merry-go-round was starting to catch up with me. They died together in a house fire at their new, well new to them, home in the Chilterns. They had bought it for their retirement; apparently, it was a wiring fault. The estate amounted to quite a considerable sum in the end. Being the only child it all came to me, it helped us put the company on a firm footing at a crucial time."

Grieve thought a return to a more relevant topic had become possible, "this must be getting close to the time you met Fiona?"

"Yes, early in 2001, just after we broke the half-million pounds turnover mark. I attended a Gulf tenth anniversary dinner. We were all in our Dragoon uniforms and she had come with one of the military liaison officers at the MoD."

"Did Fiona work at the MoD?" Grieve was surprised.

"Yes, didn't you know?"

"I understood she was a solicitor."

"Yes, well she is… God, was…. a lawyer, but the MoD need lawyers too."

"Okay. Do you feel up to talking about Fiona and her parents again?" James's mouth twisted but he nodded, "Fiona and I got on so well, I asked her out for dinner a couple of nights later, she wasn't seeing the other chap you understand; it just got better and better. Then last year we both sold our own flats and bought the place in Chelsea, with some help from my parent's legacy."

"You mentioned that you knew her parents."

"Yes, I met them first in late summer 2001 when they came down to London for a week-end. They were there to listen to some classical performance, and I think they were checking me out too. We had a meal together and got on famously. They invited us both up for Christmas and New Year. Gordon suggested I bring my gun."

"Shotgun I presume? Was that at the end of 2001?"

"Yes, we had a great time. Gordon and I went out with the guns on several occasions, he was intrigued by my Army service; I by both his and Barbara's activities in Military Intelligence."

"Was Steven Armstrong there too?"

"Ah, no, unfortunately Steven is estranged from his parents, much to Fiona's dismay as she is very... was very attached to him. He was her 'big protective brother' you understand. I met him once very briefly in early 2002; he seemed very distant. I saw him a second time, in more convivial circumstances, last December. Fiona used to meet him as often as she could whenever he was in London. But what with my work and his postings, we never seemed to make meetings happen."

"Have you seen Fiona's parents since Christmas 2001?"

"Yes, we met them in the Scottish borders last summer for a week. They have a second small house there."

"Did we know they had a second house?" Grieve said looking at Blackhall who shook his head. "Do you have the address?" He asked James and was answered with a nod, "okay, the Sergeant will take it from you later, please carry on."

"Gordon showed me where he was born and brought up. I saw a harder side to him then. He could get quite irate over Scottish politics. Surprisingly, I thought, given his background, he believed the best thing for Scotland and the Scots was to get Independence. He argued that it was the only way the Scots would stand on their own two feet again, as they had apparently up to the First War, and stop blaming the English for everything. He considered the Scottish Labour Executive dangerous puppets.

He got very angry with me when I said I judged Scotland too small to be a viable independent country. He reeled off a long list of EU and soon to be EU countries. He said they were successfully ploughing their own furrow with smaller economies, smaller populations, and with less in their favour than Scotland. He was quite persuasive. Fiona and I went on to the Highlands and climbed several Munros in the second week and I realised the truth behind some of his arguments."

"Why live in Yorkshire then?"

"Ah, Barbara is from Yorkshire. If Gordon had had it all his own way I'm sure they would have retired to Scotland, but Barbara has, had, God..." another pause and sigh, "I just can't believe they're dead. It's not the same as the Army. You expect it there. Two men I was friendly with were killed on exercise and I was sorry for their loss, but not really affected, not like this anyway."

Grieve said, "army experience or not, it'll take you some time to accept it. Would you like more tea?"

"No, but thanks. Anyway, as I was saying Barbara had her own strong views too, so they settled in Yorkshire with the small house in the Borders as a sop to Gordon.

I also know that they were concerned for their security and had spent a lot of money on their Yorkshire home. The Scottish house is modest and not such a good place to get trapped in."

"Good, now this is very relevant, can you think of any specific threat they were concerned with?"

"No, I knew Ireland contained some threat and there was a hint of threats from Eastern Europe, but nothing specific." Sergeant Blackhall opened his mouth for the first time, "what about Fiona, was she concerned, or feeling worried over anything?"

"No, she mentioned nothing to me, but then for the last few months we have largely argued."

"But that in itself might be signalling something?"

110

"We have no secrets, Sergeant she is, was my best friend, I was hers, if she had felt threatened, I'm sure she would have told me."

There was a knock on the door and a WPC put her head around the door, signalling to Grieve. He got up and went out for a couple of minutes. When he returned he said, "I think that's enough for today, it's quarter past five, you've had a big shock, can I suggest we drive you to your hotel. Get some food and some sleep. I would like to see you first thing tomorrow, say at eight-thirty. Is that okay?

Good, a car will come for you at eight-fifteen; if you could be ready, it would be a great help. Something else that would be a great help would be if you could give us permission to enter your flat in Chelsea, so that we can look through Fiona's things." James who had been dully agreeing to this point, looked startled, then angry. "Good God, no, Detective Chief Inspector, that is not acceptable, what do you expect to find?"

"I don't know, we are feeling our way, please give it some thought, we have an officer down in London already. Okay, I understand, I understand, we'll discuss it tomorrow."

Grieve was annoyed with himself as he went through the building to meet Steven Armstrong. When he stepped in, he was a little taken aback. Captain Steven Armstrong was dressed in his army uniform and had stood when Grieve came in, but what had arrested Grieve was the similarity between him and James Belvedere.

Both were blonde, both tall, though Steven was slightly shorter than Grieve so he guessed six foot rather than six two, maybe five years older than Belvedere and broader in the waist. But very similarly shaped faces, Steven's was a little less chiselled, possibly due to the extra pounds he carried. Grieve wondered if that was what had attracted Fiona to James, his similarity to her 'big protective brother'.

He introduced himself and shook Steven's hand, "I'm sorry for your loss."

"Thank you. However, I have had five hours to come to terms with it. Please tell me what happened, or at least as much as you can."

111

So, Grieve told it as it was, but he was gentle on certain details. Steven seemed stoic in the face of the description of his father's death, but flinched at the description of both his mother's death and his sister's. "Do you have any idea who did this thing?"

"We are following several lines of enquiry at the present. Some more promising that others, but it is only yesterday that they died, so the investigation is still in its early stages."

"Do you have any witnesses, anyone who saw anything?" That gave Grieve pause, "well, we did have one and we have gained a lot of useful material from him but, unfortunately, he died in a tragic accident last night." Lame, he thought. Steven looked surprised and then frowned, "isn't that a remarkable coincidence, his death so closely following my family's murder?"

Grieve was uncomfortable. "We are investigating his death too, of course."

"Was this man the only witness?"

"At the moment it seems so." Armstrong's expression was now one of incredulity and anger, "for crying out loud, you have one witness and you let him get killed within twenty-four hours, how could you make such a mistake?" Steven was barking the words.

"Hold on, it is early day's yet, please stay calm, as I said…"

"Don't talk to me as if I am some PC Plod. I am the sole survivor of my family and I have to rely on you clowns to find their killer." Grieve, not one to be calm in the face of such an insult struggled to stay reasonable, "Sir, please, could you give us a few days grace before you assume we'll fail? We do have a good track record here.

Now, can I suggest we delay no longer? We need to get the formal identification completed." Steven Armstrong said nothing more; he simply stalked out of the room. They went outside, picked up their escort, and the three departed, still in an electric silence, for the mortuary.

Fifty minutes later and they were back. The silence had finally been broken; they had agreed that Steven would be back for an interview at eleven am the next day. He immediately left, accompanied by an armed officer, to check out the undertaker.

112

The regimental chaplain had arranged the firm, provisionally, once Steven had been given the news at Deepcut. Grieve considered pointing out that planning the funeral now would be premature, but judged that the comment would only reignite the man's anger.

Checking his watch he realised he was running late, it was six-thirty in the evening, so he went straight in to meet Doyle and found him with Banks, Blackhall and Jim Prentice. Jim had just begun to report his investigation in Ilkley so he restarted for Grieve's benefit, "we couldn't find anyone who recognised the subject, but on a hunch, I went in to enquire at the estate agent who is selling Number Four, Drumchapel Close. No joy, they had no recollection of anyone fitting the description; but out of the blue the head honcho says to me, is this anything to do with the gas explosion last night? I says, why?

Well, he says, it occurred to me this morning, coincidentally, that someone rang yesterday to ask if gas was supplied in the area. That was all he wanted to know, it seemed very strange. Then this explosion happened... blaw, blaw, blaw. I says, tell me about the call. He says: the guy had an Irish accent.

I had another hunch and went outside and sure enough, there was a callbox fifty yards away on the other side of the street. So, I gets very excited and go running around the town looking for CCTV cameras again. Would you believe it? The only ones were on the entrances to some disco/bar and they weren't on. God, if only, we could have had him on film. If that had been Leeds, he would have been on four or five cameras. What is wrong with these people, don't they have crime?"

Grieve smiled, "if, is a very big word, but good idea. All the same, you have moved us forward; we now have two descriptions of, almost certainly, the same person. Has anyone been through them to extract the common denominators?"

Banks nodded, "we've given it to our artist and he will have a face and a figure for distribution at the briefing tomorrow."

"Good, and the fibres from the conifers?"

"Yes, almost certainly from the anorak."

"Does everyone know about Hastings being missing?"

"Yes, the description has been circulated," said Doyle. Grieve nodded, "can we rule out Green?"

113

Banks said, "yes, pretty much, the Plod over there interviewed some of the pub's regulars, guys that they can trust, and they say they saw him chatting up the prostitute and leaving with her at around eleven pm."

"Any news on Daly?" They all shook their heads. "McVean?"

Doyle this time, "yes, the Belfast boys are pretty sure they have him pin-pointed. Apparently, it's not possible to just knock on his door and ask for a word. It would be a breach of his security and he would be off like a hare, so they're going to go in and pick him up over-night. I have arranged a flight from Leeds/Bradford on the next available, which is at quarter to nine tomorrow morning."

"Good, any news on Kossuth, Forman, or Bulatovic?" They all shook their heads again. "Have we ruled out a local bad bugger?" He looked at Jim Prentice. Jim nodded, "there's nothing on the street, something like that, a hit on a hard, as well as, non-criminal target, would have leaked some smell by now."

"What of the buses, anything from Leeds Metro?"

Banks said, "we had three of the team, Hopper, Williams and Standing checking all the drivers and relevant routes: nothing."

"Alright, good day's work by you lot. I, on the other hand, have managed to piss both the family members off.

I will see you all in the morning; we have Belvedere scheduled for eight-thirty; you and me for that Sandy. MR M is back in at around the same time. Sergeant Banks please keep him well hidden until then. Briefing at ten as usual, hopefully the Secret Squirrels will have more for us then. Steven Armstrong at eleven; I think I will do that with Reilly.

Now I must prepare for the cameras, has anyone seen Abercrombie? Ah good, Okay sleep well."

Abercrombie had orchestrated the news conference for twenty-thirty as planned. He, Grieve, and the Chief Superintendent faced the assembled press.

It was the second news item on BBC1 at ten pm and the third on ITV, which went out at ten-thirty pm.

114

13. A Small Insight

Grieve returned to the station at eight the following morning. He found Sergeants Banks, Blackhall, and Reilly already there, sitting in the canteen with coffee and bacon rolls.

He joined them with a large mug of tea and an egg roll. "Any further insights overnight, gentlemen?"

"Nothing earth shattering," Reilly said.

"Well," said Grieve, "I was in the bath late last night, thinking things over. I found myself wondering how our killer got onto our witness so quick and what Hopper said regarding observing or overhearing us at the scene of the first murders."

No one looked hopeful, that still seemed like a dead-end. "It occurred to me, now we are reasonably sure all four deaths were the work of the same person, that he/she must have travelled back from Leeds to Ilkley sometime in the course of Monday."

The expressions of his audience remained non-committal. "Well, assuming they were in a car, the most direct and quickest way to Ilkley, not the signposted way through Guiseley, you understand, it's too busy and thirty or forty mph speed limits most of the way, anyway the most direct way is on the A660 through

Bramhope. That would be the way anyone who knew the area, or who had a map would use."

They all nodded their agreement and Grieve pressed on, "so, that road goes over the Chevin, you get that magnificent view up the Washburn valley just as you clear the zigzag at the highest point. I suddenly thought you could probably see Almscliff View from there, across the Wharfe."

The three men nodded, engaged with the speculation now. Blackhall said, "the best position would be from higher up than the main road, say, Beacon Hill or Surprise View. You can see for miles: I think the Menwith Hill Golf Balls are visible with the naked eye from there. With a good set of binoculars you could see a lot more."

"Yes, including our comings and goings at the house," said Grieve with the faintest trace of disgust in his voice. Banks was unconvinced, "still, how would that help, he wouldn't have heard anything? I can't believe a directional mic could work at such a distance."

"I don't know, but I will take some time today to have a look," said Grieve; he took a bite of his roll and a jet of liquid egg-yoke squirted out of it and onto his jacket, "shit......I can tell it's going to be a great day," he said to his smiling subordinates.

14. A Walk on the Wild Side

Sergeant Scrivener met Doyle at Belfast City Airport as planned at 0945. They drove into the city. Scrivener was lugubrious and not very talkative, but did say that McVean had been incandescent at being both found and rousted out in the early hours of the morning.

Even nowadays, when the war is supposed to have ended, such an operation is a big and very public affair. Scrivener assured Doyle that McVean had genuine reason to fear for his life; he had alienated several powerful fellow Loyalists. Hence the need for a big pick-up operation; McVean's minders had to be outgunned and neutralised. Scrivener almost managed a smile when he pointed out that all McVean's enemies now knew exactly where he was; news of such a significant arrest would be round Belfast in minutes. McVean was angry not just because he had been found, but also because he was shorn of his men. Now he had to rely on the police for his safety: it was almost designed to make him feel naked and vulnerable.

When they arrived, an MI5 man called Malone met them; he was much easier to like: amiable, talkative, and refreshingly cheerful.

117

Malone took considerable care in briefing Doyle on McVean's extensive criminal and terrorist activities. He also warned that the loyalist was an intelligent man, which was the main reason he was still free, and still alive. As they talked a steady stream of officers came by to offer their regret for Armstrong's death and best wishes on the hunt for the killer.

Scrivener was to accompany Doyle for the interview so, leaving Malone to watch unseen from the adjacent room, they went to the interview room door. Before they went in, Scrivener suddenly became animated, and clamped Doyle's upper arm in a firm, almost painful, grip. He brought his face close to Doyle's and ground out, "Gordon Armstrong was a good man, he was well liked here, he didn't take any crap, and he was a steadfast friend, when friends were hard to come by. I didn't know him; I was a young man when he retired, but we have long memories here, on this side of the water. Ask whatever you want of this bastard; he'll tell all he knows."

Doyle, slightly abashed by Scrivener's passion and irritated by the small specks of spittle he could feel striking his face, just nodded. He pulled his arm from the loosening vice of Scrivener's hand; as he opened the door he swept his other hand over his face.

McVean was standing at the back of the room with his hands in his pockets. If he had been angry before, then it had evaporated now. He smiled at Doyle, blatantly ignoring Scrivener, as he came forward.

He looked untidy with a thin shadow on his jaw; not unreasonable given the rude awakening, thought Doyle. However, he also looked surprisingly sophisticated, possibly because of the round lenses in the titanium-framed spectacles.

At introduction, Doyle was disarmed when he offered his hand, which Doyle took, realising too late that the intention was to gain a slight, but potentially significant, psychological advantage over his interlocutor. The hand did not feel particularly well muscled.

Doyle reminded himself that this man had reportedly tortured to death, in two separate incidents, two soldiers, and one policeman. The number of Republicans, and innocents, so treated was estimated to have run into double figures. McVean was still

118

free as he never left forensic evidence and no one could be persuaded to testify against him.

He was quite a bit shorter than Doyle, maybe five eight, slim, looking mid to late thirties, though Doyle understood he was a good ten years older. He was wearing a crumpled but expensively tailored suit. Dapper and handsome, went through Doyle's mind, he looked like a sepia image of Kafka he remembered, but Kafka didn't wear spectacles, on second thoughts, Trotsky without the facial hair.

Scrivener had sat down without any preamble; Doyle followed suit. McVean chose to stand until Scrivener pointed significantly at the chair opposite and made a noise in his throat. McVean patently considered challenging the clear instruction for a moment, then thought better of it, and sat.

Doyle immediately started the interview, "I am investigating the murder of Gordon Armstrong, his wife Barbara, and their daughter Fiona at their home in Yorkshire."

McVean's face indicated faithfully, Doyle surmised, that this was a revelation; his head nodded slightly as he digested the news. Obviously, no one had told him why he had been picked up; Doyle caught the slightest flicker of his eyes toward Scrivener; there was considerable calculation going on behind them. "A tragedy," McVean said, with no apparent hint of irony.

"Where were you on Sunday, Monday, and Tuesday?"

An almost sad smile passed over McVean's face, "nowhere near Yorkshire, or even the mainland. I haven't been out of Belfast for two years." Doyle was surprised at the softness of the voice; there was only a suggestion of the strong Northern Irish accent and if anything there was a slight Scottish lilt.

Doyle continued, "I understand that you knew Gordon Armstrong, am I correct?"

McVean was weighing his words carefully, "I met the man a couple of times. I can't say I knew him."

"You knew him well enough to have ill-feelings towards him?"

"I did, a long time ago…. I understand he hasn't worked here for several years."

"You're implying you haven't retained any of those feelings."

119

McVean was showing some signs of concern, and once again he gave Scrivener a short glance. Doyle guessed it might be about where the questions were headed; but he continued to respond with carefully balanced answers and in a carefully balanced tone. "That's right, Inspector Doyle, I have enough to worry me, without holding on to grudges."

"What were these grudges concerning?"

McVean had hunched forward, there was a small pull in one of his cheeks, and his lips had become a thin line. Some little time passed, then he sighed, this time he allowed the gesture to carry a message, one of impatience, "I don't recall."

Scrivener stirred in his chair: McVean tensed and straightened. Doyle had already divined the animosity between them; now there was an electric tension. Scrivener said, "tell the man."

The tension became palpable; McVean had started to breath faster through his nose; his chest moving under the shirt; a slight flush had touched his cheeks.

Scrivener waited, and the silence lengthened, then he said again, "tell the man." No louder but, coming as it did from deep and with minimal articulation, the menace the words carried hung in the air.

Suddenly McVean's faced contorted in uncontrolled rage and crying incoherently, he lunged at the Sergeant over the table. Scrivener let him come; falling backward, he used McVean's momentum against him. They rolled together sideways onto the floor and the Sergeant expertly engineered an outcome where he was on top.

Doyle, transfixed by the speed of the attack, suddenly realised Scrivener had McVean's testicles clamped in his right-hand, he could see the tendons in his wrist move as he squeezed. McVean was straining, through a clamped jaw, to suppress the scream his lungs longed to force out. His head and upper body were vibrating with the effort; animal noises were forming in his throat; forcing themselves through his clenched teeth. His body had fallen on to its side and had formed itself into a foetal position.

Doyle was ready to intervene when Scrivener released his hand and stood back; he seemed quite unperturbed. He studied the shaking, huddled shape for a moment, decided he was harmless, and walked over to pick up McVean's spectacles, which had flown across the room in the first clinch. He inspected them with the kind of casual demeanour that an optician might use: they seemed undamaged; he placed them on the table.

After a minute or so, he once again pointed at the chair opposite Doyle. Where he was on the floor McVean stared death at the Sergeant but Scrivener seemed quite sanguine and simply pointed across the table again. McVean clearly realised the reckoning was for another day and painfully hauled himself to his feet and slowly, stiffly walked around to it and sat down. He reached forward and replaced his spectacles. Scrivener waited for maybe a further thirty seconds and then said, "tell the man."

McVean sat looking at the floor, he was breathing hard but was back in controlled balance. He looked up at the two policemen. He was evidently still in considerable pain. Despite this, the words, when they came, were level. Initially he spoke softly, contemplatively, looking downward at the floor, "it's old news, no harm in its revelation now." Then he looked up; with a twisted smile and clearer enunciation he said, "you are honoured, gentlemen, I have held this silent within me for thirty years."

He paused, pursing his lips, composing. "When I was younger and much more foolish, I was interviewed by Armstrong... I hadn't yet learnt patience; I got angry; I told him he was a fool, he wasn't of course, quite the opposite." He looked at Doyle, "you must remember that this was a difficult time. In the early 70's the province was looking like it was going to explode... No, maybe implode is a better word." He stopped, eyes focussed at infinity, obviously seeing the past in his mind, "anyway, we were alone in a cell together and Armstrong looked at me. He wasn't angry that I had called him a fool; I could see that; but I could also see a dark light in his eye.

He started to torture me... Is torture too strong a word? Well, he started to inflict pain; excruciating, screaming pain. First, I laughed in bravado; but very soon, I was silent, quickly shrinking into myself. The fear of him, and it, grew gradually; eventually it consumed me.

He worked on me, very skilfully, for hours. I saw he wasn't going to kill me: that was the skill he had; there was no

121

hope of death providing a rescue. He stopped several times, when he would leave the cell; after a short time, he would always return. I can remember the horror still; it was a master-class in the anatomy of suffering. Sergeant Scrivener here is a mere novice. Eventually I lost all control of my bowels: I stank of fear; urine; excrement; sweat; vomit. Hearing the sound of him returning down the corridor, after a break, would drive me into the corner of the cell: I would cower there, whimpering, trying to burrow into the stone, until he dragged me out again.

Eventually he broke me, which was what he'd intended. I wept; hugged his legs; begged; pleaded with him to stop."

McVean's voice died, he seemed lost in another world, his hands slowly clasped and unclasped. The silence stretched, until Doyle thought to put a question. Without any warning McVean restarted the narrative, "he didn't stop but went on, through several more stages, into the night. You see he knew that I might beg for relief out of expediency, rather than because my pride was gone. He also knew I could sacrifice my pride, so he carried on beating me; bending me; tearing me, until I had nothing left. Then he threw me out."

He looked defiantly across at his two interrogators. Doyle looked at Scrivener but the Sergeant seemed impervious. McVean continued, "when you live in a place like this. The dereliction; murder; hate; fear; the smell of burnt out cars; the smells of terror; punishment beatings..." He shook his head. "Mr Doyle, did you know our Republican friends enforce discipline with knee-capping. That is shooting people through the knees. Then they realised it would be cheaper, and save ammunition, to use a large electric drill. It was also a better torture with the added benefit of being even more depraved. And why cut a beautiful woman's nose off when you can tear it off with pliers? You name the bestiality; it has found a home here. You can see the darkness around you: its primeval; anarchic; the antithesis of good; of civilization. Bestiality, in fact, is the wrong word as man does unto man things animals wouldn't do.

Well, Armstrong was my Angel of Darkness; after that, my heart burnt blacker than the blackest coal. I accepted the sanctuary of the Dark and was uplifted by it.

I debated why he had done it and I saw what his intention was. He believed I was young enough, intelligent enough to see the futility of defiance. His failure was my victory. He did me a favour really: he showed me where my true home lay: he removed the possibility of moral doubt."

sat in the one opposite. Their witness was bubbling, excited, the words fell out in a cascade, "It's very sunny out there and clear like Monday morning, that is, the day of the Armstrong murders. Because it's early, the sun is low in the sky, not as low as on Monday morning, as it's later, but just as bright."

"You wanted to tell me about the weather." Grieve said dryly. Maxwell smiled, "stay with me, Chief Inspector. Anyhow, coming from the hotel, we eventually arrived at the gate to the grounds and we were driving up the drive into the station behind a police car. I was watching it, more for something to do than for any particular reason. When they had passed the trees, the sun hit the left side of the car, just as it had done to the Mondeo the killer had been driving; the rays hit the head of one of the passengers, who was sitting in the back, and I suddenly remembered."

Maxwell paused, remembering. Grieve, left hanging, was exasperated; "Remembered what?"

"When I was rushing to get the number plate of the Mondeo with my monocular, I struggled, initially, getting it to bear. I hit the top of the car then lost it; then I got it again on the back window, and finally zeroed in on the plate. I was frantic, the car was almost at the next corner; I was going to lose it. Anyway seeing the sun like that on the guy in the police car triggered several subconscious images."

"We'll get there eventually." Grieve said with resignation. Maxwell leaned forward excitedly, gesturing with his hand, "you see, the man in the back of the police car had short blonde hair, and he turned his head to look at the sun just as the killer did."

"Right, so?" Grieve knew they were virtually there and suddenly this was interesting. Maxwell continued excitedly, "it was exactly the same as the killer, the sun on his face and hair, it almost glowed. I must have caught it for just a fraction of a second; the importance of getting the number plate forced it into the background; into some subconscious recess of my mind."

"Are you saying, now, that the killer had short blonde hair?"

"Yes, exactly, and a sharp nose and no spectacles."

126

"Are you sure, wouldn't a ray of yellow sunlight make any hair look blonde?" He looked at Banks. Banks shrugged, "it sounds fine to me."

"Would you recognise him? If we caught someone could we show you an identity parade?"

"I don't think so, it was for only a flash, at a distance, and I didn't really see a face. The only things I can be sure of, I have the image in my head now, are short blonde hair, sharp nose, and no spectacles. Other things, which are more subjective, are the face looked younger than I had at first thought and it's difficult to imagine that the profile was that of a woman."

"Well, the lack of spectacles is no surprise and the moustache was dark, so that seems like a disguise too. But it is very useful getting the hair colour and the gender, if you're sufficiently sure on that. Could it be a double bluff?" Grieve considered, "it seems unlikely, he was unaware he was being observed. He must have taken the wig, specs, and moustache off in order to drive. That would also explain the ski hat he wore in Ilkley, it was clear and cold on Monday, but I think the real reason was to hide his hair and disguise the shape of his face." He turned to Banks, "is our artist here now?"

Banks nodded, "I've checked already." Grieve looked pleased, "good, I've got to interview Belvedere. Can you feed this back to him and get him to do a further sketch quickly for the ten am briefing session?"

Banks nodded and Grieve stood, "thanks Mr Maxwell, I had a suspicion you knew more."

"So did I, Chief Inspector, I just couldn't remember what until now."

"Is there anything else lurking in that mind of yours?"

"Don't know, maybe, but nothing right now."

"Okay, in that case, I think we will send you back to your hotel with your next duty detail. Thanks again."

Grieve went to leave and Banks followed him out; Grieve frowned at him; not understanding what he intended. Banks closed the door and turned to him, "when he told me what he had seen, I checked who was in the car we were following. Obviously we didn't park together, given we are keeping Maxwell incognito: the man he saw in the back was James Belvedere."

"Really. That would be a spectacular coup if we had the killer identified that quickly. A bit hard to swallow, but there's nought stranger than fact, I suppose... All the same, I'm not leaping to any conclusions yet, Maxwell didn't say the man in the squad car was the killer; it just triggered the memory. Besides, any family member is going to be a potential suspect in a case like this.

It's good because it helps with the description, and it's good as it might just give me an extra lever to use on Mr Belvedere. I won't use it unless I must, but we have to get into his flat to go through Fiona's personal effects. So, good idea Sergeant; however, I don't want us to lock on to a particular line of enquiry just yet, it would risk excluding other more worthy ones."

Nonetheless, when Grieve went into Interview Room Two, he asked Belvedere his pardon and, excusing himself and Blackhall for two minutes, he briefed the Sergeant on the new information.

Once back in the room he enquired, solicitously, whether James was comfortable in his hotel and whether he had slept well. He found out that seemingly the hotel was fine, but that sleep had been a scarce commodity.

James, in turn, enquired about the development of the investigation. He was assured that everything was progressing well, but that it was still early days. Grieve decided to get straight down to business, "so, Mr Belvedere, I am keen to delve further into what you might know. My experience is that we are often unaware of the significance of things until we see them in their place in the jigsaw. That is exactly what we are doing, completing a large unsavoury jigsaw. Some little thing that seems totally irrelevant to you might become very significant when we see it beside information gleaned from elsewhere. We are working flat out in that hunt for material so that we can nail the person who killed Fiona and her parents. Will you help us, is that alright with you?"

"Absolutely, I will try to be as much use as I can."

"Good, I will probably have to delve deeper than I have already, please be assured that if I am asking sensitive questions then it is absolutely necessary."

Belvedere's eyes narrowed; he was clearly not happy with this statement. Still, he said, "well, I don't want to be a block, Chief Inspector."

"Fine. So let's start. When did you last see Fiona?"

"Early on Sunday morning, She went into work around half past eight to try to clear the backlog she had."

"Did you part on good terms?"

"Yes, of course we did." James bit back and his eyes flamed.

"We know from the messages you left on Fiona's mobile on Sunday night that you were in Bristol then, can you give us a rundown of your movements on Sunday, Monday and Tuesday?"

James's eyes had widened slightly at the mention of the messages, and a little flush appeared in his cheeks, he had forgotten those angry calls. Either that or he was a good actor, "I left the flat just before four pm on Sunday afternoon and went to the Cribbs Causeway Travelodge on the M5; I have an important new client near there: The Fellowship Bank."

He was clearly concerned now and his initial hostility had very quickly vanished. "Look those messages, I was angry with Fiona because she was supposed to be meeting a friend of mine who has done a lot of design work for us as a favour." He paused and put his face in his hands, "God help me, the last thing she heard from me."

"Don't beat yourself up. We are fairly sure she didn't hear them, the Armstrong house is in a mobile dead-zone." James looked up and then nodded slowly, "yes I remember now you mention it."

"You were saying, Cribbs Causeway?" James nodded again, thought for a moment and continued; "Yes I had arranged to go through the draft programme for the Bank on the Monday morning at eight am, with the training coordinator, who was my principal contact there. The Travelodge is convenient for their headquarters and there was no risk of my being late due to traffic. I arrived at the hotel just after six pm, Millie had called me while I was driving and I called Fiona just before I arrived.

I checked in and had started to review and revise the draft for the Bank that my team had prepared, when I got a call on my mobile from another client, Astons Engineering in Oldham. I had

129

arranged to meet them on Tuesday morning for a general chat on the progress of our work with them. Their Human Resources Director was ringing me to say he had had a game of golf with the Managing Director in the afternoon, and then a couple of drinks in the clubhouse. Seemingly, the old bugger was unhappy with aspects of our programme there. Tom, The HR director, is a friend and he was warning me that the Tuesday meeting with the MD, instead of being a simple review, would in fact be make-or-break. He was trying to give me as much time as possible to address the issues, which he outlined to me. This was a nightmare: Astons are an important client and I couldn't afford to mess up a potentially lucrative deal with the Bank either.

So, I worked most of the night on the Bank programme; I converted it from a draft to a final proposal. I emailed it from my laptop to the Training Coordinator at around quarter to eight on Monday morning; it was attached to a message saying I couldn't come in at eight am as planned. I asked him to review the attached final proposal and I could spend all day on Wednesday with him if he wanted changes. Fortunately, I have a good relationship with him, when I called him at eight am he was fine with this. He had already quickly scanned the final proposal that I had just sent; he was impressed: it had also made his Monday morning a lot less cluttered.

I drove up to Manchester and checked into the Travelodge at Birch Services on the M62 at around one in the afternoon. Astons are based near Junction 20 on the M62. I spent the rest of the day and half of the night completely revising their programme. When I took it into the meeting with the MD and Tom, as planned, at nine on Tuesday morning, they were delighted with the changes. The meeting only lasted an hour when I had re-scheduled it in my diary for five. My next appointment was back in Bristol with the Bank the following day, Wednesday, today in fact. So I thought with the spare time why not drive up to Otley, its only an hour away, and visit Gordon and Barbara."

"Fortunate, then, that we intercepted you first," Grieve said and went on, "when Fiona said she was going into work, did she plan to be there all day?"

"Yes, she said she expected to work until she had to come home to see Millie."

130

"She called her parents from her mobile at fourteen minutes to five on Sunday afternoon." Blackhall said.

"Did she? She should have been in the car then. As it was Sunday, she had taken it to work; she doesn't have a hand free kit in it as I do. Usually she switches her phone off when she drives, drove, to avoid the temptation of answering an incoming call."

"So she, probably, was calling them to say she was on her way. Meaning she would have arrived, assuming the call was made from London, at approximately half past eight in the evening." Grieve concluded.

Blackhall said, "remember, she had a case with her, she must have gone home, unless," he looked at James, "she took a case with her to work?"

"No, only her briefcase, there was no reason to take a case. God I must have missed her by minutes."

"So she *must* have called from London, if she had called from a point on the way, she would have met you at the flat when she went to get the case."

Grieve sighed, "well, I have to say, what you have told us suggests strongly to me that Fiona was the target for the killer, not her parents."

"Why?" said Belvedere frowning.

"Fiona is supposed to be in Chelsea, she turns up unexpectedly in Yorkshire on Sunday evening, and at around six-thirty-five the next morning she and her parents are dead, ten hours later. That tells me she brought the death with her, not that she was unlucky to be there."

Belvedere's face indicated he saw the force of this argument. Sadly shaking his head he interjected, "okay, but I can't think of any reason why anyone would want to kill her."

"Well, she didn't say anything to you, but there may be a reason for that. If I speculated, and this is speculation, for example, she may have been blackmailed, or she may have had substantial debts. There are a number of scenarios where discussing it with you might have been prevented, or might possibly have even been embarrassing." James frowned, but the slump of his shoulders suggested Grieve had got through. "Does she keep files, notes or a diary? Does she have lots of bank accounts, or credit cards, or store cards?"

131

"Well, yes some; not all, I think." But James was now sounding unsure of himself.

"Are these things kept in your flat?"

"There's nowhere else I am aware of."

"Do you see we have to look through her things in your flat?"

James nodded, defeated, "but I want to be there, and I really must attend the funeral too."

"Well, the funeral isn't set yet, and frankly, it's unlikely for some time: the coroner will not release them for burial until we have got a lot further with the investigation. We could drive you down now, the sooner the better. We can bring you back for the funeral, if by some miracle, we catch someone very quickly, and the coroner allows it."

James looked puzzled, "surely there is nothing more that can be obtained from them...them...the bodies."

Grieve looked sympathetic, "I know it may sound truly unjust, but if, sorry when, we catch someone, their defence team will have to have the opportunity to re-examine the bodies independently, or we risk a mistrial." James's lip curled but he nodded at this. Grieve went on, "right, it's twenty past nine; Sergeant Blackhall and I must attend a meeting at ten. We will send you off then with one of our team and you, and they, can get on with it today. Let's use the time until then constructively by reviewing in more detail what you have told us."

Sandy Blackhall went out and told an excited Constable Williams to go home, he lived nearby in Adel, to pack a small bag, and to try and be back by ten.

Williams must have packed a very small bag as he was back at five to the hour.

16. A Conspiracy?

The Wednesday morning briefing started sharp at ten, minus Williams, Collins and Doyle; but everyone else on the team were there, as were Harcourt and Thompson, though these two were returning to London immediately the meeting finished.

The artist had done as bidden and supplementing his first sketches was another, which included the details supplied by Maxwell in the morning. These were distributed with an explanation of how the material had been obtained. Grieve went on to brief everyone on the Belvedere interview and finished with, "so, Mr Belvedere is en-route, with Williams, to London as of ten minutes ago. They are going to meet with Collins who, as we know, is down there already. The three of them are going to go through Fiona Armstrong's things with a fine toothcomb. Remembering that he is a suspect, we have to take his testimony with a pinch of salt for the moment. Yet, if we accept it, it does seem to increase the chance that Fiona was the target, which in turn increases the suspicion of Belvedere of course. Admittedly he does seem to have a reasonable alibi."

Sandy Blackhall intervened, "I've been thinking about that, and I'm not so sure. The only person who will have seen him on

Sunday is the Travelodge receptionist at, say, five past six in the evening. The funny thing with a Travelodge is you can leave at anytime thereafter and it is easy to do it unnoticed. Assuming he did leave unnoticed the next person who certainly will have seen him was the second Travelodge receptionist at, say, one pm on Monday on the M62. After that, his third certain sighting is by the receptionist, or management at Astons on Tuesday morning, at nine, in Oldham. Remember, Belvedere talked himself out of a meeting on Monday morning in Bristol, so it's still perfectly feasible that he committed all four murders.

The critical test of his story is if anyone can be found who saw him leaving Bristol on the Monday morning, if they did then he almost certainly can be ruled out: that needs to be checked. I have a hunch, though, that we won't find anyone, and the very fact that the alibi seemed so plausible, but is in fact full of holes, itself makes me suspicious."

Grieve's expression showed he disagreed with some or all of this, "okay, Sandy. I take the point, but I was impressed that the reason he cancelled the Monday meeting was because of a, verifiable, call from the Astons Director, which might be a coincidence but it's a convenient one. However, you're right there is enough smoke to warrant a search for a fire. So, Sandy do some work on Mr Belvedere, Check the health of his company, check the two Travelodge's, check at Astons and at the Fellowship Bank that the story is, or is not, good. Get some character assessments etc. You know the form."

Sandy nodded affirmation and Grieve went on, "I want to check his army record; see how good a soldier; how good a shot he was: I'll try to talk to his old CO.

On to other suspects: there is one coming in at eleven, Steven Armstrong. Sergeant Reilly and I will take the initial interview. Nothing on him specifically, except that he is family, until Maxwell enhanced his description. Now he's just as good a fit for it as James Belvedere.

All those around at six today should meet here for a short while to compare notes. Anything from the Armstrong interview will be relayed then. Right, now, what of our other suspects?"

Grieve turned and looked at Thompson and Harcourt. These two stood, had a little debate regarding who would speak, then Harcourt sat back down and Thompson came forward talking in business-like fashion as he came. "As you know Dermot Green is off the radar now. He is back under the eyes of the Irish.

I can tell you that Frank Daly is off the radar too. The Garda found him unconscious in a bar in Sligo last night. When they sobered him up, they quizzed him; it took them only minutes to conclude that he's no longer a threat to anyone. We had speculated that he might have come into money or friends making a third party hit possible. Now, that is out the window too: he can barely afford to live, let alone fund a hit on the Armstrong family; the Garda also checked with some of his old Comrades in Arms; turns out he's become something of a pariah; the universal opinion being that he is drinking himself to death.

On to Hastings and, unfortunately, there is still nothing on him and he is still unaccounted for: he remains very much on the scope.

Gustav Forman as you know has advanced Prostate cancer. When the Czechs went to see him, at our request, they found that he had been admitted to hospital. They visited him there this morning, and apparently, he is down to 38 kilos: that's six stone in our money. He's a shadow of what he was when he was ruling the roost in Czechoslovakia.

All he seems concerned about now is the pain and the prolonged wait to die. The Czechs are sure he was unaware that the Armstrong's were dead: when they told him he seemed unmoved. They said he joked weakly; their deaths meant they had beaten him to the draw again. According to the doctors he won't be far behind them; the only thing keeping him comfortable now are stiff doses of morphine.

Czech Security checked his finances just in case his imminent death had prompted him to fund a hit, and he, like Daly, proved virtually penniless; has been since leaving jail. Even the possibility of a secret stash seems unlikely; he has been living an awful destitute existence since he was released. So, in summary, we think he is well off the radar now too.

Victor Kossuth is still very much a possibility though. In fact, our suspicions of him have increased since we found out he has acquired considerable funds in the past few months: he has been seen spending lavishly. Regrettably and damningly, neither the Hungarians nor we know where he is right now; he is not in Budapest as we originally thought. Keep him in mind and firmly on the scope.

Bulatovic is the biggest surprise. To our annoyance, he is in London, staying in a large suite in the Dorchester. He has been there since Monday morning and is having a great time. He is living it up with some old mates from the 70's and has been eating and drinking heartily ever since he arrived. He also has a cast-iron alibi. He flew by helicopter from Le Touquet on the Pas de Calais coast to the Battersea Heliport on Monday morning. He arrived at oh-seven-thirty having lifted off from France just after oh-six-hundred. He was having his documents checked at almost precisely the time the Armstrong's were killed. Everything from that point on is flawlessly documented, from the flight plan through to the air traffic record of the flight.

Unfortunately, we are not buying; there is something highly malodorous, though yet to be bottomed, regarding the whole chain of events. He hasn't set foot in Britain, well not as Gavrilo Bulatovic anyway, for over twenty years and not only does he arrive on the morning Armstrong is killed, but at almost precisely the same time. It sets all my, our, antennae going at once.

We started watching him early last night when we finally got the news through that he was in the country. Sorry about that, by the way, we should have known for yesterday's briefing. There was a glitch in the notification because he came in through Battersea. We've made amends by checking all his movements on Monday and Tuesday and they are all watertight: carefully recorded, carefully witnessed too.

Anyway, he was out for a meal with some Serbian ex-pats when he *specifically* asked the restaurant staff to put on the evening news. As soon as the deaths were reported, there was Bollinger all around. It was as if he knew that it was going to appear, and on that bulletin. They partied until three in the morning when he, his two Serbian girlfriends, and his minders went back to the Dorchester. Huge amounts of alcohol were drunk by everyone, except Bulatovic; who looked like he was to the casual observer; but closer scrutiny showed that he never looked anything other than in full control."

There was a lot of interest in this report, several questions, but no more new material emerged, and the meeting broke up at ten forty.

At eleven am when Grieve met Steven Armstrong again he discovered that he had discarded his uniform; gratingly he had not discarded the supercilious attitude: when Grieve introduced Reilly he was brusque; when Grieve offered to have some tea brought it was disdainfully refused. Reilly and Grieve shared a telling glance; pouring oil on the water, Grieve adopted a deferential style as he started the interview. "Thank you for coming back in Captain Armstrong. How did you find the undertaker?"

Armstrong looked thunderous again, and he snapped, "I judged the undertaker competent, fortunately: unlike some! He particularly impressed me when he told me that an early funeral was unlikely; only being possible when the coroner was satisfied that the bodies would no longer be needed. Something you apparently are unaware of, as you made no mention of it last night." He glared accusingly across at Grieve.

"I am very much aware of that issue, and neglected to tell you only because I judged it would upset you further." Grieve said heavily.

"Well no matter, I have agreed a memorial service at the Harrogate Crematorium; Stonefall I believe. It will be in the Chapel there at three pm tomorrow. As and when the bodies are released I will have them laid to rest in a small private ceremony."

"So soon? I mean for the memorial service" Grieve was taken by surprise.

"Why delay?"

"Well, it's your decision, of course, but it just doesn't give a lot of time to notify people, friends of your family, of the service."

"That was one of the advantages, Chief Inspector, to keep the numbers small. I myself have informed the few people I want to attend."

"What of James Belvedere? I don't believe he knows anything of this."

"Him. Does he want to attend? I understood he had a business to run." Armstrong was obviously not very keen on Belvedere. He paused, seemed to reconsider, and continued in a poor attempt at magnanimity, "no I have not told him, but he may come, to the memorial service only, if he wishes. I just don't want people there that I am unfamiliar with."

"Fine, but yes," Grieve frowned, "he, Belvedere, does want to attend. I will let him know for you if you like?" Armstrong inclined his head just enough to indicate a yes. Grieve returned to the interview proper, "okay, I am sure we can gain a lot of useful information from you that will help our investigation. Do you feel up to the task?"

Armstrong looked sour but repeated the slight inclination of his head that served to indicate a yes. Grieve, belying his thoughts, looked appreciative, "are you aware of anyone who would feel strongly enough to kill your parents and sister?"

"No."

Grieve waited for a moment to see if there would be any follow up: there wasn't. This is going well he thought. "Do you have any idea why Fiona was at your parents' house on Sunday?"

Steven was suddenly more forthcoming, "yes... she rang me and left a message on my mobile. It said she was going home to seek their advice about her relationship with James Belvedere. She said she wasn't sure now that he was as wonderful as she had at first thought. She expected to be there for a couple of days.

I don't know why she felt the need to do that, I had doubted him all along, she could have discussed it with me."

Grieve frowned, but refused to engage in any speculation, "what time was that?"

Steven sighed impatiently, "about five pm, I think, on Sunday."

Grieve nodded, "right, maybe you could give us some background on your family, where your father and mother worked, where the family lived, who their friends were, that sort of thing."

Steven didn't look pleased and pursed his lips, "is that necessary, or even relevant?"

Grieve's patience was wearing thin, "yes, it almost always is."

Armstrong patently disagreed, still, after a moment's consideration, he said, "very well." A further few seconds passed as he got over his reluctance to start. Eventually he spoke, "they; we; my parents lived in Wimbledon until they retired. They retired

138

together when my mother reached fifty-five; my father was sixty-eight then. That was in 1990.

They had bought the house in Yorkshire two years before and moved there that year. They kept a small flat in London, which they gave over to my sister when she graduated and joined a law firm in the City."

The three men sat in silence until Grieve realised that Armstrong was not going to offer any more. "Please continue; friends of your parents; friends of your sister. Tell me about your life in the family; tell me about concerns your parents shared with you; any concerns you had, and so on?"

"How can that have any bearing on their deaths?" Exploded Armstrong.

"Several of the lines of enquiry we are pursuing relate to your parents' work, some back to before you were born. Anything you remember might help us build a case."

Armstrong looked uncomfortable and Grieve could see that he was struggling with this whole line of questions. He amazed himself when he began to feel some sympathy for the man.

Armstrong reluctantly restarted. "My parents worked in Military Intelligence. When I was born, they were both in MI6. My earliest memories are dominated by how little I saw of them, and how often I stayed with 'aunties'. These were usually not actual aunties at all. If my parents had any other friends I never saw them; I can only assume they were all at work with them.

For a short while; I can just remember; it is one of my earliest memories; I must have been six or seven; I had been at school for a while, I saw more of my father." Armstrong stopped and a pained expression crossed his face, "I know, now, that was because it was 1969 and Northern Ireland was becoming a powder keg. The Army had just gone in to protect the Catholic, or Republican community, the civil rights movement; divide them from the extremist Loyalists.

My father had more time for me because he had switched to MI5. Their resources were being ramped up in response to the deteriorating security situation. Quickly though, as events turned and the Provisional IRA became active against the Security Services, he was back working seven days a week; eighteen hours a day: I saw even less of him after that.

139

The Soviet invasion of Czechoslovakia happened around then too. Again, this is not something I knew then; it's only since that some of this has come clear; my mother was deeply involved in that and so I saw little of her too. When I did see them they were both very strained."

Armstrong's face seemed to spasm, "I remember them hugging one night: both were crying. I asked them why they were upset but they couldn't or wouldn't tell me." Armstrong ground to a halt, he seemed embarrassed by what he had said; he appeared to have completely dried up. Grieve tried to kick-start the narrative once more, "I was never great at maths; am I right in saying that makes you forty years old?"

"Not yet, in two months." A very curt response.

"So you were eight when Fiona was born?"

"Almost correct, I was seven, just turning eight." Armstrong said dryly, "she was born in 1971, after that I did see my mother quite a lot. I think they had decided that my little sister deserved the attention that I had missed out on. Despite this, my father was still very rarely there. Bloody Sunday was in 1972: that was when One Para killed fourteen Civil Rights marchers, or Provo's depending on which side of the fence you were on. Of course, the Provisional IRA killed well over ten times as many civilians in the same year. That year was the peak of the murder and mayhem, it looked like a losing battle and still did three years later when I started taking an interest in it all."

"Why was that?"

"Why did I take an interest? I was twelve, almost thirteen; I was sent off to boarding school: Glenalmond, in Scotland. The other boys wanted to know what my father did; I didn't really know, so I started to learn: I was respected eventually."

Grieve went up to his office after he had ended the interview with Steven Armstrong. He had found it a frustrating business, as had Reilly. When they had asked him about his whereabouts on Sunday and Monday he had reacted with characteristic anger, probably because he had nothing to corroborate his contention that he was at home in London. As they had parted the Sergeant, an ex-soldier, opined that being a squaddie, an NCO, or a junior officer under Armstrong would have been an unbearable nightmare.

Grieve had ended feeling sorry for the man. From his account, he had hardly had a pleasant boyhood. Irritatingly he also had to agree that whilst being good background, nothing they had heard had seemed particularly relevant to the investigation.

He pulled his phone over and rang the Ministry of Defence. Eventually he got through to someone who said she could help. He explained who he was, what he was engaged in; that he wanted to confirm and develop his understanding of both Armstrong's and Belvedere's time in the forces. He explained he was particularly interested in speaking to officers who had commanded, or currently commanded, the men and who knew them reasonably well. The woman he was talking to took their details and said it would be some little time before she could call him back. She pointed out that a call back was a necessary security measure anyway; she had to establish that he was who he said he was.

Almost thirty minutes later, the phone rang and the switchboard operator put a call through: it was the lady from the MoD. Everything that James Belvedere had recounted was confirmed and Grieve was told that a Major Osborne would call him at one-thirty; Osborne had commanded Captain Belvedere in his last two years in the Army.

Steven Armstrong's history was more complex. He had gone to Sandhurst in 1982 at the age of nineteen. There he had graduated and had been invited to join the Coldstream Guards. He was promoted Lieutenant quite soon thereafter and then to Captain in 1988. He went with the Coldstream's to the Gulf and took part in the 1991 Iraq war. Early the following year, at the age of twenty-nine, he transferred to the Royal Logistics Corp where he had remained ever since. A Colonel Thackeray would call at two pm to discuss Armstrong's time in the Coldstreams and a Major Shaw would call at two-thirty to discuss his career in the RLC.

Grieve thanked her, rang off, looked at his watch and realised he had some time for lunch. As he descended the stair heading for the canteen, his mobile vibrated: it was Doyle, "I'm done here; I won't have to stay overnight. I'm having some lunch with a few officers at a local pub and then I'm on my way back. I'm catching the four pm flight from Belfast City to Leeds/Bradford."

141

"Good, how did it go?"

"Okay, I suppose. McVean… ah, it can wait, I'll be back in the station at around five thirty: we can talk then."

"You sound tired?"

"Tired? Yes, I'm tired. Anyway see you in a few hours."

Grieve heard something else besides tiredness in the voice; he tried but failed, initially, to pin it down.

Grieve feeling better with Cornish pasty, mushy peas and chips filling his stomach, was back in his office at five past one. At precisely one-thirty the phone trilled and he was speaking to Major Osborne.

"Thanks for calling, Major. I understand you commanded and knew James Belvedere when he was in the Army?"

"Yes, I got my majority in 1996 and took command of the 2nd Squadron; Jamie Belvedere was one of my Captains."

"What was he like as a soldier and as a person?"

"He was an excellent officer: well liked by the men and NCOs; well liked in the mess, except when he cleaned up at cards; a first rate fighting soldier and administrator. He was a superb tactician too. I tried very hard to keep him when he said he was resigning his commission in late 1997; he was a real loss to the Army."

"You were a tank or armoured unit were you not? Did that mean you, and by extension James, were less exposed to small arms and their use?"

"Not at all. All soldiers are trained in personal firearms; Jamie was no exception. We did one tour together in Ireland, where we leave our tanks behind in storage and venture forth naked, as it were. He was an excellent shot with rifle and pistol. Better than me and I'm pretty good."

Grieve thanked him for the background.

"No problem, Chief Inspector. Can I ask you a question?" Grieve assented.

"Thanks, how is he taking it? The loss I mean."

"He's very upset, of course."

"I'm not surprised. I met Fiona at a reunion dinner last year, 2002; she was a delight and very beautiful. Jamie was completely besotted by her; he told me he was going to marry her. Can I ask one more?" Grieve agreed again.

"Thanks. You don't seriously believe that Jamie had anything to do with these murders?"

"I'm not in a position to focus on anyone at this stage, Major."

"I understand, but if you should stray in that direction, for what it's worth, I would bet my life on him Chief Inspector; I don't say that lightly."

Grieve suddenly thought of something, "Major, how old were you when you were promoted Major? Thirty, were you especially young? Right thank you. If we wanted to speak to you face to face, where could we find you?"

"That might be difficult, Chief Inspector. If need be talk to the MoD; maybe something can be arranged."

Colonel Thackeray called sharp at two, "Steven? Yes, he was a Captain in my company in the 1991 Gulf war. I was a Major then.

Grieve followed his script from the previous call.

"I understand, Chief Inspector. He was a very good fighting soldier…"

"Why did he leave the Coldstreams? Well I am not really sure, looking for a fresh challenge possibly…"

"His ability with firearms? Yes, well, it's a valuable skill in the Army, Chief Inspector. He was an excellent shot: the best officer in the regiment; almost the best from all ranks."

Grieve said, "where are you, exactly, sir, if we wanted to ask you further questions, face to face?"

"Well there is nothing I can add to what I have said already. However, I don't wish to be difficult. My location is no secret, Chief Inspector; I work at the Staff or Military College in Sandhurst now."

Grieve jotted down the various contact details Thackeray provided when asked. The Colonel said he often worked at home, but had to be prompted to give his home address; he did so reluctantly, warning Grieve to be careful whom he gave it to.

A female Corporal called just before two-thirty to say that Shaw had been dragged away to an urgent meeting and could he call instead at four. Grieve said fine, rang off, got up, grabbed his coat, a pair of binoculars, and went out.

He took one of the cars from the pool and headed out towards the Chevin. In Bramhope, he turned up a short cut to the main Harrogate-Bradford road: the A658. Eventually he was driving along the top of the scarp on a straight road called York Gate. He decided the best view would be from Beacon Hill, so he turned into the second car park and strolled over to the viewpoint. Raising his binoculars, he leant against a tree; if he had but known it, he was in exactly the same place, stance and body position as the killer had been two days before.

The magnified image of Almscliff View swung and then steadied. He could see everything. If the killer had stood here late Monday morning he would have seen what? The activity; the forensic teams; Doyle; Grieve; even Maxwell; everything in fact.

Grieve put the glasses down, but how would that have served?

He looked around. What was it? He knew he was close to something. A glint of light caught his eye: a car was speeding along the moor road on the far side of the Wharfe valley. It had taken a bend and a window had reflected the light of the sinking sun into Grieve's eyes. Grieve stood rock still; he looked back at Almscliff View. His eyes traced the hedgerows that bounded the narrow, twisty roads. Another car was negotiating the road between Ilkley and Askwith. Grieve quickly put the glasses to his eyes and easily read the number plate.

He fished in his pocket for his mobile and called Hopper, whose number he had stored and whom he was sure was currently on the protection detail, "Hopper, it's DCI Grieve. Put Maxwell on can you?" After a short delay, the eyewitness was found and handed the mobile. Immediately Grieve stifled any small talk, "where was your car on Monday morning when the ARV took you to get it?"

He put the binoculars to his eyes again. "Right, is there only the one way from the house to there? Which way did you go to Ilkley? Did they tail you the whole way home? Right. What's your Landrover's registration? Sorry was. Thanks, I'll tell you later."

He pondered for a moment and then rang the station.

He was back at his desk at four pm and Major Shaw duly rang. "Steven is a very good officer, we were very happy to have

144

him from the Coldstreams. It's unusual for a combat officer to select the RLC: we were quite chuffed. He's a good administrator, hard on his men it must be said, but often that is a good thing."

Grieve with other fish to fry was happy with this for the moment, "Major, I think in the next day or so, I or one of my officers, Probably an Inspector Doyle, will be down in the vicinity of Deepcut. Would it be possible to see you if any other questions crop up? Great, Thank you. Can you give me some contact details? Thanks."

Five minutes after the phone call had ended, Hopper, who had been relieved of his security duty, much to his delight, knocked at the door. He was excited. "There were two PNC checks made on Maxwell's car. The first was by our own boys at thirteen-oh-eight, being ultra-proper I guess, on Monday afternoon when they took him to his car. The second was done from Scotland Yard at thirteen forty-three on Monday morning only thirty-five minutes later."

Grieve looked grim. "Who was it?"

"A Detective Constable Willis."

"Can you, Hopper, think of any reason, how or why, a detective in London would check that registration?"

"No, sir. No one outside West Yorkshire would have known it, or known of its significance."

"Give that man a coconut. Okay not a word to anyone about this yet or your balls are mine. Off you go."

Grieve went off to seek an urgent meeting with the Chief Superintendent.

Just over an hour later, a very unhappy Detective Constable Willis had been detained, cautioned and was being very seriously grilled, in London, by a very angry Detective Superintendent.

145

17. A Sad Old Man

Grieve was doing some administration work of his own at his desk when his phone rang again at twenty past five.

"Sir, I have a Mr Hastings down here, he says that he was close to Major Gordon Armstrong, the murdered...yes Sir."

Grieve called Thompson, got a recording, and left a message. He headed downstairs where he bumped into Doyle, who was carrying an overnight bag on his shoulder, "Hastings has turned up at the desk. I've told them to put him into Interview Room One; I'm just going to see him. Do you want to come?"

Doyle didn't look enthusiastic but nodded his head, "let me dump this bag."

Grieve waited in the corridor for his subordinate to return and when he did they both headed off to the interview room. Grieve glanced at Doyle a couple of times and saw, as he had finally guessed following Doyle's midday telephone call, that something was troubling him; he could see the conflict in his face and in his behaviour. He wondered whether he should take him in, but decided that it was too late to withdrawn the invitation. Anyway, he thought, better to get back on the horse and keep trying, otherwise the task may be insurmountable on the morrow.

Grieve opened the door and went forward hand outstretched, "William Hastings? Good, thanks for coming in, I'm DCI Grieve and this is DI Doyle.

No tea? That must be rectified: black; white: white no sugar, fine." He turned to the Constable who had been baby-sitting the newly arrived man, "Constable can you get us three mugs? I am white, two sugars, DI Doyle is white, no sugar too."

Hastings had stood when the two men had come in. He was around six foot, painfully thin and a little stooped. He looked his age, which Grieve knew was virtually the same as the late Gordon Armstrong.

The black and greying hair was cut surprisingly long for a man of his generation; this framed a lean and gaunt face; wind tanned, it had a myriad of stretch marks, and pockets under the eyes. Looks can be deceptive reflected Grieve, remembering the strength as the old man's hand had measured and matched his pressure as they shook. His appraisal continued to the clothing but the physical facts were as nothing against Hastings' greatest feature, which was the deep, deep sadness etched into his whole being: from his loose ill-fitting flannels; via the baggy, buff shirt with a few small neat darns spotted randomly; to the slightly frayed collar and cuffs. An old tweed jacket hung on the chair, which Hastings now slowly returned to.

Grieve had already decided this man was not the killer. What happened to your open mind, he thought? The decision stood though, this man did not fit the description, or the image of the killer that Grieve was starting to construct in his head. Either that or acting had missed out on a talent surpassing any Larry Olivier or John Geilgud.

The tea arrived and the Constable left the three of them alone. The old man spoke slowly; quietly; occasionally he would pause, almost hesitantly he said, "can you, I do appreciate I am here so that you can ask me questions, but… can you just tell me, if they suffered horribly?"

Grieve nodded understandingly. "No. They were each shot on sight with precision accuracy. If I had to go, I can think of worse ways. Any horror there was, was in the callousness that the killer showed toward the bodies. But then as you know, the dead

148

no longer care: well, one assumes so. Besides it was professional, in that the man had to make good his escape."

"It was a man then, the news report and your summary were both careful to leave the gender open."

"Yes." Grieve said. Doyle looked at his boss, why was he volunteering all this information?

Grieve smiled sympathetically. "Now, can I ask you some questions?"

Hastings, who had been watching Grieve carefully, smiled sadly and lowered his head to look at the tea. When he looked up, Doyle saw his eyes had watered; a single tear ran down each cheek; the old man smeared them away with his hand. Then he nodded, "of course, but I think I know what you need."

He paused, took a deep breath, and before Grieve could frame his first question he just started to talk, "Gordon Armstrong and I met early in July 1944. Two eager young Lieutenants parachuted into Bosnia."

Grieve nodded, "yes starting back then is right, so why you and why Bosnia?"

"Well, in my case, I came from a military family. At eighteen, I went to Sandhurst: that was in late '42. I had excelled at Latin and Greek at school and when the war was imminent in '38, I had started to study German too. What with my language skills and my good performance at Sandhurst I was picked out for Special Operations. I did some further training and was told in June '44, I would probably go to Yugoslavia: I started to learn Serbo-Croat.

In Gordon's case, he had been a Lieutenant in the Coldstream Guards and had been wounded in a training exercise for the Normandy landings, in March 1944. He had taken some Mills Bomb fragments in his back. Serious, but not life threatening.

In hospital he was in a bed next to a Yugoslavian partisan, a chap called Colonel Rodic. Rodic had been very badly wounded late in 1943 in a rendezvous with British amphibious units. At night in the Adriatic, they had been spotted and shot up by an Italian-based German night fighter.

Gordon had been entertaining himself in '43 and early '44 by attempting to learn Russian and Russian and Serbo-Croat

149

are related. By June 1944, he and Rodic were close friends and were conversing surprisingly well in Serbo-Croat. Then, at Rodic's suggestion, Gordon was invited to join the expanding British mission supporting Tito's Yugoslavian partisans. Gordon was older and more senior than me so I was assigned happily, as we liked each other immediately, to cover his back: we were a good pairing.

Gordon did some crash parachute training and then we were dropped into north eastern Bosnia where we were the liaison for a discrete partisan group, operating there under the overall command of Tito."

"A dangerous mission." Grieve ventured.

"Not as dangerous as some, Chief Inspector. Take Gordon, for instance. He had had command of a Coldstream rifle platoon. If he had gone in with them, to Normandy, when they arrived in late June, he would probably have been dead in a couple of weeks."

"Good Heavens. Why?" Grieve had thought the Normandy landings, whilst difficult in the first days, had been something of a rout for the Germans.

"For some months, it was absolute murder for the combat troops of both sides. Rifle company casualties were the highest unit losses of the lot and infantry officers below the rank of Colonel died at an even faster rate than these. Yugoslavia, while dangerous, was not on that scale."

"You're being modest, I think."

Hastings just looked sad; "We were only fighting in a guerrilla war for a few months. The Soviets took Belgrade late in '44 and we were then chasing what was left of the Axis back towards Austria and Germany. Still deadly, but more conventional."

"One of the men we are interested in is Gavrilo Bulatovic; can you tell us anything concerning him and the circumstances surrounding his father?"

At the mention of Bulatovic, Hastings' face had twisted in distaste. He became introspective and the silence stretched until he recovered himself, sighed, and nodded, "it was maybe a month before Belgrade fell to the Red Army. Gordon was temporarily in command of the partisan unit; the leader and deputy had been seriously wounded in an ambush. He executed Edvard Bulatovic, Gavrilo Bulatovic's father, on good evidence, and because he was a threat to the unit's survival.

I wasn't there at the time. I had gone to plan a joint operation with a neighbouring partisan group. Bulatovic, that is Gavrilo, always maintained the traitor was another partisan called Slavko Jovanović, but the precise attacks on our unit ceased once Edvard was dead.

I remember when Bulatovic threatened Gordon, after Tito pardoned Edvard. For several days it got a lot of publicity in the UK papers and on the News. There were pictures and interviews with Bulatovic stabbing his finger and mouthing off about British atrocities.

Fiona was nine or ten; she had come home from school crying, a few days after the story broke, saying the other children had called her father a murderer. She asked me what I thought, when Beth and I came around for dinner the following weekend. She was very upset for some days. Things died down after a while; the Sundays were prompted to write a few well-balanced articles concerning the partisans and the brutality of the campaign."

Hastings looked up at Grieve and Doyle. He was vehement, "Bulatovic has no case against Gordon, either moral, in fact, or in spirit. It was a difficult, necessary, operational decision, which undoubtedly saved the partisan unit. The accusation is a classic case of the pot calling the kettle black, as he himself is a criminal, a thief and a butcher, made all the worse as he should know better."

Grieve nodded, now seemed as good time a time as any. "How do you feel, or did you feel, about Gordon Armstrong?"

Hastings sat back; he contemplated Grieve for a few moments, "I didn't kill him. I swore fifteen years ago never to kill again. I might have been able to once, but not Barbara and Fiona; I loved, love them still. I expect you have been briefed concerning me, so I'm sure you know I had a breakdown after my daughter, Carol, was killed. I came out of that breakdown because I turned my face away from the hate; the darkness; the killing. I have spent my last few years studying all the good things we humans do: art; sculpture; music; song; literature; poetry.

I forgave Gordon for involving my daughter in the war; I know she was strong and wilful; I know, because of her involvement in Sinn Fein, she will have insisted on a role in the capture or elimination of Cahill's killers. Gordon, I can see now, only wanted her to come back to me. He was trying to help me. I behaved appallingly towards him. I paid a price too: I lost contact with Barbara and Fiona. I know, from the nursing staff, that both of them, Fiona and Barbara, came to see me in the hospital when I had completely lost my wits.

Once I had recovered sufficiently to be self-reliant, I buried myself away from any old friends. I was afraid that any contact would reopen the gaping wounds in my heart. I only unwound slowly. I was forced back into the world by Bosnia..." He paused for a long moment, and then almost in a whisper said, "yes, Bosnia."

Grieve was puzzled, "explain?"

"The latest Bosnian war; I had to help some friends in 92/93. It's not relevant to the Armstrong case at all." Hastings clearly did not want to expand further. Grieve knew he couldn't leave something like that but made a mental note to chase that story down sometime in the future, "tell me about the Armstrong family? You said you were close to them."

Hastings put his face in his hands and rocked gently backward and forward. Doyle and Grieve could see tears dropping from between the fingers. After a few minutes, Hastings reached into his pocket, pulled out a large white handkerchief, blew his nose, wiped his face, and composed himself once more, "I met my wife Elizabeth, or Beth as we all knew her, immediately after the war. I had just turned twenty-two; she had just started working in one of the banks in the City.

It was a wonderful time. We were young, alive. We danced, went for drives and picnics in the country when rationing allowed; there was a new hope: Attlee's Labour Government promised so much. We married in 1948 - the year the Welfare State came; Gordon was our best man. The three of us had such times. Gordon was a dashing chevalier and always had a new girl on his arm.

My life with Beth became simpler and calmer though, when Carol was on her way, she was born in 1953."

He frowned; the tears were threatening to escape again, but he held them back with an effort. "We began to wonder if Gordon would ever marry, he was always busy in MI6. He became more serious, introspective and care worn as the dangers in the world multiplied. The Korean War in 1950 came as a horrible shock to us all.

Then one weekend in 1956 just before the Hungarian Revolution. Gordon turned up for dinner with a brilliant, beautiful, new Cambridge language-graduate called Barbara; she had just been recruited as an analyst into Six. Gordon was thirty-four but still looked in his twenties. It was obvious immediately that she was to be his life's love.

We hardly saw them for a year, I think because of the repercussions of the Soviet invasion and repression in Hungary after the revolution was put down. Then suddenly they turned up out of the blue; they wanted to get married immediately, I was to be best man and Beth was to be bridesmaid.

For the next few years, we four tried to spend as much time together as possible, subject to the demands of their and our work, and the demands Carol made on us."

Grieve was unsure as to whether all this was relevant so he said, "can we talk about the family? When did Steven arrive?"

"They had Steven in 1963. I did feel for that boy. We often looked after him when some crisis meant both Gordon and Barbara were doing duty. I was afraid that the child was seeing too little of them and spoke to Gordon of my fears. He dismissed them out of hand: he could be a very hard man when he chose to be.

Later in the 60's, Gordon and I found we were working closely together again, like in the old days. He was covering the emerging IRA threat in the Republic; I was heavily involved in monitoring both sides in Northern Ireland. We had limited ability to influence the political agenda though. Stormont was in command of the province, and refused to bend before the legitimate concerns of the Civil Rights movement. Eventually inter-community violence became inevitable. The Army went in and the UK imposed Direct Rule. Because Gordon, still in Six, had been involved for eighteen months, he was transferred to MI5 as our need for greater resources became urgent.

153

I was very pleased as, for a time Steven saw more of his father. Unfortunately, Barbara was having a terrible time on her Czechoslovakian brief and she dropped out of Steven's life for almost a year. This was doing Steven no good. On the few occasions he came to us during this time, he really was impossible to handle. He would fly into tantrums and scream for hours at a time. We eventually had to say to Gordon and Barbara that we couldn't take him anymore."

Grieve, whilst appreciating the background, was keen to maintain some structure to the interview. He also thought that a little less 20th Century history would be good. "What about Fiona, when did she appear in all this?"

"I was just getting to that. In the following year Barbara was pregnant with Fiona and having stabilised things in Czechoslovakia she spent a greater proportion of her time at home looking after both children; despite this, though, Steven's behaviour continued to deteriorate."

"What year was this?" Doyle asked; he was taking extensive notes.

"Well, let me see, Fiona was born in 1971, so we are now around 72/73. Steven's schoolwork was poor, and he was causing problems with the other children. They had to move him to three different schools in the course of the two years before he took the Eleven Plus. He failed to get a Grammar School place and after some soul searching, they decided to send him to a good boarding school. They chose Glenalmond in the end. The school was, or is, one of the classic Scottish character-building establishments. It has a strong military tradition and they, the school I mean, seemed unconcerned by Steven's unruly behaviour, or his poor performance in the Eleven Plus. Besides, it is possible that his father twisted a few arms as well.

Gordon said to me that with that much energy, Steven would make a good soldier, and he often joked that Wellington had been a very poor scholar too. The truth was he was very disappointed really. I think he would have liked both children to follow him into Intelligence - any time he did spend with them playing, he would often teach them tradecraft."

Doyle frowned, "tradecraft, that rings a bell, can you expand a little?"

154

Hastings smiled. "Spy games." Then his face fell, "I shouldn't joke. It's the term given to good, secure, practice in the dim and dark worlds of espionage and counter-insurgency. It's what often keeps the good practitioners alive and leads the bad ones to their deaths."

Grieve sought to return to the Armstrong family, "okay, so Steven is not particularly gifted, what was Fiona like?"

"Oh, Steven was gifted, just not very academic. He was a very good athlete and proved to be a very good shot, representing the school in both. He loved the outdoors and had quite an artistic talent too; he did some beautiful watercolour landscapes in his later school years. As a craftsman, he was very good with his hands: he did have the makings of a good, if relatively simple, soldier.

Fiona, on the other hand, had picked up all the brains her parents could give her. She was extremely bright, very good at school and, I remember, she loved to learn and play the tricks of the spy trade. There was a real prospect that she would follow her parents into the Intelligence Services. Then, in her teens, her enthusiasm seemed to wane for that kind of life. I might be tempted to trace the change from around the time that Bulatovic got his press coverage. However, it could just as easily have been the emotional changes arising out of puberty; my Carol changed a lot at that time in her life too.

Anyway, sending Steven to Glenalmond seemed to work; he became increasingly strong and fit in his body. When he came home for the holidays, he would play for hours with Fiona; his unruly behaviour still re-emerged sometimes, but increasingly the overriding trait, as he became a young man, was his taciturnity. No matter what Glenalmond did though, they couldn't improve his academic performance significantly: he ended up with two poor A-levels."

Hastings paused and wiped a hand across his face. He looked up, his face had reddened, and the tears were close again, "I'm sorry, this all refreshes painful memories. This was a difficult time for me. My beloved Beth was dying from cancer."Grieve said, "take a break, if it's alright with you we can continue tomorrow." Hastings nodded, "that is fine with me, but

155

we are approaching the time when I became estranged from the family. I might as well see it out to that point."

Hastings thought for a moment then he continued. "The Army had been getting better press in '80 and '81, not least because of the extraordinary success of the SAS in the Iranian Embassy siege in 1980. Steven had come back on summer holiday in 1980 full of it. So, he was now very keen to join the Army, and got a place at Sandhurst in 1982. It was another sad reminder of his weaknesses; once more, his body excelled but his brain didn't, and that doesn't work at the Military College. He passed out well down the lower half of the year.

Gordon managed to persuade the Colonel of his old regiment, the Coldstream Guards, to take him and by all accounts, he did well initially. He worked at it for several years and it looked like a Captaincy was imminent. Then one evening Gordon rang me. He told me that Steven had decided to attempt SAS selection. I said good for him. Gordon, though, was furious. He said, 'the boy doesn't have the brains or the temperament for it, why doesn't he just work at doing well in the Coldstreams. He is going to fail and it will knock him back, I know it.' He and Steven had a very big argument over it, but Steven was determined. I began to see what Gordon's concerns were. The young man seemed to have stumbled into an impossible quest to prove his worth to his father. Later still, I realised that he was trying to demonstrate that he was as good as, if not better than, his father. Gordon feared that the boy would set his sights too high and, as he consistently failed, he would lose his dreams; it happens to us all eventually but Steven was only in his twenties.

Alas Gordon was right, as he so often was; the SAS very quickly told Steven that he should go back to his unit and they also told him there was little point in him trying again.

I knew a lot about this episode, as during this time Gordon and I were very close. Not that we had fallen apart, but I had shrunk into myself after Beth died. Following Carol's husband Cahill's death and my estrangement with her, I shrunk in even further. Then came my reunion with Carol and I was drawn out: back to life. I was so grateful to Gordon; I knew he had been instrumental in the reconciliation.

156

Agonisingly, it was all to prove short-lived. Six months later the news of the almost complete destruction of Dermot Green's IRA team flashed through MI5, and then the media. It was all down to a Gordon Armstrong initiative. I had been surprised that I hadn't been involved in the development of the case; the reason why, like a knife thrust in the vitals, became clear all too soon when I had to bury my daughter beside my wife. I ranted and raved at Gordon, but I had already begun the descent into madness."

18. A Heart to Heart

Grieve saw Hastings out. The old man had agreed not to return to his holiday in Bavaria, but to remain in the Leeds area and to come back to the station at eleven the following morning.

When Grieve re-entered the building, he found Doyle slowly pacing in the corridor outside the interview room. He was sunk in deep and melancholy thought. Grieve sought to lift him out of it with, "well, that was an interesting race through the last sixty odd years, don't you think?"

Doyle looked up and Grieve realised from his face that his jocularity was wasted. His subordinate looked lost: almost boy-like. Doyle ran a hand over his face, "it's been a truly grim day." He said and sighed heavily. Then he took Grieve completely by surprise, "you don't fancy a pint do you?"

Grieve found that he was faintly pleased. This was the first time he had seen Doyle looking as if he needed or wanted help. It was also the first time he had suggested anything as comradely as sharing a pint or two, "yes, of course. Give me a moment though; I just need to check the briefing room. We were supposed to have a short get-together this evening at six." He looked at his watch, "almost an hour ago."

159

They both went to look; they found it deserted. Their team had repaired to home or pub depending on their preference, and the current state of their marriages.

Grieve lived within walking distance of the police station and rarely brought a car with him. So they both got into Doyle's Ford Focus and drove a little further than normal in an attempt to avoid an accidental meeting with anyone they knew. Doyle was sunk in his own private hell throughout the drive, and Grieve left him to it.

After a couple of miles, they pulled into the Dog and Duck; situated in semi-rural surroundings on the edge of the city. It was an old coach-house with real, as opposed to fake, character. It had the additional merit of being one of the few Jennings pubs in the area.

Neither was a regular and the barman's bonhomie was simple professional courtesy. Grieve sought a recommendation and was assured that the Jennings Best Bitter was excellent. Grieve duly ordered two pints and took both over to where Doyle sat. He had found a quiet spot at a table in a corner of the lounge bar, away from the bustle of the bar area. "Cheers."

They touched glasses and appreciated the first flavours of the beer. Judging by the time the younger man kept the glass to his lips he was in greater need of it than Grieve. He had only two thirds remaining when he put it down. "That's a good pint," he said.

Anodyne, Grieve mused; he's still not ready to share his concerns, "absolutely," he said in reply. "It's a shame more pubs don't keep it around Leeds, I can't stand Tetley's. Maybe that's why it's so busy here, a bigger crowd than I would have expected for a Wednesday evening."

Doyle nodded absently; Grieve waited for the dam to burst. They drank in silence for a little longer and then Doyle said, "I sometimes wish I hadn't been fast tracked to Inspector. I've missed out on the hardening process that seems to take place when you remain a Sergeant for a few years."

Aha, thought Grieve, I know where this is headed, "I may seem dismissive of you sometimes, Charles, but you are a very bright; very good, young policeman. You'll go sailing past me, soon enough; I wouldn't worry too much about hardening: it'll come, all too soon."

"Yes, well, I had a belly-full today."

Grieve was sympathetic, "Belfast is a hard school."

Doyle nodded, "God knows, I've already come across some evil bastards: Murderers; muggers; rapists, you name it; somehow McVean is a class apart. The run of the mill are amoral, or stupid, or sick, or sad, or wrecked by their environment or wrecked by our society. McVean is none of these; he was quite unlike any I have encountered before." Doyle swirled the beer in his pint; he frowned down at its surface, "he knows he is evil, pure evil, and he revels in it; takes power from it. He gave me; he took pleasure in giving me, an insight into his black soul.

He was completely candid: Sergeant Scrivener must have said something to him before the interview. I can only guess he told him if he didn't cooperate he would put him out on the street, defenceless. That would be a death warrant for him apparently. After some defiance he dropped the obfuscation and gave me both barrels."

Grieve smiled sympathetically, "I shouldn't worry, that approach is just another form of intimidation."

"I know. I'm not really worried by that. It's the other things that are crowding my mind."

Doyle clammed up again and buried his face in his pint. Grieve drank his beer and patiently waited for the tale to unravel in its own time. Doyle downed a lot more of his pint before he continued, "no doubt McVean was going bad when he was a teenager, but Gordon Armstrong delivered the coup de grace when he spent a day and evening beating him to a pulp."

"Was that the reason for the hatred?"

"Yeah. McVean was quite forthcoming eventually; and therein lies the other story, but I will come to that. No, what gets me is that even if Armstrong had the best intentions in the world, what he did was criminal. And what's more, it was so counter-productive; his crime begat McVean's greater evil."

Grieve screwed his face, "when was this beating?"

"Around 1973."

161

Grieve's face showed his understanding. "Phew, that was a very bad time in Northern Ireland; it dominated the News almost every evening."

Doyle contemplated his pint, "is that an excuse?"

"Come on, Charles, you're making too much of it. The Province was literally murder then; its better now but there is still no comparison with practice here. Circumstances dictate the appropriate type and strength of policing; you know that. It can be just as criminal or evil, as you put it, to do nothing."

"No, no, no that's not what I am saying. Here we are holding the line between the bad and the good, or that is the popular image. Then I find that the bad is in our midst, or behind us, gnawing at the roots of our law, our system, even our society."

He looked deeply dejected, with his chin resting between his two knuckled hands, "I worry that we, the guardians, I worry that I myself, will inevitably be tarnished, and corrupted by our, and my exposure to it.

Even the notion of holding a line is a wrong one, as we have to fight on the flanks and in the rear too. We form schiltrom just to cover all the fronts and then discover that the enemy is our right-hand man. Standing there shoulder to shoulder, his weakness is all the opening they need: the forces of hate pour through to the centre and destroy us all."

Doyle attacked his pint in his fervour, almost spilling the remainder as he broke off to allow a further point to burst out, "another revelation of the day simply adds weight: Scrivener threatened and assaulted McVean. Admittedly, he had legitimised it by driving the man into assaulting him first. However, it was a dance that both were fully aware they were engaged in, with choreography by the delightfully mournful Sergeant.

It's just so depressing, you like to imagine you are making progress, then the world turns and the evil perpetuates. Scrivener is a mini Gordon Armstrong; doing to the villains of today what Armstrong did yesterday. Sowing the seeds of hatred in them now for the crops to be harvested tomorrow."

Doyle paused and Grieve said, "reaping the whirlwind?"

"Reaping the whirlwind is right. I began to wonder how he and his family exist in that community. Once McVean is free, back in his own protection, what revenge will he take on

162

Scrivener, his wife, and/or his children? It must be a twenty-four hour living nightmare."

Grieve, in an attempt to stem the hyperbole, saw an opening, "I am sure Sergeant Scrivener is very well aware of the risks he takes, and very well aware of the measures needed to mitigate them. You appear to be saying his concern for his personal and family's safety should affect the way he does his job. Do you do that? No, of course not, it would be fatal. Remember policing there is not the same as policing here. It needs to be more robust. The response needs to be balanced with the threat. It's still virtually a war there and in a war all the rules change."

"An evil, a crime, is the same wherever it's committed."

Grieve retorted, "that's far, far too pious. You're personalising, and over simplifying the issue. Take a step back. We are not God: we don't have that luxury. We have to act in a complicated world, where simple concepts like good and evil are way too amorphous, and only serve to complicate our job.

Imagine rather a division along the lines of order and chaos. Our job is to maintain order. The shape of that order is codified in a moral and legal framework. History, the Government and Parliament, who have been put in place by us, the people, dictate that framework. It is one of the great strengths of a representative democracy. If we had no framework, like some, our society would become a war zone, just like Ireland was, or is, or Iraq or, well you name it. Still, no framework can legislate for every situation and no framework has absolute clarity as to where the truth lies. So, almost always, there are grey areas where the end justifies the means."

Doyle had been listening, morosely, to this little lecture and immediately jumped in, "aha, yes, the end in this case was McVean becoming a really dangerous and disruptive anarchist, small a."

"But you wouldn't have a case if Armstrong's, albeit strong, medicine had worked. You can't say now, how close he came to achieving his objective. His one mistake doesn't invalidate the approach."

"How can you defend it? Would you beat a man for hours?"

163

"Well no, we can't do that here, and we can't do it now, and it's not necessary here either, yet. Maybe it'll become so, at some point in the near future; if the shift in the balance towards the violent, the organised, and the juvenile continues to tilt in their favour: the scales might need to be rebalanced."

Doyle was incredulous, "you *are* defending it: I don't believe it. I joined the police to uphold the law."

"As did I. Come on Charles, you've seen the court process; the law isn't black and white. I can't say that can I: Can I say that?" Grieve had a brief PC attack, "I mean clearly right or clearly wrong, if it were we wouldn't need the courts, would we?

We are talking about a grey world and all I am saying is, that the line is probably, getting too near one of the extreme ends. It needs to be pushed back."

Before Doyle could counter this, Grieve held a hand up, "truce, we need two more beers."

"I can't really have another, I'm driving."

"God, where did you get your halo? Relax; if need be I'll buy you a taxi ride. Let's see this talked out, it's important."

Leaving Doyle, gazing glumly out of the window at the evening and the city lights, Grieve headed off to the bar. The clientele had increased in the interim and the two bar staff were being worked hard. Grieve waited patiently for his turn. After five minutes, he got two further pints and two packets of crisps. Having considered his argument during his wait for service, he was talking even before he sat. "Look, we draw strength from the little old ladies, gentlemen, and conforming parents with their one point eight children. They are our family, the wall we can put our backs against. They are a bulwark, a passive one admittedly, but a bulwark all the same. Sure, some of them go bad, or are bad, but they're a minority. If the dirt we deal with tarnishes our shiny armour, then a few hours rubbing up on that soft wall, of right thinking, generally right thinking, people buffs it up again.

Look around you; here we are, sitting in a calm, comfortable, convivial pub and drinking some of the best ale the north of England can produce. That is what we are defending, and that is what gives us strength. Not an unchanging vision of Middle Britain, but a consensual status quo that grows and develops, as we, and our power structures grow and develop."

164

Doyle looked mildly impressed by this new analysis. He pondered on its direction, "interesting line of argument, it seems to strike a chord with the story that poor sod Hastings told." Doyle sipped the new pint; "He has escaped his ghosts by burying himself in the study of civilisation and all its works. It is almost as if, before, the thing that kept him sane and able to function was a much narrower vision of family; that is his wife and daughter: they were his bulwark, to use your analogy, and when they were gone he fell. He didn't fall into evil, as some might, by responding with violence, he fell into madness."

Doyle sat back and folded his arms. His gaze rising to the roof as he developed his proposition, "he stayed in that condition until he was able to divorce himself from the horror, and he achieved that by embracing a larger family. That heaven sent subset of our god forsaken race that operated, and operates, in the rarefied world of high art." Doyle suddenly became enthusiastic as he made a lateral connection, "it comes back to your idea of order and chaos. There is nothing so ordered as the beauty of, for example, Da Vinci's Last Supper or Michelangelo's David or Mozart's Requiem. Hastings surrounded himself with high art in order to be as far as humanly possible, from chaos or horror or evil. I rather think in this context the three words are interchangeable."

Grieve was impressed by Doyle's erudition, and he remarked on it. Doyle acknowledged the compliment and both men lapsed into beer-lubricated silence.

This expansion of Grieve's original argument had given both of them food for thought. They drank for a while, in mutually comfortable quiet. Grieve was the first to reopen the discussion with a developing reflection, "yes, Hastings told a cautionary tale. Our support must be broader based than our own families. They are a great help, though you are right, relying on them alone is dangerous. They represent far too narrow, and fragile, a prop. It wouldn't be fair on them either.

Now, in my case, Mrs Grieve is a constant source of inspiration. We took a decision, a long time ago, that I would earn the daily bread and she would run the household and family: the little homilies for me, or one of the kids; the roast dinners; the hot water bottle; her friends in the WRVS; even her apple and blackberry pie. Her life is a gentle oasis for me to shelter in if I need to. My gift to her is I don't dump on her every black mood, and every black event that I get presented with; in fact, if I did I would probably destroy the innocence, which is at the root of her charm and her restorative powers.

No, the surest thing for me in some dark moment, and it talks to your point regarding not seeing progress, is this notion of order versus chaos. Every year that goes by sees increasing order in our world. Everywhere you look: municipal buildings; office blocks; houses; amateur dramatic societies; football, rugby and tennis clubs; growing GDP; new train stations and tracks; Barbados in summer, when twenty years ago it was Blackpool; it's all being created from chaos."

Doyle looked a little askance. "Would the nature that's destroyed in the process agree with that thesis, I wonder?"

Grieve held his hands out in a gesture of appeal. Doyle relented, smiling slightly, and said, "I take the general point."

"Yes, you accept the general point, it's almost a truism. Of course, a key characteristic of chaos is always to work towards a return to the void: the graffiti; street gangs; drugs barons; terrorists, they are all part of it: but every year they lose ground.

The only time that there is a significant step backward is during war, when policing and the law are cast aside so that countries, or constituencies, can behave like children: then destruction abounds and chaos rejoices."

Grieve stopped for breath, some more beer and a bit of thinking time to round off the point he was making. "So, we have a crucial role to play, maintaining that order so that war, pestilence, and death are only visited on the few."

Grieve took a further swig of his beer and studied his companion. He could see Doyle's black mood had lifted somewhat, and he had been listening attentively to Grieve' contention. Pleased that he was getting through to his audience he went on, "unfortunately, our writ runs in only a fraction of the world, and the afore mentioned war, disease, hunger and death are visited on the many elsewhere all too often."

He pondered what he had just said and, sadly went on, "now that is something to be depressed about."

166

Doyle smiled unexpectedly. "You really are a rather decent man, Sir."

"Heavens, praise indeed, but I'm disappointed it wasn't obvious from the start." This last: a reference to the fact that Doyle had first joined Grieve's team three months before.

They smiled at each other; they had reached a common understanding. Grieve finished what was left of his pint. "Another?"

"No, I'm feeling a lot better, the wife and kid can complete the therapy; don't let me stop you though. Actually, I should be all right to drive on two pints so I'll run you home after that, if that's okay. I'll have an orange and lemonade to keep you company."

Grieve nodded happily and stepped off to the bar again. When he had returned with the fresh round of drinks, he looked seriously at Doyle, "can we talk over the investigation?"

Doyle nodded as he inspected his drink rather suspiciously.

"Is McVean still a suspect?"

"I don't think so. He hated Armstrong; of that there is no doubt. I also have no doubt that if the opportunity had presented itself, he would have done it." Doyle shook his head at Grieve and went on, "however, the hate was such that, I am sure, he now feels cheated by the fact that someone else did do it. He would have wanted to do it himself or not at all."

"Okay, we'll keep him in mind, but on the back burner."

Grieve went on to give Doyle an exhaustive run down of the day's events as he knew them. Doyle took notes on some of the details. Grieve reached the end and in summary said, "so, there is more and more focus on London and the South East: Belvedere's flat search; this link with the Met's Constable, bloody, Willis; Bulatovic in the Dorchester; the Colonel and Major down at Sandhurst and Deepcut: a lot of the investigation is down there now."

Doyle nodded. He could see what was coming.

"Would you mind heading down there, first thing tomorrow?"

"No problem at all. I'll catch an early train, there's one every hour; it should be possible to be in London by nine am, if that's okay."

When Charles Doyle got home, he gave his surprised wife a big bear hug and buried his face in her shoulder and hair for a long time. Then he went up to see their little boy. The child appeared to be reaching the end of the teething process: he was sound asleep. Doyle stood there for some time looking at the angelic face. Then he turned and re-joined his wife downstairs for their usual light, but on this occasion, belated, supper. In the morning, he caught the 0605 train to London Kings Cross.

19. A Very Unpleasant Person

Doyle was able to get some sleep on the train in the first hour. Then it became more difficult as the train filled up. In the last half hour it was so crowded it was oppressive.

At eight-fifteen his mobile rang, it was Grieve. "Did you sleep well?"

"Yes thanks Guv, did you?"

"Yes, fine. Look, Thompson just called: Kossuth was found in London last night. They had some joint operation with the Met and Customs & Excise, which threw him up accidentally. He's in the cells at the moment. Liase with an MI5 officer called Elliott. He is coming to meet you at Kings Cross and he has your mobile number, just in case there are problems.

They have also asked Bulatovic for an interview and he has condescended to see someone at nine this morning. Apparently, the rest of the day he is out and about and that is the only time available. So, you and Elliott are going straight to the Dorchester from the station. Hopefully your train won't be late.

After that, you need to head to Chelsea, and persuade Belvedere to let us continue to have access to his flat while he comes back for the memorial service. He'll have to leave Chelsea at the latest by eleven; the service is at three this afternoon. The search doesn't seem to have thrown up anything useful yet, and I need you to run your eye over it, at your leisure. Apart from that, your agenda is in your own hands. There are lots of people to see down there.

Oh, one last thing, Detective Superintendent Ingram has suspended Willis pending a disciplinary hearing, but he's sure he isn't our man. He's too stupid, according to the DS; it seems he left his machine logged on to the PNC while he went for a fag in the toilet. He was away for twenty minutes around the time that the check on Maxwell's car was done. Anyone and their dog could have accessed the computer while he was puffing away. Willis made himself very popular with Ingram when he said everyone did it; I mean not logging off when they go to the bog. So now, there are red-hot missives flying around, warning of the direst consequences if anyone else should breach Standard Operating Procedure in the future. Horses, bolts, and stable doors come to mind. Unfortunately, while it is necessary, it's going to cause the person who did do it to keep their head down for a while.

Have you any ideas concerning what else you'll do?"

"I have to be careful what I say. There are more than twenty people within earshot of me on this blessed train. Anyhow, apart from the items you've mentioned, I thought I would try to meet this Millie woman and Fiona's boss, at you know where. Also I'll go down Farnborough way, to see the two you know what's down there, and now I know about Kossuth, I will aim to see him too. That should keep me busy for a couple of days at least. Hopefully, that lot will generate some worthy leads to keep me occupied thereafter. Failing that, I would really like to come home on Friday night and spend some time with the wife and the family. She is very patient, but it's wearing a bit thin at the moment."

"Fine, speak to you later, happy hunting."

The train unexpectedly arrived two minutes early at eight thirty-one at Kings Cross and when Doyle approached the end of the platform, he saw a nondescript, middle-aged man in a grey mackintosh with a sign saying 'Doyle' on it.

170

He went forward with his hand outstretched and said, "Elliott?"

"Absolutely. Inspector Doyle I presume. Good, we must hurry, our delightful Serbian friend awaits."

He took one of Doyle's bags and headed out to the street where a grubby, light blue Toyota Corolla was parked half on and half off the pavement. A traffic warden was standing beside it writing out a ticket; Elliott flashed his ID card at him, but the man was unimpressed. "Means nothing to me mate. The ticket's been issued."

Elliott said nothing, unlocked the car, threw Doyle's bag in the back, and was driving off as Doyle closed his door and fumbled for the belt.

Elliott drove like a maniac; the car swung erratically. Doyle clung to the door handle as they defied death at every turn. As he drove, Elliott briefed Doyle on the discovery and capture of Kossuth. "We had been working with Customs and Excise to close down a newly created smuggling route into the country. We were concerned that it was guns and explosives. In the end, it proved only to be large quantities of cigarettes and cigars from Eastern Europe; when I say large, I mean tonnes and tonnes. We were exiting the operation: without the gun connection it ceased to be an issue for us. But then one of the perpetrators turned out to be Victor Kossuth; it transpires that Victor has been using his undoubted expertise to make some money for himself, and he was using the extensive Eastern European ex-pat population to fence the smuggled goods."

"When can I see him?"

"Anytime, but it's probably worth waiting a short while until we, or I should say C&E, have all the pieces in place and then we can squeeze him properly. It shouldn't be long. Jesus Christ! Where do they teach these people to drive?"

Doyle sympathised with the unfortunate woman, who had presumably assumed that the oncoming traffic would be doing thirty or less, not fifty or more.

They arrived at the Dorchester at eight minutes to nine and parked in a space in front of the hotel. As they were getting out, a smartly dressed doorman came across and, very politely told Elliott he was not able to park there. Elliott flashed his ID card: the doorman was as unimpressed as the traffic warden. He said that if Sir did not mind, if he left the keys, he could find somewhere to put the diminutive little vehicle; it assuredly could not remain in the Sheik's space. Elliott breezily agreed and handed the keys over. As they walked to the main entrance, he confided to Doyle in a stage whisper that it was a company vehicle anyway, and if the department found it in a skip, they might well reinstitute the 00 licence.

At precisely nine, Elliott knocked on Bulatovic's suite door. After a short delay, the door opened, and a hulking, aggressive looking man stood barring access. Another man, a clone of the first, could just be seen behind the half open door. He was standing two metres back and to the left.

Elliot and Doyle presented their ID cards and after studying them for several seconds, the bodyguard grunted and moved to one side. As they walked past the first, the second one moved to bar their progress and expertly checked them for hidden weapons. Doyle had the uncomfortable feeling that if the roles were reversed, they would find firearms on these two men. As he was certain Bulatovic would not have sought approval from the Home Office for such weapons, or if he had it would have been summarily refused, this gave him something of a lever. Not one he was keen to use, though, without first establishing the views of Elliott and the Metropolitan Police.

The four men were standing in a small foyer with two further doors in the rear wall. When the visitors were pronounced clean, the first bodyguard knocked on one of these two doors. Once he had heard the acknowledgment, he tentatively put his head around it and spoke in a very foreign sounding language. A second voice replied in, what sounded like, the same language and the bodyguard held the door open for him and then Elliott to enter.

They walked into a huge, beautifully furnished lounge. A large deserted soft-seated area to the left was equipped with several ornate chaise longues, arranged around an exotic low table with a chessboard incorporated in its centre. A game was in abeyance on the board. Judging by the amount of development and the relatively few captured pieces, the game was being played, by both players, at a high level. The theme of the room

172

was Persian with carpets, hangings, ornaments, and oil paintings, all dancing to the same tune.

There was a single door in the wall behind and to the left of Doyle with "Restroom" written on it, and a double door in the wall on Doyle's right.

The music they could hear was quiet, symphonic, and reminiscent of the country, Doyle thought probably Brahms and probably Symphony Number Two, though he was only an infrequent classical listener, and he could not be absolutely certain.

There was one person in the room, a man seated in a white dressing gown, at a circular breakfast table to the front right. He and it were adjacent to a wide floor to ceiling window that opened onto a terrace overlooking Hyde Park. One half of the window was open maybe half a metre and the edge of the light inner curtain wafted occasionally in the slight breeze this caused.

The man they both recognised as Bulatovic had not yet looked at his visitors. He was reading a folded broadsheet newspaper and had a cup poised halfway between the saucer and his mouth. He was engrossed in some article and when thirty seconds had passed, Elliott coughed to attract his attention. It had no effect. The silence stretched to near a minute. Elliott grimaced at Doyle and he was clearly going to take the initiative when Bulatovic stirred, sipped from the cup, returned it to the saucer, and looked around at the two standing men. "Forgive me, please, sit." And he indicated the two chairs placed at the table opposite him.

As they approached, he stood and offered his hand. Elliott took it and introduced himself as a Foreign Office civil servant. The blasé attitude he had displayed since meeting Doyle had been replaced by a guarded business-like demeanour. Doyle did likewise and they both sat.

Bulatovic looked his age of sixty-one. He was much the same height as Doyle, who was five eleven, and well built as one might expect of a recently retired professional soldier. He was not slim, though, as a slight paunch was visible through the gown. His hair was short and dark with some grey, and he had a small dark moustache.

When he had stood and now returned to his chair he seemed to move stiffly, Doyle remembered he carried some old wounds. He noticed a raised, red discolouration of skin halfway around Bulatovic's neck, which might have been a scar too.

Bulatovic tapped the paper he had been reading. "It's very interesting being a European reading an American paper." Doyle could see now, that the paper was the US edition of the Herald Tribune.

"A completely different approach to Iraq, the Americans really don't seem interested in Weapons of Mass Destruction, and this Bush administration is completely dismissive of European doubts. It is quite clear to me that war is imminent, and that they're impatient with the delays the UN is trying to introduce. They are also quite sure they'll win any war. I am as well. It's the peace that they will lose. Bombs are not nation builders."

Ever since Bulatovic had spoken, Doyle had been trying to place the accent, he finally settled on somewhere near Oxford.

"You've been on the receiving end of some American bombs, haven't you Mr Bulatovic?" Elliott said.

Bulatovic smiled broadly, "Mr Elliott, are you trying to annoy me? It won't work you know. And to be strictly accurate they were NATO bombs, several British ones too, as I recall."

"Just making an observation; you're stretching the point a little, aren't you, calling yourself a European?"

Bulatovic laughed, "you are trying to annoy me. Dear me, what fun. Well I suppose, in one respect, you have a small point, as Serbia is Slavic. However, your geography is poor. There are several Slavic countries within the accepted boundaries of the European continent."

"Can you explain why you are in London?"

"Just seeing old friends; revisiting the old haunts; refreshing my cultural soul, as well as doing a little business. I have been away for so long you know."

"How did you leave Serbia?"

"What an interesting and surprising question. Why do you want to know? It seems a little out of field for you gentlemen, surely?"

"Your departure went unnoticed. We are simply intrigued as to how you did it."

174

"Ah. Well, I drove."

"Did you pass through any border guard posts?"

"Ah. No, not all roads are guarded Mr Elliott."

"Strange, I believed they were in your former Yugoslavia."

Bulatovic smiled and shook his head. Doyle thought he would have a go, "I am sure you are aware that Gordon Armstrong, his wife and daughter were murdered on Monday?"

"Good heavens, were they? No I don't think that news made the Herald Tribune."

Elliott looked meaningfully at Doyle. "Didn't you watch the main BBC News on Tuesday evening?"

"Was it reported then? Come to think of it, I did watch some of the television news, but I was having such a good time with my old chums, I must have missed that item. How did they die?"

Doyle disliked the lightness of the tone. "They were shot, as you very well know, on Monday morning."

"Come now, what reason would I have to lie? You don't think I did it, do you? Where was I on Monday morning? Oh, that was when I arrived in London. I flew by helicopter from Le Touquet. Did the murders take place anywhere near where I was?"

"No." Doyle said dryly, "they were in Yorkshire." This man was camping it up wonderfully; laughing at them. "You were recorded as saying you would exact revenge on Major Armstrong for the killing of your father, were you not?" Doyle said.

At this Bulatovic stopped smiling. He looked at Doyle and the policeman felt a shiver go through him. God, he thought, I hope that wasn't visible. The effect had been caused by the instant transformation of Bulatovic's face and posture, without moving a muscle that Doyle could see. In a flash, he had no doubt in his mind: here was a kindred spirit for McVean.

He was a very different man though: older, stronger, refined, intelligent, obviously sophisticated, obviously very wealthy, but also suddenly, obviously a man with a black soul, if indeed he had a soul. Doyle found himself fighting to resist a reprise of yesterday's depression. As his mind struggled,

Bulatovic simply sat in silence. Elliott stepped in. "Can you confirm that Mr Bulatovic?"

Bulatovic shifted his gaze from Doyle and reached for his coffee, "Gentlemen," he said, back to his camp best, "I should have offered you coffee. Can I tempt you? No takers, very well then."

Doyle had restored his equilibrium, "Mr Bulatovic, we know that you had ill feelings toward Gordon Armstrong. Can you give us any reason why we shouldn't suspect you were behind these deaths?"

Bulatovic smiling, was about to speak when the Restroom door opened and in so doing admitting the sound of a flushing toilet. Framed in the doorway was one of the most beautiful women Doyle had ever seen. She had long straight glossy black hair that fell on to her shoulders in an inwardly cut bob; a perfect oval face; big dark eyes. And she was stark naked.

Elliott had looked, and being older and more streetwise than Doyle, had then thrown a quizzical glance at Bulatovic, who was smiling; enjoying the moment.

Doyle was still enraptured. The girl was in her late twenties and had a perfectly shaped figure and perfectly shaped breasts. She had no other hair on her body at all. She had long, very long, exquisitely slim legs and her pudendum was plainly visible, as was the gold diamond ring that hung there.

She floated, gracefully, into the room looking totally relaxed, smiled at Bulatovic, and headed for the double doors that, presumably, led into the bedroom. The diamond flashed as she moved. Suddenly Doyle realised the game that their host was playing, and tore his gaze away. Bulatovic, having achieved his objective, said, "women, they can give such pleasure, and they can feel such pleasure, greater than men I think. It is wonderful having the opportunity to study a beautiful woman isn't it. You can do so much with the female anatomy."

The girl had finally disappeared through the doors. Doyle assumed this last remark related in some way to Bulatovic's interest in fine art until he hear the next comment. "Especially when you are careless of the pain you cause."

Doyle looked aghast at this; Elliott simply looked weary. Bulatovic became business-like and grim. "Gentlemen, I am

176

ending this interview, I don't believe you have conducted it in a way consistent with the agreement I reached with your superiors. However, before I do, I will answer your question.

The reason you can be sure I wasn't responsible for the Armstrong's deaths, is because of the way they died, the speed, and the order.

Firstly, I would have insisted on being present, so that they would know who was responsible. Then I would have ensured that the old man and his wife were bound and gagged, and I would have had their daughter brutalised in front of their eyes. She would have been brutalised and used in every way possible, I'm sure your imaginations are up to the task; capable of visualising the sheer spectrum. I would have ordered every conceivable excess; I can assure you I have an inexhaustible list, especially for women. The trick, or skill, I am sure you appreciate, is to keep the woman alive for as long as possible, ensuring she experiences the full gamut of terror, horror, pain, and humiliation as her body is slowly destroyed.

When she finally is so broken and torn that she expires, I would have repeated the process with Barbara, Gordon Armstrong's wife. Only then would I have turned my attention to the true objective: I have an inexhaustible list for proud old men too."

20. A Blind Alley and A Break

The two men had returned to the main entrance in silence. They waited for the doorman to fetch the car, and then headed off to Chelsea.

Elliott drove sanely this time; his previous ebullient mood a distant memory. After a minute or so he said, "I almost landed one on Bulatovic."

Doyle nodded. "What a reptile, I would have helped you." oblivious to the irony of his words.

"The problem would have been, untying ourselves when the gorillas had finished making us into Gordian Knots," reflected Elliott.

"You know those gorillas, as you call them, were carrying." At these words Elliott looked knowingly at Doyle, "oh, I'm sure they were."

"Can't we take him and them in then? That's a crime after all."

"He's got enough money to buy the best lawyers. The bodyguards would go down; but I bet they wouldn't implicate him, and he would simply say he was unaware they had firearms:

179

he would get off. The other problem is: the possibility it might precipitate a gun battle.

Still there might be some potential in it. We need to sound the Met out."

"If we assume for the moment that he told the truth back there, that he wasn't involved in the murders, can't we get him deported as an undesirable?" Doyle knew, though, that he was clutching at straws.

"It would take time and a compliant Home Secretary. I have a feeling the Government want to use their political capital in other directions, just at the moment. If he were indicted as a war criminal they would do it, in fact, then we could have him arrested; that isn't such a distant prospect either, as the Serbian authorities have apparently compiled a damning dossier on him: we can but hope."

"Hum. Anyway, I don't want to see him again until we have something to hold over him. He had the whole thing set up; he just spent the entire time laughing at us."

They found a multi-storey car park near Belvedere's address. Elliott was leaving the car with Doyle and catching the tube to Westminster. He was returning to review the interrogation of Victor Kossuth, who had been moved to Scotland Yard. Doyle hoped to follow him, once he had discussed the flat search with Belvedere, Williams, and Collins. He looked at his watch as he knocked on the door: ten past ten. After a short pause, Collins opened it and looked relieved to see Doyle: he explained gloomily that they had found nothing at all of great note.

Collins introduced Doyle to James Belvedere and Detective Constable Farmer, the Met officer who was there to help if he could. After their introduction, given the time, James Belvedere disappeared to make some tea; he and Williams were to depart back to Leeds for the service in the next half hour. This suited Doyle; he wanted to talk to Belvedere about retaining a key to the flat; he felt sure the request would go down better in a one to one conversation.

Not wanting to broach the subject immediately, Doyle remembered that Steven Armstrong had not told James Belvedere of the service and final funeral arrangements; had even, apparently, not been particularly keen to see Belvedere there.

180

When Grieve had told James when and where the service was to be, he hadn't passed on either Steven Armstrong's antipathy or his potential exclusion, though he felt bound to tell of the decision that the final laying to rest would be private. Doyle went into the kitchen to explore these points. "You told the DCI that you had met Steven Armstrong again recently, in December; how did the two of you get on?"

James looked up distractedly as he poured tea from the pot, "okay, I guess. It was in easier circumstances than our first meeting, but we still didn't talk much; Fiona told me that isn't unusual for Steven. I tried to share some memories of the Gulf War: he just didn't seem interested in talking about it. Some people don't. He did make some rather unflattering comments concerning my business; but they didn't particularly hurt me: ignorance sometimes generates contempt, it's not the worst crime in the world."

"How do you feel about the service and proposed funeral arrangements?"

"Okay really. It must be terrible for him too, people take these things differently. I will talk to him after the service and ask to be included in the ultimate funeral too. I am sure he will agree."

None of this helped to explain to Doyle Steven Armstrong's indifference, and even animosity, toward Belvedere, but after probing gently, for several more minutes, he had made no further progress. He also felt that they were getting on quite well, so he changed the angle of attack, "okay look, DCI Grieve has asked me to supervise the conduct of the investigation down here. I want to meet various people who knew Fiona and it's just possible they will point me at something that in the greater context is important: something that doesn't seem significant at the moment. Maybe particular payments in a bank account, or credit card, or some other thing like that. You're heading off to the Chapel service, and I expect you won't be back until, say midday tomorrow at the earliest. I know it's a big thing to ask, but I don't suppose you could leave your flat keys with me. If anything of the sort that I have just described does happen, I can check it out here straight away."

181

Belvedere looked unhappy but, like Andrew Maxwell, he had immediately liked and instinctively trusted Doyle. Additionally, he had been impressed by the sensitivity the other three officers had shown the previous day. After a few moments deliberation he nodded his assent: Going to a drawer in the kitchen he fetched out a small, leather key wallet with several keys in it; he handed it over and said it would be all Doyle needed.

The Inspector also wanted contact details for some potential interviewees. James gave him Millie Ballard's office telephone number and, when asked, the name of Fiona's boss at the MoD, a Mr Jim King. By the time all this had been done, it was twenty to eleven and James was fretting to be away.

When Williams and Belvedere had left, Doyle called both Millie Ballard and the MoD to arrange meetings. Ms Ballard lived and worked from her home in Kingston and Doyle offered to come out to see her there. She, though, said she was coming into the City to meet a client for lunch, at one pm in the Ritz Restaurant, and she could stop over and talk with Doyle at, say, two, if that was okay with him. She had to tell Doyle where the Ritz was, but once that was established he readily agreed; it was a much better solution for him.

He arranged to see Jim King at four pm in one of the temporary offices the MoD were currently occupying. The man explained that there was a £400 million refurbishment of their main office currently underway. He was given directions and was told that they were within walking distance of New Scotland Yard.

Collins and Farmer had remained with Doyle in the house and, once he had finished making his arrangements, they took him through all the records and everything else they had turned up. Doyle had to agree there was nothing of any note: except the will.

A copy will had been turned up that had superseded an earlier will prepared ten years before. The new one was dated in October 2002 and made James Belvedere sole beneficiary of Fiona's estate. Doyle found himself thinking that the pressure of suspicion was mounting on Mr Belvedere.

As the will proved to be the only thing of note they had turned up so far, the review was quickly concluded: all three of them were back at Scotland Yard by twelve-noon. Farmer helped Doyle find Elliott in the tall building. The MI5 man had just emerged from an interview with Victor Kossuth, and was now in conference with an Inspector Vaughan of the Met, and a Mr Trimble of Customs & Excise: Doyle was invited to join them and Elliott summarised their analysis for Doyle's benefit; "It seems that Kossuth is the mastermind, the hired help, and the management all rolled into one in this little operation.

When he got out of prison, he somehow managed to fill an articulated lorry with twenty-five tonnes of, or approximately twenty million, cigarettes. Even in Hungary, that many cigarettes would have cost him a small fortune. The Hungarians are checking how he did it when he is supposed to have no money.

Using his contacts, he had some good quality transit documents faked and armed with these he drove the lorry over the Schengen line into Austria. Cigarettes in Austria cost a third of what they do here so the Austrian Zollamt are not as concerned with them as we are. Besides, the documents indicated they were only in transit. He drove to near Breskens on the Dutch coast, where he had hired a small fishing boat. He loaded five or six tonnes onto the boat and landed them near Chillesford in Suffolk. There he broke the consignment up into six hundred ten kilo packs, i.e. each one had three hundred and sixty packs of twenty. These were loaded into a small removal lorry and hawked around all his ex-pat Hungarian friends and their friends in London and the Southeast. The price to them meant, those they didn't smoke themselves, they could sell on to small retailers and traders and make a good return. The retailers sold them to the public for around £3.90, which is a fifteen percent discount on legal ones, and still turn a much better profit. This process was repeated every week until the artic in the Netherlands was empty; and we are pretty sure he was in the process of completing the third such operation when we picked him up. We think in total he netted at least £750k for himself.

The weakness was the number of people involved in the distribution network: some of them began to figure out the scale of the operation. Not too surprising; by then he had brought in

183

almost sixty million cigarettes. If he had stopped after two artic loads... well he would have been scot-free and sitting on about half a million pounds sterling: as it was it eventually got back to Mr Trimble's team." Elliott indicated the man on his left who was looking very pleased with himself. Elliott continued, "we, that is MI5, got involved as Kossuth, we didn't realise it was Kossuth at that time, was seeing people who were involved in illegal gun trading, as well as illegal cigarettes.

From the point of view of your investigation: Kossuth was almost certainly in the country last weekend; The surveillance had started almost two weeks ago, but crucially the team lost him on Saturday, and didn't pick him up again until Tuesday: heads have rolled, before you ask. So, he was mobile and as far as we can tell at the moment, he had the time, the opportunity, and the motive to murder the Armstrong family. We also now have a very big stick to interrogate him with."

Doyle was pleased. "So no one has suggested to him yet, that we have him down as a suspect for the murders?" They all shook their heads and Trimble added emphatically, "he does know that we have him absolutely bang to rights for the smuggling."

Doyle brought up something else. "How old is he again?"

Elliott checked a file. "Sixty-five. Ah, according to this that is guesstimate; there is some doubt regarding his precise birthday."

"I understood he had a heart condition?"

"He does have to take some pills, which are, apparently, a legitimate prescription; so, yes maybe: it hasn't stopped him doing all the work though. He has a small forklift at his base in Breskens, and the fishing boat has a short winch and crane: with their help he was able to avoid most of the manual lifting."

"If you forget the murders for a moment, you almost have to admire his endeavour!" Said Doyle earning himself a disapproving frown from Trimble and conspiratorial smiles from Vaughan and Elliott.

"Indeed." Said Elliott with mock seriousness; but as his head turned to reveal his expression to Trimble the smile morphed into a disapproving frown, gauged to mirror the one the Customs man still wore. He continued, "whether he is guilty of

184

them or not, he knows about the deaths: he and some of his friends had an all-night, celebratory, piss-up starting late on the Tuesday evening when the news came out. That was what put us onto the fact that it was him. The Five officer newly attached to the covert surveillance team did some lateral thinking, talked to someone on my team, showed them a few of the surveillance photos and bingo: we had him; he's passing himself off as a Pierre Antoine, and he still doesn't know we know he's Kossuth."

As the impending and latest interview was aimed at exploring Kossuth's links to the murder enquiry Elliott and Doyle were to conduct it. Vaughan and Trimble were going to watch, unseen from the adjacent darkened viewing area.

When they were ready and had entered the room Doyle was immediately struck by the dejection of the individual in the chair on the reverse side of the table. Kossuth sat with his chin in cupped hands; a thin trickle of smoke rising from the cigarette clamped between the first two, yellowing, fingers on his right hand. His hair was dishevelled; his tie pulled down: loose around a scrawny neck. He had a dirty white shirt on and a black suit jacket draped over his shoulders. The face was thin and pinched and the eyes had a watery look to them. Victor looked a lot older than sixty-five.

Elliott set the recording device up and introduced himself, Doyle and Pierre Antoine to it: it had been agreed that Doyle would do most of the talking and the policeman had assumed his seat in severe manner. Kossuth had watched their activity with an outward display of disdain, but his inward attention was clearly concentrated on an appraisal of this new adversary. Doyle glanced at Elliott and then turned to 'Pierre Antoine', "Pierre... we want to talk to you about Victor Kossuth."

Pierre/Victor closed his eyes in a look of despair and slowly shook his head where it still rested on his cupped hands: he remained stumm.

"Pierre (sic), would you like to offer us anything? Shall we tell you?"

Kossuth was going to talk; Doyle could see that. All the same, it was going to take a little time for him to come to terms with it. Their prisoner sat back in his chair, rested his left elbow

185

on the arm, and hid his eyes behind his palm. He raised the right hand to his mouth and took a long draw on the cigarette; the smoke remained in his chest for maybe thirty seconds, tendrils rising from his nostrils, and then slowly it was released.

Elliott went to the folder he carried and withdrew a set of mug shots dated 1991, and placed them in front of Kossuth. Their prisoner briefly raised his hand from his eyes and looked at the photos; his eyes closed after a couple of seconds and with a shake of his head, he replaced his left hand over his upper face. ·

"Victor, when did you last meet Gordon Armstrong?"

It hardly seemed possible, but the picture of dejection opposite sagged even more at this.

"Victor, Can you tell us where you were on Sunday, Monday and Tuesday morning?"

Finally Kossuth spoke. "Oh God." He croaked.

Doyle and Elliott glanced at each other, but managed to resist the temptation to smile, "Victor, we know you hated Gordon Armstrong; if you remain silent, all it does is make me think you have something to hide."

Kossuth nodded, it seemed as if he was going to burst into tears. He looked at his cigarette, saw it was nearly finished, and used it to light a fresh one.

"Victor, you are sixty-five years old, this cigarette scam is going to see you jailed for three or four years. Add a multiple murder charge and you are going to die in there, especially if you continue to chain smoke."

Kossuth had emerged from his despair and was now, evidently, calculating the best way to play his losing hand.

"We know too, that on Tuesday morning, early, the Armstrong's killer was also responsible for the killing of one of my policemen."

Kossuth's face registered consternation. He knew how police forces, world over, reacted in response to the death of one of their own.

"So what we are looking at pinning on you is: four murders, one of whom is a policeman and two of whom are women. How do you think the jury will judge you Victor?"

Kossuth had reached the conclusion of his calculation and played the first card, "okay, yes I hated Armstrong. I can still remember my friends' faces: those that were sacrificed by him. Men and women, patriotic Hungarians, being shot in the back of the neck in some dark hole somewhere.

And yes, I was very happy when I heard someone had killed the old bastard off. I was sorry that the women died, but women die too.

All the same, I had nothing to do with it, and I was nowhere near Yorkshire when it was done."

"Prove it Victor."

"Look, if I tell you where I was, and if I tell some other things that you guys would be very happy to know." He glanced at the mirror in the wall as he said this, "will you let me off the smuggling charges?"

Doyle smiled at Kossuth as he shook his head, "you know I can't do that."

"What can you do?"

"We will talk to the CPS and see if we can make things easier on you. It really depends on what you tell."

"I've got a lot of material, but it's dangerous, can you protect me? Is there a witness protection programme, like in the States?"

Doyle glanced at Elliott and saw the sceptic in him too, "there is such a thing, but frankly Victor, we don't believe you have anything worth saving your scrawny neck for."

Kossuth obviously thought he had some trumps in his hand, but was stressing over the order and timing of his play, "okay, if you can give me anonymity, I was with a bunch of would-be Pakistani terrorists here in the UK, in London."

Doyle looked at Elliott, who looked unimpressed: Elliott said, "you'll have to do better, Victor, we have tabs on any Pakistani terrorists in London."

Kossuth shook his head, "not these ones."

Elliott continued sarcastically, "come on, Victor, how would you know what we know about?"

Kossuth looked superior, but saw he had to play another card, "okay, I've got the location of a warehouse in Hungary with one hundred tonnes, approximately, of cigarettes ready to move here."

187

"Interesting, but not worth a deal, come on Victor, out with it?"

Kossuth was almost pleading, then he realised the futility of further procrastination, sighed in resignation and slowly articulated, he played his ace, "the Pakistanis have the money, and I have a second warehouse location in Hungary with six or seven tonnes of small arms: pistols, assault rifles, and RPG's plus enough ammunition for a small war. There is also fifty kilos of military grade Plastique. What sort of deal will that get me?"

Doyle and Elliott were stunned, and all three clearly heard an exclamation from behind the mirror. Elliott had recovered from the initial impact and looked very angry, "were you lining up to sell this stuff to these guys?"

Kossuth looked sly, "I meant to yes, but I don't want warfare and mayhem here, I like it to much; I was going to shop them to you boys, and then walk away with the money."

"Honest." He said in response to the dismissive looks thrown at him by his interrogators. "Very dangerous though, it needs to be planned well." Kossuth said earnestly.

Elliott terminated the interview and the two men sat down with Vaughan and Trimble again. Working on the assumption that Kossuth had nothing to gain from lying, they discussed the options.

Trimble desperately wanted the extra cigarettes; Vaughan and Elliott very much wanted the weapons and the terrorists. Doyle wanted the evidence to eliminate, or incriminate, Kossuth for four murders.

The discussion was complicated by the different agency agendas. Trimble's agenda, supported by his superiors, was the dismantling and seizure of the cigarette distribution network, right down to individual traders, if possible, plus the one hundred tonnes of additional cigarettes, plus all Kossuth's profits from the first three artic loads. In return, he would speak nicely to the CPS. On the other hand, Elliott and Vaughan's agenda; in conference with their superiors, the mandarins of Special Branch, MI5, and MI6; was to catch the prospective terrorists receiving the arms. They felt that such a prize warranted giving some trade on the cigarettes. Elliott knew that Kossuth would never disclose anything that was certainly going to get him killed. Some kind of safety net needed to be constructed. Doyle's agenda was closely related to that of Elliott's and Vaughan's: he wanted Kossuth to keep talking; his alibi for the murders was that he had been with the Pakistanis.

A decision had to be sought from on high. In the meantime, Victor Kossuth would have to stew. He was put in a police cell, and the Duty Sergeant now thought him sufficiently depressed to be a potential suicide: so, to add to his predicament he had to hold his trousers up, once his tie, belt, and shoelaces had been confiscated.

Doyle briefed Collins and told him to stay close to Elliott. He should throw the murder enquiry's weight behind Elliott and Vaughan if the negotiations looked like they were getting difficult. He left strict instructions to escalate it to him, or Grieve, if things looked like they were going awry.

Short of time now, he had only half an hour for both lunch, and the trip to the Ritz to see Millie Ballard. But he gained time when someone suggested a nearby sandwich bar. They were very quick with his order so he decided to take a circuitous route to the Ritz via some of London's landmarks. Eating and drinking as he walked, he set off through the teeming streets towards Parliament.

He went up the side of Parliament Square and onto Birdcage Walk; as he went, he marvelled at some of the architecture. The Houses of Parliament and Westminster Abbey were on the left and then, after a few hundred yards, Horse Guards was over on his right. He went past the front of Buckingham Palace, cut through Green Park and on to Queens Walk. The weather was reasonable for early spring, and he felt refreshed when he arrived at the Ritz.

In the lobby, he approached the desk and explained that he was to meet someone in the restaurant; one of the staff kindly showed him the way. He had believed he was sufficiently smartly dressed, but he began to have doubts as he appreciated the opulence of the hotel. At the restaurant, he thanked his guide and turned to the Maitre d', "I'm here to see Ms Millie Ballard."

The man bowed his head slightly, "yes, of course, Sir. She mentioned that you were joining her. Let me inform her of your arrival."

189

He bowed again slightly and went half way across the room where he bent to an attractive woman sitting with a tall gentleman. They had been conversing closely and earnestly until interrupted; both looked up at the man peevishly. Then her face cleared; she looked around and waved at Doyle: it looked like he was going to have to wait.

Whilst the rest of the hotel may be opulent, he reflected, this restaurant was sumptuous: thick cream tablecloths; sparkling regiments of cutlery; elegantly gilded chairs with red cushioning; chandeliers above; a huge gold framed mirror in one wall; gigantic classical scenes painted on the side walls; tall heavily curtained windows on the rear wall. And all so busy: the bulk of the tables were occupied, but so restrained: the staff moved gracefully between the tables. Everyone was talking, or listening, or occasionally expressing delight at the first, or subsequent, mouthful.

Doyle's mind filled with an image of his loyal, overworked wife, Sheila. She would love it here. He began to imagine a weekend where he could repay some of her support and stole a glance at the a la carte menu. The dishes were mouth watering, and he read with relish until suddenly he appreciated the prices. Any further speculation was instantly stillborn: the bill would be sumptuous too.

The Maitre d' returned and offered to take the coat Doyle had on his arm. As he handed it over, he saw Ms Ballard's companion rise, kiss her on each cheek, and come towards him. He passed; smiled; said, "she's all yours," and departed the room.

Doyle went in the opposite direction and Ms Ballard stood to shake his hand, indicating the chair just vacated. She offered him some of the bottled water in an unused glass, which he accepted, wondering how much each mouthful was costing.

Millie Ballard was very elegant, with a bouffant head of long auburn hair and a blue silk suit. She studied Doyle for a disconcertingly long time, until suddenly her expression changed, "I'm so sorry. I'm rude, I like to evaluate people I first meet, from a study of their face and deportment; it's totally inappropriate under the circumstances."

"Do you find your evaluation proves accurate on better acquaintance?"

"Usually, yes, but it could be self fulfilling, of course."

"Still, it could be a very useful skill, one that would prove valuable to the police."

Millie smiled, "if that's a job offer, I have to tell you: I don't think you could afford me."

Doyle raised his eyebrows and smiled back, "I have no doubts, it's on a par with this hotel, and I couldn't afford to eat here either."

"Ah, that's different, it's business. John is a good client, and it's always wise to give them some of their money back with a classy bit of entertainment. I wouldn't eat here otherwise."

Doyle saw the logic. It wasn't so different from the police in objective, if not in style, spending or glamour, "were Fiona and James good clients?"

A frown crossed her face, "God, Fiona, I feel so churlish now, given the way I behaved on Sunday evening."

"You weren't to know what was going to happen."

"Maybe not, but we should probably always behave in a way that would leave our conscience clear, whatever befalls."

Doyle could not disagree with the sentiment, 'Do unto others...' he remembered from church as a boy. He was currently struggling with a decision on whether he and the family should return to the Church. He felt his boy, Adrian, would benefit as he had and he also had a feeling the whole family would gain. He knew Sheila was keen; his reservation was whether they could sustain it in the longer term. His thoughts led him to say, "I am sure Fiona is happy, where she is now, and doesn't hold it against you."

She frowned bent her head and then said quietly, "I take it from that, that you believe in God and Heaven, and the Devil and Hell?" Doyle could now see redness and vestigial tears sitting on Millie's eyes.

"Yes, I do, don't you?"

"Sometimes, sometimes not. This is one of the times I hope it all does exist. Fiona and her parents are at peace in Heaven and their murderer will find himself, at some point very soon I hope, in Hell's eternal fire. God knows if anyone deserves Heaven its Fiona."

191

"She certainly sounds worthy, can you tell me about her?"

At the second prompting, Millie was ready to speak and was only forestalled by a waiter, who came over to ask if more coffee was required. She looked pleased and said, "lovely," and when she saw the hunted look on Doyle's face, she said, "the Inspector would love some too," to Doyle she directed a soothing, "it's on me," and patted his arm.

Then she addressed his question. "Right, I have known Jamie Belvedere for years. I met Fiona for the first time almost two years ago at a party for a mutual friend. She was lovely and we got on very well. We, by that I mean my partner and I, bumped into them occasionally thereafter. It was only in September or October that we started seeing each other regularly."

"Why was that?"

"Well, they bought a substantial flat together in a good location in Chelsea. Initially, they had little to spend on decor; they had rather overreached themselves buying the bricks and mortar. As time passed, though, Jamie's business improved: he won several new clients in early 2002. So, he called me; asked if I could help them do a proper job on the interior. I said: love to, once I had finished two of my existing contracts. Jamie pointed out it was Fiona's project and so we got together first in the early autumn. We had several wonderful days together planning things; trying materials and tiles; you know the sort of thing. She is very bri…"

Millie spluttered to a stop and put the napkin to her face, Doyle saw the waiter, who had been approaching with the coffee, do a world-class shimmy and pass by to serve another table, as though that had been his intention all along. He resolved there and then that he did not care how much the place cost; he was going to treat Sheila to the most wonderful weekend here: as the decision crystallised he felt a small prick of sweat on his brow.

Millie was not one to blow her nose noisily in the napkin. Her elegance had, in some respects, been enhanced by the unexpected show of emotion. She continued in a subdued tone, "Fiona was very bright in all things, she proved to have a natural talent for colour, and texture, and light."

192

Doyle could see tears still coursing down her cheeks as she talked. He had a clean, ironed, and unused handkerchief that he offered to her: it was gratefully received and immediately put to use, "I had a great time with her. Usually it is a fight with the client to save them from some madcap colour scheme or horrific furnishings, but we saw eye to eye on everything."

The waiter, timing his return perfectly, placed two new cups and saucers, and piping hot pots of coffee and milk on the table. Doyle poured; they savoured the flavour for a short while.

He was puzzled, "forgive me, but the flat, I've been there, is spacious, but very bland."

"Exactly, nothing has been done. We had largely got everything sorted out by early December and then, well, I couldn't get anything finally agreed. Have you ever read Dr Jekyll and Mr Hyde, Inspector?"

Doyle shook his head, inside he was annoyed, it was a book he kept meaning to read, but had yet to do so.

"You should it's a wonderful, if short, read. Stevenson was a master storyteller, and some of his other short stories are even better.

Anyway I stray. There was almost as dramatic a change in Fiona as Stevenson described in his book: she was no longer interested in the décor, when before she was consumed and flying with it; she was petulant and angry at the slightest cause, when before she was diplomacy personified; she would miss appointments and not appear to care, when before she would have died rather than... Oh dear, can I have your hankie again please."

Doyle waited until Millie had recovered, which took several minutes, then he went on, "I'm sure that this change is important, do you have any idea what caused it?"

"No, Jamie asked me the same thing a month ago. He thought it was SAD, Seasonal Affective Disorder, and hoped a skiing holiday would snap her out of it."

"Think back, when did you first notice the change?"

"Well, it was definitely before Christmas, probably a week before. We did see them quite a lot at that time. Let me see if my organiser can help me."

She fished in her bag and pulled out a small PDA. "Right: Saturday 7th December 2002. We had them and a few

193

other friends for dinner. What was she like then? Let me think: She was fine, her normal self.

Saturday 14th December 2002. We all attended a joint birthday and Christmas party thrown by Christian Perks. Someone I knew and Jamie went to school with. Fiona was there, but she arrived very late I remember, much later than Jamie. She was distracted but, no, she was fine. They had a karaoke machine, and she was up there like all the rest of us.

Saturday 21st December 2002. Right there was something definitely wrong here. This is a little drinks do I run for all my clients for Christmas. Nothing fancy to start with, then later the ravers among us go out on the town."

Millie had her fingers at her temples as she tried to force the memories out, "Fiona turned up late again. She was stressed and got angry with Jamie. I remember they had a big row out on the terrace about something really trivial. I know because I was doing the mixing thing, and found them there."

She played with the PDA for a little while longer, nodding to herself, "yes, that is the turning point, after that she was Mr Hyde."

Doyle spent the next ten minutes going back over this two to three week period, but nothing more came out. Eventually, thinking out loud he said, "maybe I'm wrongly assuming this is a one off change. What if it was some kind of episodic complaint? Had anything like this happened to Fiona before?"

Millie shook her head, "not to my knowledge, but I had only really been close to her for the last six months."

"Okay, I can ask James Belvedere, he should remember something."

"I don't think so. Fiona's recent behaviour was a complete surprise to him. No, really, He and I have now discussed it on several occasions, and he was completely baffled."

Doyle tried a little trick he had learnt from Grieve, and put on a very frustrated look, "this behaviour must be relevant; how do I explore it?"

Shaking his head in exaggerated bafflement, he poured them both two new coffees. As he had hoped this gave Millie an opportunity to out-think him, "look, I don't believe Fiona had a recurring mental condition, but…"

Doyle sensed this might be something useful, "go on."

"Well, about a year ago, when we met at some little do, I mentioned that I wanted some contacts in the media. Fiona gave me a name and telephone number for a friend of hers; working at the Times. I was looking for some publicity for a makeover I had done, and Fiona's friend helped me."

"Good." Doyle knew this could be something or nothing and was keeping his excitement in check, "and how did Fiona know this friend?"

"They went to school together, and apparently they went to university together too."

"Do you have the details handy: the name, a telephone number?"

Millie picked up her PDA again and searched through it, "damn, she isn't here. Ah, I know, she'll be on the phone."

She pulled a mobile out of her bag and searched it, "God, what was her name?"

Millie was cudgelling her mind. Then a bulb flashed on, "Annabel." She searched the phone again, "I've got it, Annabel Fasting."

She showed Doyle the number and as soon as he had it, he made a move to go, "thank you Ms Ballard, I want to call Ms Fasting straight away, do you mind if I go?" Doyle was half out of his seat and also half afraid he would get a bill just for sitting in the restaurant.

Millie stood and gave him a big hug, "you find the lowlife who destroyed such a lovely, brilliant girl and believe me I will make him pay, even if our bloody justice system doesn't."

Doyle did not think it politic to point out that whatever Millie had in mind, should the courts release the alleged culprit, would be totally illegal. It served further to destabilise his equilibrium. We all seem all too ready to sacrifice our civilization when presented with the lowest common denominator. As he walked out, he considered: is that a force for Good or a force for Evil?

Outside he called Annabel Fasting and got straight through. She was, naturally given her work, well aware of the murders; had been horrified by them in fact. She had been intending to attend the funeral and was surprised to learn that a

195

memorial service was, probably, underway already. Thinking it over for a short time, she rationalised it back to the fact that Fiona and she were only very occasional friends. Doyle was disappointed until she went on to say that they had been very close at school, and also in first year at university.

Doyle looked at his watch: he needed to get back to this temporary MoD building, to see Mr King. He asked if he could meet Ms Fasting in the early evening. She immediately agreed, "it's the least I can do," she said, "now that the service and funeral are out of the question." She explained that she travelled home out of Waterloo and suggested a restaurant and wine bar in one of the railway arches under the south end of Hungerford rail bridge at six pm. Doyle had a rough idea where she meant and knew that it was only a short walk from the office where he was to meet Mr King, though on the other side of the river.

21. A Psychological Exploration

At the ten am briefing, Sandy Blackhall had confirmed his suspicions. No one had seen James Belvedere leave the Travelodge at Cribbs Causeway on Monday morning, despite this particular one having a twenty-four hour reception desk. The hotel manager, concerned by the police interest in this, cautioned that his staff did not stand at the desk all the time. It was very possible for a client to leave quite normally, and for it to go unnoticed. Nevertheless, the Sergeant's suspicion mounted further, when he learnt that the key had not been placed in the box intended on Belvedere's departure. It had arrived in the post, the following morning. Blackhall rationalised that this removed any danger that the staff would notice an early deposit of the key when they cleared the box.

He was now sure that Belvedere could have left at any time between about eighteen-thirty on Sunday through to, say eleven hundred on Monday.

Blackhall's team had also established that the next person they could be sure who saw him, was the receptionist at the Travelodge at Birch Services. The Visa receipt from his payment showed a time of twelve forty-six on Monday. The machine was

197

accurately timing transactions when the Detective Constable checked it at four pm yesterday: Wednesday.

Between then and quarter to nine on Tuesday morning, James Belvedere was again without an alibi. He left Astons at around twenty past ten and the key was handed back to the receptionist at the Travelodge at around eleven am.

Blackhall had also had one of his team spend a short time investigating the health of Belvedere's company, Bel Ltd. They had obtained a Dun & Bradstreet report on its finances and credit rating. The conclusion of the report, whilst always subjective, painted a rather poor picture. It had performed well up to June 2002 when the last accounts had been submitted. Nonetheless, since then, the company's credit rating had deteriorated and the company staff numbers had declined from twelve to eight.

In Blackhall's view, Belvedere had attained the elevated position of Prime Suspect for the murders; only the motive was missing.

Grieve left the briefing just before eleven and was able to welcome Hastings when he arrived on the dot of the hour. He led him through the building and this time took the old man to his office. Once they were settled with mugs of tea he said, "Mr Hastings, Bill, thank you. Bill I want to concentrate on a narrower analysis this morning. I would really like you, if you feel able, to dust down the skills you will still have from your Intelligence experience."

Hastings looked pained, but nodded his assent. Grieve continued, "I want to explore, in more depth, the inner workings of the Armstrong family, as you knew it: Gordon's relationship with Steven, and with Fiona; Steven's with Fiona; likewise for the children's relationship with Barbara, their mother. Is that possible?"

Hastings studied Grieve shrewdly, but let whatever he was thinking pass, "you want to get inside their heads?"

"Correct, let's start with a profile of Gordon."

"Very well. This might not be in the best order, I'm very rusty." He ruminated for a while and then launched into the analysis, "Gordon was a driven man: he felt he must excel at everything he undertook. He hated failure and often regretted

198

lapses, or mistakes, he had made in the past. They never seemed to leave his mind.

He was extremely intelligent and energetic; he had a good eye for structure and form: this allowed him to make big lateral leaps in logic that often dumbfounded his colleagues and his subordinates.

Gordon considered himself a good judge of character; I'm not so sure that he always got it right, though. He dismissed several people as fools, when often there was plenty of evidence that their lack of vision was simply down to their having access to less information than he had.

He was decisive when a crisis demanded it, but to be fair when time allowed, he would grant extensive discussion with peers and subordinates in search of the best course of action.

Ruthlessness was a necessary characteristic in our job, and Gordon had plenty. But he had a good heart, and I saw his grief and tears for the innocent on occasion. All the same, he was able to put his heart aside, when a necessary decision meant pain or death for someone. I always had a suspicion, though, that the impassive exterior hid a huge turmoil. I know that on at least one occasion, when we were in their home, Barbara had to disappear with him, for a long time, when some particular episode came back to haunt him.

A lot of the pressure on him came from his over-riding characteristic: perfectionism; an enormous cross to bear, in the world of compromise, poor information, and subjective analysis that we inhabited. He demanded a high standard from himself, and also from his people, some failed to cope with this, and either left or were pushed.

In confrontation, he could dominate a meeting but, conversely, in a team he could be a good subordinate: his ego quite invisible.

He was generally gregarious and made strong friends. He also made many, powerful, enemies, the reasons for which should be obvious from this resume.

His drive extended to his leisure. He was a keen pianist and enjoyed attending performances. He revelled in reading, as much as time allowed, both the classics and modern fiction. He also enjoyed the theatre, where his taste was catholic: he would enjoy a Shakespeare; or a Stoppard, or an Ayckbourn.

I would say that he only ever loved one woman, and that was Barbara. There were a number of relationships before her, but none ever seemed like love. He saw her as a peer; often as a superior, and as someone he could trust implicitly. He trusted no one else completely, including me, and I was just about the closest there was, for a long time."

"He was a hard act to follow then."

"Yes this goes back to our last conversation, Steven was trying to do just that."

"Okay what about Barbara?"

"Barbara was not driven like Gordon. In many ways, she had a greater intellect than him. She was able to see, sometimes with supreme clarity, where effort was required; where effort was wasted. She was a better Intelligence manager for that reason. Not that he was bad at it; she was just excellent.

She had a wonderful ability to see both sides of an argument, or a discussion, or an operational schema. This made her a formidable debater and planner; something compounded by her memory, which was capable of instant recall, from her wide-ranging contemporary and historic knowledge.

It seemed that she was able to learn from her mistakes and move on. I never knew her ever to go back to an old failure and rehash it futilely, as Gordon often did. This was one of her occasional frustrations with him: she saw the pain it caused him.

Unlike Gordon, I have no doubts concerning her ability to judge character. She was spot on so often it was almost unbelievable. Even when she had identified a failing in someone, she would willingly work with them to find a way around it. On only a very few occasions did she decide that the effort would be wasted: drawing a veil over the situation or individual.

The things they had in common were: decisiveness, when it was needed; the ruthlessness, a common love, she felt for him, as he did for her, and a virtually identical appreciation of the arts. She was a good pianist too, but better on the cello. Their reading was similar; there was a large common subset, as very often the one would recommend a book to the other. Rarely would they say: I liked this, but you won't."

200

Hastings paused searching his mind for any other cogent material on Barbara. Grieve was happy with what he had heard for the moment and said, "okay profile Steven."

"Well I can't do it as I did for Gordon and Barbara, I only knew him as a boy and as a young man."

"Okay, I understand that, do the best you can."

Hastings studied Grieve and restarted the analysis, "he seemed to have inherited a greater proportion of Gordon's mental characteristics than Barbara's: he was a perfectionist and driven; often he disappeared into himself when he reran some mistake or failure: like Gordon he could cane himself over and over again, though in his case, this sometimes became violent.

I've already said Steven was a strong athlete and he drove himself in that as much as, if not more than, Gordon. He gave up on his intellect at an early stage; otherwise, he might have driven himself in that too. Both parents wanted the boy to be bi or tri-lingual, like Fiona. Steven, sadly, never showed any interest in developing the little French and German he did initially pick up.

Gordon didn't help; he'd decided Steven was a dunce and made little secret of it, even with the boy. I think this will have carved a big chip on his shoulder.

He lacked self-confidence and often found an outlet for his frustrations in violent and defiant behaviour. That's why Beth and I stopped taking him, and why he had to be moved around schools. If Barbara had had time for him at an early age, I am sure some of these pressures would have been eased.

The lack of attention from his parents created gaps in his character that, with the other problems, made it difficult for him to find friends. I am not aware of him ever bringing boys back home to play with nor, later any girls. But he did care for Fiona, and they were very close. I believe she provided that outlet for his feelings that he wasn't getting from his mother. Also, and this is a guess, she was able to see that Steven had a stronger mind than anyone else realised; her ability allowed her to tap into it."

"Okay that's good, now what about Fiona?"

"Well the same caveat applies to her, I was close to her only until she was fifteen."

Grieve nodded and Hastings girded himself again, "Fiona was a wonderful child. Unlike poor Steven, her parents, particularly her mother, put considerable effort into her early years.

She seemed to pick up some of Gordon's drive, but only just enough of his perfectionism. I think also, she seemed to have avoided much of this fault of rehearsing past failure. Most importantly, she seemed to share her mother's ability to see both sides. As I said yesterday, she had a very powerful intellect, benefiting from both her parents' genes.

Barbara and Gordon spoke English, German, and French with her from the earliest age and, unlike Steven, she enjoyed and worked at it. Gordon also spent time schooling her in Mathematics. Actually, my Carol may have been something of a role model in this too, as she talked to Fiona several times regarding life at university, and some of the esoteric maths she was doing there.

By the time Fiona was ten, she was speaking good German and good French. I was led to believe that in every subject, including physical activities incidentally, she was comparable to good twelve-year-olds. She easily obtained a place at King's College in Wimbledon; there she was so far advanced on every front, it was easy for her to stay ahead.

I remember conducting a conversation with her, when she was fourteen in virtually fluent German. Then she switched to fluent French and then back to German again. In some respects, despite her youth, her command of the two languages exceeded mine."

"A very intelligent young woman. What a waste." Grieve paused, "okay, so with these profiles can we say anything, or deduce anything about their interpersonal relationships. Firstly, Steven with his father and mother."

"Well, he had a difficult relationship with them both. Gordon expected a lot of him and reacted badly when he was unable, in Gordon's eyes, to fulfil his expectations. His relationship with his mother was never the natural one. Barbara may have been caring of those staff and field personnel that were capable of being developed, but she, in fact they both, had a blind spot where their son was concerned.

202

Gordon applied an unfair amount of pressure on the boy to achieve as he had done, yet gave him only a fraction of the support he needed to come anywhere close. I think the problem was that he fell between them; Gordon was assuming Barbara was providing support, and Barbara was assuming Gordon was: actually, neither were. With that support, he probably would have proved a normal well-rounded child. Without it, there was always a big chance he would be deficient in some way.

As he matured into a teenager, I could see a dichotomy developing. He was intensely proud of his parents, especially his father, and yet there was this resentment at being abandoned for long periods, as well as being considered backward intellectually. This bred the violence; the antisocial behaviour at an early age, and it fed the desire to emulate and surpass them when he approached manhood.

He was quite a large child, and became increasingly assertive with his parents as he went through puberty. It is not impossible that both he and Gordon resorted to blows at the worst times. It was another factor in the decision to send him to Glenalmond. After that, their relationship was calmer. They saw less of each other, and the school redirected his energies. However, the conflict or competition between them intensified as Steven got older. When they were together there was always a tension. I don't believe it openly resurfaced though, until the decision to seek SAS selection. Up until that time, they had both broadly agreed on the best way forward for him.

He was impatient, as all young men are, to achieve success. Also, like all young people, he saw the freedoms the world bestowed and not the pitfalls. This was why, I think, he applied for the SAS as soon as he met the criteria. He saw his father's old regiment as a slow road. The shallowness of his motivation may well have been the reason for his failure. His desire to succeed duped by the perception of its being a fast track to success.

After this setback, he seemed to throw himself into the Coldstreams as being the next best route for the achievement of the personal success he so desperately craved.

I can't comment further on him and his development as this was when I was committed to hospital."

"Okay then, what about Fiona?"

"Well her relationship with her parents was noteworthy only in its mundanity. She was a model child: high achieving; socially responsive; friendly. She could occasionally get angry or difficult, but no more than any other child would. It's difficult to know what else to say."

22. A New Set of Facts

Doyle found his way back to Westminster and presented himself at the temporary office, where Mr King and his colleagues were currently employed. He was ushered into a meeting room on the ground floor, once his ID had been scrutinised, and the porter had called Mr King. He was assured that the gentlemen would be with him shortly.

Doyle folded his arms and waited patiently. He used the time to mull the findings in the investigation to date. After ten minutes had passed a diminutive, bespectacled, prematurely balding man in a dark, well used, pinstripe knocked, and entered the room. He introduced himself as Jim King; sitting down only after he also had inspected Doyle's ID card.

He sat in an expectant silence, with his hands folded on the table waiting for Doyle to speak; so Doyle obliged, "thank you for seeing me at such short notice."

"You're welcome."

"As you know, I want to discuss the late Fiona Armstrong."

"Yes, it was a great shock, and a huge loss, when she was taken from us."

"Did you know her well?"

"She is one of six that report directly to me. I have, in total, a team of twenty-two. I probably knew her as well as most and saw her, until recently, usually on a daily basis. We rarely socialised though, only the occasional offsite meeting. She was close to several other team members: I can arrange for you to see them over the next week if you like?"

"Thank you, I will probably take advantage of that. Can you tell me what you knew of her as a person?"

Mr King looked troubled, "I should like to concentrate on the period up to the end of 2002."

Doyle left the obvious question for the time being, and his interviewee spent the next twenty minutes speaking very highly of Fiona Armstrong, who had worked for him for four years. As he was winding down he explained his first remark with, "it was because she was so conscientious, intelligent, and productive normally that her dilatory performance during the last three months or so came as such a surprise."

Doyle was puzzled, "I understood she had been doing substantial overtime and week-end working recently."

"Well, I very much deplore speaking ill of the dead, but really I can't think why. I had become very frustrated. I think I have seen her on only a handful of occasions since the New Year began. She had taken several days sick leave, and almost all of her five-week annual holiday entitlement, already this year. Several of her projects are running late, and in reviewing her work since her death, I have found a disappointing number of problems."

Doyle knew this was potentially very important, "do you have any explanation for this behaviour?"

"None. I had arranged to discuss her conduct with her last week, on a personal, one to one basis: she called in sick on the appointed day. I rearranged it for yesterday afternoon and I'm afraid, as a result of her cavalier attitude, I had escalated it to a disciplinary matter. An HR consultant was going to attend this second meeting too: in order to record the formal warning. Sadly, her death intervened."

"Has she ever demonstrated anything, even the smallest lapse, like this before?"

206

"No, not at all, as I said before she was an excellent employee, one earmarked for promotion. Also, I can say quite categorically, she came very highly recommended to us. I know her previous employer extremely well."

"Can you pinpoint the time when her behaviour started to deteriorate?"

"I'm afraid that the best I can say, is that it probably started just before the New Year. Possibly some of her other colleagues can be more precise."

"Does she have a desk, or locker, or other similar thing where she might keep personal material?"

"Hum, yes, she has a desk and some filing. There are certain personal things in them." King suddenly seemed less accommodating, "she may also have a locker at the leisure club some of our staff are members of. I can check with HR whether she is a member."

"Yes, Thank you. Can I also look through the desk and the filing please?"

"Hum, let me think that over."

King picked up the phone that was sitting on the table and dialled an extension. After being redirected, he spoke briefly; receiving confirmation that, if Fiona was a member of a fitness club, it was not the one that HR had an arrangement with.

Doyle was fretting about the desk and the filing, and eventually King agreed, reluctantly, to allow him access. Suffocatingly, he insisted on being present whilst Doyle conducted the search.

They left the room and King escorted him through the security checkpoint and up to his department, which was already half deserted. There he showed him into a corner by a window where Fiona Armstrong had worked. Doyle spent half an hour checking all the potential storage areas. At the end, he had found two lipsticks, a deodorant stick, a comb and hair brush, a couple of postcards of skiers on snow covered Alps and a plastic wallet that was three quarters full of business cards. He asked if he could keep the postcards and the card wallet. After some soul-searching King decided that this would not compromise the security of the nation, and he agreed to their removal. He showed Doyle out just as five-fifteen was chiming on a church nearby.

Some time before this, Grieve had attended the memorial service. There were very few people there. Steven Armstrong, James Belvedere, Harcourt, Thompson, Hastings, three from Northern Ireland representing the police, the Army and MI5, two couples who had lived near the Armstrong's in Wharfedale and three other people from London who were very friendly with Harcourt. Some of the people were very annoyed with Steven that it was such a muted affair.

Grieve casually spoke to everyone who attended. But he didn't learn much. Only that Steven was driving back to London that evening and that Belvedere was staying overnight in Leeds at the same hotel he had used before. After the ceremony, a disgruntled Grieve regretfully acknowledged that it had been mostly a waste of his time.

Doyle headed over towards the south side of the Hungerford Bridge at five-thirty. Within easy reach of the café/wine bar where he was to meet Annabel Fasting, he stopped and leaned on the wall overlooking the Thames. For several minutes he enjoyed watching the prosaic, calming movement of the water and the craft plying it. With time to kill, he took out his mobile and called his boss. In great detail he told of: the degeneracy of Bulatovic; Fiona's new will; Kossuth and the dilemma he had presented; Millie Ballard's help and the crucial fact that King's, and Belvedere's stories did not tie up. Once all that was done, he enquired after the memorial service; Grieve grumbled that he had returned from the muted ceremony empty-handed. The only thing of note being his gentle intervention when it looked like there would be angry words between Steven and James. Doyle told him James was going to ask to attend the funeral when it happened, and he guessed the anger stemmed from a refusal. Grieve digested this and then went on by giving Blackhall's assessment of James Belvedere, but also that he remained yet to be convinced; he said he had an outstanding enquiry, which he thought would shed light on the question. Doyle listened as he watched the world float by in the centre of the Capital; he felt a million miles away from his workplace, and his boss.

When the conversation reached a natural end, Doyle excused himself and meandered the embankment, soothed by its calm environment. Slowly he approached his prospective rendezvous in the stylish café cum wine bar, where he realized he needed, and ordered a cappuccino. He still felt aggrieved that Mr, bloody, Jim King had neglected to supply a coffee when he was with him; yet was sufficiently pedantic to stand breathing down his neck, when he was searching Fiona's desk.

At five past six a medium height, buxom, blonde woman in her early thirties came in and looked around uncertainly. She fitted Ms Fasting's description. Doyle had described himself too, so when he stood up her face cleared and she came over, "Inspector Doyle?"

Doyle nodded and handed her his ID to check, "can I get you a drink?" He asked expecting her to match his coffee.

"God, yes, it's been a crazy day, I'll have a large glass of their Chilean Cabernet Sauvignon." She smiled broadly at him, "it's after six: I'm allowed to imbibe."

A huge bulb of deep red wine arrived in the hand of a tall, dark, very cheerful waiter; his perfect white teeth a counterpoint to his tanned skin. Annabel watched lasciviously as he walk away. Dragging her eyes from his posterior, she turned her attention to the glass. She put it to her nose and appreciated the bouquet, "they do have a good wine selection here; you should try some."

"Maybe later, what made the day so crazy?"

"Oh, it's often like that, it's just more so now. The paper is trying to get every angle under the sun on Iraq before the Americans obliterate it forever: the activity has reached fever pitch."

"Do you think there will be war?"

"Well, that isn't my field. The boys there whose field it is say 'yes' and probably in the next week or so. The biggest issue is whether Britain will join in; one of the legal boys is convinced that any invasion now has to be illegal; that the British military might refuse to fight. It all depends on the Attorney General and his deliberations with the US."

Doyle took a keen interest in current affairs and was surprised that there was a prospect of the Army defying the government. Annabel continued, "anyway, we must talk about poor Fiona, how can I help you?"

209

Doyle had been reluctant to force the conversation in that direction and was pleased; this was a refreshingly quick start, "can you tell me about her; your time together?"

"Okay." She pursed her lips, "let's see, we met first when we both started at Kings College in Wimbledon. We were twelve and got on immediately: strange really because I had struggled to get into the school, whereas Fiona had waltzed in. She helped me a very great deal, it was as if she had taken me under her wing; was looking out for me."

Annabel was doing everything in double time, she talked at double time; she drank at double time. "That initial period can be quite vicious: with bullying and the disorientation of a new school. Being together like that, from so early on, insulated us both from most of it. I know some girls, those we befriended later, had a difficult first few months."

There was a half pause dedicated to the wine, "by the end of the first term there was a little group of five of us, all drawn together really by Fiona. We all benefited from our association with her, and she was protected from the detractors by our support. I am really proud though that I was her first, and best, friend."

Doyle smiled at the happy picture Annabel was painting, "it sounds like she was a natural leader."

"Oh she was. She was hockey captain in each year after the first. And she had a seriousness about her that always got her respect: even from the teachers. Especially the poor language teachers, they were almost afraid of her."

Slurp.

"She was too polite to pick them up on anything though; on several occasions she said afterwards that they had made mistakes. No, the problem for them was when they conducted conversations. Sometimes in her enthusiasm, Fiona would leave them behind. It could be very funny."

Doyle was surprised that a young girl could be so proficient, "why was she so good at languages?"

"She was so quick, and besides her parents are, were both multi lingual, and they had spoken German and French with her from when she could first talk."

Slurp, hic.

210

"When they went on holiday, which they did increasingly as Fiona had got older, they always went to the French, or Swiss, or German, or Austrian Alps. I went with them as company for Fiona on several occasions. That's why I'm moderately good myself: when we were in France, we always talked French; when we were in Germany or Austria, we talked German; and when we were in Switzerland, we would experiment with Swiss German and Italian, as well as the other two.

A game Fiona often played was to try to fool the locals into thinking she was a local too. That's very difficult to do given the spectrum of dialects; but she often made them think she was a native, just from some other part of the country."

"What was her relationship with her parents like?"

"It was excellent, it was more fun being with her and her parents than it was with mine. They treated us like little adults, when my parents still treated me like a small child."

"What about her brother?"

"Oh, Steven used to get us girls really excited. We were in our middle teens and we were so interested in boys anyway; Steven would come back from the Army in his uniform. He was so tall, and strong, and handsome, and the uniform, God! I used to cream my pants when I saw him."

Annabel smiled at the memory and took another gulp of wine; she seemed quite oblivious to the risqué comment, "he was very quiet though, and usually; when he did appear, Fiona would limit the time she spent with us in order to spend time with him. They were very close. He seemed only really comfortable in her company His parents, particularly, seemed to disturb him. He hardly every stayed in the house; staying in nearby cheap hotels often, rather than be too close to them."

"That's unusual." Doyle said thoughtfully, "why was that?"

"There always seemed to be problems, he would bristle if they told him to do something, or if they offered advice. He just seemed to value his independence."

"So, he was still rebelling, is that what you're saying?"

"Pretty much, yes, but Fiona was always mediating, she hated the ill-feeling that often existed."

211

"I don't wish to be rude, but Fiona almost sounds too good to be true. Didn't she ever do anything bad?"

Annabel smiled nostalgically, "she was very mischievous, and would play practical jokes on everyone, except Steven I should say. That got her into trouble a few times with her parents, and once with the school Head: I think that's why she never made school captain.

You don't mean that, though, do you: you mean did she ever do things that were selfish; did she ever feel sorry for herself; did she ever have a temper tantrum. Well yes, of course, but no worse than anyone else and probably less so really.

Look can I get you a drink?"

Doyle realised that her wine was down to a last mouthful. He was surprised it had gone so quickly. Relenting he had a small version of Annabel's Chilean red while she took a second huge bulb. He joked, "I hope you're not driving when you leave your train?"

"No, I walk, I only live five hundred yards from Virginia Water station."

Doyle, sipping his wine, had to agree it was an excellent choice, "so, you remained very close throughout school, what happened then?"

"Well, we were both going to University and Fiona had such good results, she could have gone anywhere. I, on the other hand, didn't do so well; I was limited in the places I was offered. In the end, I chose Nottingham. I remember being really pleased when Fiona said she would come with me: but I did, honestly, try to persuade her to go to Oxford or Cambridge. This was the one time I really saw her have a big bust up with her parents. Her mother, Barbara, was furious that she wasn't choosing Cambridge, and her father wasn't much better: he wanted her to go to either, Oxford, Cambridge, or Edinburgh."

"How big a bust up was it? Say, on a scale of one to ten."

"Oh, five, a standard sized teenage fight with parents, it blew over after a couple of weeks."

"Okay, so you both went to Nottingham University, what happened there?"

"After the initial few months, when we were still very close, we started to drift apart. The main reason, I am sure you

212

have guessed, is that we found men. Fiona met a nice boy called Graeme in Second Year Law and I, unfortunately, met my future, and now ex, husband Hugh. These new sexual interests, different courses, and different hobbies eventually drew us along separate paths. We still would get together, but it became less and less frequent.

That went on into our careers; we both came back to London. I had got a 2.2 in English and started in journalism. Fiona had got a first in Law and started with a leading City firm.

She was a bridesmaid at my wedding in '94. I recall we got horribly drunk together; had a great chat and a laugh. That was the closest we had been for maybe two or three years.

We would see each other every couple of months for lunch, or at a party held by mutual friends; that sort of thing."

"Did she ever show any signs of any mental instability?"

Annabel looked shocked, "God no, absolutely not, someone with her feet more firmly planted on the ground you could not find. No, if anyone in that family was going to go off the rails, it was Steven. Latterly, he was bottling up such a lot, you sometimes expected the top of his head would blow off."

Annabel paused, with the wine glass at her mouth, as she saw Doyle jot this down: she reconsidered her remark, "look I didn't mean he was going to: he was likelier to blow-up than Fiona, but she wasn't likely to at all."

"Okay, I take the point. Did you see Fiona in the course of the last three months?"

"I saw her at a surprise early Christmas party that her brother threw one Friday night: can't remember the date. He hired an entire restaurant for the evening and paid for all the drinks; champagne; food: everything, it went on until two in the morning."

"That was the only time you saw her?"

Annabel looked sadly into the remains of her wine, which had sunk so much it barely covered the bottom of her glass, "I'm afraid so; the last time I saw her."

"How was she?"

"She seemed fine, she was very concerned over the amount of money Steven was spending on the party. I saw her having a very serious looking word with him; but he just laughed

213

it off: said he was celebrating not being forty yet; that his fortieth would be a very dull affair."

"How big a party was it?" Doyle was surprised at his interest. "Pretty big, he probably spent five or six grand. But then, once in a blue moon, people can do that, can't they?"

Not Police Detective Inspectors, or at least not this one, flashed through her companion's mind, "can you think back and try and pinpoint the date?"

She sat back with a hopeless look on her face; then she concentrated and said, "well, it was definitely in December and it was definitely a Friday before Christmas. Actually well before Christmas."

She looked up and called across, "Carlo, can I have a look at that calendar?"

Carlo came over with the calendar; he was beaming so much his teeth flashed; Doyle tried not to see the way Annabel caressed his derriere when he arrived. Carlo, who was, in Doyle's opinion the 'The Italian Stallion' of legend, obviously had his derriere caressed so often he was quite immune. When he left, Doyle thought Annabel looked, well, quite flushed and she was seeking to hide her elevated heart rate by concentrated on the dates. Each month had a page and each page had the previous and following month summarised at the bottom; she was looking at the December summary on the January 2003 page of the calendar. She distractedly reached for her glass and was surprised that it was so easy to empty; without a glance at Doyle, she held it up meaningfully, and Carlo beamed. Beaming seemed to be his thing. Annabel looked at Doyle, and when he shook his head, she went back to studying the calendar, "right, we have Friday the 6th, Friday the 13th, and Friday the 20th. I am fairly sure it wasn't the last one. So either the 6th or the 13th."

She deliberated a little more, but was distracted by Carlo who this time placed the glass in such a way that Annabel was unable to reach his body. Doyle got the distinct impression that an intricate dance was being played out and that Carlo was the lead. Disconcertingly, he winked and flashed his teeth at Doyle, who was irritated when he felt himself reddening slightly. Annabel shook her head, "no, it is one of those Friday's but which one - I can't be sure. I might be able to ask around?"

"No, no need, either is close enough." Doyle already had a good idea which one it was. He looked at Annabel, who was in the process of demolishing the third third of an entire bottle of red wine, "how well did you know James Belvedere?"

"Oh, he's such a hunk." Annabel made a face that Doyle would not have been surprised to see a man make, "Fiona was totally, madly in love with him, and he was with her. He was so good to her, and for her."

"You obviously liked him?"

"Oh not just me, there was a collective wail from us singles when Fiona snared him. It isn't just that he is so physically beautiful. He is also so gracious and so lacking in any form of malice. He can be depended on in a crisis, and yet, sometimes he could be so boyish. You could just cuddle him, and love him to bits."

"Really." Doyle said disingenuously and continued, "when you saw them last at this party. I understand James and Steven didn't see eye to eye, did you see anything of that?"

Annabel shook her head, pouted a little, "I saw them talking, I can't say there was any disagreement. They didn't talk for long, I suppose that might indicate something, but then Steven was never very talkative."

"Did you see Fiona acting strangely, was she angry, or out of sorts?"

"No, as I say she was concerned about the cost of the do, but apart from that, all I saw was Fiona and James being disgustingly happy together; that's all."

Doyle sighed, it was late, and he let his guard slip. His frustration was obvious, and Annabel looked apologetic, "I'm sorry, I'm not helping a lot am I?"

"No, you've been great, I'd just hoped to understand Fiona a bit better following this conversation."

"Well, you're asking the wrong person."

Doyle's interest quickened, "why, who should I be asking?"

"Fiona, of course, she's the best person to ask."

Doyle was disappointed: he frowned and decided they had better pay the bill before Annabel drank all the wine the bar had. She understood his behaviour immediately, "no, no Inspector

215

let me pay. You're right I have drunk too much. However, I'm serious. After I had known Fiona for a while, I discovered that she kept a diary. She didn't broadcast the fact, but when she was fourteen another girl, an awful cow named Belinda, caught her writing it at school. Belinda like the horror she was, grabbed the book, and ran off with it. Seemingly, she took pleasure in sharing the juicier parts with some other girls. Fiona was furious and tearful, but couldn't get it back. In the end a friend, Isabel, and I retrieved the thing. We had had to threaten the thief with grievous bodily harm to secure it.

You remember I mentioned a practical joke that landed her in trouble with the Head. Well, the bedraggled fall-girl was Belinda.

I don't know for certain if Fiona maintained the diary into her adult life: it was never seen or discussed again, but my guess is, she did."

23. A Constructive Search

Doyle escaped at quarter past seven, as he rushed off to find a taxi, he called Grieve.

His boss was at home, with slippers on, feet up watching snooker on BBC2. He was patiently waiting for Mrs Grieve to finish the preparation of the evening's Coq-au-Vin. It was a sacred process where the only person allowed in the kitchen was his wife.

He was just as excited at the prospect of a diary as Doyle was. Doyle went on, "I'm going back to the Chelsea apartment now to see if I can find it. It must be well hidden if it's there."

"Charles it's late, take a rest."

"No, I'm on a roll here. Different topic: I have to say I think we may be barking up the wrong tree chasing Belvedere. Everything I have heard relating to him and all my instincts too, suggest he isn't our man."

"Well, as I hinted earlier, I'm reaching the same conclusion. Sandy Blackhall is very keen, but what he doesn't know is that some of the timings on Tuesday don't work.

Belvedere was recorded checking in at the M62 Travelodge at twelve forty-six according to the Visa payment slip. But in order to have seen Maxwell leave Almscliff View and pick up his car, he would have had to be on the Chevin before one. That's impossible, they are forty-five minutes fast driving apart, unless there are two of them, and there's no evidence of that. I have spent much of the day trying to think of other ways to square that circle and have failed.

I am still waiting for a call from this Tom Humble chap, the HR director at Astons, to support my conclusion. Sandy's team didn't probe him regarding the telephone call he made to Belvedere; they just confirmed that it took place. I have some pertinent questions to ask him, which if answered appropriately will, in my view, lift Belvedere off the hook."

"If he's innocent and telling us the truth, then how do we explain Fiona's behaviour? Belvedere believed she was spending inordinate amounts of time at work, when in fact she wasn't."

"Well, if there's a diary, and you find it, there might be an explanation in that. Unfortunately, I never find life's that kind; you never know though, hope springs eternal."

"Let's hope then. Something else that needs considering is a link between Fiona's changed behaviour and her brother. This expensive party he threw was, apparently, completely out of the blue. I'm guessing it was probably on Friday 13th December: unfortunate date to get thrown up.

Anyway, Millie Ballard said the change in Fiona happened around Saturday 21st: but that was when she first clocked it. I think it started before then. Besides, she hinted at something different about Fiona on Saturday the 14th, the day after the Steven Armstrong party. Annabel Fasting said Fiona and Steven had something of a disagreement concerning the cost of the do."

"Maybe James Belvedere can shed some light on that conversation?"

"Yes maybe; another thing: Steven Armstrong, in contrast to Belvedere, is looming larger in my mind by the minute. He is looking increasingly flaky the further I go with this investigation."

"Yes I have to agree with you on that one too. I had a very useful discussion with Bill Hastings this morning, regarding the relationships in the Armstrong family, precisely for that

218

reason. Everything I learnt increased my interest in our angry friend.

Sometime soon, you should go and squeeze the Colonel, Thackeray, who commanded Steven when he was in the Coldstream Guards. He knows a lot more than he told me on the phone. Also, I think, after dinner I might go and have a little discussion with James Belvedere at his hotel, see if I can jog his mind about some of this."

"Oh, well in that case, something else cropped up which you can ask him. Was Fiona in a fitness club, and which one? When she turned out not to be in the MoD one, it made me wonder if she might have storage in some other club."

Immediately Doyle rang off Grieve got through to James Belvedere at his hotel. He just caught him in his room before he departed for dinner. They agreed to meet in the hotel bar, at half past nine that evening.

Meanwhile, Doyle had found a taxi and was soon back in Belvedere's apartment. He explored the various rooms initially. There was a huge lounge, a dining room next to the king-sized kitchen, a master bedroom en-suite, two other bedrooms, another large bathroom, and a big cloakroom off the entrance hall.

Doyle knew James hadn't mentioned any diary when quizzed over Fiona's relevant documents, even though that specific question had been put. That meant, if he was now to be believed, that Fiona had kept the diary from him too, assuming there was one of course. It also meant that firstly, she would have had to have somewhere convenient to hide it quickly, and secondly, somewhere that Belvedere would not stumble on it.

Where would she have written it? Probably somewhere that would be perfectly natural to be: she wouldn't be able to explain regular visits to the cloakroom for instance. Also, if she wrote it in the bedroom and hid it, for instance, in the cloakroom there would be a chance that James would catch her during the process of hiding. That reasoning seemed to rule out a hiding place in the main bathroom, the hall, the cloakroom, and the two spare bedrooms. All were unlikely sites for both the writing and the hiding of it.

Doyle started methodically to search the master bedroom and en-suite. He checked all the conventional storage; checked boxes and bags in the wardrobes. He looked under, around, behind, and inside the bed. He pulled at the carpet to see if anywhere it was loose. He tested the roof panels for movement; went around tapping the walls looking for hidden cavities; looked for hollow walls, or safes behind the few pictures.

In the en-suite, he felt the bath panels, looked in the cistern, burrowed through the towels in the airing cupboard. He strained his hand into, and up and down, the basin pedestal. Like the bedroom, he searched floor, walls, doors, and roof for a hiding place. Nothing remotely like a diary turned up.

Undeterred he started on the lounge. He repeated the whole process there too. Still nothing. He checked all the books on the bookcase: every book was as the cover proclaimed. He ran his hands over the TV, the HiFi, and the speakers.

He was becoming tired and hungry, but he persevered. He started and finished the dining room. From there, he went through every possible location in the kitchen: still absolutely nothing.

His mobile rang. It was Grieve in the hotel bar with Belvedere. God, Doyle thought, it's ten to ten in the evening. Grieve relayed that James knew absolutely nothing about a diary: he was rather shocked that Fiona would have kept such a thing from him. He was able to confirm they were both members of the South Kensington Fitness First Club, which was only a short walk from the flat. Neither, though, had kept any storage there. Grieve had yet to broach the subject of Fiona's unaccounted-for time, or the discussion at the party. In a whispered aside Grieve also confirmed that the argument at the service had been about James's continued exclusion from the private funeral: apparently he was still seething. After this they drew the telephone conversation to a close.

Doyle gloomily considered the next steps. If the diary existed it almost certainly had to be here, or possibly, somewhere he had overlooked at Fiona's work perhaps. He went and sat down in the lounge. He was desperately hungry now, but was like a terrier at a bone when something like this cropped up.

He had checked everything, had he not? He closed his eyes and spent some time trying to imagine Fiona moving around the house, sitting, eating, drinking, watching television and

220

writing. He remembered that Belvedere worked hard; was often away seeing clients. This implied that most of the time she could safely write, knowing there was no chance of interruption.

He opened his eyes again and they focussed on the writing desk next to the bookcase. He had been all over it, and there was no diary. Not withstanding, as his mind traced the imaginary Fiona around the room he became convinced that she sat and wrote the diary at the desk.

He went to the desk and sat in the chair, he opened the top central drawer. Plenty of pens, many well used, judging by the amount of clear plastic tubing he could see. He lifted one likely looking one, a Uni-Ball; the column of ink had been shrunk to an inch from the head. He pulled some paper out. He signed his name, and thought, nice feel to the pen. He wrote a short text at the top of the page:

'Twinkle, twinkle little bat
How I wonder what your at
up above the world you fly
Like a teatray in the sky'

He smiled nostalgically. Something else came unbidden to his head and he wrote, careful to retrieve the exact quote:

'What need we fear who knows it, when none can call our power to account? Yet who would have thought the old man to have had so much blood in him?'

Doyle, at first pleased with his recall, then looked, aghast, at what he had written; he shivered, but found another quotation coming to mind; he almost felt impelled to write it down:

'But Mousie, thou art no thy lane,
In proving foresight may be vain;
The best-laid schemes o'mice an' men
Gang aft agley,
An' lea'e us nought but grief an' pain
For promis'd joy!'

Bloody hell, apposite or what, hopefully it's the killer's plans that will 'gang agley'. Doyle's heart pumped a little harder when he suddenly wondered if putting himself in Fiona's mind had had some kind of supernatural effect. He shook his head. Get a grip man, your blood sugar's low. He folded the paper. Where would he hide it? He looked around again, trying *not* to emulate Fiona now.

He looked at the modern and rather striking painting that hung on the wall on the other side of the desk from the bookcase. Because of its size, maybe six foot tall and four foot wide, the wall behind it had been one of the first things he had checked when he started searching in the lounge. He was turning away to look in the other direction, when his eyes widened, and he spun back to look at it again. There was no external frame; the canvas was stretched around, and onto an internal, sturdy, wooden frame, so that the modern art painted on its face reached right to the edge. Because of this, the work was quite deep, at over an inch, and hung vertically, flush with the wall. Doyle got up and pulled the lower edge part way from the wall, as he had done before, but this time he looked at the back of the picture. Nothing. Then he looked up. There were two wooden battens running horizontally across the back. They divided it into three sections. Two thin pieces of plywood were nailed to the upper sides of these two central battens; each was eight inches deep. They spanned the whole breadth of the painting and the lowest was just above Doyle's eye level.

When he had looked the first time, his eyes had gone nowhere near it. Even so, it could be interpreted as part of the frame's necessary strengthening: the tension of the canvas must impose significant forces on the wood. What was clear now though, was that there were two pockets an inch in breadth, eight inches deep, and four foot in length in the back of the picture. He easily reached up to the lowest one and sure enough, there was something there.

His heart pounding with excitement, he took the painting down. In the lower cavity, there were six black books and some loose papers. In the upper cavity, eight identical black books. He put it all on the desk and returned the painting to the wall.

He opened the book from the lower pocket that had been nearest the desk-side of the painting. It had very fine paper in it and was just less than an inch thick.

Writing covered about two thirds of the pages, the last third was blank. He found the last written page and…was baffled.

222

There was a series of horizontal, diagonal, and vertical lines; many point marks, small circles, squares, and triangles on it.

On the penultimate page, there were further patterns but these looked more like the doodles he himself would design when he was sitting in a boring meeting or lecture. The last page looked as though there was a meaning to the markings but these looked meaningless.

Then there was writing, but the date at the top was December 10th 2002. The page before that read December 6th 2002. He leafed through the book and found this structure repeated back through time to August 6th 2001. Sometimes every day was recorded; sometimes there were gaps of as long as five days.

The next book was full and covered the period May 17th 1999 to August 4th 2001; the next the previous two years approximately. In all, there were ten books with material; the earliest date was 1st January 1980. Four of the books in the upper cavity were still blank. The loose papers had patterns on them similar to the last page of the last diary.

The entry for December 10th read: 'Mummy tells me Jamie has bought a diamond ring!!! I have been sworn to secrecy; must give him the impression that I am totally surprised when my darling asks me for my hand. I am so lucky: the only man I have loved, and he loves me just as much back. Mummy and Daddy are delighted too. Maybe, he will wait until Christmas Day. That would be wonderful.

Steven has invited us, at short notice, to a party this Friday. It is unfortunate timing with Christian Perks' do on the Saturday. But happily, Steven sounded very cheerful: an excellent development considering his depressions over the last year or so. I have promised faithfully to attend. He surprised me by insisting that Jamie come too. Hopefully, he is reconsidering his antipathy toward my poor love. I am just a little worried by the cost of it all though. He mentioned at least fifteen others who were coming and he is determined it is all on him. I told him not to be silly, we are all capable of funding ourselves, but he would have none of it.

At the beginning of the week I had one of my thought-provoking meetings with Millie: she has such wonderful ideas. It should be possible to transform the apartment for as little as £60k.

Millie is sure, as am I, that the changes will add at least £100k to its value. That's not the reason for doing it though; it really will make this rather dull place into a home for us both. If we marry in summer it should be possible to return from honeymoon to a transformation.'

Doyle felt a little seedy reading these private reflections of a beautiful, intelligent, and human woman: who was now cold and dead. The image of her body, lying in the upstairs corridor only three days before, clear in his mind. He closed his eyes. God, I hope she is with you. He looked at his watch; it was almost twenty to eleven. He tried Grieve's phone and discovered that he was still in the bar with Belvedere, and was now sounding just a little merry.

"I've finally found the diaries."

"Great news, are they a gold mine?"

"I think they will be very valuable, but you were right to caution that they wouldn't be a panacea. My guess that Steven's party was on the 13th December was correct. Also, the diary entries end at that time too; further evidence of a connection to the party.

Can you ask James how many people attended it?"

Grieve passed on the news concerning the diaries, asked the question and passed on the answer, "ninety-ish, or maybe slightly more, but not probably as much as a hundred."

"Well, that explains the discussion with Steven. Fiona though his paying for fifteen or twenty was going to be too expensive; she must have been appalled when she arrived and saw so many. Has Belvedere given you anything on the conversation?"

"Just a minute, excuse me for a moment James."

There were noises off and then Grieve spoke again, "right, now I can talk. Steven boasted that he was going to spend ten grand on it. As soon as James realised that this angered Fiona he ducked out and didn't hear the rest of the conversation. Fiona joined him five minutes later with an impenetrable look on her face. That's all he knows. I asked him if he enjoyed himself and he said it was a funny do; hardly anyone knew anyone else. Quite a few hardly knew Steven."

"Well, everyone says he didn't make friends easily.

Look sir, there's something else. Following the last entry on the 10th December, there are two pages of something that looks like doodling, except, there is sufficient structure on the last page for it to have a meaning. There are several loose pages with similar meaningful markings on them too. Unfortunately, it's a meaning lost on me. I'm going back to Scotland Yard now, I'll copy them and send them to you."

"Bloody Hell, Charles you're the one with the brain for that kind of thing, not me. If it's some kind of convoluted code it'll go straight over my head."

"Two brains are better than one, Sir."

"You're making a very flattering assumption there, my boy." Grieve said ironically, then he sighed, "on the other hand, I have had a thought. Can you fax them?"

"I can, but the problem with faxing is the quality. Some important detail in the pattern might get lost. I would do better to have them couriered to you."

"Expensive, but okay, do it. And then go and get some food and sleep. Well done by the way."

Doyle took the ten diaries and the loose jottings; went and found the car park where the Corolla was still sitting, and drove to the Yard and photocopied all the patterns.

He labelled them all, put the photocopies of the diary patterns and the loose originals in a big envelope a Met officer found for him, and waited until he could hand it directly to the courier.

Then he found a steak restaurant, stuffed himself with medium rare Aberdeen Angus, as many trimmings as possible, and finally crashed in his hotel in Fulham: He was in bed by twelve.

Grieve had made a phone call of his own after finishing with Doyle; after a brief conversation he had obtained the affirmation he had sought. Then he went back for another drink with James Belvedere, whom he was growing to like more and more as the evening went on.

24. A Little help from the Military

Doyle woke when his watch alarmed at seven thirty. He was still very tired and got up slowly. He thought a weekend of sleep would be no bad thing.

He showered, dressed and went to breakfast with the two most recent diaries and the one spanning 1992.

As he ate, he leafed through the two recent ones looking for clues to both Fiona and Steven's lives; fortunes and misfortunes; and their mental state. He was particularly interested in finding an explanation for the depression that Steven had been exhibiting and that Fiona had alluded too, given that it had, so dramatically, lifted in December.

Fiona seemed to have been enjoying life with James Belvedere: not surprising, if they had both planned to marry. The decision to sell their separate flats and buy the Chelsea apartment was hers as much as Belvedere's.

Her work was enjoyable and she believed that she was progressing well. Her health was good and she was attending the gym three or four times a week. She was a keen runner and had entered and done well in several road races in and around London: all fine, happy stuff.

No, the only cloud on Fiona's horizon that Doyle could track down in this first quick review, was Steven. There were several references to his depression.

Doyle flipped to the first page of the first of the two diaries, it was headed 17th May 1999, in an attempt to trace when this, seemingly prolonged, period of depression had started.

Steven was obviously based in the UK at this time as he was living in his flat in Chiswick and seeing Fiona quite regularly. There were several references to having a nice lunch or dinner with him. He was reported as being cheerful: even happy.

His research was interrupted when his watch alarmed again at eight twenty. It was a reminder to call the office number Colonel Thackeray had left with Grieve. A secretary answered the call and she told him Colonel Thackeray was at home all day working on a lecture course.

Doyle thanked her and said he had all the necessary details. He looked in his notebook to check the house address and telephone number Grieve had given him, and rang Thackeray at home. When it was answered, he asked if he could come down to Sandhurst to meet the Colonel in the next hour or two.

Thackeray was not in good humour: he was at first furious that Grieve had passed on his personal details. Doyle soothed him by saying Grieve was unable to be everywhere at once; that Doyle was the only other person with the information. Thackeray calmed somewhat, but said he would still call Grieve to establish Doyle's credentials. Doyle had no problem with this, and went on to say that he would try to be there for ten am.

The next call was to Major Shaw at the RLC HQ in Deepcut. He asked for an appointment at eleven thirty, which, in contrast, was politely and graciously granted.

Before leaving the table, he picked up the third diary and started to leaf through it from January 1992. Five minutes gave him what he wanted: Fiona had just found out about Steven's decision to leave the Coldstream Guards. Her father was enraged at Steven's choice: he saw it as a deliberate slap in his face. Fiona wrote of her own feelings and her concerns for Steven: it was almost as if Steven had given up on his ambitions, she could not understand why, and Steven was offering no plausible explanations. The next entry, three days later, lacked any hope of compromise. Fiona had guessed, knowing him so well presumably, that the Major had used his connections, despite being two years retired, and had sought further information from the regiment. The result was that he and Steven had had a vicious argument on the telephone. Neither would explain the reason for the argument and both had washed their hands of each other.

A week later, the schism had deepened and strengthened; nothing Fiona could say would bring the two men together. Even her mother had turned her back on her son. Doyle looked and looked but there was no further elaboration or explanation.

Reluctantly, he put the diaries into his briefcase, went out to the Corolla, and was soon traversing the Thames on the Chiswick Bridge. Down the A316, through Twickenham, he looked out for the home of English Rugby: Twickenham Stadium. He had to be satisfied with a fleeting glimpse of it, off on his right. Eventually he was on the M3. The journey had gone well: all the traffic congestion was on the other carriageway heading into London. At Junction 4, he left the motorway and headed into Camberley, where he pulled into a petrol station. He topped up the tank and bought a local AtoZ. So armed he drove past a giant shopping complex where a huge M&S was twinned with a huge Tesco, and headed for Owlsmoor: a large housing estate on the outskirts of the villages of College Town and Sandhurst. Following the map closely, he turned onto Acacia Avenue and was immediately buried in the maze of roads and houses. After two hundred yards, on the left, he saw Cardiff Close. Being ten minutes early, he drove past, pulled in, and switched the engine off.

He took the moment to call Collins, who was staying close to the deliberations on Kossuth. He was with Elliott and the MI5 man was back at his bubbling best. The decision on Kossuth looked like it was going his and Vaughan's way. This was good news for Doyle; it meant that Kossuth would keep talking. The decision should be reached by mid-day, which suited Doyle; he reckoned he should be back at the Yard by one thirty. He rang off, restarted the car, and pulled up in front of number three just before five to ten.

Spending these last few minutes studying the surroundings, he was not impressed: the estate was very claustrophobic. He thought substantial houses like these if they were in Leeds and its surroundings would have had three times the space around them that these houses had.

Seconds before ten, Doyle got out of the car and walked up the six yards of front paving to knock on the door. Colonel Thackeray, unlike his behaviour on the phone, was relaxed and amiable when he came to the door, "good timing."

He took Doyle's ID and studied it closely. "Sorry about the tirade on the telephone. With a war pending we have all been warned, once again, to be careful with our security."

"Really, don't be concerned; I can well understand the problem." Doyle said, but privately reflected; you were also worrying that you might have been found out.

Satisfied with the identity card, Thackeray led him through to a small study. This was furnished with a small rich, dark red leather, sever sided sofa; a heavy looking Georgian desk with red leather panels and a red leather, swivelling, bosun's chair. A computer monitor and keyboard took up a quarter of the desk space, and there was a neat pile of papers in the middle with a pair of spectacles sitting on top. The other wall was completely obscured by a bookcase full of books. Thackeray turned, "can I get you some tea?"

"Lovely, white, no sugar."

The Colonel went out and Doyle, seated on the sofa, studied the array of literature. At one end, there was an obvious military theme, at the other an obvious classical one, some in original Greek and Latin. In the middle, there was an eclectic collection spanning civilization, science, art, philosophy, maths and mechanics, music, economics, and much more besides: in fact it was a fairly comprehensive, if small, reference library.

Thackeray returned with a tray on which sat a teapot, two cups and saucers, a jug of milk and a small bowl of sugar, "shall we let it brew for a minute?"

Doyle nodded. The Colonel made himself comfortable in the bosun's chair. Doyle could see that the man was quite relaxed. "So, what can I add to what I told DCI Grieve?"

"I would like you to go into greater detail concerning Steven Armstrong's conduct in the Coldstream Guards, and what led him to leave?"

"I'm afraid, I would just be repeating what I said to your superior."

"Interestingly, the DCI didn't think you had told him very much. That surprises me, as Steven's departure from the regiment was a very significant and unpleasant event for the Armstrong family."

Thackeray frowned, "I can't imagine how you would know that. I'm quite certain Steven didn't volunteered such a thing."

"Well I do know it, and from an impeccable source. I also know that it led to the complete estrangement of Steven from his parents. I'm sure you can see that in the light of the murders, this event could be very important to the understanding of what happened."

"You suspect Steven of doing this thing?"

"We haven't ruled anyone in or anyone out. It is only Friday after all; the family died just four days ago. However, we have to track down every angle, and this is looking increasingly relevant."

"It's a shame I can't help you with it then."

Doyle decided to embellish what he had learnt from the diary, "Colonel, I also know that Major Armstrong, Steven's father, obtained information from the regiment concerning the reasons for his son's departure. It resulted in a very unpleasant argument between the two of them."

This shook Thackeray. His earlier relaxation was now well and truly forgotten. Doyle gave him some time to think by indicating the tea. Thackeray, stiff and tense now, whose mind was clearly racing, turned, and filled the two cups. He put three sugars in his own and handed Doyle his, "I really am very sorry, Inspector, I am unable to help."

Doyle decided to stop pussyfooting, "Colonel, believe me, I assuredly will find out what you are keeping from me. It will waste some precious time though. I'm sure you can see that this will, almost certainly, amount to obstruction of our investigation. Do I need to spell it out for you."

Thackeray now looked worried and angry in parts, "no, I have no trouble recognising a threat when I hear one," he spat back.

Doyle switched back to softly, softly mode, "look, is it sensitive? If it is, I'm sure something can be done to mitigate any ill effects on you, or the regiment, or the Army."

Thackeray was weighting the balance in his mind, "if there were something, I'm not saying there is, but if there were, and there was a subsequent trial, could anything I told you be kept out of the case… out of open court?"

Doyle sensed victory, "we are talking of an event that happened over ten years ago. If it proves relevant, and I think it will, in building our understanding, I cannot see how it would be proximal to the murders. If that is the case, and I am unable to give you a guarantee, it should be possible to keep it from the court. Other more recent information should be sufficient." Doyle reckoned his nose had remained the same length during this clumsy little speech: a minor miracle. He went on, "I will discuss it with my superiors, and we will do the utmost to keep it back."

Thackeray still looked worried and sat thinking for some time; eventually reaching a conclusion he said with some vehemence, "I think what you've just said is a complete load of *horseshit*. Nonetheless, in my estimation, what I can tell you will simply add to a picture of Steven's psychology. As such, in one small, but important respect, you are right; it is difficult to see that it is directly proximal to the murders.

I also, am quite sure, that Steven's developing estrangement with his family started long before his time with the Coldstream Guards. Though, yes, it might have been the final straw."

Doyle was quite happy to be ticked off, if he got the information. Thackeray threw in one last small defiance, "I will be very disappointed if this ever sees the light of day, Inspector."

Doyle supplied the obligatory nod. Thackeray took a deep breath, "Steven started well in the regiment. He was enormously ambitious, but then all young officers are, by and large.

I believe he attempted and failed SAS selection after three, or maybe, four years. That failure seemed to calm him and he flung all his effort into the Guards. As I said to DCI Grieve, he was a good soldier. He achieved his Captaincy in; oh I can't remember, two to two and a half years before the 1991 gulf war,

232

so probably in '88 or '89. He started putting enormous pressure on his Lieutenants and Non-Comms to hone the men. That was no bad thing, but sometimes he went over the top; I started hearing tittle-tattle of him losing control of his temper, which wasn't good. His relationship with some of his fellow officers, never easy, started to deteriorate.

Then Saddam invaded Kuwait. Ambitious junior officers are excited by war. They are still young enough to think themselves immortal, and it's an excellent chance for rapid promotion: for a variety of reasons. Steven was no exception and enthusiastically prepared for our deployment. I remember his infuriation when we were assigned a support role, rather than being in the front."

Thackeray paused and considered, "this didn't mean we were divorced from combat: there were some difficult moments for us. Sometimes the Iraqi prisoners changed their minds about surrendering. Occasionally they had local superiority and, as they'd often retained their weapons, a small unit of Guards if isolated could have faced annihilation.

Unfortunately, Steven's company was encountering these situations more often than others. There were rumours that the encounters were engineered. If that were the case, it would have been a potentially very dangerous game. Steven lost no men, but several were wounded; though it has to be said, none was serious. In addition to this problem, there were also suggestions that some recalcitrant prisoners died unarmed in Steven's care.

When I investigated these issues, potential testimony evaporated. Given the fluidity of the situation, I couldn't establish whether this was due to pressure and threats, or because the rumours lacked substance.

After the war, one of Steven's Lieutenants resigned; a very promising young officer, he very much regretted leaving the regiment, but left his feelings towards his Captain unsaid. There was a thorough internal investigation, and I do mean thorough, of all the allegations and nothing came out of it.

Steven, though, had become very unpopular in the Officer's Mess. He and I had a lengthy discussion at the end of 1991; I told him that he had no future in the regiment. This came as a body blow to him. He had convinced himself that his performance in the Gulf meant he would soon get the majority that he so patently wanted. His poor relationship with his fellow officers he had put down to jealousy at his impending elevation. I'm afraid that I told him he was in cloud cuckoo land, and was very unlikely to ever see a majority; certainly not in the Coldstreams."

Doyle drove to Deepcut sure that he now had virtually the whole truth from Thackeray. He had probed mercilessly, but the essence of the initial summary provided by the Colonel had remained unaltered by any of the further detail obtained.

Whether there was anything in the suggestion of manipulation and murder of Iraqi prisoners was irrelevant to the current investigation. Thackeray was afraid that if the story emerged in court, the tabloids would leap on it and discovering that they could not establish evidence of any fire at the base of the smoke, they would manufacture it. The man himself might probably feel exposed because he was responsible when the alleged deaths occurred. He also had probably failed to investigate it properly at the time, presumably as he was preoccupied with the conduct of their part of the war. To be fair to the Colonel too, Doyle had seen that the man was intensely proud of the old regiment. He wanted its long and worthy reputation unsullied by allegations of illegal or inappropriate conduct by one man.

He now understood the entry in Fiona's diary. He guessed that when Major Armstrong asked for the background, he would have received the unadulterated truth regarding Steven's activities, and his newly acquired pariah status in the regiment. That neither parents nor son had enlightened Fiona to this history was no surprise either.

Major Shaw welcomed him into his office and offered tea. Doyle, who lived on it, or coffee, accepted as usual. Once they were seated he wasted no time, "I would like to discuss Steven Armstrong in a lot more detail than DCI Grieve did with you on the phone. He was engaged in other aspects of the enquiry when you called, and so left a lot for me to ask now."

Shaw shook his head; he appeared fatalistic, "Captain Armstrong has just left here; you've just missed him. He is still on leave, regular and compassionate; there is no reason for us to

234

want him here. Sadly, he requested a meeting with me, which turned out to be because he wants to resign. I told him with a substantial war pending, it would have to wait. Anyway, I pointed out that making an important decision like that when your emotions are running high, was probably a mistake."

Doyle agreed. "Had there been any suggestion of this before the murders?"

"I suppose maybe, he hasn't been happy for some time. Having said that I must say his demeanour recently has been much better."

"Say for the last three months?"

Shaw look surprised, "yes approximately, since Christmas."

"Can you think of any other reason why he would wish to resign now?"

"No idea, really."

Doyle considered the import of this news; he failed to see the context at the moment. He decided to leave it until further investigation might suggest a reason, "okay, thanks for that, we will ask him about it when we see him next. In the meantime, can I review some of his history with you?"

"Is he a suspect then?"

"Major, we just have to rule people out, even the bereaved, my asking questions doesn't imply anything."

"I understand; fire away, I will try to be as helpful as possible."

"Steven joined you in early 1992, is that correct?"

Shaw nodded, but still referred to the file open in front of him.

"Has he always been based here since then?"

Shaw laughed, "God, no. Very soon after joining us, eight months in fact, he was deployed in support of the new Bosnian mandated UNPROFOR force, which was operational in November 1992. There was already an UNPROFOR force in Croatia: with British troops in it. But with another two thousand five hundred British troops committed in Bosnia, we needed considerable logistics there too. He ran a large supply depot in situ, in difficult circumstances, for two almost three years, though he was able to take leave, occasionally, in that time.

In July 1995, he had a two-year assignment in Germany, which probably felt like a rest after Bosnia. In August 1997, he was back here for almost two years. Then he was off, in July 1999, to the Balkans again to help plan the supply side of the NATO deployment to Kosovo. He was in Kosovo throughout 2000 and then back here since January 2001."

"You mentioned that he hasn't been happy, can you expand on that?"

"Not really, it has been prolonged, and I did tackle him concerning it, but he said it was nothing. I'm sure if you have met him you will have seen that he is very taciturn."

"He has been a Captain for some time, well over ten years, is there any prospect of a promotion: to Major, is that right?"

"Promotion in support is not as rapid as in front line combat units, Inspector. It isn't my call but a majority is a possibility in the next four or five years."

"Would you recommend him for one?"

Shaw frowned and thought for a few seconds before answering. He was evidently in two minds, "I would support it, I think, but not now, in a couple of years, maybe."

Doyle tried very hard during the next half hour to develop information pertaining to Steven's ambition, drive, and happiness whilst with the RLC; Shaw did everything he could to help. The problem was that the variety of postings left the Major with only a partial picture of the man. Doyle left in some frustration to drive back to Scotland Yard.

25. A Puzzle, A Key and A Horror

DCI Grieve arrived at Weetwood station just before eight am. He picked up the couriered envelope sent by Doyle, which had arrived overnight, and went into the canteen. He got a mug of tea and considered a fried egg sandwich, but took pity on this new jacket, pressed into service so that the other could be cleaned, and ordered a bacon buttie instead.

Sitting down at a table, he opened the package, removed the papers from inside, and spent ten minutes looking at the various patterns from every angle. He even looked through some of the original loose flimsies in a sunbeam that was traversing the room. He was as baffled as Doyle had been, and was saved from further futile study when his mobile rang, "Detective chief Inspector? Hello, its Tom Humble, from Astons."

"Ah, yes thanks for calling back. I have a couple of questions for you, do you have five minutes?"

Grieve looked at his watch: five or ten minutes should be okay for him too.

"Of course, Chief Inspector, more if necessary."

"James Belvedere mentioned that you had played a round of golf with your Managing Director on Sunday. Can you confirm that?"

"Yes, our Managing Director, and our biggest shareholder."

"During that game he expressed concerns to you about the BelL Ltd programme at Astons. Is that correct too?"

"Yes, it came as a very unpleasant surprise, I was over-the-moon with the programme."

"Right, so there had been no warning of these concerns to you or James Belvedere?"

"None; absolutely none. It was, between you and me, extremely irritating. However Max, as I said before, is not just MD, he owns 26% of the stock and also controls another 32%: what he says goes."

"The first inkling then, that Mr Belvedere had that there was a problem, was when you called?"

"Yes, I told him every one of Max's issues. I rang him straight away because I believed saving the programme was so important. I was very gloomy though, I couldn't see how Jamie could address everything before the Tuesday morning meeting. Max had made it clear that unless there was substantial change, he was going to insist on terminating the contract there and then."

"How much work was involved in changing the original programme to the one Mr Belvedere presented at the meeting?"

"A huge amount, which was why I was so upset by Max's ultimatum: Jamie must have worked night and day on it; I was amazed and very relieved. Max was completely won over; he now thinks Jamie is something of a management icon. He has been going around telling our senior people of his professionalism, his strength of purpose, and exhorting them to emulate his example."

"Thank you, Mr Humble, that's all I need for now. Thanks again."

It was twenty-five past eight so he got up and went to reception. He had hoped to bump into Sandy Blackhall and give him the bad news that his Prime Suspect was in the clear. Sergeant Banks came by and Grieve only said good morning. It would be unfair to shoot all Sandy's hard work down third hand.

238

He was also reluctant to spread too widely, what he had discovered on the Chevin: the breach of security at the Met.

Hastings arrived as requested at eight thirty. Grieve took him to his office, this time via the canteen for some self-service drinks.

When they were seated at Grieve's small circular conference table, he shook the contents of the envelope out onto the surface. Hastings looked, and then reached into his jacket pocket for his spectacles.

With the help of these, he studied the patterns for several minutes. Then he sat back with a thoughtful expression on his face. Grieve looked a question at him, and the old man nodded, "yes, I know what they are."

"Don't keep me in suspense."

Hastings removed the spectacles, cleaned them, and returned them to the case, which was, in its turn, returned to his jacket. He looked across at Grieve, "I'm sure you are aware Chief Inspector, that when you are following someone; when you don't wish to be discovered in that enterprise; that it is very helpful if there are several people involved: working as a team. Each participant can take a turn; they can switch places every little while. That way if the target looks back, they never see the same face or car repeatedly; if they stop, the immediate tail doesn't have to match the target's behaviour. It is in this way, as you know, relatively simple to maintain the target's ignorance of your surveillance.

The labour requirement increases further, if the target is well versed in the art too. Then the surveillance has to be more subtle. maybe both sides of the street; others anticipating the route, and possibly coming in from other directions; some on foot; some on bike and some in a car. Each participant when re-used seeks to change their appearance modestly; take their coat off or put one on; wear a homburg one time: remove it another.

An even larger team of qualified personnel is required, if the target is actively seeking to lose a tail, even if they have no reason to think they are compromised. Then you have to cover all of the route options so that when the target makes a rapid departure, you still have them and they are still oblivious of their pursuit: Good tradecraft, you understand."

"Yes, it can be a very expensive, resource intensive, business."

Hasting nodded; he knew that Grieve and he were talking the same language, "now," he continued, "what happens if you have insufficient personnel? Maybe even, you are on your own. How do you do it then?" Hastings looked at Grieve, searching his face for realisation. This time though, the DCI was quite happy to let the old man get there in his own time, and quite happy to let him do all the thinking. Hastings obliged, "it is nigh on impossible if the target knows the game as well, and your task requires you to remain in contact: then it is only a matter of time, a short time, before your presence is noted." Hastings paused, "but... but, if you can break contact, if you have the luxury of a static target, then there is some hope. If you have the time, even the best operative will start to display a pattern. The less adept will reveal their favourite route choices sooner."

Grieve sought some clarification, "when you mean a static target, you mean someone who you can pick up again and again, from the same point: their home for instance?"

"Exactly, you start to map all the route options: say there are two possible routes from the front door, two from the back. Once these are established, you can then map the next route decision. Say on route one, after one hundred yards, there are three options to choose from and so on. The number of combinations expands exponentially: an impossible task. Happily, there are three saving graces. The first is that, even the best player will relax their behaviour after, say, five or six route changes, if there is no sign of a tail. The second is that even if the target *is* one of the better exponents of the art, it's virtually impossible for them to be rigorously random: some routes will be more popular than others; some destinations will be used repeatedly. The third saving grace is that most targets are very far from being the best: it's easy to fall into a false sense of invulnerability."

Hastings looked at Grieve, "do you see it yet?"

"Yes, these patterns are a record of a surveillance of the form you have just described."

"Exactly; right again, they are a shorthand for mapping movement. They are all written in one hand indicating a solo operation. A female hand I should say. From looking at them, I

240

would speculate that four of them relate to one location, three relate to a second. but I can't be sure of that yet. Most are, I think, incomplete, but one, here, does indicate a destination: speculating, probably the most frequently visited covert destination. Crucially, they are using a form of shorthand that Gordon Armstrong developed for his own use and, by way of security, was only known to a very few of his closest associates. My guess is: you have recovered these papers from Fiona Armstrong's effects." Hastings had taken a punt and had caught Grieve's expression as he said it.

Grieve was disconcerted that Hastings had deduced so much, but given the context and his inside knowledge, it was hardly surprising. "Why would Fiona know an operational code of Armstrong's?"

"I told you, if you recall; when he played with them, he usually played at tradecraft. Surveillance and counter surveillance methodology are a crucial part of that art. I knew them to go out into Wimbledon and tail people. It was actually great fun; when it wasn't work; I know as I joined in occasionally: Fiona loved it. Even Steven came along once or twice when he was home from Glenalmond in the holidays. Gordon would buy Fiona an ice cream if she could tail someone for thirty minutes without that person realising.

Admittedly, that wasn't the type of surveillance that we have been discussing, but it comes as no surprise to me that Gordon taught Fiona the shorthand. It's a form of language, not too difficult to learn and use; she would have found it stimulating, and fun, given her intellect; her interest in languages; her interest in maths."

"I take it you can read this shorthand?"

"Yes I can."

"Could you follow it then?"

"If you can provide me with the starting point, yes."

"Ah. Can we deduce that I wonder?" Grieve sat back thoughtfully. So, Fiona has spent a lot of time recording the movements of person or persons unknown. And it was recent as the patterns were immediately following the last diary entry of the 10th December. Something came to him, "an AtoZ would be a useful aid in this exercise?"

Hastings agreed.

Grieve continued his deliberation. Well now, we know what she was spending her time on during the last few months. And the whole thing started after Steven's Christmas party on the 13th December. There were no more diary entries; why was that... security? He looked at Hastings again, "if I found a London AtoZ and suggested a starting point, could you follow these notes using it now?"

Hastings looked at him for a few seconds with an impenetrable expression on his face, then shook his head, "not really, you've got to be on the ground. An AtoZ will help in the mapping process, but there are things like... for instance, going into a department store by one entrance and out of another on a different street, maybe even, on a different floor. You can't follow that with an AtoZ, you can only do it if you're there."

"Is there anyone in London, in MI5 or MI6, who would know this shorthand?"

"I wouldn't know, I would guess not, though. Only a few people knew it, all old guard really, and Gordon retired almost thirteen years ago."

"Right, in that case will you come to London with me now: I wish to strike whilst the iron is still hot."

Hastings nodded, he appeared to have anticipated the request. "Very well. Let me pick up my few things from the hotel and check out. And then yes, of course I'll come, if it will help."

"I'll drive you there."

They went down and Grieve took a car from the pool. He drove Hastings the short distance to his hotel. He said he would return in forty-five minutes and went straight back to the station. Eventually Sandy Blackhall was found, and they sat down together for five minutes. He thanked Sandy for his efforts and explained why he believed Belvedere was in the clear. The Sergeant was at first disappointed, then philosophical, and then excited for Grieve that he had such a promising lead. For the moment, Grieve was releasing most of the team to go back to other duties. Blackhall offered to come to London, but Grieve gently pointed out that Collins and Doyle were already there.

Then he drove home, quickly packed a small overnight case, and when the forty-five minutes were up, he was back at the hotel: Hastings was standing thinly, patiently, nondescriptly outside with his own diminutive case.

They drove down the M1; Grieve, whilst being generally law abiding, and being a very careful driver in town, did not extend this to observing a motorway speed limit, and they cruised at eighty-five mph.

For the first thirty or forty minutes neither spoke much; each had their own thoughts about the investigation, and what they might find in London. But Grieve eventually broke the silence, "when we talked on Wednesday, you were describing your self-imposed exile from the human race."

Hastings nodded agreeably. Grieve went on, "you mentioned that you were forced out of your exile by the need to help friends in Bosnia."

Hastings closed his eyes and shook his head: this was not a welcome topic. Grieve persisted, "when was it, 1992?"

After a short pause Hastings quietly said, "yes."

"Did you actually go there then?"

a further short pause; "yes."

"Wasn't that an awful time, was that when all the ethnic cleansing was going on?"

"Yes." Hastings almost hissed the word, his stomach had knotted; he had not discussed his trip to Bosnia with anyone in Britain; it was very painful recalling it.

Grieve realised he was on uncertain ground and let the silence lengthen. Hastings was lost, staring out at the fields and towns speeding by. His hands worked unconsciously in his lap. Ten minutes passed, then Grieve caught a movement in the corner of his eye and he looked at the complex that was Bill Hastings: he was looking down at his hands, open palmed in his lap; he spoke, "I was watching the news; I was lucky to catch the item. A small village in North Eastern Bosnia called Tarčin, about twenty kilometres due east of Derventa, had been attacked by elements of the Bosnian Serb Army: the inhabitants massacred. It was a small event really, only thirty-two dead; compared to the one hundred and fifty thousand and more, who died in Bosnia between 1992 and 1995."

Hastings stopped and looked out of the window again; his hands were in the same position, open in his lap, almost as if they were the hands of a Shakespearean tragedian drenched and dripping in blood. Steadfastly looking out the window Hastings said, "it was a big event for me. I was very familiar with Tarčin, and the Bosnian Croats that had lived there."

He dried up for ten further minutes and spent the time alternating between looking out of the window, or looking down at his hands, which remained in this curious opened palmed position. When he eventually spoke he looked across at Grieve, "Gordon and I both made life-long friends when we were in Bosnia in the War. My closest male friend by a long way, apart from Gordon, was a Croat called Ivan Despoja, we were the same age and Ivan saved my life when we were fighting together. After the war he returned to his father's farm, which was relatively large for Bosnia. He was the only surviving child and so when his parents died, he inherited it. He married a local girl, Maria, in 1950 and had two sons, and two daughters. Ivan was tireless in building his enterprise and the farm expanded. All the children married locally, and all four families lived in beautiful houses, which the whole family, pulling together, had built on their land.

Beth, Carol and I used to go there on holiday and some of my happiest memories are in the summer fields and orchards around the village.

When Beth died and Carol was estranged, I spent a substantial part of the summer of 1984 with Ivan: he kept me sane. I had never satisfactorily repaid his bravery in the war: my debt to him: now he was saving me again. At that time the next generation ran to eight healthy, beautiful boys and girls: I had watched them all grow. The village they lived in was twenty kilometres east of Derventa; it was called Tarčin."

Grieve was wondering now, at the wisdom of having precipitated the memory. Hastings, however, made no attempt to stem the flood, "I was forced out of my unreal, surreal life, and I eventually managed to get into Bosnia. I discovered that the two twin boys, Ivan and Ivo, born to Ivan's son, the eldest, had survived and were in a refugee camp in central Bosnia. I was able to get them out; I moved them to a small, cheap hotel in Split.

They had been several kilometres away from the village playing in a quarry. They were too far to hear the gunfire, but they eventually saw the smoke. They ran back, fortunately only in

244

time to see the trucks leaving. All the houses were burning. All the people were dead. Even you, Chief Inspector, do not want to know how some of them died.

I will tell you, that my friend Ivan, a sixty-eight-year-old Yugoslavian war hero, was hanging by the neck from a tree. He had been eviscerated and castrated, his entrails hung from his gut to the ground. He was still alive when the boys arrived in the devastation; the rope had been deliberately arranged in a simple sling to avoid breaking his neck. The whole of Ivan's family, excepting the twins, were dead right down to the babies. All the women and girls in the village, including the twin's nine-year-old sister, Theresa, had been repeatedly raped in the road that ran through the middle of the village, and then they had been executed. The other twelve odd people who lived in the village had died beside them."

Hastings stopped and sat staring down at his hands. Grieve glanced at him and was surprised that he was dry-eyed. Tears had come easily on Wednesday, but then maybe he had cried all he could cry, for these dead from ten odd years ago.

"The boys, I hadn't seen them for almost seven years, were bright, sturdy fifteen year olds. They had already tried to join the Bosnian Croat Army, but it was in chaos and had more than enough volunteers clamouring for training, and weapons, and blood. They were told to wait until they were sixteen.

I desperately wanted them free of the horror; it was a vicious war, like all Balkan wars, if they did fight there was no certainty they would survive. I saw it as my duty, my belated duty, to Ivan to rescue them from both the reality, and the mental torture they were putting themselves through. I didn't think I was in a fit state to adopt them; I didn't think it would be countenanced in the UK anyway.

So I went to Augsburg in Bavaria. The boys had spent two months on an exchange with a Catholic family, the Köck's, there, eighteen months before; they and the family had thoroughly enjoyed the experience. Josef and Theresa Köck had a boy and a girl of similar age to Ivan and Ivo and I asked them, if I gave financial support, if they would take the boys in.

They were delighted to help, once they had got over the horror at the circumstances, and we managed to sort out the

245

legalities surprisingly quickly. Possibly Josef's employers helped, I don't know, certainly the church did: being Croats, the whole Despoja family had been devout Catholics.

I went back to fetch the boys and they refused to leave. They had determined to stay and find the perpetrator of the massacre. They were quite happy to die in the attempt. I pleaded with them to forget their revenge, to turn their backs on the hate: it was useless. Eventually, I got them to agree to go, by promising I would stay and investigate the crime for them. I told them that because of my contacts in the intelligence world, and in the newly arriving British contingent of UNPROFOR, I stood some chance; when they stood none. I promised to deliver the man to them."

Grieve suddenly had an inspiration, "it wasn't this Bulatovic character by any chance?"

"No." Hastings smiled bitterly, "he was in Bosnia and he was on my list, but I struck him off when I received reliable reports that he was committing similar atrocities in East Central Bosnia. When the Tarčin massacre took place, he was a hundred kilometres away. As a Serbian Army officer, he shouldn't have been in Bosnia at all, but it was an open secret that the regular army was supporting both the Croatian Serb and the Bosnian Serb forces."

Hastings finally moved his hands and folded his arms, "I saw him in action, you know: Bulatovic I mean. The Serbs were attacking a town, it was... I forget, one of the many. There was a British UNPROFOR observation post on a hill west of the place.

I was in the area, on my mission, and the young Lieutenant who was in command there invited me up to watch the assault."

Grieve shook his head, "why were the UN troops looking on? Why weren't they intervening and separating the factions?"

Hastings looked at him with what might almost have been pity. "We are talking about the UN here, Chief Inspector: a hopelessly divided executive, and the men at the coalface: the troops; had no mandate to intervene in a civil war. Besides, they had insufficient troops on the ground to enforce their will. When they did eventually take firm action, do you not recall...? The Serbs took hostage several hundred of them, including some

246

thirty British. Then the international community started to move, but all too slowly."

Grieve was confused, "I remember a sizeable military campaign. Bombing missions by NATO; artillery; I remember seeing the big British guns firing on Serbian positions."

"Yes, that was IFOR/SFOR in 95, eventually NATO and some non-NATO countries, notably Russia took action."

Grieve's face cleared as he remembered. The old man proceeded in a tired voice. "Where was I? Ah yes, it was quite a substantial town and there was a rich suburb on the south-facing slope of a gentle hill, on the north side of it.

The main thrust was in the centre from the east but there were flanking attacks on both sides. The Serbs were leaving a corridor for the inhabitants to conveniently 'cleanse' themselves westward.

The Lieutenant told me that a Major Bulatovic was in command of the flanking attack through the northern suburb. From what I learnt later, it was no surprise that he was on the rich side of the town.

The commanders in the centre and on the left opened up with artillery and tank fire on the defences, but Bulatovic didn't. In the night, he infiltrated several hundred special troops into the suburb and they took and held ten buildings. These strong points disrupted the relatively weak defence, their supply, the manoeuvring of their mobile reserve, and their communication lines. His main advance was able to break the line piecemeal. I was impressed at first; it almost seemed as if Bulatovic was trying to preserve life and property with this novel and quite dangerous approach. I was wrong though, two days after he had overrun the suburb the massacres had taken place of those trapped or unwilling to leave, and all the buildings, those I had believed he was preserving, were in flames."

Grieve considered but eventually said, "I'm sure you're going to explain his rationale."

"It was simple; he was committing theft on a grand scale. It became obvious to me, during the next few weeks that he knew where to find all the best hauls. You see, unlike the other brutes, he understood when he saw something beautiful that often it was valuable, sometimes fabulously valuable, and as much as his duties allowed he stole them.

The purpose of the special units was to take the properties that, probably, contained the best material; preferably too, trapping the owners. These unfortunates would wait, in vain hope, only to find that Bulatovic's arrival precipitated wanton torture and interrogation; he sought their concealed treasures: when they had given all, they were executed: allowing him to argue he had obtained the booty and the works of art legitimately. Then their buildings were razed, eliminating any trace of both the murders and the theft.

Militarily it worked, as it was unusual. The defenders expected to be bombarded initially; they organised the defences in the best way to mitigate the attrition it caused. In other words, they didn't hold a watertight single line; they established a defence in depth with mutual support.

He repeated the process in a significant number of actions. Sometimes when the Bosniaks or Croats organised their defence to counter his type of threat all it did was give him a wonderful target to decimate with artillery."

Grieve expressed some surprise that there was such a potential for stealing valuable artwork. Hastings shrugged. "You have to remember; Yugoslavia is just around the corner from Venice and the other Italian cities of the Renaissance. The Croats are Roman Catholic and have traded extensively in the region for centuries. They and the Bosniaks had their old, wealthy, trading families just as other countries did. Remember too, that Tito and his legacy kept Yugoslavia stable and wealthy until the late 1980's. Besides valuable artwork isn't restricted to Western Art, Eastern and Muslim artefacts can be hugely valuable too. No, the Croatian war, the Bosnian war, and to some extent the Kosovan civil war were a golden opportunity for Bulatovic, with his knowledge of fine art, to line his own pocket."

"So, Bulatovic, nasty though he may be, didn't kill your friend and his family. Did you find the bastard who did?"

Hastings looked sadly out of the window. "I narrowed the list to four. Two of them have since died, one from wounds and one from ill health. The other two, are on the run as indicted war criminals. The NATO forces in Bosnia have been very active in

248

pursuit of all the indicted, but they have had only limited success, my chances of getting them are nil."

"The twins must be in their mid twenties by now, is that right?"

"Yes, they settled well, they are loved in the Köck family, they took to German schooling brilliantly, and they went to university, did medicine, and are now junior interns."

"So they've accepted the fait accompli? They're happy with their new life in Germany?"

Hastings signed heavily; yet another burden he carried; "No, I have failed them, as they constantly remind me. I promised to deliver a man to justice and I have, in the past ten years, singularly failed to do so."

"You're too hard on yourself Bill, your not Superman."

Hastings sighed heavily again. "Clearly... the twins are right though, in the logic of the Balkans, I still owe them. They are becoming increasingly restive; the only thing keeping them in Germany is their desire to complete their training. They want to return, albeit for good reasons as medicine is valued in Bosnia, but they will also start the dangerous quest for their *bete noire*."

Grieve had been surprised by how much the story had moved him, given the things he had seen in his police work. He ventured, "I have some sympathy for them, if I had a bunch of murdering thugs, like the Serbs, next door I would probably want to do the same."

"You're wrong to assume the Serbs are all thugs, they're not. Just like any country or race, they have criminals, and they have saints. The Croats and the Bosniaks committed multiple war crimes too. The Bosniaks even fired mortars on their own people in order to blame the Serbs. Like I said war in the Balkans is a vicious business."

After this, Hastings slowly subsided into a depressed, distant shell; no matter what Grieve said, he could not lift him from it. The rest of the journey was largely conducted in silence.

249

26. The Prime Suspect?

Steven Armstrong had travelled back from the memorial service the previous evening. He had eaten in a motorway service restaurant at five pm and had called Major Shaw to arrange the ten-thirty meeting and the family solicitor in Wimbledon to arrange a meeting with him afterwards at one pm.

He had got back into the outskirts of London at eight pm in time to miss the worst of the rush, which was mostly going in the opposite direction anyway. He parked his Audi in its small garage and finally was able to close the door of his flat, shutting the world out. He put the case down, went into the kitchen, poured himself a big glass of Glenfarclas, and added some still Highland Spring to double it.

Going into the small lounge, he sat in the darkness with his whisky. He dearly wanted to talk to Fiona. He leant forward and put his face in his hands. Why is life so cruel? Did he ask so much? He fell asleep in the chair, and woke at one am with the glass of whisky sitting only half drunk on the table.

Doyle got back to Scotland Yard at one thirty in the afternoon. The decision had been made. Kossuth was talking to Collins and Vaughan when he arrived.

There was to be an elaborate operation to catch the potential terrorists as they were returning with some of the weapons cache from the exchange with Kossuth. The Hungarian police were already on the move to the two warehouses to impound the bulk of the weapons, and the cigarettes. The plan allowed for Kossuth to return to Hungary, keep his cigarette profits, and hopefully, be unsuspected of being the Pakistani group's nemesis: Kossuth seemed comfortable with the plan anyway, which was the important thing from Doyle's perspective. Whilst Doyle was happy for Vaughan and Elliott, what he was interested in was Kossuth's whereabouts on Monday and Tuesday.

After twenty minutes, Collins came out of the interview and sat down with Doyle, "he met his contacts from the mosque at seven on Monday morning in a West Ham supermarket car park. He says it has CCTV. He was laughing at the muppets for choosing it and was calling them amateurs. He left his car there and went with them. As soon as he was in the car, they blindfolded him and he was taken to see an Imam and a small group of young men. The meeting was in the mosque. They took his blindfold off just as he went in and he saw they had CCTV there too, on the outside. Kossuth asked the Imam about it in the meeting and he was told they had had to install it in mid 2002. Seemingly, Molotov cocktail throwing BNP supporters had attacked them three times since the Twin Towers Atrocity.

Inspector Vaughan has sent someone to see if the supermarket still has the tapes for Monday. That would be enough to clear Kossuth of the murders anyway, if they are good enough to see Kossuth clearly."

Doyle nodded, "good, stay on it."

He decided to treat himself to a lengthy lunch: one that he could justify, as he was going to give the diaries a thorough read. He was just approaching the canteen when his mobile rang. He screwed his eyes but felt duty-bound to answer: he could see it was his boss. When he answered, Doyle was surprised to be told that Grieve and Hastings were in Chiswick: his boss told him of the old man's ability to decipher the patterns. Apparently, Hastings had already established that the Chief Inspector's choice of start point was consistent with four of the patterns. Grieve asked Doyle to join them in a street adjacent to Steven Armstrong's flat, and he also asked him to bring an armed Metropolitan police officer, just in case. He reminded Doyle that there was someone in the Met with a connection to the killer: he needed to keep that in mind. As an afterthought, he also said to bring, or buy, a good AtoZ of London.

Doyle had to cancel his leisurely lunch and again grab a sandwich. He retraced his steps to find Detective Superintendent Ingram and explained what Grieve had requested. Ingram agreed and said that he had utmost confidence in Constable Farmer whom Doyle had already met at the flat. Ingram confided that the Constable had passed his Sergeant's exams and would be elevated shortly. Farmer was called in and told to arm himself. Ingram asked Doyle what his firearms certification was and when Doyle told him, he gave him clearance to draw a pistol too. Then Farmer and Doyle both got into the Corolla and headed off to the rendezvous.

When they arrived at two-thirty, they left the Corolla and got into the car with the two older men. These two explained why they needed help: Hastings said he had to walk the routes with the pattern in hand, and the problem was their suspect Steven knew Hastings and had met Grieve. The job had to be done in a way that allowed the maps to be followed, without putting anyone at risk, and without alerting Steven.

As Armstrong had not met Doyle and, presumably, did not know Farmer, the solution obviously revolved around one of them. Doyle suggested he himself walk the route. The other three could stay in the car and talk to him on his mobile. He could use his hands-free cable to disguise the fact he was receiving directions, or at least make it less obvious, and the car could probably follow him at a distance, but in short bursts, or hops; better that than creeping along behind.

As no one could think of a better solution, Doyle got out of the car and fitted the hands free in his ear and on his lapel. He slipped the phone into his breast pocket and Grieve called him to check the system; it seemed to work satisfactorily. He was ready to move off to the front door of the block of flats when he heard Grieve hiss in his ear, "it's Armstrong; he's coming down the street."

He immediately gunned the car and drove out of sight. Doyle looked up at the surrounding buildings as though admiring the architecture, which was stretching a point as, here, it was appalling. Armstrong stormed past, sweeping around the corner towards his block of flats. Doyle said into the mic, "he didn't look very happy."

Hastings spoke to him on Grieve's phone, "that's quite common for Steven; the good thing is we know where he is now. Off you go then, make your way around to the door."

Doyle did as he was directed and waited for his first directions, which Hastings duly supplied, "okay, the route we will use is the only one that looks complete; it goes left from the door for one hundred and fifty yards." Doyle paced off and arrived at a corner.

"Turn full left and go thirty yards." Then, "turn full right, cross the street and go two hundred yards."

Doyle turned right and saw a narrow walkway between two buildings on the other side of the road. He crossed and went down the walkway and stopped after he had paced out two hundred yards, "I'm at the bottom end of Gordon Crescent; I appear to have three options."

"Wait for us to drive round." Three minutes later the car appeared at the other end of the road and Hastings said, "okay, turn full left and go forty yards." Doyle did as bidden and he came out at a junction with a further three options: Straight on, half right and full right. The half-right option was a street with a number of shops in it.

"Turn half right and go one hundred and sixty yards."

He walked up the street and saw the car pull up two hundred yards in front of him. When he stopped, he had a Kwik-Fit tyre and exhaust centre on his right and a Comet electrical retailer on his left, "turn full left, over the road, and go through the building. There is another entrance slightly left of centre at the back."

Doyle went into the Comet store and walked through the washing machines and fridges; sure enough, there was the rear exit and entry. He arrived outside in the customer car park, "I'm in the parking area at the back."

"We can see you. Okay, turn full left and go one hundred yards." Then when he had done that, "now go full right fifty yards and you're there. Where ever he was going, it is on your right. Seven should figure in some way."

Doyle found himself walking beside a line of garages with numbers on them. The other side was a row of identical blocks of flats, with walkways between each block. He stopped after fifty yards. Looking over his right shoulder, he saw he was beside a garage with a number 7 on it: he told Hastings.

"We can see you; we're at the end of the road. Come back and we'll start again." Grieve whispered to Farmer, he nodded, got his phone out, and started to research the ownership of the garage.

They took Doyle back to near the front door of Armstrong's block of flats, and the team went through a second route option. It ended at a junction about 500 yards from the garage, "well, that appears to be going in the same direction but Fiona obviously hadn't been able to complete it." Hastings said to the delighted Grieve.

A third test took them in a slightly different direction and stopped in a small shopping centre. Hastings said, "this is probably not going to the garage," Grieve frowned, "but we are still in broadly the right area, I wonder if there is an apartment linked to the garage?" The last test brought them to a standstill at another junction. Hastings speculated it could be the garage, apartment or somewhere else. Farmer got off his phone and said the agent renting the garage also rented its apartment; "To a mister Brian Lockhart, the apartment is Flat Seven, Marlowe House, Corunna Rd."

Doyle got back in the car and they drove, what turned out to be a short distance, to Corunna Rd, and sat looking at Marlowe House. Meanwhile Hastings looked through the patterns again, "these other three patterns definitely do not fit with Steven's flat: does anyone have any ideas?"

"Deepcut?" Doyle suggested.

"What now?" Grieve thought aloud.

Hastings said, "really we should, for completeness, test the other route alternatives on these first four sheets. There are maybe five on each. However, now we know about the flat and garage, the probability, from my reading of them, is they will, if completed, all come back to these two locations: the flat and the garage."

"I would like to see inside them: the flat and the garage." Grieve said.

Hastings looked concerned; "One: Mister Lockhart might object, if he exists, and two: it risks tipping Steven off. as tradecraft would dictate the placing of telltales, which we could hardly help but disturb." Hastings cautioned. Grieve looked at him defiantly, "that would suggest then, that the garage is the best bet."

Hastings looked very unhappy at this turn of events. Grieve made a decision and drove around to the garage. They all looked around to see if there was any possibility of being overlooked. There were several windows with a view: none though, seemed likely to have Armstrong, or Lockhart, behind them.

Grieve turned to Farmer, "this is your patch, do you have any problem with me having a little look."

Farmer smiled mischievously, pulled some wires out of his pocket, and handed them to Grieve, who studied them professionally, "these are better than mine, not as well used, thanks."

Hastings was still agitated, "I really think you'll give the game away. Don't underestimate Steven." But Grieve was determined; "I need some corroboration before we go to the next stage. Come out with me; help me look for these telltales, if there are any."

Hastings saw Grieve was unbending and grudgingly acquiesced: they both got out and spent five minutes studying the door. Hastings found two human hairs stuck, probably with saliva, across the gap between the frame and the door.

"Okay, so we can replace them." Grieve said blithely. Hastings remained unconvinced; but that was what they did. Grieve quickly unlocked the door and lifted it to reveal... a black BMW M3. They noted the registration and Grieve took samples

256

from each tyre, bagged them, and labelled them. They quickly closed it and replaced one of the hairs as precisely as possible. The other Grieve bagged too.

Grieve asked Farmer, whose hair was the nearest to blond of the four of them, to pull some out. He selected one from the bunch that looked like the hair in the bag and placed it where the original one had been. Then they drove off; the whole operation had taken ten minutes.

In a nearby, anonymous road, three hundred yards away, Grieve pulled over and called Weetwood Police Station: he got through to Sandy Blackhall, "Sandy, Get Jim Prentice to coordinate the garage search in Chapeltown that he suggested on Tuesday morning. I'm couriering up some samples from the tyres of a suspect car to see if Forensics can get a match: with that, we may get him.

There's also a bagged hair coming. See if we can get some DNA from it; have it checked for a relationship to the DNA from the various Armstrong samples."

Farmer had submitted the vehicle registration for checking and was listening to the feedback on his phone. It was registered to a Brian Lockhart, resident of Flat 7; Marlowe House; Corunna Rd; Chiswick. Grieve could see everything falling into place, "right, we need to set up surveillance on the garage and the flat. When that is done, we need to see if we can get the hare to bolt here and catch him red-handed." He looked at Farmer who nodded, "I'm already on it." He had the phone to his ear; he was explaining everything to DS Ingram. When he rang off, he said it was going to take some time to set up a proper surveillance. "In the meantime the DS is sending three cars to watch both these sites and Armstrong's flat discreetly. He told me to tell you that he will only be using CID from outside Scotland Yard. They should be here in half an hour. I'll go back and watch the garage until they arrive."

Grieve was pleased, "thank you. I will say the same to DS Ingram when we get back to the Yard."

He turned to Hastings, "thank you too, you've been marvellous; I think you can go back to your holiday in Bavaria now. Can we arrange anything for you?"

Hastings still looked very concerned. He frowned, "no. No, I have a number of old friends here in London; I think I'll look them up."

"Can we take you anywhere?"

"Actually, no, this is fine."

Hastings got out and took his case from the boot. The three men shook his hand warmly. Farmer left to watch the garage and the other two got back in the car. Grieve casually glanced in the mirror; then in some surprised, he swivelled left and right; he looked puzzled and Doyle sought clarification: Hastings had completely vanished.

27. A Best-Laid Scheme

Major Shaw had been surprised to hear the reason for the meeting, and Steven had enjoyed telling him that he wished to resign. He could see that the pathetic little man was panicked by the prospect: the person who kept the whole place afloat preparing to jump ship.

When he left, he turned onto the London bound carriageway of the M3 at Lightwater and given the time of day steered the car onto the anti clockwise London orbital M25. Two junctions brought him to the A3 and he drove up this to Wimbledon.

He had some time to spare, so he stopped for a quick lunch at a pub he knew, and suitably replete, he presented himself at Thomas, Hamble, and Frank Solicitors at five to one. He was feeling in buoyant mood.

He was shown into Mr Kelly's office and the family solicitor stood to shake his hand and to offer his condolences. Steven sat down and got straight down to business, "I've decided to resign my commission in the Army. I am therefore keen to liquidate the family estate as quickly as possible."

Mr Kelly was a little surprised. "You are aware, I know, that your father and mother changed their wills at the time they retired."

"Yes, I was to get a third, and my sister two thirds. But I also know that my sister's will made both my parents, and me beneficiaries of her estate. We discussed it when she had it prepared, just after my parents altered theirs."

Kelly sat looking at Steven for a few moments, a worried look on his face. "Regrettably, that second bit is out of date. You are, obviously, unaware that she had a new will prepared in October last year."

Steven said nothing, but Kelly could see this was surprising, unwelcome, and irritating news for his client. The solicitor continued, "I had sent her a routine letter, asking if her circumstances were still the same; it was ten years since she had made the will. She rang and told me that she and her boyfriend James Belvedere now owned a Chelsea apartment together; that they had been discussing the possibility of marriage. If it happened, as it was most likely to do, it would be in the summer." He paused, looked down at the desk; rubbed his fingers distractedly on the wood, and then continued quietly, without looking up, "sadly, this now is not to be."

He sighed, "as I had sent her the necessary documents, she said it was easy to make him sole beneficiary, there and then."

Steven's face metamorphosed before the solicitor's eyes, he was now verging on the puce: clearly struggling with his rage. He managed to splutter, "I'm not interested in Fiona's estate: I'm concerned with my parent's legacy. Fiona's will isn't relevant; they all died at the same time."

Kelly was looking very uncomfortable. "Ah no. Sorry, I checked with the Police. Gordon and Barbara died before Fiona," he closed his eyes and shook his head, "appalling to think of it. It was only a matter of minutes, admittedly, but in those minutes, Fiona came into her inheritance. Then when she died, her estate passed to James Belvedere."

There was a long, searing, silence before Steven slowly said, "you mean the lion's share of my family's estate is going to go to him?"

"That is, I can see, unfortunately for you, correct."

"How much are we talking?"

"Well, I can't say at this time. The principal assets are the two properties, but there are also a variety of investments in both cash and stocks."

"Guess?" Steven was going to break the little man into two halves if he refused. Kelly, who had known the family for some time, knew that Steven had a violent temper. He guessed. "If I consider your two parents only, it is unlikely to exceed £800k, but it could come quite close. There will be inheritance tax to come off, of course. We did take some measures to mitigate this; the most obvious act, being the gift of the London pied-a-terre to your sister nine years ago.

You can probably expect between £220k and £250k give or take."

"Belvedere will get almost half a million then?"

"I am not at liberty to discuss his position with you, Steven."

His furious client catapulted out of the chair and crashed out of the office.

By the late evening, the surveillance of the garage and the flat in Corunna Rd had been organised. A vacant flat, advertised in another block, had been taken. It had a window at the back offset from, but still overlooking, the garage. Behind this window all the paraphernalia associated with such an operation was set up. Flat Seven was to be observed from vehicles parked in the road outside the entrance.

Doyle inspected the arrangements at around eight-thirty in the evening and then drove back to his Fulham hotel where he found Grieve checking in. A police car had dropped him there after his lengthy meeting with DS Ingram.

They were both ravenous, but they both wanted a beer first. Doyle went to set them up and Grieve joined him in the lounge bar five minutes later, "cheers, here's to a good day's work." Grieve saluted Doyle: he responded in kind with a quirky smile. The beer was welcome but nowhere near the quality of the Jennings they had drunk last time they'd shared a pint. "So, we've learnt a lot today," Grieve opined thoughtfully, as the working robes fell away and the contemplative period began. Doyle

261

agreed, "yes you were right about the Colonel, he was worried that Steven's alleged behaviour might unfairly stain the reputation of the Army's oldest regiment."

"What did he do?"

"It's all rumour and innuendo, but it would appear that Steven's ambition caused him to prosecute the Iraq war too enthusiastically. He was suspected of creating conflict in order to demonstrate his ability as a soldier, a dangerous form of self-promotion. His real crime was achieving ostracism in the Officer's Mess: thereafter his future career in the regiment was dead.

The interesting speculation from this is how did it play in his head. It happened eleven years ago, so he was twenty-nine. He had been told, apparently in categorical terms, that he would never achieve the rank of Major. A rank, I think, he had set his sights on, i.e. his father's nominal rank. Fiona remarked in her diary that he seemed to have lost his ambition: a young age to have achieved that sad state, assuming she was right in her observation."

"I'm not sure when I lost mine; I just know they aren't there anymore." Grieve smiled and Doyle said, "I hope we're still talking about ambitions," and laughed back. "Seriously though, what would happen to a man as wound up as Steven Armstrong, if he believed there was no further hope?"

Grieve looked grim, "exactly."

He reflected for a moment, "he's been competing with his father; actually, I'll stretch that to both his parents, most of his life. He's been following legitimate routes up to this departure. If they are all closed to him now, where does he turn?"

"I wonder if that was at the root of the estrangement. Was this a speculation that had engaged Gordon and Barbara too? Did they see it as an unequivocal step away from legitimacy? I was surprised, and I think Fiona was too, that both of them turned away from him at that point."

Grieve looked interested, "is that what the diary said, both parents?"

"Yes, both parents."

Grieve was thinking hard, "Hastings mentioned that Barbara was an almost unbelievable judge of character. He

262

considered that Gordon's character judgement was flawed, but that Barbara's was razor sharp. I wonder did she see the way the future would develop."

Doyle raised his eyebrows and considered this proposition; then he shook his head, "okay, I'm going to pour cold water on this, now. Major Shaw says he is a good officer, and he has completed several postings with distinction since he joined the RLC."

"I understand what you are saying, but we have found evidence that Steven is leading a double life."

"Have we? Maybe Brian Lockhart exists and simply allows Steven to borrow his car."

"Possibly, but it seems unlikely when Steven regularly visited the garage, at least, but was trying to hide his connection to it. Also, I believe Fiona's change of character is because she discovered that he had this inexplicable second persona. Something made her sufficiently suspicious to start following him and, I think that an event or a revelation she stumbled on, ultimately led her to flee to her parents. On that Sunday she went out with the car, she said she was going to work. We now know she wasn't going there; she was tracing Steven's movements. Something happened during the day that set her running. She called Steven, remember, after she called her parents, what would she have said? Was it a 'How could you? Telephone call': what had she seen, or heard him do?"

Doyle largely agreed with this speculative line of thinking, he continued its development with, "I've thought of something else. She was spying on her brother: remember they were close and she worried about him. It probably started out as a game, as a necessary evil to help him in some way. Gradually, though, it became serious.

That's why she was stressed, but that also explains why she didn't say anything to James, she didn't want to shop her own brother. It also explains why she started to jeopardize her work; it had assumed a primary importance. It also explains why there was no diary record after 10th December. She was consumed by Steven's behaviour, and yet she didn't want to commit anything to paper."

Doyle ran out of points and drank the last of his beer. Grieve looked at the bar, "shall we have another?"

"God no, I could eat a horse. Let's have dinner; then I think we should give the diaries a thorough read."

The restaurant and the food it served were surprisingly good, given the shabbiness of the rest of the hotel.

By ten-thirty, they were both back in the lounge bar. Doyle gave Grieve the three diaries from his briefcase and went upstairs to his room to fetch the rest. When he came back with them, he saw Grieve was leafing through the two most recent books, "I had been looking earlier, for a reason for Steven's depression. A depression that the party on the 13th of December suggests seems to have been lifted by then."

"Yes, well, I think it had to do with money: that seems to be a theme that is occasionally hinted at."

Grieve was going through the latest diary, so Doyle picked up the penultimate one and again flipped to the first page headed 17th May 1999. He had had a quick look at this diary in the morning, and had deduced in that time that Steven was in fine fettle.

He started to put some flesh on the bones. He discovered Steven and Fiona had had a very pleasant meal at the Roux Brother's Waterside Restaurant out in Bray, near Windsor, to celebrate Steven's 36th birthday. Fiona had considered the Thames-side setting wonderful and the food out of the world.

He leafed through more pages where there was no mention of Steven. There were some private and quite bitter deliberations on the shallowness and duplicity of men. Some satisfied reflections on her developing role at the MoD and some concerns regarding her weight and the exercise she was taking to keep it in check.

He got to mid July and suddenly exclaimed, "bloody hell."

Grieve looked up, "what is it?"

Doyle had an astonished look on his face. He looked around to establish there was no one within earshot and then started to read the entry, "Friday 16th July 1999. Steven rang me on Monday to say that he has been told he will probably be deployed to Kosovo. He suggested that, as he might not see me

264

for some time, we should go out for another evening meal together. I had immediately suggested that we go back to Bray, but he said that a new Scottish chef called Gordon Ramsay was doing wonderful food at a Restaurant called The Aubergine; he had won two Michelin stars. Steven had presumptively called them and told me that he had, with a lucky cancellation, booked a table for us for Thursday evening i.e. yesterday. I was very happy to go along with this idea.

It proved to be truly wonderful, a lovely atmosphere and Steven had been right, the food was even better than the delicious food we had had at The Waterside.

He spent a fortune. We had vintage Bollinger to start, which wonderfully complemented the meltingly beautiful hors d'oeuvre and first course. The main course consisted of the most exquisite dishes, whose taste, whilst based on beef and veal, quite frankly defy description. This was accompanied by a truly magnificent bottle of 1982 Chateau Haut-Brion. The wine was almost a meal in itself.

Unfortunately for my liver the drinking continued; we had a half bottle of a classy Sauterne, which I'd never had before, with the delectably petit dessert of summer fruits and parfait.

I was decidedly sozzled by this time, but they had a rare cask strength Glenlivet, which Steven insisted on us both having to finish. I'm very partial to a good Malt, but it was a bridge too far, we rolled out of there both very inebriated. Steven spent almost £2,000, the bad boy. He is going off to war, though, and he tells me his stock portfolio, amazingly, is now valued at £860,000. I have been astonished at his skill in selecting investments, he has just got better and better over the last three or four years."

Doyle and Grieve looked at each other; they were both trying to fathom this newfound little bombshell. "So, he isn't short of a penny or two. Where did he get so much money? Not from his Army pay that's for sure."

Grieve frowned down at the diary he had, "I don't understand it: he seems to be depressed in this one because of a lack of money."

"Let's keep looking; there may be an explanation yet."

Doyle looked at his notebook; "He came back from Kosovo at the beginning of 2001 and has been in the UK since then."

He skipped forward to January 2001 and searched forward in time, Grieve with the other diary continued to work backwards. After a period of twenty minutes of reflective reading, no talking and slow sipping of beer, Doyle looked up, "he doesn't seem so extravagant in 2001, there's been no mention of money, but also no big blow outs. They are still eating out every few weeks but at up market pizzeria's and homely pubs. It comes across as pleasant and unstressed, but not as expensive."

Grieve nodded absently, as he read and leafed another page. Doyle eventual reached the end of his diary, the last dated entry being 4th August 2001. He was no further forward. He looked at his watch and it showed it was nearing half past eleven, "I'm off to bed. I'll see you for breakfast, as we agreed, at half past seven. Sleep well."

Grieve packed up too, leaving a slip of paper marking where he had reached in the diary. They walked up the stairs together.

28. A Window on a Mind

Steven had swept past Doyle in the street, oblivious to the detective's presence. He banged through the main entrance of the apartment block, deliberately ran hard, and fast up the stairs: soon he was in the sanctuary of his home.

Without removing his coat, he turned to the wall and smashed his fist into it again and again until the sensation of pain submerged the rage.

He stood there with his chest heaving and eventually calmed enough to remove his outer garments.

He went into the kitchen and looked at the bottle of Glenfarclas; it was still three quarters full. He reached for a clean glass, poured a smaller measure than he had the previous night, and then rummaged for the bottle of water in the fridge.

In the lounge he sat down and imagined the pleasure he would get from blowing James Belvedere's head apart with a carefully doctored 9mm round. He knew he was dreaming, he would be an immediate suspect for such a killing, and it wouldn't get the money back. But after a few minutes of deep cogitation, he began to question this: if Belvedere simply disappeared there would be no murder hunt, surely. They might even think the disappearance was because he was the killer of his family; had absconded before he was caught: what a truly happy thought.

No, the question revolved around retrieving and keeping the money. He spent a long time thinking of more and more exotic and fantastic ways to recapture his rightful property. This man that had seduced his sister; had driven a wedge between them. A man so supercilious about his success, his business acumen, and his shitty little company.

He must get the money, it was a stain on his honour, but if he did get it, well, it would have to stay very clear of his bank account: the police would definitely investigate his financial affairs.

He started to hatch a plan that revolved around, either a threat to disrupt the company, or kidnap and extortion, or... well there were several other possibilities. He spent a number of hours constructing an elaborate plot, which he eventually considered, in his current state, was the height of ingenuity. Unfortunately, it was a plan that would, when tested in the sobriety and cold of a new day, be seen to be almost certainly unworkable.

Cheered by his perspicacity, he got up and went out for an evening meal. Then in an indication of his improved mood he popped into his local The One-legged Parrot, which was the only place in the area where he could sit, drink, and feel reasonably at home. Sid, the owner, saw him come in and set his usual tipple up without asking. He and the regular clientele simply accepted Steven as he was; there was no judgement, just friendly, though distant, acknowledgement.

He sat there enjoying the anonymity of the busy little pub. He liked to sit at the bar near the model parrot that gave the pub its name. It stood in the centre of the back wall between the bottles and optics. In fact, the parrot had no legs, just an extremely large and dexterous penis that was wrapped around the horizontal of a tee-shaped perch. Every now and then, someone new to the pub would give Sid a coin to put in the slot in the base of the device. After a second's pause the bird looked around, winked, whistled; said, 'Cor' blimey, that's a nice bit of fluff.' and then, with a despairing squawk, would promptly fall off its stand, accompanied by gales of laughter from the newly arrived revellers.

Late in the evening, Steven wended his way home where he fell into bed and was out for the count immediately. He was deeply asleep for several hours, but then his consciousness rose into the shallower regions and he began to dream: He found himself back in the Coldstreams. Major Thackeray was telling him he was a swaggering idiot: why, and why here in the Mess? Captain Franks, standing at the bar, made a remark that Steven could just overhear; all the other officers laughed and some looked in his direction: Steven felt his skin crawl, go hot and then the prickly sensation of sweat. He went outside and some men marched by saluting; did he see glances and vestigial smirks on their faces?

His sleeping form rolled one way and rolled back. He was back at school; the boys were taunting him because he was thick. A master came to break up the Cabal but it was, horror, his father. He asked them what they were laughing at and they told him. He looked at Steven and started to laugh as well. The boys joined in.

Steven's body rocked from side to side in the bed. His sister had come to him to comfort and calm him. She reached forward and caressed his head, he turned his face into her hand and kissed it, his hands reached out and they kissed, mouth on mouth, he ran his hands over her body, but then her eyes disappeared; blood poured from her neck, her mouth, her nose; her head lolled to one side and fell off. Jets of heart-driven arterial blood shot six feet into the air. He tried to stop it with his hands and the blood, redirected, sprayed everywhere: into his face, onto his body. He reached down and tried to put her head back on again; it dissolved into ash: he woke screaming.

29. A Trap is Laid

Grieve came down to breakfast with the copy of the Times that had been put under his door, and the unfinished homework of the diary.

Doyle was already seated reading The Independent and tucking into juice, muesli, and toast, before his fried breakfast arrived. Grieve ordered the cooked breakfast too, and helped himself to a cup of tea from Doyle's newly arrived pot.

They were both on good form, despite being away from home at the weekend. Both had slept well and both had been considering how the day would pan out, particularly the first few hours.

Doyle asked if he could scan the Times, so Grieve surrendered it and picked up the diary. He told his colleague that he had reached March 2002.

The first plate of heart attack arrived and the younger man began to tuck in, but stopped when Grieve made a noise, "I think I've found part of the answer. Steven had a big investment in WorldCom shares; seemingly they went into freefall in February 2002." A few seconds passed and he looked up gleefully, "aha, even better, he has also admitted to Fiona that he

271

had taken out a second mortgage on his flat in 1998 to fund his equity purchases. He has got a huge mortgage now and Fiona is very worried for him."

Grieve carried on reading and after a further five minutes, "his equity is heavily weighted towards the higher risk US Technology stocks, Fiona is urging him to get out, but he won't listen, he still clings to the hope they will bounce back."

Ten minutes went by and Grieve was now so absorbed he ate the cooked breakfast without once taking his eyes from the book, "aha," he said again, this time with his mouth full. He swallowed and went on, "December 2001, Enron collapsed. He had a big chunk of their stock too. I think we can see where the depression stems from. He had been riding the crest of the stock market wave; he had lapped up his sister's, admittedly naïve, adulation, and then came unstuck. Suddenly instead of looking like an astute investor, he has started to look like a patsy. Now his sister knows not only that he is no investment guru, but also that he borrowed heavily to fund his purchases.

This stuff is not my forte at all. I'll try and get some informed advice at Scotland Yard when we've set the hare running."

They tidied up the last scraps of toast and other goodies; then set off in the Corolla to Corunna Rd. They arrived at eight-thirty and checked in with the surveillance team in the flat. They learnt from these two that the two man team put on to watch Steven, the previous evening, had tailed him to a local eatery, then a local pub, and then home. They confirmed over the radio that he was still in his flat.

The two Yorkshiremen thanked their Metropolitan brethren and drove around to park near the front of Steven's block of flats. Bang on nine, Doyle rang Steven's bell at the main entrance. The intercom crackled and Steven's voice, even more belligerent than usual, asked who the blazes was ringing his doorbell on a Saturday morning. Grieve obliged. "Ah, Captain Armstrong, its Detective Chief Inspector Grieve and Detective Inspector Doyle from Leeds."

There was a prolonged silence.

"Can we come up? We have a few questions we would like to ask you?"

272

"I was just about to go out."

"Really, Sir, it won't take long."

There was another silence and then the speaker crackled with a reluctant, "well, if you must."

The door lock buzzed and the two men went in, and up the stairs to the third floor. Doyle knocked on Steven's door. When it opened, Steven stood to one side to let them in. Grieve offered his hand and thought God, he looks terrible. Armstrong took the hand warily and Grieve introduced Doyle. Steven shook the Inspector's hand with a little frown on his face: he was trying to remember where he had seen him before, Doyle said, "may we sit down?"

"Be my guest."

The two policemen sat down, but Steven remained standing. "We are down in London as your sister, Fiona, kept a diary. Were you aware that she did?"

Steven's face showed that he had been completely unaware, and that this was another unwelcome development, "Fiona started to exhibit a change in her character from just after you had your big Christmas party on the 13th of December. Did you know that?"

"I didn't see her again after the party; that was the last time I saw her." Steven turned away and dropped his head into his hands but quickly recovered himself as the comment sunk in. With a slight frown he turned back, "what kind of change?"

"She seemed preoccupied: very engaged in some project."

"It was probably associated with her work then." Steven looked at the men as though they were stupid.

"Well, maybe, but we have good reasons to doubt that. No, we are rather interested in the possibility that her concerns stemmed from something to do with this Christmas party of yours." Grieve was talking in a confident and direct way to the plainly troubled soldier: he was almost issuing a challenge.

Doyle took up the baton, "we are told that you and she had a disagreement during the event; that she was angry with you. Maybe *this* was the trigger. Are you aware of anything that might explain it?"

273

Steven's face, despite his efforts to hide it, indicated that he could think of a connection, and it was as much a revelation to him as it had been to the policemen. "No, I can't think of anything obvious."

"Did the event cost you a lot of money?"

Steven reacted badly to this remark. "You've no right to ask me such a question; you are treading a very narrow path here."

"It's just that the diary indicated that your financial position is, how should I say it, unhealthy."

Steven visibly seethed, "your gall is quite staggering; that is no business of yours. I'm tempted to see if the courts can prevent you reading any more."

"You can try, I think it would be doomed to fail. Your financial position is very relevant you see: you're a beneficiary of your parents' will. It could be construed as a clear motive for murder."

"Out: get out of my house." Steven moved threateningly and the two men stood, "I wouldn't do anything stupid Sir, we are going. However, I suggest that you keep yourself available; I'm sure we'll be back soon."

They walked back down to the car in silence; when the doors were closed, though, Doyle said, "well, that'll have given him something to think about."

"Yes, let's hope he panics."

Grieve started the engine and they headed off to Corunna Rd again, nodding, as they passed, to the two Met men who were to tail Steven, if he left.

Steven was pacing up and down the room, thinking furiously. They suspected him. How the fuck had they reached that conclusion? The house of cards was falling about his ears. It had worried him when he had seen Grieve talking to that old bastard Hastings at the chapel service; he was aware of altogether too much of the dirt that had flowed under the Armstrong family bridge. But what hard facts could the police really know: it must be guesswork and feeling in the dark, surely? Could he ride it out? The problem was he was quite sure they had only told him a small amount of what they knew, or suspected. They were also deliberately trying to panic him; why, so he would do what?

What else did Fiona put in the fucking diary? Is the diary a fiction? He found it inconceivable that Fiona would have had one and not told him. Why would she have kept it from him? Also, what was this project she had been on, had she been checking his finances somehow? Could he believe the fucking police anyway?

It had come as a horrible shock to find out she had followed him to Hyde Park. One that was painful, nightmarish, and lonely for him: fatal for her. Had she been doing it for longer? Surely not, impossible in fact: he would have seen her if she had been routinely following him. He had been preoccupied when he was heading to that meeting: that's why he'd been careless; that's why he'd not clocked her. Generally, though, he was alert to a potential tail: it must have been a one-off: a huge, costly, and unfair one-off, but a one-off nonetheless.

Steven would not have recognised the word 'hubris' if asked to define it; did not recognise it in his own behaviour now either. What was clear was the police were watching him. If they got a warrant and searched here, they would find several items that would increase the pressure on him.

He wished he could call his inside contact at the Yard to establish what the West Yorkshire police knew. But, unfortunately, on Thursday the man had emailed that with the suspension of a colleague and the clamp-down on company procedures, he was now concerned not to do anything that might draw attention to himself. Besides, Steven couldn't think of any way the man could get enough detail about the investigation to help him reach an informed decision, without exciting some degree of suspicion.

After a couple of hours of stressing, he decided the safest option was simply to drop out of sight. It was just too much of a risk to stay visible and end up arrested. Then events might well spin out of control; now he still had attractive alternatives. Interestingly, he found the fact that he was only to receive a third of his parent's estate was making the decision easier. Dropping out meant the fucking mortgage company and the other loan companies could whistle for their money. They could fight over his flat: which would cover, at best, three quarters of the accumulated debt.

He had already moved all of his remaining equity holdings into Brian Lockhart's name: he had £169k there. The *piece de resistance*, though, was the Titian, could he continue with the Sotheby sale?

He went to the phone and let his hand hover there for a moment; then he thought better of it. He would have to ring from somewhere else. The Brian Lockhart mobile was in the Marlowe House flat. He could use that, or he could use a call box.

He looked around for the few items, incriminating or otherwise, that he needed to take, but there were really only two. The first his laptop he picked up and put in its slim carry case. The second, the wallet with the Lockhart passport, driving licence, and credit cards, he retrieved from its hiding place. There was no need for clothes as he had a ready sack in the other flat; it would cover all his immediate needs. He took one last look around and said goodbye forever to his little home.

When he got outside it took less than two minutes to clock the tail. Two more minutes established there were only two of them: amateurs. He led them a merry dance and quickly lost them. He jinked and dived for twenty more minutes, until he was absolutely sure there was no one else in contact with him, and then he headed for Corunna Rd. On the way, he saw a builder's skip down an alleyway. He looked around to ensure no one was watching; then smashed the laptop several times on the corner of the steel. When it looked sufficiently unusable, he chucked the mangled ruin and the case in under some broken plasterboard. He took his mobile out of his pocket; removed the battery and pocketed it; smashed the SIM card; smashed the rump of the mobile, as he had done to the laptop and threw that into the skip too.

A little further, he saw a telephone box. He felt in his pocket for coins and found a couple of pounds in loose change: he called Sotheby's. The phone rang three times and then an answer-phone kicked in: shit he had forgotten it was Saturday. Whatever the decision, he could do nothing with the painting until Monday at the earliest. He suddenly felt out of control: on the run and separated from this his greatest asset. His heart pounded, but slowly he calmed; the auction house knew him as Brian Lockhart; there was no possible connection to Steven Armstrong. Besides the police would only slowly realise that he had disappeared for good.

Switching tack, he considered the merits of arming himself, and eventually decided in favour. It would increase his options. His weapons cache was in his backstop little safe flat in Hounslow. So changing direction he headed for the Lockhart garage rather than the flat.

He was feeling in his pocket for the key ring with the garage key on it when he stopped: something was wrong. He always placed four telltales and two had moved. The two head hairs seemed fine. But he always would pick up some sand particles, smear them into the little gap around the edge of the rotating lock barrel and, quickly, one or two would lodge. There was none there now. The other was that he would wet and roll a small ball of paper. This he would balance on the top of the door, just as he closed it: it was virtually out of sight, unless you knew exactly where to look... He knew exactly where to look; he was looking there; it was gone too.

The dawning horror that the garage was compromised was eclipsed by the even greater horror that that meant Brian Lockhart and the flat were compromised too. He was rooted to the spot; he had to walk away· but it was too irrevocable, too big a wrench. He had lost his insurance. He had lost his painstakingly built creation: Brian Lockhart. The work during the past three months to construct an escape route had all been wasted.

He willed himself to move, but nothing worked - it was just such an enormous loss: loss of his equities, loss of all the cash, almost physical pain engulfed him, even loss of the Titian. Or no, maybe not, he could get that yet, they had met him at Sotheby's: they would recognise his face. They had sought payment in advance for the restoration work and he had called in when he had got back to London, to check again that nothing was outstanding and that all was on schedule, so they had seen him very recently. Hopefully... it was likely, in fact, the police knew nothing about it. With the realisation that he might still be able to recover the painting, a tiny hope rekindled and he forced himself to move, stiffly away. Sure enough, as he came out onto the street and walked around the corner he had a tail. He spent the next hour, making absolutely sure he had lost it. He was still furiously thinking; his mind continued to play alternatives. Could he act as if nothing had happened and go back to his, Steven Armstrong's, flat: simply try and tough it out?

He thought and thought till his brain hurt. No, impossible, the painting was at Sotheby's in Lockhart's name. It would be national news when it was sold, the money would be paid to Lockhart. He had a suspicion that the proceeds and the recipient would have to be notified to the police under the anti-laundering legislation, either by Sotheby's or by the receiving bank. He could not go back.

He stopped at a bank-telling machine. He needed cash. There were ten debit and credit cards in the two wallets on him, five in each name. The machine would honour them now; but he guessed not for much longer. He used all ten and ultimately withdrew a total of £2,500. Then he lost himself again and eventually found himself outside his little bed-sitter in Hounslow. He checked the telltales and thankfully, they were all intact. This, his final only to be used in absolute extremis, refuge was still secure.

Safe now inside, he slowly sat down on the bed; he was dazed: the police had known of his second persona. That was why they had wanted to panic him, to connect Steven Armstrong with Brian Lockhart. He had walked straight into it; though all he had done was stand in front of the garage. He lay back on the bed and tears of frustration ran down past his ears. Hours went by before he roused himself. He watched the news on the tiny TV and, thankfully, there was no mention of him.

He got up and moved the bed; pulling the corner of the carpet, he gently lifted it from its tacks. He worked the floorboard and lifted it out. Leaving the package that was the rifle he took out the large biscuit tin. He sat on the bed; removed the two pistols, the spare magazines, and the boxes of loose ammunition. He reached for the wallet at the bottom and checked that the £2,000 in twenties was untouched inside. His cash now stood at a little over £4,500. He could probably try to take another £2,500 tomorrow and maybe also on Monday. He would have to use anonymous teller machines and he would have to be quick off the mark. He could probably expect to garner almost ten grand. Not a lot if you are on the run without an identity, and buying a

278

watertight new identity would absorb a significant amount of money.

He only had two passports, Steven Armstrong and Brian Lockhart, both useless if he was ever to enjoy life again. He had not foreseen the need to spend money on a third false identity: these days it was a very expensive business. Unfamiliar, as he was, with how the police had found Brian Lockhart he assumed that somehow they had linked Lockhart to the killing. This led him to the conclusion that his parsimony had been a folly. He should not have mixed the creation that committed the crime with the creation he needed to escape. Two hours of self-recrimination followed before he started to think of the future.

The bed-sitter was paid for with cash every quarter; no questions asked. He was safe here for at least two months, but it was not going to be a life worth living. No, a pleasant future revolved around the Titian; he had to get it ASAP, and be able to sell it: for that he needed a new identity and a quiet foreign sale. It seemed he had no alternative; he must seek help from a quarter he had hoped he could now be independent of; someone to whom he had wished to be a peer. He reached into the tin and took out a mobile. He switched it on, checked that the battery was fully charged and called a number, "I need us to meet, same place as last time, same procedure, three pm Monday, okay?"

Grieve, Doyle, and the two Met officers had watched Steven approach the garage; had watched him stop in front of it; took pictures of him; had willed him to open it. Grieve even let the words slip from his mouth, "open it, you son of a bitch, what are you waiting for?"

Yet, Steven stood like a statue; he had been like that for a minute; two minutes "He's rumbled it," said Doyle and he looked at one of the Met men who nodded and got on the radio to the watchers at the front that included Constables Farmer and Collins.

Grieve said, "shit."

Doyle looked back and saw Steven walk slowly away. The policeman on the radio relayed the information and he and his partner raced off to join the other four. It availed not. Thirty minutes later and Doyle got the news that Farmer, Collins, and the four others trailing Armstrong had lost him. Grieve was sitting head in hands, "Hastings warned me and I ignored him."

"We've still got the samples you took."

"Yes, but you know that the only one of those that will be admissible in court is the hair. The others were taken from a locked garage. It may link him so we know he is connected to the crime, but they won't help us put him behind bars."

"At least we got them, if we had let him drive away without getting them we might have got nothing."

The two men left the teams patiently staked out at the three locations and went back to Scotland Yard.

Just as they arrived, Sergeant Banks called from Weetwood in Leeds, "the DNA test is back. The hair is almost certainly from a sibling of Fiona Armstrong and from a child of the Armstrong parents. That puts Steven Armstrong squarely in the frame unless there is a third, yet to be revealed, child out there."

"Good news. Nevertheless not enough, we need to link him to the abandoned Mondeo."

"We're working on that, but it's a nightmare trying to get permission to enter some of these garages."

"Yes, that's what I'd anticipated would be the problem, it's a necessary evil though, you'd better keep looking."

"We've got everyone that can be spared on it."

"Okay, keep at it and good work."

Grieve rang off and looked at Doyle. "Have we got enough, now, to get a search warrant?" He already knew the answer and Doyle provided the confirmation, "not yet, I fear, we have still to establish a credible link between him and the crime."

DS Ingram, unusually for him, was in his office on this fine Saturday morning. He noted their glum looks, but smiled at them. "Don't be downcast. Just when you're least expecting it, the sun comes out."

Grieve was not in the mood to play ball, "we need more to get a search warrant."

"Well, maybe this will help." Ingram threw two wallets over. One had passport documentation for Steven Armstrong with a photo in the top left corner. The other had passport documentation for Brian Lockhart with another photo in its top

280

left corner. The photos differed by virtue of hair colour, spectacles, and a moustache. It was evident, though, with them side by side that they were both photos of the same man. With the two Yorkshire-men studying the documents, Ingram continued, "we got a handwriting expert to check the signatures too, he is prepared to testify that they are the same hand. So, he obviously lied and provided false documentation and that, as you know, is a crime. I think there is enough accumulated evidence of dastardly deeds now for us to have a look at his properties, don't you?"

Raising and approving the search warrants was set in motion. They also decided they had enough to put a watch and detention order out to air and seaports, for both men. While they waited for the warrants, Grieve asked Ingram whether there was anyone he could ask about the stock market information in the diary. Ingram said there was during the week: Saturday would be a problem; but he searched out a telephone number, gave Grieve the telephone, and said, "call Hamish." Half an hour later, after much conversation, some confusion, and a lot of explanation, Grieve had the answers and rang off with a heart felt thank you.

He leafed to Friday 16th July 1999, where Fiona had told of the meal at Gordon Ramsay's restaurant, and tapped the page. "I think I understood all that; I'll try to explain.

Mid-July 1999 was very close to the high point of both the US and UK stock markets. Since then there has been an exceptionally long bear market." Doyle signalled that he wished for some expansion, "apparently, a bear market is the opposite of a bull market. A bear market means there are always sellers and not so many buyers. A bull market is the reverse, i.e. prices are rising with the pent-up demand."

"So a bear market is bad news for investors and a bull market is good?"

"Hum, well, apparently, it's not quite that simple, but you're broadly right. So, if Steven had a fully diversified portfolio, that means spread about to reduce the risk, say, following the Dow Jones and/or the FTSE indexes, then his £860,000 then, would be down to between £400k-£450k now."

"Bloody hell, that's a huge loss."

"Yes, that's because the whole market slumped. The only way to have avoided that kind of loss would have been to move the assets into safe, but low yielding, cash investments. If he had done that, the next day, with all his equity, he would now have in the region of £930k, in other words, it would have grown, very slowly, but it would still have grown. Like everything in life, if you bet and you know what the future holds you'll win. It's a very big 'If' though.

Anyway, it's clear from the diary that not only did he stay in equity, but also that he was biased towards the high-risk end of the market. That's why he was doing well; the stock prices were surging; and why he had such a lot in WorldCom and Enron: they had maintained their high share price growth by dubious accounting. We don't know how much bias there was, but his £860k could now be down to…it's anyone's guess, about £200k. That may seem like a lot, but it needs to be set against his borrowing. Hamish had a blue canary when I told him Steven had borrowed at fixed rates in 1998 to fund equity purchases. He said that is, generally, an absolute no-no.

That's all the help Hamish could give but he did say my subject must have had some money to start with: Fiona had said that he had only been active in equities since 1995. Therefore, there remains the question of where did he get the money to start his stock portfolio? Given that he isn't the skilled investor Fiona believed he was, it seems unlikely that he built it through the wily identification of good, high-growth businesses."

Doyle had listened attentively to the explanation and offered a point of his own, "the other important point is, as we mentioned to him, it gives him a motive for killing his parents: we know he only gets a third of the estate, but that might yet amount to several hundred thousand."

A knock came at the door and a policeman said that the warrants had been granted for both flats. All three men trooped out of the door. Grieve went to Steven's flat with Ingram; Doyle went with Collins and Farmer to Marlowe House.

Doyle allowed Farmer to effect an entry and they found a very sparsely furnished flat. A bed, a small TV, some long-life foods in a cupboard in the kitchen, a holdall packed with all that would be necessary for a week's trip, and a mobile phone on charge in the kitchen.

Doyle pounced on the phone: it was a Nokia. He looked for messages: nothing. So he looked at the call register; missed calls: nothing. Received calls: there were several, but the last two where both on Monday, the day of the Armstrong murders, at eight-fifty-eight and at thirteen-thirty-one and they were both from the same mobile number, which he jotted down.

Dialled numbers also had several recorded. The number he had just written down was dialled at both eight forty-eight and at thirteen-twenty-five on that fateful Monday.

Doyle recalled that Maxwell had been taken to his car at about thirteen hundred on Monday and the drive to Ilkley probably had taken at most thirty minutes. He called Grieve and asked when the Met PNC check had been done, Grieve could only remember it was at about a quarter to two. Doyle thought that that was close enough, told of the discovery of the phone, gave him the number, and heard him passing the information on to Ingram. Grieve called Thompson in MI5 and asked him to see if he could locate the phone, which he agreed to do. Additionally the three of them devised a simple plan.

30. A Friend in Need

Gavrilo Bulatovic had put the mobile down and swore colourfully in his native tongue. Janica and Natascha who were engrossed in an intense chess match had looked up in surprise.

Neither girl spoke particularly good English so Bulatovic switched language and lowered his voice. "Fucking Armstrong, this is the third, and last, time he has fucked with me."

He obviously could still be heard if not completely understood as Janica, the blond, said disingenuously, "again, you with us want fuck?"

Bulatovic looked around and glared at her, she pouted and returned to the game.

Thinking he had better bring his plans forward to Monday, he debated whether it was possible. He had some more disposals to make. They were minor though, he could let the pieces be auctioned; simply transferring the funds remotely. After a lengthy period of calculation he decided it would be no bad thing to close this episode sooner rather than later.

He went over to study the chess match and was impressed by the quality of play. A testament to his teaching, he thought; until a few weeks ago, neither girl had even seen the game.

Steven had spent a stressed, worried, and tormented weekend. He was thankful when he woke at six fifteen on Monday. Going out, he visited another, distant, bank teller machine to further augment his cash, and then on his way back found an anonymous café. Several mugs of tea, a large fry-up, and a couple of newspapers occupied him for the best part of two hours. There was no mention in the paper of him or his alter ego. Arriving back at five to nine he waited these last five minutes impatiently and then lifted the mobile and rang Sotheby's. After a five-minute wait, he was put through to Manvers, the specialist who was dealing with the painting.

Irritatingly, before he could say anything Manvers started to tell him how beautiful the painting was now that it was properly mounted and framed. Eventually Steven was able to get an angry word in, saying that he had decided both to withdraw the work from sale and to collect it within the hour. Manvers tried to argue: he was upset, not just for the lost sale, but also that the world would not now benefit from seeing the wonderful piece. This strengthened him in his contention that the painting could not be prepared and boxed for travel, as required, before 11:30 at the earliest. Steven bowed to the inevitable, but demanded too, that the documentation that he had supplied in support of its provenance be returned as well, with any copies that had been made. Manvers was truculent but eventually agreed. Fortunately, Sotheby's had sought payment in advance for the work required in raising the piece to a saleable condition; only Steven's request for it to be boxed would require payment.

At Scotland Yard at virtually the same time, DS Ingram had called a group meeting of the CID team that worked around and with Constable Willis. The ostensible reason was to introduce Grieve and Doyle to the thirty or so men and women.

In fact, Farmer was in an adjacent room and at the appointed time, just as the meeting was to start, he used Brian Lockhart's mobile. He dialled the number that had been called twice on the previous Monday morning. Grieve, Doyle and Ingram were all watching the assembled team; but, courtesy of Thompson, they knew who their target was. They had desisted from picking him up on Saturday as the use of MI5's extra-judicial tools ran the risk of being challenged in court.

286

All three saw the man make an involuntary move to his left breast pocket and then think better of it. Unsurprisingly, no one else moved. DS Ingram growled, "God, I hate mobile's in meetings, muted or not." And he went up to Constable Chalmers, hamming it up wonderfully, he angrily asked him if he had a mobile on him. The man sheepishly acknowledged the fact, but when asked to switch it off, he reached into his right breast pocket. Ingram impatiently said he had seen him go for his left pocket and held his hand out.

Chalmers was caught on the hop. Still unaware of the trap he simply believed Ingram was suffering from mobile rage; he extracted the phone and made to switch it off, but, Farmer, who had now entered the room, conveniently called the device again.

Chalmers, though, saw the writing on the wall when Ingram dismissed everyone but the three Leeds officers, Farmer, and himself. He was shaking when Ingram read him his rights. He was singing even before they got him to an interview room. Once they were settled, and the recording device turning, he told his story, which according to him, was very simple.

He said he had done the PNC search for an old friend but he had no idea why. The old friend was Captain Steven Armstrong whom he had worked for when he had been in the Army's Logistics Corp in Bosnia. Chalmers had left the Army in 1995 and had joined the Metropolitan Police.

Grieve and Doyle were jubilant: Monday morning, only a week after the murders, and they now had Lockhart and Armstrong linked and Armstrong well and truly in the frame. Once their initial excitement had passed though they realised that a conviction, with what they had, was still not a foregone conclusion. They needed more, but first and foremost, they had to find him.

A press release was prepared and issued citing Steven Armstrong and his alias Brian Lockhart as wanted for the murders of the three Armstrong's and of PC Nichol. He was described and both passport photos were released. The bank accounts of Steven and his creation Lockhart were put on watch and frozen.

Grieve rang Andrew Maxwell to say that they had a suspect pinpointed, but that he was still at large and he, Andrew, would have to remain hidden until the man was caught. Maxwell was relieved to hear, though, that in Grieve's view the threat was now negligible.

Before leaving, Steven had had to make a decision: whether to take a pistol and, if he did, which one. The two he had were his Walther P22 and the Browning that he had used the previous week. He preferred the Walther; it was very light and highly accurate. But, there were two problems with it, firstly the magazine had a capacity of only ten rounds, and secondly, as the calibre was .22, or 5.5mm, it had a much lighter punch than the 9mm: good for an assassination; but not to stop and down a man in a fluid situation. Once again, he had to take the Browning.

He left for the second time at ten, stole a car from half a mile away, and drove it to near Ealing Broadway tube and rail station; he took the Central Line tube direct to Bond Street.

Warily, he approached the Sotheby's building, but in the end, he just had to bite the bullet. He strode, as confidently as he could, through the door, and was relieved when he was greeted solicitously: an army of police officers failing to descend. Minutes later he was ushered through to Manvers.

The man fussed and fussed around the crated painting, which encased as it was, was now almost a metre and a half long, a metre high, and thirty centimetres deep. It was also, to Steven's dismay, surprisingly heavy with the wooden packaging, the new mount, and the frame. He was not going to disappear, inconspicuously, with it into the underground.

Manvers wrung his hands and asked about insurance, and security, and atmosphere, and humidity, and a whole host of other things. Steven was desperate to get away, and took little notice until Manvers did say something that sounded interesting; he just caught the end of it, so he looked up, "can you repeat that?"

"I said please don't sell it privately; the world needs to see this: it has been in private hands, unseen, for hundreds of years."

"No, the other thing you said?"

"My auction estimate of £4million-£4.5million, is just that: an auction estimate. A private sale may generate as little as £3.5million."

"Yes, I understand that, but I meant the other thing; you said something regarding waiting?"

"Ah, well the economic situation at the moment, the slump in the market and the doldrums in the US, and the City here, are holding the art market back too. If you waited until activity picked up again, maybe for another year or so, this painting might exceed some of the prices paid for Titian in the past."

"Like what?"

"Well, let me see, Christie's, our arch rival, sold 'Venus and Adonis' in London back in 1991 for $13.5 million: that's approximately £8million. Just weeks ago the National Galleries of Scotland bought the 'Venus Anadyomene' for £11.6million from the Duke of Sutherland's collection. That is an especially important work, though, the price reflects that, and there was a risk of it leaving the UK.

If sold at auction in eighteen months time, assuming by then that the economy has picked up, this might fetch in the range of £5million to £6million."

Steven nodded and said, "good, well I will think on it, now can your people help me get it, awkward as it is, into a taxi."

The taxi driver pulled away from the kerb just as the twelve-noon news came on the radio. Suddenly Steven was listening. He, either as Steven Armstrong, or as Brian Lockhart, was now wanted for the murders of last week. The taxi driver looked back at him and said, "they should bring back hanging, hang both the bastards, if there's two of them. In fact hanging is too good for them; they should do what they did to Mel Gibson in Braveheart: Hang them, cut them open, and chop them up."

Steven relieved to be clear, in possession of the Titian, and unsuspected was in upbeat mood; he nodded enthusiastically. The taxi left him near Ealing Broadway station and when he had driven out of sight Steven eased his encumbrance into the back of the stolen vehicle. Several people watched him with interest.

He drove back to Hounslow and manhandled the painting into his little flat. He checked the time and, as it was just after one fifteen, he immediately returned to the car, drove into Knightsbridge, and left it in one of the back streets behind Harrods: the large, ostentatious, department store. He stopped for some food and a drink and at quarter to three he made his way to Edinburgh Gate on the south side of Hyde Park. Once in the park he slowly walked west towards the Albert Memorial.

31. A Lesson in Death

Gavrilo Bulatovic caught the midday news on TV and smiled when he saw the report regarding the search for Steven Armstrong, or Brian Lockhart. He had briefed the minders on the need to slip the tails he had; they were to help, and they had spent an hour in the late morning discussing this plan, and the rest of how Monday should develop.

He was drawing a line at this point and when the men were finished with this last task they and the two girls were to return to Serbia and he would never see any of them again.

All three men left the Dorchester at one pm and took a taxi to Piccadilly Circus. There they separated and Bulatovic headed in the general direction of Soho. He dawdled up Shaftsbury Avenue, took a right; dawdled some more, and then a left. Browsing still, he walked a further two hundred yards, then he suddenly ducked down a side alley and ran surprisingly fast along it where at the end he cut right.

He was heading for a specific spot where he was, briefly, to meet his two minders again; they should have shaken any tails they had by that time. He ducked, weaved, and after a few minutes, came out at one of the entrances down into Tottenham

291

Court Road tube station. One of the minders was waiting halfway up the stair. After Bulatovic passed him, while he tore through the subterranean complex, he heard a crash and a burst of swearing from behind him. He headed for the exit where the other minder was to have taken position; sure enough, there he was, at the head of the steps. He started to descend slowly when his boss came into sight; as Bulatovic fled down the street, he heard another crash from behind; another furious burst of invective. A dive into a small alley; several twists and turns; through some shops and he was working his way back towards Oxford Circus tube station. He had three underground lines to choose from here, and when he was safely on the Victoria line, he decided he was probably clear of all the tails. He was still wary, though, and got out at the next station: Green Park. He got on the Piccadilly Line and went to Knightsbridge station. Now, absolutely sure he was clean; he stepped into a coffee bar and killed time until two-thirty. Then he walked into Hyde Park and found a quiet spot by a tree. He got a small pair of binoculars out and waited for Armstrong to appear at the Edinburgh Gate. When he arrived, Bulatovic watched him, and the people around him, for twenty minutes until he was sure that he was alone. Only then, did he come out and approach Steven from behind.

"You're late," Steven said. Bulatovic looked coldly at him, "yes well, if you recall, when we met here last Sunday you brought your, fucking, sister in your wake. I've been watching you for twenty minutes in case someone else was tailing you: I definitely do not want a repeat of that, especially now that you are wanted. I was very disappointed in you, Steven.

When I got your panicked phone call last Sunday evening, I had to decamp to Heathrow and fly to Paris; else, I would have struggled with a credible alibi. I don't like being put into such situations."

"I solved the problem, didn't I? You wanted my parents dead; you got it. The threat my sister suddenly presented to you, and to me, was solved at the same time."

Gavrilo rounded on him, "the fucking threat should never have occurred in the first place, you arse."

He was very angry. "Something else that has seriously pissed me off: our agreement was *not* that you clinically execute

292

them. When I saw the news on Tuesday, I found myself having to brave it once more. I wasn't very happy with you, at all. You were supposed to kill them slowly; to make it clear to them that we were partners in their end."

Now it was Steven's turn for anger. "For fucks sake, I'd to move fast. There were three of them in the house. It was perilously dangerous as it was, without putting bells on it. There was no way to square the circle. I had to shoot them on sight. The old bastard was carrying, in a shoulder holster. If there had been only two of them I would have stood a chance: I could have used my mother, wrinkled old crone that she was, to force him to disarm, but I couldn't risk it with Fiona upstairs. Besides I could never have tortured her."

"I didn't ask you to torture her. She was involved, you had been forced to rush, and you had three to deal with, all because you carelessly allowed her to see us together in the first place. She'd still be alive and kicking otherwise." Gavrilo spat back at him.

"Give me a break, for crying out loud. It's no skin off your nose, it's me that has to live with her loss."

Gavrilo took a few breaths. "So why did you want to see me?"

Steven frowned, pursed his lips and said, "I need your help."

"Help, help with what? I understood you had your legend and an escape route planned down to the last detail. If you recall, on Sunday, the need to construct it was the reason you gave me for the delay in completing your side of the bargain."

Steven slumped looking depressed, "it's all been compromised: the police know about my alias."

"I hope you haven't lost the Titian." Bulatovic's voice carried the suspicion of a threat, which Steven missed.

"No, and incidentally, your estimate of £2.5million was light. When Sotheby's came back in early December confirming its authenticity, they estimated, at that time, it would fetch between four and five million. They think if the sale is delayed for a year it could fetch as much as six million."

Bulatovic smiled ever so slightly at this news, which actually wasn't news to him at all, "where is it?"

293

"I have it in a safe house." Bulatovic looked faintly pleased. "So what help do you need from me?"

"I know you come and go easily between here and Serbia. I want you to get me out; help me create a new identity; possibly change my face."

"Is that all? And is this supposed to be charity, or are you offering something in return?"

This whole conversation differed from any Steven had had with Bulatovic since he had known him. Steven was shocked: unused to Bulatovic taking such a hard line with him. Ever since they had met in Bosnia in 1993, Bulatovic had acted towards him like the father he had never had, "I thought a man of your wealth, with your connections, would help a friend out: surely it's peanuts to you?"

Bulatovic looked at Steven for a few seconds, "I did you a huge favour giving you the Titian in the first place. It was worth a lot more than simply paying someone to take out your parents. You had had the taste of the good life, and then you lost it, I was giving it back to you again."

Steven hung his head and eventually, showing some humility, nodded, "I know. I am grateful." He looked at Bulatovic uncertainly, "what would you like from me?"

Bulatovic was still studying Steven; unexpectedly he smiled. "That's all I wanted to hear, my boy, that you would give something if I asked. But you are right a friend shouldn't ask, what are friends for after all. As to the problems during the last week, well, all's well that ends well."

Bulatovic slapped Steven's back and the younger man smiled nervously. Bulatovic continued, "possibly, when you do sell the Titian, maybe you can find it in your heart to repay my expenses at least?"

Steven nodded, still upset at his patron's earlier stance. Bulatovic clapped his hands together, and looked around with an air of decision, "right, we'd better get you out of London; over to France or Belgium, as quickly as possible. Come with me."

They walked together, back through Edinburgh Gate, crossing first Kensington Rd, Brompton Rd, and then Sloane St. Ten minutes saw them in the NCP car park on the other side of

294

the busy, broad Knightsbridge carriageway. Bulatovic took him to a Silver Mercedes C class estate and threw him the keys. Steven drove out; at the barrier, Bulatovic used a credit card in the name of Harold Dennis.

Armstrong looked questioningly at Bulatovic who indicated south and east. They went down the back of Buckingham Palace gardens, past Victoria station, across to Parliament Square, over Westminster Bridge, and eventually, onto the Old Kent Road. They were now headed east out of London on the A2. Every now and then Bulatovic would take a prolonged look out of the back, a frown of concentration on his brow. A couple of times he ordered a detour; watching carefully for any untoward behaviour by vehicles behind. After ten minutes he relaxed and studied Steven instead. "Tell me, why did your sister react so violently when she saw us together?"

Steven glanced at Bulatovic, not entirely sure whether there was some agenda behind the question. "You created a big impression on her in 1980 after your father was pardoned by Tito; you threatened revenge on her "daddy". You got a lot of news coverage here. She was nine, nine and a half; the kids at school made her life a misery for a while. It was different for me, I was in my last year at Glenalmond; I basked in the adulation of the other boys: I had a father who had shot another man to death for spying."

"Yes... I should have been more circumspect; it would have made life much easier. It was an empty threat at the time; I could see where the wind was blowing in Yugoslavia: Tito was dead: his iron grip gone; there was a great opportunity for advancement, Serbia and," Bulatovic smiled malevolently, "the acquisition of wealth and art from those who didn't appreciate either. The planning, and preparation of that occupied me for a long time."

Bulatovic contemplated the horizon for a while, and then looked at Steven again. "Was it difficult for you to kill her?"

Steven look sick, and took his turn to look out of the window, "yes, it was horrible." He paused, "I had to close my mind to it, treat it as an operational task, think of them, well her anyway, only as targets."

He looked at Bulatovic and there was blurring in his eyes, "I wracked my brains, but there was no alternative. She was furious with me; left a message on my mobile: she couldn't understand why I was so hand in glove with a reprobate such as you. She was going to my parents to seek their advice. My fucking father would have shopped me, without a second thought, to the police or more likely to Military Intelligence. He would see it as a 'wrong act' despite our relationship. Everyone would be wary of me; when my parents eventually did die unpleasantly, I would immediately have been suspected: hauled in. Even if I then sold the painting as Lockhart, my face would have been plastered over the news. It would have been very difficult to escape with the proceeds. You too would have been suspected, whatever alibi you had.

The alternative was not to kill them at all, but then I would have lost the Titian: I would have had to return it to you. Anyway, my debt to you is greater than any debt to my parents: I couldn't let you down.

In the end, it was a choice between the proceeds from the painting or my sister: that was a Hobson's Choice, in effect."

"Did you use that little Walther you've got?"

"No, the situation was too dangerous. I needed something that would put any one of them down with one or two shots: good shot I may be, but I couldn't guarantee that with the small calibre Walther. Also using a .22 would, being unusual, leave a signature, when a 9mm wouldn't. I had planned to get a Sig or a Glock in the next two weeks, but Fiona pre-empted that. I have a Browning as well, so I used that, and poor though it is, it has the merit of being anonymous, given the tens of thousands that are around on the black market."

Thirty minutes went by, largely in silence. Bulatovic started to look back again at the following traffic, but just as before after ten minutes he relaxed. They had left the conurbation behind and they crossed the M25 orbital. Still they bore east: past Gravesend. Arriving at the start of the M2, they ignored it and cut left on to the Rochester relief road. Now they were heading north, back towards the south shore of the Thames estuary. The roads were smaller here as they came onto the coastal peninsula that was called the Isle of Grain.

They passed a sign for St Mary's Hoo on the left and then a sign for Allhallows on the right. Bulatovic indicated a track that led to an isolated house and a boat shed on the right edge of St Mary's Marshes with the sea lapping only a hundred yards away. The boat shed opened onto a small sea inlet and there was a narrow bar of sand.

Bulatovic said he rented the house, had a couple of men based here, and kept a boat in the shed that was capable of negotiating the English Channel in most weathers.

There were two Mercedes saloons in front of the house, and when the two men went to the door it was opened by one of these men. He was hard looking with a broad chest and a grim face. Bulatovic asked this man in serbo-croat if anything suspicious had transpired over the past few days and the man shook his head. Steven didn't understand the conversation but the explanation the man gave appeared to satisfy Bulatovic.

As Steven walked in, the bodyguard politely stepped aside, and as he passed, in a fluid movement the big man punched Steven in the kidneys and brought a cosh down on his head.

Steven regained consciousness in the boat shed. His head continued to spin and he remained groggy, but it was quickly obvious that he was tied to a chair in the centre of the building. The chair, in turn, was connected, in some undefeatable way, to one of the columns supporting the roof. He could see through the slatted walls that it was not yet dark outside. Looking around he realised there was no sea-going boat in the shed. The only craft was a sturdy looking inflatable with a large outboard motor on the back. He could feel that the Browning was no longer between his belt and his back.

Steven strained at his bindings, but there was no escape. He heard a door open behind him; a different, but equally large, minder to the one who must have attacked him came in. He studied Steven for a few seconds then nodded and left. Five minutes later both minders and Bulatovic came in. His friend of ten years pulled up a chair, reversed it, and sat down with his arms resting on the top: he was two metres away. He had an orange, and a short, wicked looking knife in his hands, "I'm sorry Steven; you've been out for half an hour. Stephan must have hit you harder than he should have." He looked over at Stephan and wagged the knife at him, the man's impassive face creased slightly. Bulatovic looked back at the bound man appraisingly, "Steven, did you ever wonder why you and I met in Bosnia in 1993?"

Steven shrugged as best he could. Bulatovic used the knife to cut the top off the orange. "You know I love to play chess: you and I have had some good games in the past, did we not?"

He pointed the knife at Steven and wagged it as he had at the minder, "I think maybe you were born in the wrong age. I was always impressed by your tactical flare, your eye for terrain, even your strategic thinking. In an older age you might well have been a very great soldier." He shook his head sadly, "but you never had the social skills, or the wider intellect, to excel in the present day British Army did you? Your parents really shat on you as far as that was concerned; shat on you like your father shat on me; my parents; my hopes; my prospects."

Bulatovic studied Steven for a short time while he peeled a strip of skin from around the bare patch on the top of the orange. "Anyway chess, a superb tactical and strategic game: a model for life possibly? We used to discuss how life was like playing a game, didn't we."

Steven saw no particular reason to engage in the discussion; he could feel himself getting angry. Bulatovic shook off the air of reflection and went on purposefully, "I digress. When I heard, in early 1993, that there was a Captain Armstrong running a British UNPROFOR supply depot in Bosnia, I couldn't help but be interested: the name Armstrong does that for me. I had some investigation done, and what a pleasant surprise, the son of my enemy had turned up in my sphere.

My immediate reaction was to plan your killing, but soon I realised it would be a poor way to take my revenge; I also recalled the lesson of chess: playing the game well involves patient manoeuvring to get positional advantage, as you know. A good player takes time to build a strong strategic position. I began to wonder if you were a pawn that I could employ in a larger game; perhaps you were more valuable: a knight, or a bishop, possibly even strong enough to play a rook?

I set one of my Lieutenants, you remember Captain Broz? Dead now sadly..." Bulatovic grief stricken (sic) shook his head; "Anyway, I set him to get to know you, in the course of our relations with UNPROFOR. You had a couple of meetings, and some drinks together, remember. He reported to me that you hated your father and your mother and, additionally, that you had achieved a level of cynicism that might be useful. So we tested it: he suggested to you that knowing the timing, and direction, of the next escorted humanitarian aid convoy would be valuable information for us."

Bulatovic smiled at Steven. "And you said, do you remember? How valuable? Excellent, I thought, he's corruptible; so, we paid you $5,000 for the information. Unknown to you, though, I had photographs and tape recordings made of the exchange. Just in case you changed your mind later about continuing to supply information, you understand." Bulatovic smiled maliciously this time. "But, you didn't change your mind did you? You became more and more enthusiastic. You had seen a new way to excel, wasn't that it? Instead of succeeding as a soldier, you could succeed as a businessman. You liked the friendship we; I extended to you: you liked the fact you had befriended your father's enemy. We would drink together, have great fun, all the time you were building a pile of cash, and I was building a damning portfolio on you.

It was good for the Bosnian Serb Army too, every third or fourth convoy would be intercepted, we would take maybe a third of it, not enough for the escort to fight, you understand, and of course we had to be careful we didn't kill the Golden Goose.

There was that time when, what was his name? Lieutenant Roberts, he started to take an unhealthy interest in you. He began to suspect something was leaking, so we kidnapped him for you; that little Walther you have came in handy, didn't it. A single shot in the side of his head. Oh, by the way, you know we videoed that too, your execution of a fellow British Officer; I know exactly where he's buried: his disappearance never was explained."

Steven was patently struggling to contain his rage now. Bulatovic's tone was winding him and winding him. Bulatovic was enjoying himself; "You didn't restrict yourself to just intelligence on the aid convoys either did you? By the time you went back to the UK, you must have amassed, what $350-$400k from your little treacheries. We discussed what you should do with it; I gave you the benefit of all my investment knowledge: for a long time our stock portfolios were very similar in profile, if not in size.

I remember meeting you a few times in London; we had a wonderful time there too; profligate in our spending; it was hedonistic, you loved it; people are so friendly when you're wealthy and spending it: suddenly you were a success."

Bulatovic paused, looking at Steven from under his eyebrows. He cut a further strip of skin from the orange and sliced a piece of flesh, which he ate. Then he continued; he was enunciating deliberately now. "What I didn't tell you, was at the end of 1998 I got out of equities completely. Do you know the name Warren Buffett, Steven? He's a very good judge of the market: that's why he's the second wealthiest man in the world. I listen closely to his investor advice. He had got out into cash and I decided: if it's good enough for him, it was for me too.

The chess game was reaching a decisive point; I needed there to be a release of pressure, a bout of piece exchange; a bloodletting. So, I still prompted you to invest in sky-high, high-risk stock. I knew a crash was coming, I couldn't say when, but it was coming and I wanted you to be burnt, very badly burnt." Bulatovic grinned and almost gleefully, he went on: "And you were, weren't you?" He laughed out loud.

Steven had been listening to all this in silence but his colour had been deepening by the minute; suddenly he lunged at Bulatovic, and whatever it was that bound the chair to the upright parted. He staggered towards his tormentor, still encumbered by the chair, but it was useless: the bodyguards had been alert to the risk; they simply pushed him back and rebound the chair to the column.

Steven was screaming obscenities at the man he had believed a friend. Bulatovic smiled indulgently and allowed the outburst to subside. "You see, I needed you to have tasted from the cup, then to lose it, and to yearn to taste from it again."

Some more of the orange vanished. "We were getting to the end game. I had accumulated a huge amount of art, which I was slowly selling off and investing. Now Serbia is a spent and pathetic shadow of its former majesty. The new Serbian Government is sucking up to the Europeans. They might actually indict some of us war heroes in Serbian courts: unbelievable. I resigned my position, a course I had planned for some time anyway. Now I'm in the process of clearing the decks of all my outstanding issues; one of which being the destruction of your family."

The orange was down to a third of its original size, "the game I'd been playing with you was the delightfully symmetric use of you, Armstrong's son, to take revenge on him for his destruction of my father, my mother, and my life. It's almost worthy of a Greek Tragedy. I had raised you high, and I had helped to bring you low, you were ripe to be tempted by the offer of renewed wealth. Ripe for the offer of the Titian: something you couldn't resist. And in return," the last of the orange vanished, "in return, all you had to do was torture your parents to death."

Bulatovic was grim now. "Something you singularly failed to do; I swore never to forgive you that error, Steven."

Bulatovic smiled darkly. "You really have messed things up The plan I had originally mapped out was:

Step 1; you torture and kill your parents.

Step 2; at some appointed time, I pick you, and Fiona up.

Step 3; use and abuse your beloved sister to death in front of you.

Step 4; torture you for the whereabouts of the Titian.

Step 5; kill you thereby wiping away all trace of the Armstrong family.

Step 6; well, I think I'll keep step 6 from you, just for now, Steven.

You've robbed me of the torture of three of your family. I'm afraid Steven you are going to have to make amends." Bulatovic opened his hands as if there was no other way, "First though the Titian. That was the best piece I found in my little sprees through Croatia, Bosnia, and Kosovo. I liked the fact that it was going to help me destroy your family. I told you it was in payment for your patricide, but I didn't *really* intend to let you keep it, or sell it. The only reason I gave it to you with all the fake provenance, back in September, was so that you could have it authenticated; you mistrusting, pathetic piece of shit."

Bulatovic stood up. "So tell me where it is Steven and I promise, what is about to follow will be swifter and less painful for you."

Steven knew, with absolute certainty, that he was going to die; he also knew that he would, eventually, tell Bulatovic what he wanted: he had seen him torture people in Bosnia. But he was damned if he was going to give in straight away. "Go fuck yourself, you Serbian cunt."

Bulatovic signalled to Stephan one of the guards; the big man came forward and grabbed Steven's head. Bulatovic coaxed, "tell me Steven."

"Knowing what I know now, only a traitor could have spawned you, you evil shite."

Bulatovic's eyes narrowed, and he brought the point of the knife close to Steven's right cornea: Steven closed his eyes. Bulatovic retreated and Stephan moved his hands to pull the lids apart. He had experience of just how strong the protective response of the eye was, so he hooked his index fingers, painfully for Steven, under each lid. When he was ready, Bulatovic returned the knifepoint to the cornea, "tell me Steven?"

Steven struggling as best he could; was breathing rapidly; was preparing himself for the pain: he didn't offer an answer. Bulatovic increased the pressure and the knife slowly penetrated the eye: Steven started to keen. When the knife had penetrated an inch and a half, Bulatovic began to twist it slowly through ninety degrees; the trickle of fluid and blood became a torrent: Steven screamed.

Bulatovic removed the knife from the wrecked eye, and told the minders to tear Steven's clothes from his body. When it was done the two men wrenched Steven's legs apart, Bulatovic took a pinch of his scrotum, and slowly carved through it to make a hole about an inch in diameter. Steven bucked and fought, but Bulatovic squeezed one of his testicles out of the hole, and started paring thin slices from the end. The well-muscled bodyguards had to work hard to keep the screaming and thrashing man steady. Eventually, with one testicle destroyed Bulatovic squeezed the other out. "Ready to tell me yet, Steven?"

302

All that came from Steven was grunting and more thrashing. Bulatovic smiled sadistically and started to pare away at the other testicle. Steven screamed and started to urinate, but Bulatovic kept steadily working, inflicting the maximum amount of pain.

When he was finished between Steven's legs, he cut a flap of skin on his stomach. Once he had sufficient purchase he pulled the flap and slowly tore a strip of skin and flesh two inches wide and a foot long across his victim's torso. He looked apologetically at Steven. "You see, Steven, there is almost unlimited scope for me to skin you alive for hours, why inflict so much pain on yourself? Tell me where the painting is?"

Steven had always considered he had a high tolerance of pain, but he had never been subjected to such bestiality or such unrestricted brutality. He looked up at Bulatovic, pleading with his one good eye, "why, you bastard? We were friends... Why" Red tears dripped. Bulatovic's lip curled, "you're pathetic. You have nothing. I have everything. You are your father's son; that's why. A sorry offspring admittedly but still carrying his loathsome genes."

Steven was defeated; he screamed as Bulatovic approached again, "okay, okay... I know it's hopeless... Will you end it... if I tell you?"

"Yes... you can be certain I'll kill you when I have it. If you persist with your silence, or you lie to me, I will make this little exercise last for days."

Steven told him the address of the Hounslow flat. Bulatovic looked at Stephan and the bodyguard pulled out Steven's keys. Bulatovic looked at his prisoner. "Which key is it, Steven?" Steven nodded when Stephan held up the correct one. Bulatovic smiled slightly, "good. There aren't any booby-traps to singe Stephan's crew cut are there? It would be very painful for you should that happen."

"Good," greeted the shake of his victim's head.

Stephan made to go and Bulatovic restrained him. He wiped his bloodied hands on a cloth, put some latex gloves on; then he removed Steven's confiscated Browning from the small of his back. Wiping it all over with another, clean, cloth he took the magazine out and cleared the breech. When it was safe, he put it into Steven's right hand and closed his fingers around the butt. Steven had slumped, but felt what was going on; he started to buck again, but the two bodyguards held him firm. Once Steven's fingerprints were well and truly imprinted on the gun, Bulatovic took a plastic bag from his pocket and dropped the gun into it. Then, for good measure, he put Steven's index finger and thumbprint on the magazine and dropped that in too.

Once this minor operation was complete, Stephan was given leave to go to Hounslow and Bulatovic went back to the house. He left Steven guarded by the other bodyguard, Dimitry: taking no risks, this man unholstered his pistol and sat several metres away by the inflatable where he could cover the door, the prisoner and the entire shed. An hour and a half later Stephan rang to say he had the artwork. Bulatovic told him to stay put with it and went back to Steven. "So Steven you told me the truth: that was very wise... Sadly, I lied. I feel the need to torture you some more. There is still the price to be paid for the quick deaths the rest of your family had."

Bulatovic, true to his word, tortured Steven until his body looked like it had been turned inside out. The boatshed stank of every fluid and semi-fluid product his body was capable of producing. Steven's pulse finally flickered out at nine-ten in the evening. The remaining bodyguard punched holes through the corpse with a pick and fed a heavy chain through and around the skeleton. He padlocked the chain, buried the pick in the body's chest, and then drew the tarpaulin, which had been on the floor from the start, around the trussed carcase. Lacing the tarpaulin, he dragged the whole thing to the inflatable where, with Bulatovic's help, he loaded it. Half an hour later, it was dumped unceremoniously into the sea five miles out.

When he came back, he stripped and threw all his clothes into the boat; he threw the pile of Bulatovic's clothing sitting on the beach in too. He emptied the outboard's fuel tank over everything and flipped a lighter, which was also thrown into the ensuing blaze. He bathed in the sea and then walked up bare-footed, naked, though still armed, to the deserted house.

Bulatovic had similarly stripped, bathed, walked to the house, and redressed half an hour before. With a new set of gloves on he extracted two padded, stamped envelopes from his briefcase. He took his PDA out, tapped some further material into it, and saved the new material onto the half gig SD card. He took the card out, put it into its little protective box; then put it, and the bagged Browning into the larger envelope. He took another half gig SD card from the case and put that in the smaller envelope. He addressed both and returned them to his briefcase.

Then he drove off in the Mercedes he and Steven had arrived in. Driving back onto the A2, he turned clockwise onto the M25 around the south of London. Occasionally he concentrated on the rear mirror but always, after maybe five minutes, he dismissed his suspicions as paranoia. Pulling into the Clacket Lane services, he posted the two packages and quickly returned to the motorway. He got to Steven's Hounslow address at eleven-twenty five and Stephan helped him load the Titian into the back of the Mercedes. Then they both went their separate ways. The bodyguards had some minor tidying duties to perform before they could return to Serbia.

Bulatovic drove to an address in Engelfield Green where he parked the Mercedes in the garage, closing the electric door behind him. Once the door was soundly shut, he hauled the Titian out and manhandled it into the house.

He was starving hungry after his exertions and he knew there was a good, late opening, Indian restaurant down the hill in Egham. He also rather fancied a drink, so he called ABC taxis and was soon tucking into poppadums, nan bread, and chicken tikka marsala. He washed it all down with several glasses of Indian beer.

He took another taxi back to the address in the Green, having booked a further one for seven-thirty am, and fell gratefully into bed where he immediately sank into a deep, uninterrupted sleep.

At seven am he was up, vigorously showering in the power shower and by eight am he was at Heathrow. He flew to Zurich with Swiss, the humbler phoenix drawn from the wreckage of Swiss Air. A car was waiting for him and took him direct to Kreuzlingen, still just inside Switzerland, but on the

German border, and adjacent to what some call Lake Constance; some call the Boden See.

Kreuzlingen, a rather sterile little town, especially compared to the old town of Konstanz, its German siamese twin over the border, had the merit of being crammed with private banks and private, very secret, medical clinics.

He checked into his chosen clinic as Harold Dennis.

32. A Pair of Puzzled Policemen

Grieve, Doyle, and Collins returned to Leeds on Monday evening. They all took two deserved days off. Doyle spent most of it at home with their little boy, Adrian, cooking and cleaning the house. His wife Sheila had a part-time job, so this went some way towards relieving the pressure on her.

Doyle was a good cook when he turned his hand to it. He presented a casserole of chicken, mushrooms, apples, cream, and cider, with sautéed potatoes, baton carrots, and courgettes on the first evening. On the second he tried the wok for the first time, using strips of fillet pork and a variety of sliced fresh vegetables with saffron rice: the experiment got a guarded thumbs up from his nevertheless impressed wife.

Afterwards they had a little cuddle on the sofa whilst watching a video of The Last of The Mohicans. Sheila expressed admiration for Daniel Day Lewis; Doyle kept quiet about his secret desire for Madeleine Stowe.

The following morning, he arrived at Weetwood police station at around eight am and found Grieve, Reilly, Banks, and Blackhall together in the canteen.

They were discussing a new piece of puzzling information that had emerged via Scotland Yard. Someone at Sotheby's had finally connected Lockhart the Titian owner with the Lockhart that the police were searching for. The description and address details all fitted so there was no mistake: Armstrong was in possession of a masterpiece worth several million pounds. It complicated the case's logic as it undermined the putative motive: gaining from the legacy. However, it also raised the possibility of criminal theft, though apparently the painting's provenance had been cast-iron.

Then the discussion turned to the garage search, which was still progressing slowly. New and legitimate samples had been obtained from Lockhart's and Armstrong's cars during the searches of the London properties and at the moment, this was the best hope for linking Lockhart/Armstrong to the stolen Mondeo.

The next topic was the character of Steven Armstrong; Reilly reminded everyone of his assessment of Steven as the Army officer from Hell. Doyle picked up on the theme and offered some reflections that he had given form to in the past two days. He looked at Banks, "do you remember in the first briefing, you were surprised that Barbara didn't seek to arm herself, when she left the washing in such a hurry." Banks nodded and Doyle turned to Blackhall, "and you believed the polymer frame pistol in the gun cabinet was specifically for her."

Blackhall nodded too. Doyle said to the whole gathering, "I think these were clues pointing at Steven all along. Easy to say now, of course, but I'm guessing that the phone call and message Fiona left on Steven's answer-phone said, she knew he was up to no good, and she suspected him of something illegal. She was obviously very suspicious concerning his newfound blasé attitude to money. It seems clear that that was the trigger for her to start following him. Maybe, it had something to do with this painting: there is no mention of it in her diary, even though Sotheby's had the painting since September. Anyway, If Fiona revealed all to her parents over the evening meal they shared, I bet that Barbara half suspected that Steven would follow Fiona, but that the outcome would be a big argument. The possibility of murder, despite her intelligence and experience, by a child she had borne, never even entered her mind. Even when she might have heard the pistol's action, she still wasn't prepared to believe."

This provoked a considerable bout of discussion about, such things as, the clarity of the sound the pistol would have made, or what the content of the message Fiona had left Steven was, and even whether Fiona and Steven had actually spoken. Grieve departed shortly after to his office and the day's routine got underway for the rest of them.

At around nine-twenty, Doyle's phone rang: Grieve wanted him in his office. He walked upstairs, knocked on the door, and went in when he heard Grieve's invitation. He sat down and studied the sliced open, padded envelope that was sitting in front of Grieve. The contents looked intriguing. Grieve said, "this arrived this morning. It was opened very carefully, because of its size, shape, and weight, by the people who know about these things: as you can see it isn't a bomb."

Grieve had some gloves on, he lifted the bag with the Browning and magazine in it. "What do you think, a 9mm pistol, the Armstrong murder weapon? If it is, why has it been sent to me?" He put the bag down and picked up the little clear plastic box with the SD card in it. "Do you think the answer will be on this little thing? I'm bloody sure." He said forcefully.

There was a knock on the door; a Constable took the items away for both forensic evaluation, and for the SD card to be investigated. The telephone rang and Grieve answered it. He listened and then looked up at Doyle. "Just a minute, Sir, can I put you on speaker."

Grieve pressed the secrecy button and said, "it's the Editor of the Times."

Then he pressed the speaker button and put the receiver down. Grieve said, "you're talking to me, DCI Grieve, and DI Doyle."

"Thanks Detective Chief Inspector. As I was saying, we received a half-gigabyte SD card in the post this morning. We've had a look at the contents: I realised I needed to call you." Grieve urged the man to continue. "Well, the man you are seeking for the murders of last week, Steven Armstrong, is the subject of a large number of files on the card.

309

There are photos, taped conversations, video footage, and some text files. All of which, if it is to be believed, suggests that this man really is a very nasty piece of work."

"Like what exactly?"

"Well, the most damning, seems to be a video of him shooting a badly beaten British Lieutenant in the head. But the tape recordings indicate that he was taking bribes in Bosnia, and some conversations indicated that he longed to confront, even to kill, his parents. The photos appear to show the exchange of cash. A text file offers a commentary, and one gives the location of a grave in Bosnia."

"Is there any indication of who sent the material?"

"None: Look, Chief Inspector, this is *very* newsworthy stuff, very public interest. I'm guessing though, actually it's a near certainty, that if I publish it, it will compromise any trial."

"From what you've said that does sound very likely. Can we have it please?"

"Of course I'll send it to you. Can I have your assurance that we get exclusive on it, when it is possible to publish?"

"Absolutely."

"Thanks, I'll courier it to you. Best of luck in catching the bastard, and thanks again."

When the phone clicked off Grieve looked at Doyle. "This investigation has gone so well, I had begun to notice queasy feelings creeping up on me; almost as if we were being manipulated: now I am feeling positively ill. Someone wants us to know, without any shadow of a doubt, the identity of the killer. They are also determined to blacken his name, and they have probably been so determined for some time…Who could possibly have that level of insight… without being implicated." He shook his head, "the connection with Bosnia is interesting; don't you think?" He added meaningfully.

The SD card sent to Grieve had the same material on it as that sent to the Times, but with one addition, an address in Hounslow, which the Met investigated on West Yorkshire's behalf. They found among other things, a sniper rifle, a Walther pistol, and two passports.

310

The Browning's ballistics matched the three rounds from the Armstrong house and it had, clearly imprinted on it, Steven Armstrong's fingerprints, and no one else's.

The British Army exhumed a body in Bosnia. It was identified as the remains of the missing officer. Eventually, its sad form was buried with full military honours, accompanied by truly poignant images of parents and family grieving for the loss of a strong, brilliant, righteous son.

The Walther, which also had Steven's prints on it, proved to be the murder weapon: initially this was achieved by study of the video footage, but subsequently through matching it to the round that had failed to exit Lieutenant Roberts' head. Roberts' murder was added to the list of Steven's crimes.

Weeks went by and there was no sight, or sound, of Steven Armstrong, or Brian Lockhart. West Yorkshire Police issued a statement that they were looking for no one else in connection with the murders, and the investigation was mothballed.

33. Nachspiel

As April turned to May in 2003, the bandages came off Gavrilo Bulatovic's face. He now had the face to match the photo in the Irish passport. He was, to all intents and purposes, the Patrick Gallagher represented in the little booklet. He had already bought the house and stud farm about fifteen miles outside Dublin. In fact, he had flown from Dublin to London in order to have the first, fateful meeting, in Hyde Park with Steven: a step the man had forced on him by his delay in killing his parents. The scarring was almost healed and within another two weeks, he was ready to face the world.

The only slight sour note in this period was that the Times had not published any of the material he had sent relating to Steven. It was what he had called 'Step 6' when he had been taunting Steven: not only the destruction of the Armstrong family, but also the tarnishing of the name. It was some time before he realised why they hadn't, and he began to wonder, with some disappointment, if they ever would.

A lot of his recovery time had been taken up by following the Coalition invasion of Iraq. He had watched, from mid March through to the de facto UN resolution, several different channels on TV; avidly consumed newspapers, and had even spent time reviewing material on the Net. His interest was primarily professional; intrigued by the weapons technologies on display, by the tactics, and by the strategy employed.

He was much trimmer too, a combination of enforced light eating, and exercise. Both the surgeon and the physician had advocated regular exercise in the clinic's private gym as part of his rehabilitation. This had occupied virtually all the balance of his spare time.

His slimmer waist and hips meant that the clothes he had brought now barely fitted him. The first task he had given his newly arrived bodyguard was to go and buy him some reasonable clothing; enabling him to go shopping himself without looking like a scarecrow.

This new man, Graeme, was supplied by a good agency in London and was an ex Paratrooper and ex SAS NCO. He was not huge like his last two minders, but he was efficient, if his clothes' shopping was anything to go by.

Bulatovic felt better than he had done for some time. He felt he would have easily been able to sate Janica and Natascha's unquenchable sex drives, had they formed part of his new life. They were part of his old life though; there was plenty of time to find two, or more, new ones.

Feeling well dressed in his Italian cotton flannels, short-sleeved Versace shirt, a cool cream cotton blazer, and dark Gucci sunglasses he stepped out into the increasingly hot weather. He walked down the road with his new shadow a respectable, and respectful distance behind.

The man was unarmed, at least with a firearm, which had irritated Bulatovic, but he could see, even in gun-obsessed Switzerland, it would have been difficult for the agency to arrange. They would not countenance illegal weapons, and so it became a necessary evil; the agency's above board establishment image was what Bulatovic had wanted.

Shopping in Kreuzlingen was a waste of time so he headed down the gentle hill through the town towards the border crossing. He was surprised at himself, he felt excited at the prospect of testing his new look and new passport.

He went through the Swiss side unremarked and the unsmiling German guard looked at his face closely; then down at the document, then jerked his head unemotionally in acceptance.

Bulatovic wandered into the interesting little streets and lanes of Konstanz. The town was well supplied with classy clothes, shoe, perfume, and leather shops; interspersed, there were bars and quaint coffee shops and restaurants. Alfresco seating extended into the pedestrian zone every fifty metres or so. In the end, the choice of apparel was so great he felt unable to decide, and only bought a couple of shirts. He would have to think over what he had seen and come back in the next few days. He promenaded down to the edge of the lake. He looked at the sails, near and far; slack in the heat, and relatively slight wind. He began to ruminate on the purchase of a yacht: possibly in the Mediterranean; based somewhere on the French Riviera.

Working his way back, in a very good humour, he liked the look of a display of cakes and confectionery in a particular window. He entered the shop, which was a long established, up market, bakery cum café. He sat at a table at the back. Graeme sat at another near him, but far enough away so as not to crowd him. Bulatovic was impressed by his tact and style.

He had a coffee and a savoury dish of cheese, ham, tomatoes, and asparagus that was a specialty of the house. Because of his svelte like shape, he felt able to indulge in a dessert: one of the cakes he had seen in the window.

Heading back in the general direction of the border, there were tables and chairs set out in front of an ancient looking beer house. Bulatovic went over, sat down, and indicated to Graeme to join him. Graeme, diplomatically, did as directed, sitting looking outwards with his back to the wall, his eyes hidden by the Rayban's. Bulatovic ordered a Weizen beer, and asked Graeme what he would have. Graeme turned to the waiter and said in good German, "haben Sie alkoholfreies Bier?"

"Ja, natürlich."

Graeme nodded his decision and the man departed. Bulatovic was impressed. "You speak German?"

"A bit, not very well." Graeme, still very much on duty, never let his gaze fix anywhere for long, and appraised anyone who came remotely close.

315

"It's not a language I ever had any desire to learn."

"It's definitely a language to learn young, it's not easy to get beyond a basic level."

Bulatovic nodded, took his sunglasses off and cleaned them; he changed the subject, "do you have any problem working for an Irishman?"

Graeme frowned, "no, why should I?"

"The war that was fought with the IRA; your history suggests that you were heavily involved, were you not."

"Yes, I was, but active IRA players were, or are, a tiny minority of the Irish nation. It was clear from the pan-Ireland referendum, the vast majority favour democratic change to the rule of the Armalite."

The conversation was interrupted by the arrival of the beers. They drank in silence for a while, enjoying the cool beer in the warmth of the sun. Then Bulatovic stirred; he looked at Graeme appraisingly, "I have houses and farms in Ireland and Tuscany, I have flats in London and New York. I've been impressed by your conduct; how you handle yourself; you have a good head on you too: would you consider a permanent position with me? I'm likely to spend equal amounts of time at each location, when I'm not travelling elsewhere."

It was early days, but Graeme was developing a poor opinion of Patrick Gallagher; character was an important factor in choosing an employer. Diplomacy prevented him saying as much; instead, he inclined his head. "Thank you, it's rare in this business to be complimented. I will consider the offer. I should say, though, that at the end of the day, I'm a bodyguard: you don't know how good I am at that yet."

"You come highly recommended."

Graeme acknowledged the fact and they subsided into silence.

When the beers were finished, they resumed the pattern they had used before, with Graeme a short distance behind.

Back at the Border crossing it was the German guard's turn to ignore them. The unsmiling Swiss border guard looked into Bulatovic's face and then looked into his passport. "What is the purpose of your visit to Switzerland?"

"I'm receiving treatment at a clinic here in Kreuzlingen, I only visited Konstanz for a few hours."

The man looked up; Bulatovic suddenly felt uncertain. "Have a nice day, Mr Gallagher." The man, expressionless, handed him his passport back.

Bulatovic moved off and studied a shop front as he waited for Graeme to clear the checkpoint; then he slowly walked up the hill. After walking two hundred metres up the road, Bulatovic sensed something; he turned just as Graeme shouted, "run." A car was pulling up beside him and three men were jumping out; he had nowhere to run to. A second car had already pulled up beside Graeme and a battle-royal had started between him and the three men who had leapt from it; as the outcome looked in doubt, the driver was getting out too. Bulatovic was quickly searched and bundled into the vehicle, but he had enough time to see the border guard pacing back to his office: watching the commotion but doing nothing to intervene.

The car sped away with Bulatovic, in the back, sandwiched between two hulking men. The third in the front was looking back at him with a pistol pointed at his head. The safety was off, and Bulatovic held his breath, until he realised that the hammer was down; the gun was uncocked. He let his breath out, "what's going on, I'm not a well man, I must get back to my hospital."

The driver looked in the mirror at him. "We weren't very happy to learn you were in Switzerland, Mr Bulatovic."

"I don't understand, my name is Gallagher, Patrick Gallagher, I'm an Irish citizen."

"You're Gavrilo Bulatovic. We are well aware of your history, and we know you entered the country using false papers in the name of Harold Dennis."

"I'm Patrick Gallagher: an Irish citizen."

"Save your breath."

"I'm... upfff." One of his back seat companions had punched him in the stomach.

The car sped on, Bulatovic could see the lake over on the left, it was coming closer. After a few minutes, they entered a small town called Münsterlingen on the south shore. The car pulled up beside a small motor cruiser and the men got out. They cuffed their prisoner's hands together, but Bulatovic was pleased, not behind his back. All four boarded the boat with their captive. It was immediately gunned, and headed away from the shore.

At this point, the huge body of water was quite narrow at about seven kilometres, or just under five miles, wide. There were a lot of sail and motor craft dotted around but it soon became clear they were heading for a similar motor cruiser sat roughly in the middle of the lake.

Two of his captors went out to kick tyres down the side, and when the boats bumped gently, they expertly caught the thrown lines, putting a few turns on the fore and aft cleats.

The driver, the man who had accused Bulatovic, jumped into the other boat and warmly shook hands with the occupant. That man looked over at him and... did he know him?

The two men on the deck had returned, one looked on with a pistol as the other two forced Bulatovic over the gunwale, and into the other boat.

They left him in the company of the two men there. The Swiss reached into Bulatovic's pocket, drew out his passport, looked at it, then glanced at him with a grim expression on his face. "We never want to see you returning to Switzerland, Mr Bulatovic, whether you be guised as Mr Dennis, Mr Gallagher, or any other fiction. If you should make such an attempt, it *will* prove to be a grave error."

He pushed the passport back into the pocket, without taking his eyes off Bulatovic's face.

He turned to the other man, shook hands again, smiled, and leapt back into the Swiss boat. The lines were released, thrown, and the other boat sped away.

Bulatovic looked around, this man seems to be alone, and he is old: I could maybe... He looked back and found the man had moved back to the opposite gunwale and had a pistol levelled at him. He spoke softly, "I know what you're thinking; it would be foolhardy."

"Who are you?"

Hastings said, "you're not entitled to ask questions, especially risible ones. What *I* want is: you down in that cabin, now."

Bulatovic didn't move. His captor looked bored, "it would be unfortunate if you died now... but not a catastrophe, move."

Bulatovic moved, but not toward the cabin; he took a step towards the man and his gun. Instantly, he stiffened: he felt the shock wave of a bullet whipping perilously close to his left ear. Strange that he sensed it even before he seemed to register the report: he was sure the pistol had to have a subsonic muzzle velocity.

"The next one goes through your head."

Bulatovic conceded defeat for now, and acquiesced; he turned to the small door, and went into the open sided cabin. The exercise involved some steps; he almost tripped; with his hands cuffed, as they were, he might have landed on his head. It was with some relief that he eventually made the bench seating.

He sat quietly, but internally he was thinking furiously. At the same time, he felt the boat move slowly for ten minutes. It stopped and, inexplicably, half an hour passed with no sign of his jailor. Then he felt it moving for a further ten minutes. Bulatovic was forestalled from shouting for some kind of explanation by the appearance of his anonymous captor at the top of the steps, where he sat down, pistol still in hand. He studied his captive briefly before speaking, "the Swiss were very grateful when I told them you were in the country illegally. They owe me some big favours from the old days; were glad to be rid of you by the back door... and I'm short of cash. You on the other hand are swimming in it: surprise, surprise, I want some."

Bulatovic's mood lifted somewhat. Of all the options he had considered this was the best: simple extortion; it was good news if that was the logic behind this. He responded guardedly, "how did you get the information on me?"

"Another pointless, risible, question. I'm the master here, it's my agenda we are following, and the substantive point is, the transfer of one million Sterling from you, to me."

Bulatovic laughed, "I don't have that much money ready to hand."

"How much do you have?"

Bulatovic had an easy-access account he could transfer sums as large as $1 million from, simply by using a telephone, and

319

a rotating numeric key. Currently it had a balance of more than $2.5million in it. He said, "I could probably get you $500,000 in the next few hours. The rest will take days."

Hastings looked angry; then frustrated; then philosophic, and then suspicious. "You aren't likely to tell me the truth are you. Let me guess that you can actually reach, say, $750,000." Bulatovic shook his head in feigned disbelief.

Hastings considered Bulatovic for a short time; he said, "I'm going to assume $750,000 whatever you say. That will have to do; approximately half a million Sterling."

"I can't get it to you, I'm not as wealthy as you think."

"That's tough shit for you then." Hastings said brutally.

"I can get you $500,000, but I won't give you anything unless you let me go."

"I thought we'd been over this ground, you aren't in a position to bargain. I hope for your sake that you can transfer the money by phone."

"What do you propose to do with me?"

"If you transfer the money to me now, I will take the boat over to the German shore, and drive you to Friedrichshafen Airport. There are short-haul services from there to various national and international locations."

"How do I know I can trust you?"

"You don't."

"I won't transfer any money then."

This bullet almost grazed his right ear as it cleared the gunwale through the open sided cabin and impacted the water ten metres away. The report's echoes died; his captor had lost patience, he spoke softly, chillingly, "you are only cash to me. If you don't transfer the money, $750,000 of it, within ten minutes, in eleven minutes you will be on the bottom of the Boden See with a hollow head." Hastings looked at his watch; Bulatovic silently debated. After a minute, Hastings said, "nine minutes."

A further minute passed in silence, Hastings said, "eight minutes. Maybe I didn't make myself clear; the money must be confirmed in my account within the time limit: if not the result will be the same." Casually he continued, "how long does the transfer take?"

Bulatovic swore inwardly and quickly said, "okay, I'll do it." He thought, but when I'm free, I'll spend a fortune hunting you down you old bastard; your death will be a living hell for you and a great pleasure for me.

Hastings chucked a mobile into his lap, and Bulatovic dialled a number in Switzerland. He identified himself, gave the correct key, not the alarm one, specified three quarters of a million in dollars, and looked at Hastings for the recipient account, to which he said, "the details are taped to the back of the phone."

Bulatovic looked, found the paper, and peeled it away just as Hastings said, "five minutes."

Bulatovic gave the details on the paper, requested that the transfer be expeditious, and switched the phone off. Hasting indicated Bulatovic should throw the phone over the side of the boat, then he keyed a button on another phone and listened to it, occasionally breaking to look at his watch. As one minute came and went, he straightened his arm, cocked the hammer, and pointed the gun at his captive's head. Bulatovic cringed and cried, "no, wait." However, seconds later, Hastings said into the phone, "ah, thank you, and a very nice evening to you too." He switched his phone off, decocked the pistol, and looked at his watch; coolly he said, "just in time."

He got up, went out, and the boat started to move again; soon it was pulling in by a deserted jetty at the end of a road on the German shore. "Out," he called into the cabin.

The boat was bumping gently against the wood. Hastings took the boat keys, hopped onto the low platform, and moored the stern of the boat. His captive appeared as he secured the bow. Bulatovic climbed ashore awkwardly and with Hastings a few metres behind he walked up to the waiting VW Touareg.

Hastings unlocked it with the remote, told Bulatovic to open the tailgate door, and sit in the back. After a short hesitation, he did as directed, but with some difficulty given his cuffed hands. Eventually, he was sitting with his back supported by the rear seats. Hastings cocked the pistol again, so that it was on a hair-trigger, and told Bulatovic what he had done: his captive knew exactly what had been done and was sitting as still as a statue.

Hastings took a second set of cuffs from his pocket, and clipped one of Bulatovic's ankles to one of the luggage lugs in the floor. The rigid man ground out, "for fuck's sake, be careful with that gun." Hastings smiled at him, closed the tailgate, and walked around to a side door, which he opened. He dropped one of the rear seats to reveal his prisoner's back and put the muzzle of the gun in the depression between Bulatovic's spine and the base of his skull. If anything, his prisoner became even more rigid. He reached around and unlocked Bulatovic's left hand. "Put your hands behind your back." There was no response. Hastings pushed the muzzle hard into the man's neck. "Do it, or die." Bulatovic did it, and Hastings re-engaged the cuffs around the left wrist. He removed the gun, raised the rear seat, closed the door, and gently decocked the weapon's hammer.

They drove a few kilometres away; up quiet, clean, winding roads edged every few metres with neat white posts; into gentle rolling hills in the verdant farmland of the Linzgau and Baden-Württemberg. The cloudless azure sky kissed the swellings of the emerald horizon in a boundary sharpened by the clear air and brilliant sun. The open driver's window directed a refreshing, cooling breeze into the hot car's interior and carried the rich aroma of hot leather upholstery to Bulatovic's nostrils. He was impervious to it, his mind, and thoughts, concentrated on the planning of his retribution; a strategy that would commence the moment he was freed.

Eventually Hastings pulled off the road onto a well-graded farm track; white against the lush green of the surrounding grass. Five minutes and he stopped at its end; at a building that was a cross between a barn and a house, in an open field, well off the main road. The field was bounded on two sides by deciduous forest. He opened the tailgate and Bulatovic looked around suspiciously, "you said we were going to Friedrichshafen."

"I've been using this as a base; I have to collect my equipment: or to be more precise you're going to collect it."

To Bulatovic's dismay, Hasting cocked the gun again. He unclipped the luggage lug, but left the other cuff on his left ankle. He stepped back and indicated for Bulatovic to get out. They walked to the building; at the door, Bulatovic hesitated again.

322

Hastings calmly said, "remember, this pistol is on a single-action hair-trigger; it's pointing at the back of your head."

Bulatovic grimaced, opened the door, and went in with Hastings a few metres behind him. They walked into the centre of an open, raftered space. Around were piles of baled hay; neat stacks of split firewood. There was a dry musty smell: but no sign of recent occupation.

Hastings aimed at the back of Bulatovic's right knee and squeezed the trigger. An explosion of bone, tissue, and blood erupted from the impact area. Bulatovic screamed, as much from the shock as from the injury, and collapsed on the ground. Hastings had aimed off centre so as to avoid a rupture of the Popliteal Artery, which ran centrally down the back of the knee. When he was sure Bulatovic was incapacitated, he unclipped a rope with a karabiner on the end from a ring in the wall. He bent to the writhing man, who was lying face down on the ground. He clipped the karabiner onto the bracelet between the cuffs; went to the rope's other end, which was on a three-way pulley, and hauled the screaming, shocked man to his feet, or more accurately to his foot. He had had to stand; the strain and pain in his shoulders from having his cuffed arms raised up his back was, obviously, excruciating. Eventually with the rope taut, Bulatovic's arms were just a little over the horizontal; the man had to lean forward on his one good foot to relieve the strain on his shoulders.

The damaged leg hung limply: leaking blood, but not enough to threaten the man's life. Hastings clipped the open end of the cuffs that were still around his prisoner's good ankle to a ring on the floor. Bulatovic screamed, "what are you doing? You said you would release me."

Hastings looked at him steadily; after a prolonged pause, very deliberately, he said, "sadly, I lied."

Bulatovic frowned, "I thought this was about the money?"

"No, that was a ruse to direct you away from my true intent, I didn't want to kill you then; the money will go to a good cause though." Hastings continued in a light conversational tone, "symmetry, it's only symmetry. You saw symmetry in accelerating Steven's descent into corruption; your own

323

corruption working on him, to destroy the targets of your…" He sighed, "your misdirected enmity."

Bulatovic thought, did Stephan or Dimitry talk? No, that can't be it: neither understood enough English, they only had a smattering of functional words.

Hastings started to tell the story of the Tarčin massacre and of his friend Ivan Despoja: the story that he had told Grieve in the car. Given that he was talking to Bulatovic he went into much greater detail concerning the behaviour of the Serbs. He explained how the women were all in the road with their skirts over their torsos and underwear ripen off, how the youngest girl to be raped; little, sweet Theresa, the nine-year-old; had obviously been the favourite of the attackers, given the tearing and other damage to her genitals; the amount of puddled semen.

How the men, in their enthusiasm, had broken arms and legs and torn joints as they sated their hate and lust. Warming to the story, Hastings told how the men-folk had obviously been made to watch their multiple rape and then their ragged, near decapitation with knifes.

He told how many of the men and boys, had then had their legs and arms systematically broken with sledgehammers: gradually from foot to hip, from hand to shoulder, the pelvis, and the ribs. The final fatal blow to the head had left them virtually decapitated too: their heads and skulls exploded, like watermelons, by the heavy impact.

He seemed oblivious to Bulatovic, who was screaming at him, "why are you telling me this? I didn't do it! I was hundreds of miles away. I didn't do it!" He repeated the words over and over.

Hastings eventually stopped. He had either run out of story; run out of breath; or run out of energy. Sitting on a stack of wood, he was slumped, looking at the ground with the gun dangling loosely from his hand, between his knees.

"You old bastard, didn't you hear me, I didn't do it. I do know who did do it, and he's dead. I heard he was hacked to death by a mob of Bosniak women."

Hastings roused himself. Bulatovic repeated what he had just said and Hastings nodded slowly, "I know you didn't do it."

324

Bulatovic looked relieved. Hastings looked at his watch, and then at Bulatovic sadly, "I know of, I saw in fact, your appalling behaviour elsewhere in Bosnia though." Bulatovic revised his mood.

Hastings looked steadily at his prisoner for some minutes. He seemed to be considering his next words, "do you know how I found you?" Bulatovic looked as impatient as a man could do, in such a contorted position. Hastings, though, seemed too drained now, to expand on the point in depth. "Well, suffice it to say, I had a lot of good help from a lot of old retired friends; friends with time on their hands, who were only too happy to track the Armstrong killer. Your monitoring of Steven, when he arrived in Hyde Park, did you no good: ten of us had him boxed; there were two more of my team in the Park already, in anticipation that that was his destination. I was the only one, though, who went in close on the Isle of Grain. I watched, through the slats, the whole sordid business in the boatshed. I didn't intervene: I reckoned Steven deserved everything he got.

So, you see, I know from watching your exploits both in Bosnia, and also in Britain: you are totally, irretrievably, depraved. I can see no redeeming feature in you at all.

We are full circle, back at symmetry. You saw symmetry in the son destroying the parents. I see it in you, innocent of the crime of Tarčin, but paying for it, just as all those other innocents that you tortured and killed, paid for your greed and dissolution."

Hastings got up and stood grim and sad in front of his captive. Bulatovic strained to look up into his face. Hastings was matter of fact; polar cold, "I sentence you to death, Gavrilo Bulatovic: in your death you will repay some of your evil. Your dying will even, I hope, confer a good: it will be a closure for the only two survivors of that massacre ten years ago."

They both could hear the unmistakable sound of a car pulling up outside. Bulatovic looked around wildly; he bucked, forgetting his shattered knee he cried out again.

Hastings was oblivious. "Unfortunately for you, they are Bosnians, and you know what that means. Their closure will mirror your destruction of Steven. They, though, are not rushing to catch a plane: they have taken three days leave to do it properly."

Bulatovic was no coward, but he knew what his tormentor had just said was horrifically true; his next few days were going to be a pain racked, screaming, nightmare. He had never had any trouble with rapid and difficult decisions: he reached one very quickly here. He looked steadily up at Hastings. "Mercy, mercy... please, I can see you're a good man. Kill me; kill me before they come in."

Hastings shook his head sadly, "what mercy did you ever show?" Two tears squeezed out and down his cheeks. The door opened and two tall, strong, strikingly handsome, young men came in each carrying a heavy bag, "hallo Vater."

"Hallo meine Söhne."

They shook hands and embraced him one after the other. They looked at the gently swinging captive. "Ist er das?"

Hastings turned to look and said, "ja, das ist er, der Metzger aus Tarčin.

Bulatovic knew no German but understood enough: he shouted. "He's lying, I didn't do it. He can't deliver the real killer; he's using me."

Ivan walked up to Bulatovic; the young doctor casually kicked the man's shin below the shredded knee. Bulatovic screamed; Ivan smiled. He studied his contorted victim for a short while, then came back, and helped Ivo unload the bags. The young men had brought everything they needed for an exercise of several days: food; water; sleeping bags.

They had also brought a strange assortment of household hardware and medical equipment. There were electric drills, electric cables, pliers, knives, scalpels, probes, syringes, needles, clamps, tweezers; just to name a few: in fact a veritable cornucopia of torture.

The two men took some black bread and cheese and went over to Bulatovic. They stood there for some time, having a professional discussion regarding the best way to extract the most pain for the longest period. They walked around the gently swaying man, probing at the injured knee, feeling his head, neck, and torso: just as two doctors would do in examining a patient. All the time they munched at the bread and cheese, mulling the possibilities.

After half an hour, they had constructed a plan.

326

They dressed in plastic suits, and enthusiastically started their work. Bulatovic now began to experience the pain, horror and terror he had visited on Steven and so many other innocents over the past many years.

Hastings watched, appalled, and transfixed for some time, but the horror eventually overcame him and he stumbled outside. He could feel the mental stability he had nurtured for years deserting him. The walls he had built to keep the pain out were crumbling. He sat on a bench at the wall, still hearing the horror from inside. He looked out across the green hills, the fields, and trees, towards the wide expanse of the Boden See in the middle distance, sparkling in the evening light. He could see the dozens of sails and boats plying the huge expanse of water. Night was closing in: in the far distance in the Alpine foothills, the darkness was accumulating and growing. It was coalescing and descending on the peaceful lake.

Hastings put his head in his hands. How far was Bosnia from here, barely three hundred and fifty miles? And Ireland too, how far distant in geography and time was that green country? Tears came again for himself and all the innocents as the darkness marched inexorably on; slowly it consumed the hinterland, then the far shore, then the sails; the fields; the trees; the people.

Epilogue.

DCI Grieve was watching the early evening news late in May 2003. The Iraq war was won; Tony Blair, in stark white shirt, was touring Basra, Iraq. He was thanking the British troops for their part in the invasion of the country.

Tony believed that they and the Coalition had achieved a great thing for Iraq and the world. He said it would prove to be a defining moment of the century. The whole region, once riven with strife, was already changing for the better: moving toward that Beacon of Democracy; moving towards a peaceful future.

Grieve listened, but did not hear any mention of right and wrong. It was there though: Tony was saying that, despite all the pain and death - "Mainly Iraqi," Grieve added mentally - the war had been the right thing to do: a word that he used promiscuously, in just about every other context.

Grieve had supported the war, reasoning that the British Government had to know far more regarding the threat than they could possibly say in public. Yet despite the certainty regarding the Weapons of Mass Destruction, none had yet been found. He now doubted they ever would be found. He recalled Blair saying in Parliament that Saddam posed a clear and imminent threat to the UK: he no longer trusted the Prime Minister.

He also had a fear that the US Army, unused to a mix of war and policing; would revert to a model more akin to the appalling behaviour of the Israeli Government and army in the Palestinian lands, than that of the, albeit still controversial, British in Northern Ireland. That the policing action would, breaking the critical rule of balanced response, swamp any threat that presented itself. He hoped he was going to be proved wrong; but he suspected deep down, that there were many dark years ahead.

His mobile rang: it was Thompson. "Hello Chief Inspector. We haven't spoken for some time. I hope I find you at a convenient moment?"

"Yes, I was just watching our Glorious Leader on the News."

"Hum," Thompson invested the word with heavy disdain. "Well, I thought to pass on two pieces of information: one of which, I would guess, could appear in summary on the late News; and one which won't."

"Go on," said Grieve expectantly.

"Well the first concerns that delightful chap Dermot Green: the IRA man that you had the pleasure of meeting at the beginning of the Armstrong Murder Inquiry."

"Yes, I remember; delightful is right."

"The news is he's now an ex-IRA man. He's been found on some waste ground in Dublin: been dead for several days. It probably happened some after he, once again, managed to slip the Irish surveillance.

That's what will make the News. The bit that I doubt will be expanded on is; he'd been cut to shreds. There is no one discernable cause of death: there are about thirty vying for pole position. I've seen the pictures; he was brutally tortured, it must have taken hours, or days, for him to die."

Grieve frowned and his mind raced.

"The other bit of news concerns Steven Armstrong: he's never going to face a trial. I have it on reliable authority that he is somewhere on the seabed of the North Sea. The man who put him there, and who supplied all that material in the envelope was, believe it or not, Mr Gavrilo Bulatovic: I knew he was up to something. Well, anyway he is also, apparently, feeding the little fishes: couldn't happen to a nicer chap. I think you can probably

330

release the shackles from the Times, they will find out soon enough anyway..."

Grieve's face screwed as the disparate items percolated through his mind. They danced and twisted together there, along with every other item from the recent inquiry. As they arranged themselves into the semblance of a logical pattern, he bent his head sadly into his free hand.

"Chief Inspector? Chief Inspector, are you still there?"

"Yes... yes I am, thanks for the information."

"Okay. It was good working with you. All the best."

"The same to you."

Grieve put the phone away, got up, got his coat, and yelled that he was going out. He walked down to the Mouse and the Elephant; his shoulders slumped; his hands buried in his pockets. As he approached the empty stool, situated at the end of the deserted bar, Ernie, the old barman, looked at him with concern, "in one of your dark moods, Mr Grieve?"

"I am." He said grimly, "the usual please Ernie." Ernie shook his head sadly, but did as he was bidden. Grieve proceeded to get completely hammered.

+   +   +

That evening Bill Hastings was at home in North Wales. He had just finished writing a cheque for £500,000 payable to reputable medical charity which had agreed to employ Ivo and Ivan as young doctors on their return to Bosnia. His plan for them appeared to have worked. The destruction of Bulatovic in atonement for the massacre did indeed appear to have been a catharsis. They had sworn to him that they would now dedicate the rest of their lives to caring for their Bosnian brothers and sisters without prejudice or favour.

When he was finished, his head and hand stayed frozen in place for some time. Their catharsis, whilst welcome and he did not regret any part of the horror that had been necessary in achieving it, had been at his expense. Eventually he slowly turned from his writing desk and looked over at the Titian hanging on

331

the end wall. It showed the Assumption of the Virgin Mary: she was depicted, beatific, rising unaided from a group of Apostles to an expectant God in his Heaven. It was exquisite and majestic, a smaller version of his masterwork: the Frari Altarpiece.

Hastings was still not sure whether he could live with it. Occasionally he took hope from it: Far more often, though, it plunged him into days of wracked despair.